CONVERSION
A NOVEL

R. J. Albanese

E. T. Sherman

Conversion

ISBN 979-8-9867592-2-7

eBook ISBN 979-8-9867592-5-8

Copyright © 2024 R. J. Albanese, E. T. Sherman

www.rjalbanese.com

Printed in the United States of America. All rights reserved under International Copyright Law. Contents and/or cover may not be reproduced in whole or in part in any form without the express written consent of the Publisher.

Dedication

This book is dedicated to our fathers.

A. J. Albanese, a true American patriot. A veteran of World War II and the Korean War, he understood adversity and encouraged me never to give up in a difficult endeavor. At the age of 97, he passed into glory, but I know he would have loved this book.

Tom S. Teetor, a compassionate visionary who loves his family and his country. Age 96 at this writing, he continues to use every gift and resource available to push back the darkness of oppression. Freedom, integrity, and wisdom run through his veins and inspire me always.

CONVERSION

IS THE ACT OR PROCESS

OF CHANGING SOMETHING

INTO A DIFFERENT STATE OR FORM

Prologue

David Parks had the uncanny ability to discern if someone was telling the truth. He knew who could be trusted in any situation, and he knew the only person he could trust right now was Reuben Katz. MacArthur had always referred to Reuben as his "rabbi and priest," but the moment David had looked into the man's eyes — in that brief encounter years ago — he had known the day would come when Reuben Katz would be the key to his survival on the planet. He had dismissed the thought back then because it made no sense. Today, he would discover why it made perfect sense.

He trudged along the final block before turning off Broadway onto the snow-bound side street. Laboring up the steep hill to the entrance of an old, brick apartment building, head down, he continually surveyed his surroundings, trying not to be distracted by the blinding rays of sunlight that were bouncing off the cloud of white around him. With his stomach in knots and his heart shattered, it wasn't hard to appear much older than he was. For a moment he thought he might pass out, but he took a deep breath and kept moving toward the entrance. No one was following him. His hat and sunglasses obscured his face from surveillance cameras, and the padded coat hid the shape of his athletic body. For once, he was glad to be in frigid temperatures.

He forced his long legs to take the last strides up the steps to

CONVERSION

the double-door entrance. Then he grabbed the right door handle and pulled the door open, pausing to use it as a crutch. The musty smell provided a strange comfort, but before he could press the button of Reuben's apartment, the obnoxious buzzer sounded. He quickly pushed the inner door open and entered the foyer, where he saw the elevator arrive through the small pane of glass in the outer door. He pulled it open, pressed 6 as he entered, and rested his forehead against the back wall of the elevator. He heard the inner door slide across behind him and dropped his bag like a barbell. The small cage creaked and groaned as it crawled to the top floor. He turned and was careful not to raise his head to the camera in the corner. Finally, the door slid open. He lifted his bag, and in a moment's time he was knocking at 6L.

A door opened directly behind him.

David turned to see Reuben grinning in the doorway across the hall. He motioned to come into the apartment and said with a soft, resonant accent, "Nice disguise."

David dropped his bag and removed his hat and sunglasses. "Nice decoy."

Reuben shrugged his shoulders. He helped David out of the heavy coat and hung it on a hook near the door. "*Shalom*, Superman."

David swallowed hard and clenched his jaw while he slung his hat over his coat and tucked the sunglasses in his shirt pocket. MacArthur had always told him he looked like the famous hero. "I don't feel like a man of steel today."

"Good. I can't help those who live in fantasy." Reuben

PROLOGUE

motioned for him to move down the long hallway, "Please, go to the front room and rest. Would you like tea?"

"That would be...nice."

David walked slowly down the narrow hallway and entered a warmly furnished living room, basking in the afternoon sunlight pouring through its windows. He stared at the old church across the street, then turned and collapsed on a soft leather couch, stretching his legs under the coffee table and supporting his head by threading his fingers behind his neck. He closed his eyes. The pain seemed bearable in this place, but he had to remember in order to forget. He had to move past the pain or he was in danger of drowning in it.

He winced, remembering the cliché MacArthur had thrown at him just days ago, "Don't let the pain beat you! Find the purpose. Get the understanding. Then you can defeat it and be a better man." He had laughed in derision then, but now he was sliding into the abyss again, so he shook himself and took another deep breath. *Get a grip.* He glanced down at the coffee table and stared at his friend's face on the front page of *The New York Times*. The headline read the same as all the others: Super Bug Kills Young Senator.

He vaguely heard footsteps. Not like an older man's. But he couldn't seem to take his eyes from the familiar photo, as though the intensity of his gaze could alter reality. Reuben handed him a steaming cup of chamomile tea.

David looked up into eyes that alarmed him with kindness, but he knew this man was not soft. No, this was someone who

CONVERSION

would never break but knew how to break others. He would die before he would betray anyone he loved or anything he believed. He suspected Reuben had passed that test more than once. He wondered if *he* would be up to it.

"Thanks." He concentrated on cooling his tea, blowing on the surface of the hot liquid. Reuben sat down in the armchair facing him. Finally, David offered what was expected, "I'm sorry for your loss. I know what he meant to you, and what you meant to him." He sipped his tea and avoided eye contact. If he saw Reuben's grief, his own would surely kill him.

"All is well, David. We haven't lost MacArthur. I know exactly where he is."

David grimaced. "I know what you *believe*." He wanted to change the subject. "That's not why I'm here."

Reuben's eyebrows rose slightly. "Why are you here?"

David placed his mug on the newspaper and forced himself to meet Reuben's gaze. "MacArthur was assassinated. And I know who did it."

1

Growing up is always hard, but it is easier when there is at least one good friend to go through it with you, and David Benjamin Parks had MacArthur Edward Wells. They met in the fall of 1963, when they were both twelve years old. The US Army sent MacArthur's father to the Panama Canal Zone and, as it turned out, he was just the person to deal with a volatile situation that developed shortly after he arrived. In truth, the United States was beginning to feel the strain of an enemy within, fomenting discontent and rage, and the Americans in Panama were not immune.

The American youth rebellion of the 1950s had involved smoking cigarettes, racing hotrods, and occasionally getting drunk. Sometimes a high school girl got pregnant after parking in lovers' lane with her boyfriend, and sock hops were all the rage. Elvis declared that rock 'n' roll would never die, as his swiveling hips replaced Frank Sinatra's crooning. Music superstars were here to stay.

In the sixties, rebellion began to roar across the nation. Kids went from blazers and ties to bellbottoms and beads, from crew cuts and ponytails to long hair and even longer hair. The new look reflected a revolution in core beliefs. Sexual purity and the sanctity of marriage vows were antiquated notions and "love the one you're

CONVERSION

with" was celebrated in the public square. Sex, drugs, and rock 'n' roll were the path to self-realization and freedom of the soul.

Cole Porter had no idea he was being prophetic when he wrote "Anything Goes" several decades before. So the Beatles landed in the States, wanting to "hold your hand" through it all, and many believed it was the dawn of the Age of Aquarius, when there would be "harmony and understanding" among all the peoples of the Earth. This generation was a transitional one for the country, and although they had no line of sight to see it, David and MacArthur were the prototypes.

David was born in Cuba, where his father was a dentist and his mother a schoolteacher. His father gathered an amazing amount of information through his practice. You would think people in a dentist chair would not have much to say, but Ben Perera made time for them. His patients were diplomats and wealthy business people, who understood where Cuba was headed and who was destined to lead it. They spoke of the young rebel Fidel Castro, and Ben was a good listener. He listened so well that, after Castro's first failed coup, he moved his family to Miami in 1954, when David was three years old.

As Ben anticipated, Castro and his band of communist rebels took control of Cuba and began tearing her down in 1959. Ben and his wife Elena were deeply saddened, but grateful to be in America. By then they were well on their pathway to US citizenship, and when this dream was realized in 1961, they changed their name from Perera to Parks. It was their show of loyalty to the nation that had given them a life they never would have had in Cuba.

CHAPTER 1

In 1962 David's father accepted a job working as a dentist for the Panama Canal Company. Since they spoke Spanish, they got on well with the locals as well as the other Americans. Like his mother, David had a light olive complexion, but his jet-black hair and striking blue eyes came from his fair-skinned father. He was a nice blend of both of them: the quiet, affable dentist and the mama he never wanted to cross. Mama's fiery personality complimented Papa's almost sedate sense of purpose, and they filled their home with passion and joy. His father loved to tease, "She's my fireworks," and the glint in his eye confirmed that her love always exceeded her temper.

In junior high school David met the new boy the first day of seventh grade. They were in the same homeroom and were seated next to each other in the back row. It was the perfect set-up to talk or pass notes and not get noticed by the teacher, if you timed it right.

David turned in his seat. "Hi, I'm David."

"MacArthur," the boy extended his hand with a big, toothy grin.

David tried not to laugh. He shook his hand firmly and asked, "Like the general?"

"Yeah, but you won't have trouble remembering my name!" smiled the boy who looked as different from General MacArthur as possible. He had short, golden curls that betrayed the crew cut his father had forced him to get a few weeks ago. His mischievous smile and dancing, hazel eyes revealed the heart of a boy who considered the world his personal playground.

CONVERSION

Not knowing how to respond, David defaulted to what he knew. "Do you play any sports?"

"Yep! Anything that involves a ball."

"That's neat. My favorite is football, but I play baseball and basketball too."

"I like football, but we didn't get here in time for summer practice. Can I try out?" asked MacArthur.

"I'll introduce you to the coach. You must be fast because...no offense...you're not that big for a football player."

MacArthur shrugged his shoulders and continued to smile, "Yep. I'm fast. And most of the time people don't know what I'm going to do."

David wondered, *Is he trying to say he'll change the play without asking?* "What you need to know is that we just play ourselves."

"Huh?"

"There aren't any other junior highs on our side of the canal, so coach breaks us into two teams and we play each other."

"Oh, I see." MacArthur didn't seem to be disappointed. "What about high school?"

"Well, the Balboa High School coach watches our games to see what's coming, and the high school only has a varsity team; but freshmen can try out."

"Does the high school play anyone?"

"Oh yeah. Balboa plays Cristobal, the high school across the Canal, and the Canal Zone College, and the Athletic Club."

"Aren't those guys too old?"

"Well, the college is just two years, so they're not that old. But

CHAPTER 1

in the Athletic Club, they can play as old as thirty-one."

"Wow! High school must be a blast!"

"Well, we'll find out. Meet me at the gym after school. I'll tell coach about you."

"Thanks." The bell rang, and their homeroom buzz began to quiet down. MacArthur waited until the bell had stopped then whispered, "See you then."

They were an unusual pair. MacArthur would always look short standing next to David, but what he lacked in height he more than made up in confidence. David's quiet and shy nature appreciated — and sometimes envied — a friend who was able to blend into any social situation and charm his way out of any misdemeanor. MacArthur often wondered how a guy as handsome as David could be so smart, so nice, and a great athlete besides. He counted himself lucky to have found a friend with *all* those qualities. And from the beginning, they could tell each other anything.

Their fathers were pleased when, after several months, it became apparent their sons were inseparable. The week that school started, the Colonel had developed a toothache. He had always had trouble with his teeth, and he was not pleased to have to spend several hours with Dr. Benjamin Parks when he had so much to do at his new post. However, he liked the soft-spoken dentist, and he was trained to size up people in short order. While the Colonel was in his chair, the dentist talked about world affairs and particularly the Cold War, mentioning his timely departure from Cuba. When the last rinse and wipe were over, the Colonel remarked, "Never met a dentist like you! Do you talk to all your patients like this?"

CONVERSION

Dr. Parks smiled. "Please excuse me. It's my habit from years in Cuba, sensing a revolution was sure to come. Many of my patients did not know they were supplying me with information to keep my family safe — and free." His smile faded and his eyes narrowed. "It was conversations with people like you that let me know when it was time to move to America."

That night the Colonel told his wife, "Our new dentist is impressive."

"Was he easy on ya?"

"Oh, the pain wasn't bad. In fact, he had me so interested in what he was saying that I almost forgot why I was there."

"Ya don't say?"

"I should bring Parks in to demonstrate to my staff just what a briefing should entail!"

Discovering Colonel Wells had served under General Patton in World War II and General MacArthur in Korea, Ben Parks found him fascinating. Nearly all the military brass in the Canal Zone were engineers, but the Colonel was a combat soldier. The two men also enjoyed a mutual love of history, so there was never a lack of conversation after each rinse.

November 22, the Colonel cancelled his afternoon appointment because President John F. Kennedy had been assassinated. Americans were in shock and mourning, and that generation would always remember where they were and what they were doing when they heard their president had been shot and killed. David and MacArthur were in gym class when their physical education teacher-football coach was called out of the gym. When

CHAPTER 1

he returned, everyone stopped what they were doing. This rock of a man was wiping his eyes and blowing his nose, visibly upset. He managed to tell them the news and then broke down again.

David and MacArthur looked at one another. MacArthur didn't recognize the look on David's face. *What was that?* When he asked him about it later, David explained that he had been in shock and didn't know what he was feeling. MacArthur said that he had felt the same way. School was cancelled for the next few days as Americans watched history on television, culminating in the funeral on November 25th.

The Colonel finally came to see Dr. Parks the second week in December. Ben could see by the look on his face that he was in no mood to talk. Over the years, he had learned when to ask questions and when to keep them to himself. His survival had depended on reading people in positions of power, and he sensed his new friend was shaken under his thick skin.

The Colonel was truly shaken, but as always, he found solace in his wife. She was the love and strength of his life, and they made the most of every moment they had together. At one hundred pounds dripping wet, Jeanne Wells was no pushover! She had given him five healthy, rambunctious children and ran their home with precision and charm. Raised in a Mississippi home that resembled the White House, she was a southern belle with impeccable manners and immovable morals, and people loved her for her warm hospitality and delightful sense of humor.

They met when the Colonel was stationed at a base in Mississippi, near Jeanne's hometown. Her grandfather was "The

CONVERSION

Judge," which made her the cotillion princess. Since Wells was a lowly lieutenant, she was completely out of his league. Moreover, she was Protestant and he was Catholic. So when he strolled in to do some business for the army at the Chamber of Commerce where she worked, they spoke briefly, he went on his way, and no one suspected that she thought he was dreamy like Frank Sinatra, or that he told his army buddies he had just met his future bride.

The bold lieutenant began courting the lovely Miss Talley, and he soon discovered he also had to court the Judge — who hated him at first sight. MacArthur told David that his great-grandfather was a Ku Klux Klan Confederate who never stopped fighting the War Between the States (which he called The War of Northern Aggression), and Lieutenant Wells was from Gettysburg, Pennsylvania! Undaunted, he persevered and won the begrudged respect of the Judge and the hand of his granddaughter.

After a world war, a "police action" in Korea, and several other postings states-side and abroad, the Wells family were now stationed in Panama. They lived in a large, comfortable home at Fort Amador, near a golf course, which was fortuitous. The Colonel was an avid golfer, a passion he passed to his son and a couple of his daughters.

They looked like a typical military family except for a few anomalies. One of them involved religion. At the post chapel, the children attended the Catholic service with the Colonel and the Protestant service with their mother. This ecumenical arrangement seemed perfectly reasonable to both parents, and their children obliged them with few complaints.

CHAPTER 1

MacArthur was outgoing and charismatic like his mother and athletic and unusually perceptive like his father. He was placed on the same football team as David and proved to be exactly what he had declared: fast and unpredictable. By January, the boys were playing basketball, where David's increasing height and MacArthur's scrappiness were a winning combination. Both were team players, but there was a special connection between them that their team counted on when not at their best. You could safely say that separately they would not have been as successful or as popular as they were together.

Being competitive athletes was not their only bond. Academics came easy to them, which often happens to kids who spend a lot of time with adults. They were always able to finish their homework in study hall and rarely took books home. If one of them did not understand something, the other invariably did. They were learning but were quite unaware of it. To David and MacArthur, school was simply a requirement they breezed through while playing sports and having fun.

One warm, January day, they left school at the beginning of the lunch hour to enjoy their empanadas on the hillside of Quarry Heights. This was where all the generals lived. Up there, they could see Panama City to their left and Fort Amador below, with the great canal just beyond it. They loved to go there, part of the draw being that the area was entirely enclosed by a chain-link fence and two gates, all heavily guarded by US military. However, they knew where there was an cut in the fence.

The sun shone through the clouds as they stretched out on the

CONVERSION

grass. David asked, "How'd you get the name MacArthur?"

MacArthur launched into the explanation. "It's funny and it's serious. After having four girls, Mom and Dad finally had a boy, me. They were really happy, but I guess my dad said, 'Damnit, Jeanne, this boy has to have the backbone of MacArthur to stand up to all you women, especially when I'm away.'" They laughed at his imitation of the Colonel. "And then my mom said, "Weuull than, let's cawl'm MacAaaaaarthah.'" They laughed even harder at his attempt to mimic his mother's Southern drawl.

"You were really named after General MacArthur?"

"Yep. My dad said that what he did for Japan after the war, helping them rebuild and not rubbing their noses in it, was historic. He really respects the man, even though he didn't always agree with him in Korea."

"Yeah. Truman fired him!"

MacArthur shook his head. "My dad says that sometimes the news reports things in a 'simplistic, outrageous fashion that betrays the whole truth.'"

"That sounds like your dad!" said David.

"Well, he said that MacArthur got part of it right and part of it wrong, and if Truman really understood war, like, well, he would've let MacArthur do the part that was right. Eisenhower did — understand war, I mean — and that's why the whole Korean conflict ended right after he was president."

"So *MacAaaaaarthah*, are you going to win wars, rebuild countries, and piss off presidents?" David teased.

MacArthur stared at the clouds passing overhead. David was

CHAPTER 1

discovering that his friend got serious at the strangest times. He finally answered, "I don't know, but ...." He sat up. "Do you hear that?" Shouts were coming from below. They jumped up and ran down toward the fence line to get a better look. The sentries were closing the gate, so they knew something important was happening.

"Sounds like it's coming from the high school," offered David. Slipping through the cut in the fence when no one was looking, they carefully made their way in that direction. As the high school came into view, David was the first to see it. "What the heck?" Kids were streaming out of the building and gathering around the flagpole, where Old Glory was waving in the wind.

"Why's the flag up?" MacArthur wondered out loud.

At that moment a hundred or more Panamanian college students came over the hill, marching toward the school. A couple of them in front were holding a Panama flag. The mob was taunting the American high school students as they approached the flagpole. They began to surround the Americans, who encircled their flagpole protectively.

MacArthur started jumping up, trying to see better. "Do you see my sisters anywhere?"

"Yeah!" David pointed. "There's Joanna, right in the middle." Joanna was a junior and was screaming with everyone else. Sarah, who was a freshman, stood on the outskirts of the crowd, so they didn't see her. The boys began to move closer to the mob, trying to find a way to get through the Panamanians and join the Americans.

Suddenly they saw Sarah running toward them. She was the

CONVERSION

closest to MacArthur in age, but since MacArthur had grown an inch taller this last year, strangers in Panama thought she was his younger sister, which vexed her and thrilled him. She had her mother's slim figure and her father's quiet demeanor, but to be heard, she yelled, "What are you doing here? Why aren't you in school?"

Her excitement was contagious. MacArthur cried back, "What's going on? Why's the flag up?"

"The Panamanians decided to fly their flag, but some college boys got wind of it and put our flag up before they got here. Some of us looked out the window and saw our flag, and we started cheering. The teachers got into it too, and they didn't stop us from coming out here. We surrounded the pole, and now the Panamanians have come with their flag. It's a mess." They all stared at the flagpole. Angry words in Spanish and English were being exchanged, and soon an all-out brawl began.

"You need to go back to school!" cried Sarah. "If Dad finds out you're here, you won't sit down for a month!"

"If it's dangerous for us, then it's dangerous for you too!" David blurted out. He had a crush on Sarah, even though she was older. He didn't know what had given him the courage to speak to her like this, so he froze and stared at her. Unlike her brother, she had auburn hair, but she had the same sparkling, hazel eyes. He was shocked when she smiled her amazing smile, put her hand on his arm, and said, "Thanks, David. I'm staying out of it, but I don't know about Joanna."

"Don't worry, she can take care of herself!" MacArthur grinned.

CHAPTER 1

Joanna was the tomboy of the family, and he could always count on her to push the envelope with him. Just then, he saw her running toward them with a look on her face he never thought he'd see.

Breathlessly she said, "The Panamanian flag tore, and they're blaming us. This is crazy!" She took Sarah's hand and began to pull her toward the school. "We're going back inside, and you guys get back to Diablo before you get hurt! Now!" MacArthur thought she sounded like the Colonel, but he didn't have time to ponder it. The mob was moving toward the road, because a group of American high school boys had decided to chase the Panamanian students out of the schoolyard.

MacArthur and David stayed out of the way and made sure his sisters got inside the school before they ran to join the pack of high schoolers, who followed the Panamanians down Balboa Avenue toward Fourth of July Avenue, the boundary between the American Canal Zone and Panama City. The two boys shouted like warriors as they gained on the others ahead of them. They were invincible! They had almost caught up when MacArthur winced. Someone had gripped his shoulders and spun him around to fly in the opposite direction. When he landed, he turned to face the Colonel.

David stopped and ran up beside him, just in time to hear, "Get your butts home. Now!"

With a duet of, "Yes, Sir," they walked quickly back up the road, looking over their shoulders to see the Colonel, in uniform, jump in his jeep and head the other direction. They moved slowly, glancing back to see the American students stop at the Panama City boundary. The Panamanians had already crossed over and had picked up stones and whatever they could find to throw at them. It was hard for the boys to keep moving away from the action.

They walked in silence toward the intersection, where David would turn toward his house in Balboa and MacArthur would turn toward his home at Fort Amador. David saw that his friend had that look on his face. It was a combination of reckless abandon and steely determination. "Let's get back up the hill so we can see everything that happens. I bet this isn't over."

David's face lit up. "Just what I was thinking!"

The boys took off running.

2

Sometimes one event can cause another, and that certainly was the case on January 9, 1964. Two boys cut school to watch what became an historic moment for the United States and Panama — and for them. There had been an ongoing dispute over whose flag should fly in the American Canal Zone: US or Panama. And if both flags flew, which flag should fly above the other? Until the issue could be resolved, the governor had ordered no flags flown. The clash over whose flag would fly at Balboa High School led to an all-out, anti-American riot in Panama City. What no one reported was that MacArthur discovered that he and David had a purpose, and David was the catalyst.

The boys ran to their best lookout on Quarry Heights, as the chaos increased in Panama City. Canal Zone police faced hundreds of rioters near the Canal Zone boundary, and the US military was on site as well. MacArthur was glad David was such a good Boy Scout, always carrying his pocket knife and a small pair of binoculars. "Oh my God, Mac. There're men with guns! I can't believe this!" He handed his binoculars to MacArthur, who noticed one particular Panamanian man directing men to sniper positions.

"Yeah, that guy's running the show," said MacArthur. They heard rifle shots, but smoke from a burning building kept them from making out where the shots originated. Then the smoke

CONVERSION

cleared enough for MacArthur to see that a Canal Zone police officer was shot and trying to crawl to safety. "Man, I never thought so much blood could come out of a person. Oh, there's my dad!" He wondered why his father seemed to be in charge and handed the binoculars back to David.

What the boys learned later was that because most US military brass in the Canal Zone were engineers, and the only general with combat experience was out of the country, the Colonel took charge. When the onsite engineer general was informed, he called the combat general to inform him of the riot and that Colonel Wells had taken command. The combat general replied, "He's a good man, and he's the right man," and hung up.

The Colonel's men shot tear gas in the direction of the Panamanian rioters, who retaliated with more rocks and taunts in Spanish. Then the strategically positioned shooters fired upon his men. Several were hit.

"Why don't our guys shoot back?" cried David. He handed the binoculars to MacArthur.

"I don't know. Maybe they aren't allowed. I think the president has to okay it." For the first time in his life, he was afraid for his father's life. *Oh God, keep him safe!*

Meanwhile, the Colonel made a strategic decision. After an hour of getting nowhere, trying to get the president's approval to return fire, four brave men in his unit were dead. That was enough for Colonel Wells to take the offensive and give the order to fire.

"Something's happening! Look!" MacArthur handed the binoculars to David.

CHAPTER 2

Their adrenalin raced as they watched the Colonel's troops fire bazookas at the buildings harboring the snipers, to flush them out. "My God. The Panama National Guard is just sitting there, watching. Why don't they do anything?"

"Let me see." MacArthur took the binoculars to get a closer look. "Yeah, I see what you mean." Now more Panamanian blood was being spilt. MacArthur described what he was seeing and swallowed hard. The Panamanian rioters were looting and burning as many buildings as they could. The US embassy was being evacuated. Panama City was on fire, but the Panamanians filled the streets to keep fire trucks from getting through. "Why are they burning the best buildings?" he cried. "That's crazy!"

David didn't have to think to answer. "They're *American* buildings, and they hate Americans. I mean, we came in here and took over their country."

"But this country would be in the dark ages if it wasn't for us. How could they hate us?"

"We take advantage of them. Use them for cheap labor. I mean, we came in with our money and know-how, and along with a few rich Panamanian families, we own the whole country. To them, Americans are capitalist pigs. And not just here. It's the same way in the entire third world. My father told me all about it so I would never go into Panama City. They hate us."

"Americans aren't capitalist pigs!" retorted MacArthur. "Who got rid of the mosquitoes and built this canal for them, anyway? Who got the Russian missiles out of Cuba last year and kept the Canal Zone free? We keep the world safe! How can they hate us for that?"

CONVERSION

"My dad says the only people that like Americans are other Americans. Everyone hates us, even our allies. They need us, but they don't like us."

MacArthur was deeply troubled as he handed the binoculars to David. How could his friend say these things? "Well, I'm going to ask my dad. He's been all over the world."

David didn't like being at odds with MacArthur, but he knew he was right. They sat on the hill and watched quietly for a while, hardly believing what they were seeing. Much of Panama City was obscured in smoke, and many people were dead. They had never seen anything like it except in the movies. But that was not real. This was really happening — yet it seemed unreal.

MacArthur got up, and David figured he wanted to go home before his father got there or their parents became worried. It was past the time school was out. But MacArthur just stood there, staring at the burning city, and then tears began to roll down his cheeks.

"Are you okay?" asked David. He had never seen MacArthur even remotely sad, and here he was, crying!

"I see it. The suffering. Look at those people. I have everything, and they have nothing." He took out his handkerchief, wiped his eyes, and blew his nose. "We have to do something about it." He stuffed his handkerchief back in his pocket, turned, and clasped David's arms. "David, something is terribly wrong! The world is broken. It needs fixing." David was speechless. MacArthur let go of him and turned back to the city. "I don't know what it is, but I'm going to find out, and I'm going to do something about it. We've

CHAPTER 2

got to do something about it!"

At that moment a beam of light burst through the sky and blinded them. They covered their eyes at first. Then they realized they could see. They felt weightless and carefree. In what seemed like years later, the light faded away and they "came to." They were lying on the ground, staring at the sky — laughing the deepest laugh they had ever laughed. Slowly, they turned to face each other, eyes wide and mouths open.

David managed to get the words out. "What...was...that?"

MacArthur cried, "Don't...ask...me!" They rolled around on the grass, punching each other and continuing to laugh, gasping for breath. As their laughter began to subside, they managed to pull each other up. "Oh my God, David!"

"Jesus, MacArthur!" David stared at him and then spit in his hand. He held it out, his expression deadly serious. "We tell no one."

MacArthur spit in his hand and shook David's with equal intensity, then broke into an incredulous grin. "Who would believe us, anyway?" They began to march down to the cut in the fence, giggling for no reason. "But it's crazy — I feel so...so..."

"Yeah. Like...peaceful."

"Yeah, even after what we just saw."

David Parks and MacArthur Wells were not old enough to drive, to drink, or to vote, but they had just witnessed the kind of human hatred and blind rage that nearly always leads to war. It was thrilling and grotesquely illuminating, and MacArthur had had his epiphany: He and David were supposed to change the world.

CONVERSION

As for the light...what did it mean? The only thing they knew for sure was that its brilliance had given them a serene sense of wonder in the midst of horror. It was an oxymoron they pondered for years to come.

Neither of these incidents, however, was the one that bound them together forever.

3

MacArthur, his sisters, and his mother didn't see his father for three days. Meg was a freshman at the Canal Zone College and was the first to greet the Colonel when he came through the door. She threw her arms around him and said, "So glad you're home, Dad." She knew better than to ask him about it. If he had something to tell them, he would.

"Meg. You look so pretty today." He kissed her on the forehead and squeezed her tightly again. "Where's your mother?"

Before she could answer, he heard: "Welcome home, Colonel." He turned and kissed his wife, then picked her up and whirled her around. Only he could make her laugh like this, and their children loved it. By this time Joanna, Sarah, and MacArthur gathered around him also, Joanna doing most of the talking. He gave each daughter a bear hug and then shared a firm handshake with his son. His eyes said, "Don't ever do that again." MacArthur hoped that would be the end of it, and as it turned out, it was.

For the first time in his life, MacArthur felt he had something significant in common with his father. Since he could remember, everyone in the family had told him he was like his mother: never knowing a stranger, on a mad dash to get everything he could out of life — and most of the time making it an exhilarating ride for all around him. He was unabashedly a mama's boy but all boy.

CONVERSION

MacArthur had watched his father do his job, and now he marveled at how the Colonel didn't act differently than he usually did around his family. He didn't swagger through the door boasting of victory, nor did he withdraw from them or become angry and violent because he had experienced the worst of humanity. Somehow, he managed to walk through the door and act like everything was okay. MacArthur began to question what "okay" was, because he had witnessed something that definitely was not okay.

Joanna told the Colonel about their adventure at the high school, Meg recounted what had gone on at the College, and Jeanne told him what the news had reported. He assured them all was well — making very little information sound like a lot. He called Rebecca, MacArthur's oldest sister, who was a junior at Ole Miss, and was joking with her on the phone in no time. The father who always came home to them, sometimes after a long absence, who was generally quiet except for the occasional witticism or "setting the record straight," had become a multi-dimensional being in the eyes of his son.

What else has he been through? MacArthur wondered. Now he understood why his father rarely talked about what he did or where he did it. There was no doubt he wanted his family to be happy and safe, *and* that he didn't want them to know what their freedom and security cost him — or could cost all of them.

On the one hand, MacArthur was greatly relieved that no questions were asked about what he and David had done during the riot. He had managed to get home soon enough after school

CHAPTER 3

so that his mother's curiosity had not been aroused, and for some reason his father didn't pursue it. On the other hand, he had a great desire to discuss the experience with him.

Today MacArthur also realized that, although he was like his mother in personality, he was like his father in his life's purpose. His father stopped conflict and restored peace, and MacArthur wanted to find the root of human conflict and pull it out, to eradicate it from the Earth. The world was sick, and he wanted to heal it. That was as far as he had thought it through, but he couldn't talk to his father about it. Not yet, anyway. Thank God, he had a best friend, the best he'd ever had.

David arrived home later than usual, and his mother gave him a hug that said she was more pleased he was home safe than she was angry about his tardiness on this of all days. When his father arrived, they discussed the riot, speaking mostly in Spanish. Because he was an only child, David had a unique relationship with his parents, very unlike MacArthur had with his. David told them everything, and today was no exception — other than the incident with the bright light. That was too weird, and he and MacArthur had made a pact not to discuss it with anyone else.

"You took great risk to follow MacArthur into such danger," his father admonished.

"I know, Papa, but as we watched from Quarry Heights, he finally recognized why the Panamanians hate us. It shook him up." He recounted his conversation with MacArthur.

"David, that is most significant." His father looked at him intently.

CONVERSION

"Yes, you are a very good influence on your friend," added his mother.

David felt proud and important. Several days afterward, he decided to do some more influencing and talked to MacArthur about his Boy Scout troop. "You should join. We learn a lot and have a blast."

"Sure! I was in a troop back in Virginia and really liked it. After all, the men in my family look great in a uniform!" he joked.

David watched MacArthur tackle scouting with the same competitive spirit he did everything else. He wanted to achieve the highest awards and do things few others would do. He pursued the God and Country Medal, which was something no one in their troop had attempted. The medal took a year to complete, and it required an extensive amount of work. MacArthur had to study and be able to describe the major religions of the world, and he had to spend a number of hours serving in a religious institution. As usual, he went overboard by being both an acolyte in his Protestant service and an altar boy in his Catholic service. He also delivered flowers to sick congregants of both congregations and polished the brass. A year later, in the spring of their 8th grade, the medal was his — and David dubbed him Saint Mac.

The subject of religion was the one issue of contention between the boys. Eventually they avoided discussing it. Despite the fact that his parents were Catholic and attended mass regularly, David recently had decided it was superstitious nonsense. An extremely intelligent boy, he was a great thinker at an early age, and his good looks easily belied the depth of his philosophical inner life to those

CHAPTER 3

who did not know him well.

MacArthur was also given to meditating the issues of life, but he never had trouble with leaps of faith — or leaps of any notion. Whereas trusting a power you couldn't physically see or scientifically define was too much of a stretch for David's rational mind, MacArthur had no problem believing in a God who could supersede his own natural laws and alter the course of human history. He sometimes wept when he looked at Jesus on the cross, always blessed his food, and thanked God every night before going to sleep — a practice David witnessed on their first sleepover. Although it irritated him, he endured MacArthur's commitment and hoped that one day his friend would come to his senses.

In the summer after eighth grade, the boys attended Boy Scout camp. They liked being able to concentrate on badge work and loved the whole camp experience. MacArthur discovered that he excelled in archery, and he spent as much time as he could practicing to compete. In just a few weeks, he was almost as good as the instructor. David's favorite activity was riflery, and he was well on his way to becoming an expert marksman. He felt an adrenalin rush every time he took aim, fired, and felt the powerful release from his rifle, while MacArthur preferred the quiet whir of an arrow shot from his bow.

With his new passion for the bow and arrow, MacArthur convinced David they should pursue the Order of the Arrow, an honorary service group he perceived to be the Army Rangers of the Boy Scouts. The program taught the ways of the American Indian and the meaning of brotherhood. They had to be recommended

CONVERSION

by their peers, and being well liked, they were chosen one day after lunch. All the campers were assembled, and two scouts dressed in Indian-like garb took David, MacArthur, and eight others down a short jungle path to a campsite. There, they were met by a group of older scouts dressed like Indians, "war paint" and all, and a "chief."

The chief gave each scout two solid taps on his right shoulder, signifying that he had been "tapped out" for initiation into the Order of the Arrow or OA. If they passed the test, called the Ordeal, they would be members. Two OA members, who were not counselors at the camp, led their Ordeal. David and MacArthur had seen them around the camp and knew their names were Chuck and John. They looked like they were in their mid-twenties. It had been rumored that they had been in the special forces of some branch of the military, but Chuck didn't look or act the part. He was truly an Indian, from one of the Dakotas, had a ponytail, and was quiet and laid-back. They didn't know where John worked, but they knew he was a guest professor at the college, because Meg had talked about him on several occasions. Evidently, all the girls considered him quite "the catch."

Chuck and John gave each recruit a heavy backpack of supplies and tools, including a knife and a canteen of water. A string with a stick attached to it was tied around their necks. John declared, "If you violate any rules or disobey any commands, you will carve a notch into your stick. Three notches and you're out. You will act honorably and honestly with yourself and with others, and take a vow of silence until instructed otherwise." He waved his hand, indicating that they should follow him.

CHAPTER 3

Chuck was the last in line, and the recruits were curious about the unusually large pack he carried on his back. John led them into the jungle, and David took note of the path and the terrain. They were hiking uphill, and a couple of times they took another path, once to the right and once to the left. He thought he heard flowing water, and a few minutes later stepped into it. The water was cold, refreshing, and came almost to their knees in the middle of the stream. About that time, they began to leave the jungle and enter the forest, always walking a steady rise.

Finally, they stopped. Although on much higher ground, they couldn't see anything because of the trees around them. They were in a small clearing, and they could still hear the faint sounds of the jungle below them and a rippling stream nearby. Despite his efforts to be brave, David fought visions of dying horrible deaths by wild animals and snakes that inhabited the woods. He glanced at MacArthur, who stood opposite him with a look that said, "This is the best, isn't it?!" Part of David wanted to sock him in the jaw, but the other part was relieved to see his friendly, if ignorant, face.

John barked their orders: "You will work together to transform this area into a new campsite, which must have a diameter of fifty feet. You will find the equipment you need in your packs, although what *you* need might be in someone else's. The big trees have already been cleared, but they will need to be cut for firewood." Then he assigned the boys various tasks. Forging a path from the campsite away from the stream and digging a latrine at the end of the path fell to David and two other boys. MacArthur and two others were to dig a fire pit and set a ring of rocks around it in

CONVERSION

the center of the campsite. When they finished, they would gather tinder and cut sticks and logs and set them in neat piles, using the small trees that had been cleared by the remaining four boys.

The OA recruits soon realized that none of these assignments could be tackled without first unloading and organizing the contents of their backpacks. The difficulty of doing this in silence affected each boy differently. MacArthur relished the challenge and immediately devised creative hand signals the rest could understand. It was his nature to take the lead. David studied how they attempted to communicate. He was fascinated at his new awareness of the other boys and their sudden interdependence. Eventually, they managed to put the blankets in a pile, consolidate the food in a few packs, and distribute the appropriate tools to each boy. They wondered what the ten pencils were for, but each took one.

Stopping only for a sandwich and an apple for dinner, they finished the work just after ten o'clock. The now brisk mountain air caused them to enjoy the heat of the fire as they sat roasting marshmallows. It was strange to eat in silence, especially for MacArthur. He was used to sitting around the table, joining in the chatter of his sisters and mother, with the occasional comment from his father when he was there. He took a long drink from his canteen, and the cool, night air sent a chill down his spine.

Chuck stood, brushed off his pants, and spoke for the first time, "Good work. Fill your canteens. Visit the latrine. Grab a blanket and find your place in the woods. Sweet dreams." He smiled, and then he and John got their blankets and hunkered down next to the

CHAPTER 3

dying fire. David felt someone punch him gently on the arm and turned to see MacArthur, who was making a ridiculous face while performing what could only be called silly sign language. David shook his head, and they went their separate ways. The moon was full, so the boys had just enough light to find a solitary place to sleep in the woods.

MacArthur was thoroughly content to brave the elements alone. He found a nice grassy place and was asleep in no time. David couldn't get MacArthur's silly face out of his mind as he wandered away, trying to find the right spot. Then it hit him: *My God, he looked just like Harpo Marx!* The image was so funny, he almost burst out laughing. Only the fear of having to carve a notch in his stick kept him mute.

He finally settled on a place, checked for snakes and spiders, and lay on his back, shifting his weight and trying to find a comfortable groove in the ground. Soon he stopped and gazed at the few stars he could see through the trees. It was peaceful, quiet, and the vast universe was stretched out before him. It told him that his life held infinite possibilities, and soon he was asleep.

The boys were awakened by the steady but increasingly strong beat of a drum, just as the sun began to brighten the sky. When they returned to the campsite, Chuck was putting a large Indian drum back into its special pack. They also noticed more tools, a bunch of sawhorses, and a large container. Other OA members must have brought them up. They put their blankets in the designated pile and lined up to get their breakfast of beef jerky, fry bread, and oranges.

CONVERSION

This time Chuck gave them orders. "Remember, anything you don't eat goes in the latrine, and never leave the camp without a full canteen." He stifled a smile, realizing he had just rhymed. "Today you're going to build a tipi." The boys' faces lit up, and two yelled, "Neat!" and "Wow!" Each had to put a notch in their stick for breaking the vow of silence. The other boys felt sorry for them, knowing how close they had come to doing the same thing. It put them all on edge.

"Seventeen poles, twenty-five feet long." Chuck pulled some plans from a duffle bag and opened them as the boys gathered around him. "Fifteen poles for the frame." He pointed to illustrations of both the frame and each kind of pole. The end of each framing pole came to a sharp point at the bottom, tapering up to a four-inch diameter at the butt. Then the rest of the pole was tapered to a two-inch diameter at the top. "The other two poles are called the smoke flap poles and are two-inch diameter instead of four.

"Other recruits have already cut pine trees suitable for the poles. These trees were planted here in the National Forest in the 1930s and are not native to Panama. They are stacked about a quarter mile due north of here. Find them, carry them back, and set them on these sawhorses to remove the bark, branches, and any knots with your hatchets. You'll mark them, and then use two-handled drawknives to trim them." He and John proceeded to illustrate the process.

The boys watched them trim with their hatchets, measure and mark the naked trunk to indicate where and how it should be cut (so that's what the pencils were for!), saw the excess off the bottom

CHAPTER 3

and top, and use the drawknives to slowly and carefully form the pole. Each boy was given a turn with a drawknife to get the feel of it. Chuck said, "When the poles are the right size and John or I have approved them, you'll leave them on the sawhorses to cure."

John continued, "The poles should be turned regularly for three or four weeks while they are being cured by the sun and weather, then you would apply a sealer, which would take a couple of days to dry. Obviously, you can't hang around for weeks, so you and your partner will make one or two poles to be used for another tipi for this campsite later. Other recruits have already finished poles, which you will use tomorrow."

Chuck added, "You may have noticed that many things were done before you got here. We thank the Creator for those in the past who have worked to make our lives better, and we honor them by working to secure a better life for those who will come after us. This is the Indian way. It is the Great Spirit's way." Then he commanded, "Line up!" and he and John separated the ten boys into groups of two.

John said, "There will be a half-hour break for lunch and dinner. Set up your sawhorses, then move out and get the cut trees. AND, be careful with these tools. They are sharp and should be used with respect. Don't hurry. One good pole is much better than two with cut fingers."

David and MacArthur were separated again, and all the boys soon discovered that carrying the long, slender trees back to camp was the easy part. Nevertheless, by sundown each set of two boys had finished at least one pole to either John or Chuck's satisfaction.

CONVERSION

After dinner, John motioned to the pile of blankets. The boys were so tired, each grabbed a blanket and returned to the place he had slept the night before.

The next morning they were awakened again at daylight by the beckoning drum. They walked into camp and saw that the sawhorses and their poles had been moved to one side of the campsite, and there was a stack of finished poles at the other side. After breakfast, Chuck said, "Choose a different partner, someone you don't know that well, if possible. You're going to set up the poles and cover them the Indian way. If the tipi is not done by the end of today, no one will have passed their Ordeal." The boys forgot how tired and sore they were and became more determined than ever.

Chuck and John opened the large container and motioned for several recruits to pull out the large, white canvas. They rolled it out flat on the ground. "You need to mark where the canvas hits the poles at the top. You'll see why later. So each of you pick up a pole or two and set them on the canvas like this." John had placed a pole on the canvas, with the butt at the outer edge.

Once the poles were marked, they returned them to the side of the campsite. John motioned them to roll the canvas and set it to the side again. He motioned for the recruits to set three poles near the fire pit, in parallel fashion. Chuck said, "You will tie the three main poles together with rope at the mark, where the top of the canvas will be." He knelt next to the three poles, and John handed him the end of a very long, half-inch, coiled rope. "Watch carefully." He used one end of the rope to connect the poles with a

CHAPTER 3

clove hitch knot, wrapped it around all three poles four times, and finished with two half hitches.

"If you do this correctly, this is what happens." He and John used a fourth pole to lift the three poles. They moved two of the poles apart and placed the third so that the three formed a stable tri-pod that tilted slightly. This was to ensure that smoke could escape but rain and snow could not come in the hole at the top.

"Take a good look," said John, and a minute later he and Chuck used the fourth pole to collapse the tri-pod, lower the poles, and remove the rope. "Now each of you will do this with your partner." MacArthur eagerly stepped forward with his partner in tow. It took them four tries to get it right, and the other boys had the advantage of learning from their mistakes, but MacArthur was having too much fun to be embarrassed. By the time David and his partner knelt down and he took the rope, he knew exactly what to do and succeeded with the knots on the first try.

Once all the boys had had the experience of tying and setting the first three poles, Chuck and John jammed the sharp ends into the ground until only the butts were visible. Chuck took hold of the rest of the rope, which dangled from where it secured the first three poles. John placed the fourth pole between two others, jammed it into the ground, and Chuck secured it with the rope. John said, "Get a pole with your partner." Each twosome placed and secured a pole with the rope, with Chuck helping those who needed it.

By lunchtime, the frame of the tipi was finished. They devoured their lunch, and afterward they hauled out the canvas again. Chuck

CONVERSION

and John showed the boys how to roll the cover over the frame by using the two smoke flap poles. They told the recruits to retrieve the connecting pegs from the canvas container and showed them how to insert them in the overlapping canvas door.

When the canvas was secured around the frame, Chuck and John used the smoke flap poles to place the smoke flap cover piece around the top of the poles. The smoke flap poles remained attached to this piece, and Chuck demonstrated how to open and close the smoke flap cover piece with the two poles, which were set at the back of the tipi. "It's open when you have a fire and closed when the weather is bad." Then he removed the cover and each group of two did the same.

The last task was to pound wooden pegs through the loops at the bottom of the canvas to secure the canvas. When they were finished, they were in awe of what they had accomplished in silence and even more in awe of the Indians who had done this for centuries. It was now past dinnertime, and they ate their meal with great satisfaction.

"Because you have achieved your goal and built this great tipi for others to enjoy, you have the honor of spending the first night in it," said John. Thrilled, the boys got their blankets and entered the tipi. John and Chuck showed them how to close the tipi door flap and left. All was quiet except for the usual night sounds of the forest and the jungle below. MacArthur wondered what it would be like to live like the Indians. He dreamed of dancing a victory dance around a great bonfire. David had a nightmare that he was being scalped.

4

On the third day, the OA recruits were allowed to sleep an hour longer. Chuck, John, and three other members of the OA served them a huge breakfast of eggs, bacon, sausage, fry bread, fried potatoes, and all kinds of fruit in the tipi. The boys were sure they were being rewarded for passing the Ordeal and wondered why they were still keeping the vow of silence.

After cleaning up their breakfast, John declared, "You will count off one-two by holding up your fingers, and each group of two will begin the last part of your Ordeal."

Standing next to each other, David and MacArthur were paired together. Each OA member took two recruits. Chuck slipped on a backpack and stepped in front of David and MacArthur. He blindfolded them and instructed David to hold onto his backpack and MacArthur to hold onto David's canteen strap; then he led them into the forest. The boys tried to mark the terrain and sense what direction they were taking. They went uphill and downhill and crossed a stream, only a couple of inches deep.

After what seemed about thirty minutes, Chuck stopped and removed their blindfolds. He gave them the following instructions as he unloaded two blankets, two hatchets, and an army issue water pouch from his backpack: "There is enough water in the pouch to last twenty-four hours. You will spend today and tonight working

CONVERSION

together. What you do in this time should reflect the honor and service of the Order of the Arrow. Be here tomorrow at sunrise, and I will take you to the sacred ceremonial ground, where you will be sworn into the brotherhood." He started to walk away. "You can speak after I leave." Then he disappeared into the woods.

MacArthur was the first to speak. "Now we know —" he squeaked, and they laughed — "why they gave us a big breakfast."

"Man. Your voice sounds really weird," David laughed at his own strange-sounding voice. Their voices had begun to change, but being quiet for so long had made them sound even more bizarre.

They looked around. "I don't see any paths, do you?" asked MacArthur.

"No. Maybe that's what we could do."

"Yeah. We could make a new path. Then other boys can get lost in the woods too!" MacArthur laughed and looked up at the sky to check the position of the sun. "Which way do you want to go?"

"Let's be safe and go back the way Chuck brought us. Wait. What if Chuck left a different way than he brought us?"

MacArthur was baffled. "Oooh. Well, I think he brought us from the same direction he left. That's what feels right."

"I think so too. It was just something I thought of."

"Sometimes I wish you didn't think so much," said MacArthur. "Let's leave the water pouch here to mark this spot, since we have to meet Chuck here."

"Mac, we're making a path *from* this spot, remember?"

"Oh yeah! On second thought, you keep thinking."

"Let's just take the hatchets. We can come back for the pouch

CHAPTER 4

and our blankets later."

"Gotcha." They moved slowly in the agreed direction, clearing the foliage away, forging a path a little more than two feet wide and going around anything that was too big to cut with a hatchet. "Hey, there's a clearing up ahead that looks perfect to make a campsite."

David followed MacArthur to the clearing. It was a rough oval with only a few small bushes to remove and lots of green grass. After finishing the path to the clearing, they collapsed on their new green bed, taking a long drink from their canteens. David looked up at the sky, "At least it's clear. From where the sun is, it must be after lunchtime. Hey Mac, look at that tree."

MacArthur jumped up and ran to it. The tree was what all kids who love to climb trees call the perfect climbing tree. Its lowest limb was far enough from the ground to reach with a good jump or a leg up from a friend, which meant the tree was mature enough to be tall and strong. You could climb higher and see more. MacArthur leapt up to grasp the first limb and proceeded to climb more than fifty feet from the ground. "This is one of the best I've ever climbed!"

David wasn't far behind and whistled. "Wow, it's great up here! Look, there's our tipi," and he pointed to the left. "Chuck went around and around to get here."

"Hey! There's the stream we must've crossed. It gets bigger down there." MacArthur pointed to the right.

David's stomach wrenched. "God, I'm hungry. I guess we should think about picking some fruit or something."

MacArthur surveyed his new kingdom. "How 'bout we kill a

wild boar? We'd be the hit of the Ordeal!"

"Now you're thinking like a swine!" David's voice cracked on "swine," and their laughter floated above the trees. "Let's get to that stream. Maybe we could catch a fish. We're up high enough, we might find some trout."

"We can make spears and spear them, like the Indians here do it!"

As it turned out, the flowing brook was teeming with trout. "Mac, look at the size of those buggers!"

"Yep. It looks like fish on the menu tonight. We just gotta catch 'em." The boys cut small branches with their hatchets and sat down to sharpen the ends with their knives.

"This is easy compared to shaving tree trunks," David remarked. As they worked, they tried to ignore their hunger pangs.

MacArthur remembered how tame his previous scout trips had been in the past. "My troop did a lot of camping in Virginia, and that was really neat; but it wasn't anything like this."

"What's it like there? I've only lived in Cuba, which I don't remember, and Miami we did a little camping, and now Panama."

"Virginia was beautiful, green like here, only cooler — I mean, in temperature. Our first scoutmaster was the best...personality-wise. Like, he was always cracking jokes and doing crazy stuff. Then we got a real 'by-the-book' guy. If we had done anything wild, we'd have been, like, court-martialed or something."

"Wow," said David, "court-martialed. That would freak me out for sure."

MacArthur grinned mischievously. "Speaking of being freaked

CHAPTER 4

out, when you gonna call my sister?"

David's face turned red, even in the heat of the day. "She's like *two* years older than me."

"Actually, not even a year and a half, cause you're older than me; but I think she likes you."

"Yeah, like another little brother! Besides, you haven't exactly gone after Jennifer Westin."

Now MacArthur looked uneasy. "She's just nice to me because I do all the dissecting in science lab."

"Oh come on! When you became lab partners, everyone saw the chemistry." David laughed at his pun.

"That's bad! Really bad!" MacArthur put his knife back in its sheath and felt the tip of his spear. "Mine is ready. Yours looks good too."

"Okay," said David, putting his knife away and feeling the sharp tip of his spear. The boys waded into the brook, poised to stab their prey.

"Whoa! Shoot! Damnit!" After minutes of near misses, they looked at each other in frustration.

"This is harder than when I saw the Indians do it," said David. He picked out a fish swimming toward him and positioned his body to strike. *Not now. Not yet. Now!* He stabbed at an angle, pulled out his spear — nothing. "What the...?"

"YabaDabaDooo! I got one!" cried MacArthur, holding up his spear with a flopping fish on it. It was a nice-size trout. He lowered the spear, admiring his catch. "Okay, your turn!"

David shook his spear like a warrior and stared. *What? Was that*

47

CONVERSION

the same fish? Couldn't be. Was it taunting him? More determined than ever, he leaned over slowly, took aim, and a moment later rammed the spear into something that felt more dense than he thought a fish would be. "I got something!" The spear was heavier than he expected as he pulled it out of the water, and that's when he saw three fish trying to free themselves from it. One of them tore loose and splashed back into the water, but the other two had been speared firmly through the middle and were stuck fast.

"Wow!" yelled MacArthur, who had run to his side.

"I can't believe this," marveled David. "It's like a double play... well, almost a triple play."

"What are the odds? This is, like, a miracle or something!" said MacArthur. They found some rocks that were flat enough to clean the fish, throwing the discarded parts into the stream. "Ever eaten raw fish before?" he asked.

"Mmmmm, *ceviche*, but the fish have spices and stuff on 'em. I like it when Mama makes it with plantains and sweet potatoes. God, I'm hungry."

"Our cook makes it for us, but I never eat raw fish. I only like it cooked. Mom has her cook mine." He stared at the fish he was cleaning and his stomach growled loudly. "We need to build a fire for tonight anyway. I'll go get some wood as soon as I finish cleaning this."

"Okay. It's going to take me a little longer..." David chuckled, alluding to the fact that he had caught more fish.

"Right," MacArthur finished and began to wash his knife in the water. As he wiped it on his pants, he said, "Hey, since we're doing

CHAPTER 4

this Order of the Arrow Indian thing, I was thinking it would be neat if we became blood brothers."

"You mean, like cut ourselves and mix our blood together?"

"Yeah. What do you think?"

David threw the second fish head in the water. "I think it's cool. You wanna do it after we eat?"

"Yeah, at our campfire tonight." MacArthur watched David remove the bones from his second fish. He looked around. "This sure is a pretty place."

David cleaned his knife and gathered the fish, while MacArthur picked up their spears. They hiked back to the clearing in silence. "I'll get the wood and all our other stuff while you clear a place for the fire," said MacArthur.

"Okay. Don't get lost." He watched MacArthur disappear with a hatchet along the path they had made hours ago, but it seemed like days. The pungent smell of the fish overwhelmed him and he took a bite of one. *Not bad. Probably because I'm so hungry.* He finished eating it and took a long drink. His canteen was almost empty, but MacArthur would be back with the pouch soon. *Time to get to work.*

With his hatchet, he tore away the grass, digging into the ground to make the fire pit. He had cleared just a couple of square feet when he heard MacArthur yell, "Help! David! Hurry!" For some reason, he dropped his hatchet and grabbed his spear, then ran as fast as he could toward his friend's voice, which was away from the path they had just made. Swiping at branches along the way, he heard MacArthur crying, "Oh God, help me. Agh!"

"I'm coming, Mac!" he yelled back.

49

CONVERSION

He saw MacArthur on the ground, holding his right knee, looking pale and scared. Pieces of wood and tinder were scattered behind him on a blanket. "Snake bite. It hurts. Bad."

"Where's the snake?"

"Over there, by that big tree," and MacArthur pointed. It was about twenty feet away and surrounded by brush. "But I don't know if it's still there. I felt something awful, like it hit my ankle, and decided to get away from whatever it was. And then it hurt, so I stopped to see what had happened and saw this." He pulled back his bloody sock.

David saw two large fang marks with blood seeping out of them. "Wait here." He raised his spear and scanned the woods as he slowly approached the tree and underbrush. There it was, curled up, with its head sticking out about six inches from the rest of its body. Fortunately, it was looking away from him. It was a very large fer-de-lance. He estimated it to be seven feet long and as round as his forearm. He thought about killing it, but that would only waste time and put his own life at risk, and MacArthur needed help now.

Every scout in the troop had been taught what to do if someone was bitten by a snake. First, you identified it or, if you didn't know what it was and you had time, you would kill it and bring it or the head to a medical facility. Then the correct antivenom could be administered. After identifying the fer-de-lance, David ran back to MacArthur, who was breathing heavily. He threw down his spear and patted him on the shoulder. "You're gonna be okay. It's gonna be okay."

MacArthur relaxed, and David looked at the bloody sock again.

CHAPTER 4

With this kind of snake, it did no good to cut the wound and suck the blood out, because the fer-de-lance venom acted like a blood thinner. There was only one thing that would help — antivenom — and it had to be administered fast. Fer-de-lance venom not only acted as an anti-coagulant, but also it caused flesh to rot and could be fatal.

"Look Mac, we've got to get you back to the camp infirmary. I bet the nurse has antivenom. Can you get up?"

"I think so."

David helped MacArthur to his feet. He cried out in pain as the blood rushed to the wound. It bled more steadily, and his ankle was already turning red and beginning to swell. David hoped a lot of the venom was coming out. He put MacArthur's right arm over his shoulder and acted as a crutch, but it was slow going. MacArthur tried to be brave, but he cried out with every step. Soon, it felt like his lower leg was exploding. His mind began to slip, and he could only hold onto one thought: *God, help me.*

They managed to get back to where they were to meet Chuck the next morning. "I feel really sick at my stomach," murmured MacArthur, and he passed out. David lowered him to the ground. He took the canteen from around MacArthur's neck, dropped to his knees, and filled it from the water pouch. Then he put it around his neck and under his right arm. He rose and pulled MacArthur's body up. "Mac, you should be really glad I'm bigger than you," he murmured, trying to forget that his best friend could be dying.

MacArthur came to and screamed in pain. "Ahhh! God!"

"Sorry Mac!" He waited for him to steady himself. "Can you

walk?"

"I...think...so," he mumbled, trying to remember where he was and what had happened. At the first step and shooting pain, it all came back to him. "Oh God!"

"Here. Try to drink some water." MacArthur managed to swallow several times, and they set out again, down the path they had just forged through the brush. His right arm was wound tightly around David's neck, and each step was agony. After a couple of yards, he leaned to the left and retched several times, but only water came out.

David let him take a few breaths and then said, "Mac, we need to keep moving. All right?"

MacArthur took a deep breath. "You're Superman, you know that? You even look like him." The comic book character was one of their favorites. He took the next step. "Oooooh, Jesus!"

David was suddenly enraged. *Superman? I have to be Superman because you rush around and crash through life without thinking about where you're going or what you're doing!*

"David...where are we...going?"

David realized that he had not thought about where he was going! He forced his mind to remember what he had seen when they were up in the tree and deduced that the tipi was to their left. "We're going back to the tipi. Remember Mac, we saw it when we climbed the tree." He looked up to mark their position by the sun, then turned and began helping MacArthur through the woods. Absent a path, it took much longer, and he had to stop and look at the sun periodically to see if he was still going in the right

CHAPTER 4

direction.

He thought, *There's got to be someone — or maybe some other recruits — nearby.* He yelled as loud as he could, "Help! Snakebite! We need help! If you're out there, please come! Help!" He whistled. He shouted, and his voice cracked from time to time. But he crept forward, hoping he was still going toward the tipi site. The worst part was MacArthur's cries of pain. His lower leg was sensitive to any kind of contact, which was impossible to avoid in the dense woods.

MacArthur felt heavier with every step and David's neck ached. "David, I feel...really..." and he fainted again. David shifted MacArthur's body onto his back and began carrying him. He continued crying out for help when he could catch his breath. Sharp pains stabbed his neck and back, his throat was sore, and his legs were like jelly. He thought he heard someone.

"Over here!"

5

"What happened?" Chuck asked. He helped David set MacArthur on the ground and examined his bloody ankle.

"Fer-de-lance."

"How long ago?"

It's been almost an hour, I think."

"We're not far from the tipi." He gave his backpack to David. "Let's get MacArthur there first."

"Do you have any antivenom?"

"No, but there's some at the camp infirmary." Chuck threw MacArthur over his shoulder, and what happened next was what David would call classic MacArthur. He opened his eyes, threw up his arm, croaked, "Tally ho!" and passed out again.

Chuck burst out laughing and almost dropped him. When they got to a path, he said, "You go ahead of me — and watch for snakes!" A few steps later he asked, "How did you know what direction to go? You were headed almost right toward the tipi site."

"We climbed a tree and saw where we were," said David.

"Ah." They were silent to preserve their strength, moving as quickly as they could. Chuck's backpack was much lighter than MacArthur, but David was getting dizzy scanning the ground and trees for any sign of another snake. With every step his heart seemed to beat, *Just live, Mac. Just live.*

CONVERSION

When they entered the tipi site, Chuck called to John, "We've got a snake bite, fer-de-lance!" David helped Chuck slide MacArthur off his back onto the ground and held his head in his lap.

John yelled through a bull horn in every direction, "All recruits return to the tipi! Emergency! All recruits return to tipi! Emergency!" Then he walked over to MacArthur and looked over Chuck's shoulder, "There's antivenom in the infirmary." Seeing MacArthur's swollen and bruised leg, he said, "We need to make a stretcher." Two recruits came running and assisted as he removed the smoke flap poles from the tipi. "Get a blanket."

Chuck stood and frowned. "I'm taking him on down the trail, and you can catch up to me." He looked up. "It will be dark in a couple hours." He pulled MacArthur over his shoulder, which brought him back to consciousness.

David fought back the tears, hearing his friend's cry of pain. There was no "Tally ho!" this time. He felt desperate to do something and followed Chuck. "Hey," he said. "I can run to the camp and get the antivenom and meet you on the trail. That will save some time."

Chuck looked at him intently. "Are you sure you're up to that?"

David nearly skipped alongside him. "Yeah. I ate a fish and feel pretty good."

Chuck stared at him. "You had a fish?" When David was about to explain, he cut him off with a wave of his hand. "Do you know where you're going?"

"Yep. I memorized the way up here." David took off running.

CHAPTER 5

Most of the trail was downhill, which was good and bad. It got easier breathing and gravity was working with him, but also it was a lot easier to slip and fall. Halfway there, he realized he was in a zone, like when he was at the end of a baseball game, the score was tied in the bottom of the ninth, and the bases were loaded. He remembered each turn and his feet flew over the ground, leaping over tree roots, impervious to stones that might have caused him to stumble — his heart beating steadily, *Just live, Mac. Just live.*

When he reached the camp, a bunch of scouts and a couple of counselors watched him race past them and yelled, "What's going on?" He kept running until he reached the infirmary and burst through the door, panting, "Snake bite...need antivenom...up on the trail."

The nurse hurried toward him, "What kind of snake?"

David bent over, and she rubbed his back. "Fer-de-lance. I need to get the antivenom...and meet them on the trail." He tried to regulate his breathing and straightened up. "They're carrying him here, but it's taking a long time."

She motioned for him to follow her. "How long ago was he bitten?"

"I think it's been almost two hours."

His eyes fixed on the nurse like she was his lifeline, and she responded the way he wanted her to: "Okay. Let's get you ready." He opened his canteen and drank while she unlocked the door to the storage room, took down two vials of fer-de-lance antivenom from an upper shelf, and opened a drawer to pull out a couple of syringes. "Here are two just in case. Is Chuck or John with him?"

CONVERSION

"Yes, Ma'am."

"Good. They know what to do." She placed everything in a leather pouch and handed it to him.

"Thank you, Ma'am." He looked at her for the first time and realized she was Indian, from one of the tribes in Panama.

She followed him to the infirmary door, opened it, and walked out with him. "God put wings on your feet!" she cried as he took off.

For this occasion, he set aside his atheism and yelled back, "Thank you, Ma'am!"

It seemed hours later when he met Chuck and John and the other recruits, who were taking turns carrying MacArthur on the makeshift stretcher. He was obviously in horrendous pain and unfortunately conscious. "David...uh." Tears had made paths down his dirty cheeks. They lowered him to the ground, and he groaned. David handed the bag to Chuck.

"It's all there. The nurse said you'd know what to do." He knelt beside MacArthur and patted his white hand, which was gripping the pole of the stretcher. At each stabbing pain, his head and uninjured leg jerked.

Chuck took his hand and held it over his heart. "Try to hold still, MacArthur, so John can give you the shot. You're going to start to get better now." Chuck looked up at John, who stared at him blankly for a second. It unnerved David. *What did that mean?*

David glanced at the leg. Most of the calf was badly bruised and swollen. MacArthur was also having trouble breathing. David squeezed his other hand and said, more for his own benefit, "You're going to be okay. You're Saint Mac, remember?"

CHAPTER 5

John administered the shot. "Did she give you anything for the pain?"

David was crestfallen. "No. I didn't even think about it. Sorry Mac." He swallowed hard.

MacArthur grabbed his hand. "It's...okay, I—"

Chuck interrupted him and gave him a drink of water. "Don't talk. You need to be still and rest." He and John picked up the stretcher, and David and the other campers followed behind. Time seemed to press in on them as they navigated the twists and turns and downhill slides, trying to move as fast as possible but mindful that every jolt caused MacArthur excruciating pain.

By the time they reached the camp, a medical helicopter was waiting. Chuck told the medic everything they knew while he and John transferred MacArthur to the gurney. "Sounds like you did the right thing," said the medic. "We'll take it from here. Don't worry. We'll do everything we can," and he patted David on the back.

"I'm going with you. I'm not leaving him!" he shouted.

When they began to load the gurney into the helicopter, MacArthur cried out, "David! David!" Chuck and the medic relented, and David hopped on board, strapping himself into a seat near his friend.

Chuck yelled to David, "I'll call his dad!" From the way he said it, David wondered if he knew the Colonel. The medic went to work as they lifted off the ground. He put an oxygen mask on MacArthur's face and inserted an IV in his arm.

David watched and his heart continued to cry out, *Just live, Mac! Just live!*

6

"I want to do it now," MacArthur said adamantly, straining to sit up in his hospital bed.

David gripped the foot railing of the bed and tried not to lose his temper. "Let's wait until you're well."

"I'm well enough. It's been...how many weeks? We need to do this now. I know it."

"The doctor...your parents will kill us. This is crazy. We need to wait. That's the safest way."

"Safe...not right." This was not the first time David had heard his friend say this. And then there was that look: reckless and determined...usually a bad combination for both of them.

"Okay. I'll talk to Hernandez. If he says we can do this, then at least we'll have an ally when we talk to your parents. If we're going up against the Colonel *and* your mom, we need huge back-up."

MacArthur laughed and fell back on his pillows. "I won't say anything until you get him on our side."

David shook his head, rolled his eyes, and walked out of the hospital room to find the doctor. The last couple of weeks he had thought a lot about how the Ordeal had become more of an ordeal than anyone had anticipated. When the helicopter had arrived at the hospital, both MacArthur's and David's parents were there. The Colonel had no trouble getting access to the landing pad. He shook

CONVERSION

David's hand as he jumped out of the helicopter. "Chuck told me what you did, Son, and I thank you. He said you probably saved his life."

The medic and an orderly lifted MacArthur's gurney out of the chopper. The Colonel took his son's hand and squeezed it, glancing at the swollen leg. MacArthur opened his eyes and smiled back at the Colonel, that same goofy smile David remembered from their first day in homeroom. He seemed to be breathing easier. Once inside, he was wheeled into the large, private elevator and taken to emergency surgery. David and the Colonel took another elevator.

When they entered the waiting room, he heard, "Aww David," from MacArthur's mother, wrapping her arms tightly around him. She kissed him on the cheek, and he felt her tears.

He whispered in her ear, "He was so brave, and he would've done the same for me."

Then he saw his parents. They hugged him and told him how proud they were of him. Suddenly he felt completely spent. He slumped into a chair and said, "I'm really hungry."

"Elena smiled and said, "Let's get you home."

He looked up. "No. I can't leave until I know he's okay."

"Mama is right," said Ben. "It might be some time before MacArthur is out of surgery and the doctor can report to us. We've already asked. He's in wonderful hands — Hernandez is the best — and you are going to be no good to your friend if you get sick too."

"Yes. That's an order, David," added the Colonel.

"We promise we'll cawl ya if anithin' happens," said Mrs. Wells.

Her accent sounds so strange yet so soothing, David thought.

CHAPTER 6

Back in his bedroom, he felt like he was in a foreign land. Nothing seemed real, even though it was familiar: the posters on the walls, the books on his desk, and his old army men on his dresser. He didn't recognize himself in the mirror. His face was covered with dirt and his hair was oily and matted. *My God, Mrs. Wells hugged me, and I probably smell like dead fish!*

He removed MacArthur's canteen, then his knife and belt. He walked into the bathroom and let his filthy clothes fall to the floor. His body warmed under the hot shower, while his mind drifted to MacArthur, sitting on the ground next to the blanket and scattered wood, holding his knee. *He must have gone back to the water pouch and gotten a blanket to carry the wood. That's why the blanket was there.* He dried himself off, put on clean pajamas, and combed his hair.

By the time he dropped his filthy clothes in the laundry room, smells of Mama's cooking were calling to him. He ate heartily, telling them all that had happened. Elena patted his hand periodically as he spoke. She got up to refill his glass and kissed the top of his head. Ben was deep in thought.

"You have done well. Very well."

"MacArthur wanted to be blood brothers, but he got bit before we could do it."

Ben sat even more straight. "This will affect your entire life," he said soberly. "When you become his blood brother, you will be bound to him forever."

"Yes Papa."

"Benjamin? What are you saying?" Elena set the pitcher of milk on the table.

CONVERSION

He turned to his wife, took her hand in his, and looked deep into her eyes. "You know what I am saying."

She pulled her hand away and shook her head. "Men and their games." She grabbed the pitcher and looked at David. "Do you want seconds, Mr. Hero?"

David and his father laughed. "No, Mama." He patted his stomach. "Now that my stomach is full of such good food, the rest of me is falling asleep."

He kissed them goodnight, crawled into bed, and slept for twelve hours. By the time he dressed and came into the kitchen the next day, his mother was fixing lunch and his father was at his office. "Good afternoon, sleepyhead."

"Good afternoon, Mama. Have you heard from the hospital?"

"Your father visited after his morning patients and just called to say that MacArthur is doing fine. They had to remove some of the flesh on his leg, but he came through the surgery fine. He's fine. He's just fine."

"Then I guess he's fine!" quipped David. She waved her big wooden spoon at him menacingly. He held up his hands in surrender. "Sorry!" he laughed as she pulled him into her arms and kissed him on the side of his head. Before the Ordeal, he would have resisted her, trying to be less of a boy and more of a man, but today was different. Everything was different.

After lunch, his mother drove him to the hospital. And so he began a new, daily routine, staying by his friend's side and helping as much as he could. MacArthur was in a lot of pain, and Dr. Hernandez tried several painkillers until he found one that worked.

CHAPTER 6

It caused MacArthur to sleep a lot. When he was awake, he acted goofy. David thought, *So this is Mac on drugs.*

Chuck and John visited briefly at the end of the first week. MacArthur was heavily sedated when they were there. "Everyone in your group passed the Ordeal, and we went ahead and had the ceremony," said John. "As soon as you're on your feet, MacArthur, we'll have a special ceremony for you and David."

"Thanks. Thank you so much!" He grimaced. "But I dropped the wood, and I couldn't find my knife. Where is it?" He sat up and began feeling around his bed. They all tried not to laugh.

Chuck took his right hand and shook it. "We're keeping it for you. No need for a knife right now. You have a different assignment." He had MacArthur's full attention.

"Yes, Sir."

"You need to rest, give your body time to heal, and think about your future. Can you do that?"

"Yes, Sir." He laid back and closed his eyes.

David followed Chuck and John out of the room and closed the door behind them. "Thanks for coming. It means a lot to him — well, if he remembers!"

John laughed softly but Chuck only smiled and said, "We covered the area you were working and found the path and the beginnings of a campsite."

"It was good," said John.

"What happened out there, before I found you?" asked Chuck.

After David briefly described what had happened, John shook his hand. "Well, no doubt about it. You guys had the most

CONVERSION

challenging Ordeal of anyone I've known. We're proud to welcome you into the Order of the Arrow."

Chuck smiled and shook his hand. "Are you coming back to camp?"

"No. I'm going to stay with Mac until he's able to walk out of here."

"Understand."

David sensed Chuck understood in a way that he didn't, which reminded him. "Can I ask you...do you know Colonel Wells?"

Chuck and John shared a quick glance of recognition. John said, "We served under him."

Chuck added, "He's a true warrior. And it looks like you and MacArthur are also."

Before David could respond, John ended the conversation. "Let us know when you're ready for your ceremony."

"Okay. Thanks for everything!" He watched them walk down the hallway to the elevators. It was a great day among many long days.

The one good thing about MacArthur's lengthy recovery was that his family members began to take turns visiting. Because Joanna had a part-time job and Meg was in summer school, Sarah and her mother visited most often. Rebecca flew home to spend a week with her brother, and she and David had lively conversations. They discovered they both were punsters and entertained MacArthur with their dueling wits.

The Colonel came whenever he could, which was special, but David loved it when Sarah was there. Of course, it always turned

CHAPTER 6

into a disaster. His stomach flip-flopped and his mind deserted him the moment she walked into the room. She was nice to him, but at the end of the day, he was even more certain that she viewed him as just another little — and somewhat deranged — brother.

7

The hot summer days crawled by, and David learned that healing from this kind of snakebite was an extensive and painful process. MacArthur had three more "clean-up" surgeries, and Dr. Hernandez told them that several skin grafts were necessary. The venom had destroyed a sizable amount of flesh above the ankle, and MacArthur's entire leg below the knee was encased in a special bandage. Dr. Hernandez recommended a specialist for the grafts, and the Colonel arranged for him to fly in from the States to do the surgery, which was to take place in five days.

With another major surgery ahead of him, MacArthur's only concern was that he and David become blood brothers. He was so adamant, David called Dr. Hernandez' office and pleaded with the nurse, "I just need ten minutes. That's all. Ten minutes." She finally agreed to give him a few minutes at the beginning of the doctor's lunch hour. David had just enough time to catch the bus and get there.

"Hello David. What can I do for you?" the doctor asked as he chewed a bite of his sandwich. He was a character study to David and MacArthur, who had spent a lot of time speculating about the private lives of the doctors and nurses that attended him. Hernandez was their favorite. He was jovial and even playful at times, but what they really liked were his dark, bushy eyebrows,

CONVERSION

which resembled a sun visor hanging over his eyes. When he was funny, he looked like Groucho Marx; but when he was serious, and he was extremely serious about the practice of medicine, he looked ominous. This was how he appeared now, so David nervously blurted out the whole scheme.

"MacArthur and I were going to become blood brothers just before he got bit by the snake. Now, he's got it in his head that he needs for us to do this — I mean, cut ourselves and put our blood together — before he has the skin graft thing."

The doctor stopped chewing and swallowed. His first reaction was to laugh and shout an adamant no, but then he had an image of the boys cutting themselves with knives contaminated by fish guts and whatever else they had used them for in the wild. It occurred to him that if he oversaw the procedure, he could ensure their safety. He had become quite fond of them the past few weeks.

David saw the frown on the doctor's face, that his eyebrows had come together menacingly, and noted that he had stopped eating. He was about to launch into his well-prepared argument, when the doctor shrugged his shoulders and said, "Okay."

"Really? What?"

Dr. Hernandez was amused but kept scowling. "Yes, but with the following terms. First, I will do the cutting and dress the wounds. We'll do it tomorrow morning, after I examine him. If I see any reason not to do this, it won't happen, understood?"

"Yes, Sir."

"Second, you must get written permission from his parents and yours. I will issue a consent form, stating my opinion on the matter

CHAPTER 7

and what I intend to do, which you will give them to sign."

"Yes, I can do that. Thank you so much, Doctor," said David.

"If they refuse, I cannot allow it."

"Yes, Sir."

"You can pick up the form between four and five today," and he took another bite of his sandwich as if to say, "Dismissed!"

"Thank you, Sir. I'll be there. I promise." David stuck out his hand and shook the doctor's while grinning from ear to ear. Then he bolted out the door.

When David walked into MacArthur's room, he found him sitting up and surprisingly lucid. He said, "David, I have to tell you something, and you might think I'm crazy, 'cause I know you don't believe in God or Jesus or anything."

"Okay, Saint Mac. Fire away." David thought, *How bad can it be?*

"When I was bit by the snake, I guess I went into shock pretty quick. I don't remember much except being in a lot of pain and begging God to help me. I also remember screaming at you not to leave. I think that was when the helicopter came." David nodded. "Well, I was really out of it through the first surgery and kind of through the second. Did I thank you?"

David shook his head and rolled his eyes. "You thanked me constantly. It was ridiculous."

"After the second surgery, I could see things better. I could really understand what Doc Hernandez was telling me about what was happening to my leg and why he had to operate again. But when I was out during this last surgery, I went somewhere. It wasn't Heaven — or Hell, thank God — but it wasn't here. It was like I was in the sky, but above our atmosphere. You remember when we got hit by that light during the riot?"

"Yeah...."

"Well, it was like I was inside that light again, with no pain and like, totally happy, only this time I wasn't laughing. Jesus was standing next to me. I didn't really see him, but I knew it was him. He said, 'You are healed by my blood,' and he showed me his hands. They had these big scars on them, right here, not in the palm where everybody thinks they are. Then he disappeared, and I woke up in the recovery room, really in pain. I thought, *If Jesus was right beside me, how could I be in pain?*"

David immediately found the reasonable explanation. "It was the drugs! I mean, they've kept you high the past few weeks, and you've said some pretty crazy things."

"It was as real as you and me sitting here right now," he insisted. "I know this is weird, but it really happened, and I believe him."

"Believe who?"

"Jesus. I mean, I can't explain it, but I know I'm healed, just like he said."

"But that doesn't make sense, Mac. You've seen your leg. You still have pain. You know what they have to do to fix it. Maybe — I can't believe I'm saying this — maybe Jesus meant that you are going to be healed by the next surgery. That's what makes sense."

"No," MacArthur was shaking his head. "I *know* I'm healed. I don't need more surgery. I'm going to tell Dad not to waste his money by bringing the specialist. The only thing I need to do is

CHAPTER 7

for us to become blood brothers. Don't you see? That's why Jesus showed me his hands. He wants us to cut our hands, because healing has something to do with blood. That's all I know."

David decided to change the subject. It was obvious that his friend was out of his mind. "Well, I have good news on that. Hernandez okayed it—"

"Great!"

"But we have to get our parents to sign off on it. I'm supposed to pick up a form for them to sign this afternoon. He said if they sign, he'll let us do it tomorrow morning, but he has to do the cutting."

"That's okay. The important thing is that we mix our blood together, right?"

"Right. Oh, and if he examines you and finds any reason not to do it, we'll have to put it off."

"Well that's not going to happen, because I'm already healed. Jesus told me."

David sighed. "Look, I gotta go get that form. Are your parents going to be here after dinner?"

"Yeah. If they try to leave, I'll stall them until you get here."

"Okay. See ya later alligator."

"After 'while crocodile."

David walked out of the room wishing he hadn't heard what MacArthur had told him. He had to have been hallucinating! He was often reckless and thoughtless, but he was not a liar.

That evening, all was forgotten in light of facing the Colonel and Mrs. Wells. He walked back into the hospital room and bravely

73

CONVERSION

greeted them. The Colonel was standing and shook his hand with a smile.

"Hello David," Mrs. Wells said quietly from a chair on the other side of the room. Something was definitely wrong there.

The Colonel said, "MacArthur has filled us in on your intention to become blood brothers tomorrow morning. Mrs. Wells is a little unsettled, but I think it's a fine idea. It would have been better doing it in the mountains, but Hernandez has the right plan under the circumstances."

"Yes, Sir," said David. The Colonel was great! The man understood what it meant to be a warrior. He handed him the form, which he read, signed, and handed to David.

MacArthur gushed, "Thanks, Dad. Thanks, Mom. This is great. This is really great. Now I need to tell you something really important." He took a deep breath and David knew what was coming.

"Excuse me, but I need to get home and get my parents to sign this too. Thanks again, Colonel. Mrs. Wells. See you tomorrow, Mac."

MacArthur waved goodbye as David ran out of the room. Then he proceeded to tell his parents about his visit with Jesus. "So you see, Dad, you don't need to bring the specialist. I'm already healed. I know that sounds strange, but I *know* it's true."

His parents were now standing on either side of his bed, each holding a hand and looking concerned. "Macaaathah," his mother began. "Ya know we believe in God and that he can do miracles if he wants to, but we have to do owha paht too. God helps those

CHAPTER 7

who help themselves, right?"

"Yes, but this is different, Mom. I don't know how. I don't understand it. I just *know* that what Jesus said to me is true."

The Colonel frowned. "The facts say something else, Son. I admire your faith, but as your father, I would be remiss if I didn't do everything in my power to get you well."

"But I am well!"

"I don't know how you can say that," said the Colonel, struggling to be patient. "You cannot deny the present condition of your leg. I'm sorry. I have to do what I think is right." He saw how upset his son was getting and softened his tone. "Look, tomorrow you and David will become blood brothers, and then the specialist will fly in to examine you. If your leg is not healed by the time of the surgery, then you will have it. You will be healed that way. Is that fair?"

MacArthur's heart sank. His parents didn't believe him. They probably thought it was the drugs, like David. "Yes. But I'm telling you, I won't need another surgery." When he heard himself say it this time, he wondered if he had imagined Jesus' words. He was suddenly uncertain.

They tried to make small talk until MacArthur received his pain shot for the night. He faked falling asleep, and as soon as they were gone, he opened his eyes and called the nurse.

"What do you need, MacArthur," she asked.

"Rosita, is there a Bible somewhere around here? Can you get me one?"

She cocked her head. "I'll see what I can do."

CONVERSION

Five minutes later she was back. "The Gideons always leave a bunch of these in our chapel, so you can keep this one."

"Thanks," he said, and she closed his door behind her.

He opened the book and thumbed through it, reading a verse here and a verse there. He was about to go to one of the Gospels and start reading when he saw: "by whose stripes ye were healed." It was in the book of 1 Peter, chapter 2, and verse 24. *So Peter wrote that.* He read the whole verse: "Who his own self bare our sins in his own body on the tree, that we, being dead to sins, should live unto righteousness: by whose stripes ye were healed." *What does all that mean? I know Jesus died on the cross for our sins so God could forgive us, but does that just mean spiritual healing? Can it mean physical healing too? Is that what Jesus meant when he told me, "You are healed by my blood?"*

His thoughts were like a prayer, asking God for the full meaning of the verse, but nothing came to him except one, absolute truth that he had nearly lost in the face of everyone's doubt. He said aloud, "God, I don't understand it, but I know one thing for sure: Jesus said his blood healed me." He turned to the first chapter of the Gospel of Matthew, looking forward to reading about Jesus' life, but after six verses of "the begats," he was asleep.

The next morning David handed the signed permission forms to Dr. Hernandez, who inserted them in the chart at the foot of the bed. Then he and MacArthur waited nervously for him to finish his examination of MacArthur and particularly his leg. "Looks good, considering," he murmured.

"Does that mean we're a go?" asked MacArthur.

CHAPTER 7

"Yes," he sighed. "Now, where were you thinking of cutting yourselves?"

Without hesitation, MacArthur said, "Right here," and he tapped his index finger on the heel of his hand.

Dr. Hernandez stopped. "Why there?"

"That's where the nails went through Jesus' hands."

"Hmm. That makes sense, because if the nails went through the palms, the weight of his body would have torn his hands apart." He pointed to the heel of his hand. "Here, between the first and second carpal bones, the ligaments are much stronger and would be better able to support his weight."

MacArthur was grinning wildly at the doctor, but David did not know what to make of this conversation. He plunged ahead with, "We don't want any painkillers. We want to do it like real warriors, like we would've in the woods."

The doctor smiled and swabbed each boy's right hand with disinfectant. Then he disinfected two scalpels, using one for each small incision. David took a deep breath and stifled a cry of pain. His blood was darker than he thought it would be. MacArthur made one of his silly faces and realized the pain was nothing compared to what he had been suffering. Blood flowed immediately, and the boys shook hands, gritting their teeth and grinning as they moved their wrists together so their blood would be mingled in each other's cuts.

"No doubt about it. You are now blood brothers," declared Dr. Hernandez. "Better not operate any heavy machinery, David, now that you've got all those drugs from MacArthur in you."

CONVERSION

MacArthur laughed, but David's mouth dropped open. "Don't worry," the doctor smiled as he wiped each of their palms with disinfectant again. The boys cried, "Ooooh, that stings!" Then he placed a thick gauze pad over each wound.

"Apply pressure, like this, to get the bleeding stopped." They did as they were told and now they were both smiling. When the bleeding ceased, he applied an antibiotic ointment and a Band-Aid.

"MacArthur, the nurse will be checking this and changing the Band-Aid, just like she does your leg. Your blood has been clotting normally, so I don't anticipate any problems, but if you notice anything unusual, let us know immediately."

"Okay."

"Thanks Dr. Hernandez," said David. "But really, am I going to get loopy or something?"

Hernandez shook his head and raised his eyebrows. "No *loopier* than you two usually are."

David held out his bandaged right hand, but the doctor waved him away.

"I'll see you tomorrow morning, MacArthur." He scribbled something on the chart, placed it at the foot of the bed again, and left the room. The nurse came in and removed the surgical tray.

David sat in the chair facing MacArthur's bed. His father was right. He felt like his life had changed. He hoped it wasn't anything drug-induced.

"Thanks, David," murmured MacArthur.

David groaned. "Not again!"

"No! I mean it. You got this done." He yawned and shut his

CHAPTER 7

eyes. "I couldn't have, by myself, and I…we had to do it…I know it sounds strange…because of the blood, you know, and…." He dozed off.

David took a long look at his new blood brother and then closed his eyes. He would stay until MacArthur woke up again. Maybe Sarah would come today, and maybe he wouldn't act like an idiot.

8

When David got to the hospital the next morning, he sensed something was amiss. At the ground-floor receptionist desk, on the elevator, and as he got out on MacArthur's floor, people were whispering in small groups and looking at him. Then he noticed the crowd of doctors and nurses around MacArthur's door. He froze. *My God! Is he dead? Did cutting his hand push his body too far?* He forced his way through the crowd and almost fell over the foot rail of the bed. To his relief, MacArthur was sitting up, smiling his silly smile. Dr. Hernandez was scratching his head, and David followed his gaze to see what all the commotion was about: MacArthur's lower leg was covered with new flesh and skin. "Did you have the surgery already?" asked David.

Dr. Hernandez looked at him as though he was insane. "The surgery is scheduled in three days, David."

MacArthur laughed, "Can I get up, Doc? Let me get up!" And before the doctor could answer, he had leaped out of bed, grabbed Rosita, and began waltzing her in a circle. She laughed and cried in Spanish, "God be praised! It's a miracle!"

"I told ya! I told ya Jesus said I was healed!" he yelled at David as he twirled Rosita and let her go. Another nurse came in to give him his pain medicine, shook her head in disbelief, and walked out. Then the Colonel and Mrs. Wells arrived. They were shocked

CONVERSION

and overjoyed at the same time.

The boys were finally alone when MacArthur's parents went to arrange his discharge. Dr. Hernandez had performed a thorough examination and had found nothing wrong with his leg or any part of him.

In a stupor, David packed in boxes the things family and friends had brought the last few weeks, while MacArthur showered and dressed. He couldn't stop staring at his leg. He pulled up his pants leg. "Take a good look at it, blood brother. It's real. I told you Jesus said I was healed."

"I see it, but I don't believe it," said David. His mind was whirling, trying to find a logical reason for what he was seeing.

"Well, all I know is what that guy in the Bible said, 'I was blind and now I see.'"

David smiled impishly. "Wait a minute. It makes perfect sense. When we became blood brothers, your blood was mixed with my *Superman* blood, and it caused your leg to make new muscles and skin!"

MacArthur laughed. "I think *my* drugs have affected *your* brain! And Hernandez sure doesn't know what happened. I just know we did what Jesus showed me to do, and he healed my leg. David, look! I don't have any pain, and it feels stronger than ever!" He began doing jumping jacks and squats like a madman.

David was baffled. This was not a bad dream, but it sure wasn't a good one for an atheist. "Would you come over to my house? I want Mama and Papa to see this."

"Sure, but I think my family's gonna want me to hang around

CHAPTER 3

for a while. I'll see if I can get Joanna to drive me over tonight. Maybe *Sarah* will come too."

David smirked. "Very funny."

As it turned out, Jeanne Wells invited David and his parents to share in MacArthur's homecoming dinner. She instructed the cook to make his favorite meal of spaghetti and meatballs and set the table like royalty was coming to dinner. She had come to terms with her son's miracle by simply being glad he was well again. She didn't want to ponder the how and the why. It happened, and she was grateful. Life was fun again.

The Colonel, on the other hand, looked at his son with new eyes. He had always known MacArthur was intelligent and bright, but now there was something more to the boy. He had never known anyone who had had a visit from Jesus, and he still wondered if it was the work of the drugs, but the result was indisputable. His son was well, and not by human effort. Only MacArthur had believed. Indeed, he had exhibited a kind of faith — or was it a strength of mind? — the Colonel had never seen. It was unnerving.

Elena Parks gasped and began weeping when MacArthur pulled up his pants and showed her his leg. He thought she'd never let him out of her arms. Ben stared at his leg, knelt down to examine it, and looked up at the Colonel, who shook his head and shrugged his shoulders. The Colonel wondered why his friend looked so stricken. The Parks were such devout Catholics, much more than he.

When they were all seated at the dinner table, the Colonel said a simple grace and thanked God for his son's miraculous recovery.

83

CONVERSION

He barely uttered "Amen," when Joanna demanded, "Tell us everything that happened, Mac!"

MacArthur began with Jesus' visit during the last surgery, told them how he and David had become blood brothers, and continued, "Then I had this dream last night, or I think it was a dream. I was lying on my hospital bed, and a doctor was working on my leg. He was dressed all in white, but he didn't have a mask on, and his head was, like, draped in a white shawl with, like, markings on it. But he had hair to his shoulders. I just remembered that! So it must have been Jesus! But he could have been an angel, I guess."

"Okay, okay. Go on!" goaded Joanna.

"Well, my leg tingled, like when it's asleep, and then for a few minutes it felt like it was on fire. That's when I woke up, and I noticed that I didn't have any pain when I moved it. My covers were off, so I sat up. Then I saw that my bandage was cut down the middle and was, like, flopped over on either side of my leg. At first, I thought the specialist had come to look at it. Then I just stared at it, because it looked like it did *before* the snakebite — except for the two little scars where the fang marks were." He got up from the table and sat on the floor. "Then I tried bending my leg and moving my foot, like this. It was amazing! It was completely normal and no pain at all!" He jumped up, plopped in his chair, and grinned as he twisted spaghetti around his fork.

"What did Dr. Hernandez say when he saw it?" asked Meg.

"Well, I got up and skipped to the nurses' station, and they went bonkers when they saw me. I think that's when they called the

CHAPTER 3

doc. They tried to get me to sit in a wheelchair, but when I showed them my leg, Rosita screamed and started yelling in Spanish. I understood most of it. She was the one who usually changed my bandage in the morning. But then they made me go back to my room and get in bed, and they wouldn't let me get up. It was crazy! By the time Doc Hernandez and you all got there, like, all these nurses and doctors were crowded around. Well, you know the rest." He shoved the bite of spaghetti in his mouth.

The phone rang, and Sarah went to answer it in the kitchen. She returned and looked at MacArthur, "It's Rebecca." He jumped up, threw his napkin on his chair, and a moment later they heard him recount the story to his oldest sister.

"Do ya think we'll evah heah the end a this?" Jeanne asked quietly, her eyes fixed on the Colonel.

"Most likely not," he answered.

There were a couple of weeks of interviews with local journalists, which MacArthur relished. He loved being the center of attention almost as much as he loved telling a good story — and his was a *very good* story. Both their Protestant pastor and Catholic priest came to see him and shook their heads in wonder, as did many of their friends. And they had another celebration when David and MacArthur went through their Order of the Arrow ceremony.

David was glad when tryouts for the Balboa High School football team began. Before MacArthur's miracle, he had been dreading it, knowing his friend would be sitting in the stands their freshman year and might not play again. Now, they could play

85

CONVERSION

together, just like always. In their usual dynamic-duo style, they made the football team, and practices began.

The back-to-school inquiry, "How was your summer?" caused the story of their Ordeal and MacArthur's healing to remain a headliner in their lives for the first few weeks. MacArthur's attention span being what it was, however, the event was eventually forgotten in the throes of homework, ball games, girlfriend drama, and class cliques.

And then there was puberty. When boys and girls begin to become men and women, their ideas about who they are and what they want in life are intense. In the sixties, sex was in the air more than usual. *The Catcher in the Rye*, by J. D. Salinger, was the book to read. There was talk of introducing sex education as part of biology class in the public schools. Hiding a *Playboy* magazine under your bed and sharing it with friends provided a rare education, and the news reported a sexual revolution in full swing on college campuses. David and MacArthur reacted uncharacteristically for their temperaments and proceeded according to their religious (or lack of religious) beliefs.

Thoughtful and cautious David wanted to have sex as soon as possible and with as many girls as possible. Often reckless and always carefree MacArthur wanted to wait for his wife, that extraordinary girl he was sure God was saving especially for him. As upcoming star athletes, their popularity soared, so they had no trouble getting dates. Unfortunately for David, the demands on their time and energy allowed little opportunity for sexual exploits.

The rivalry between their high school, Balboa (on the Pacific

CHAPTER 8

side of the Panama Canal), and Cristobal High School (on the Atlantic side) was extreme. The coach at Balboa had been impressed with both David and MacArthur. Since the quarterback was graduating and the sophomore and junior quarterbacks weren't nearly as good, the boys anticipated sharing the responsibility for leading the Balboa football team to victory as sophomores.

Then fate dealt them a terrible blow. The Colonel was assigned to the Atlantic side of the Canal, and the Wells family was moving to Fort Davis. MacArthur would be attending Cristobal in the fall, and he and David would be playing *against* one another!

"At least we'll still see each other. I mean, it's not like we'll be living on different planets." MacArthur was conditioned to move into the next phase of his life and make the most of it, but David was irritated by his friend's habit of always looking on the bright side. In this case, for him, there was no bright side. The best friend he'd ever had was moving across the Canal to fight against him, and every upbeat comment coming out of MacArthur's mouth infuriated him. He ground his teeth and tried to be helpful as MacArthur packed his room in boxes.

"Might as well be different planets. You know what it takes to play ball and keep your grades up. And what about our social life? You'll be busy, and so will I. We won't see each other except when we play *against* each other. And that will be a real fun time." He slammed a box on MacArthur's desk and began to fill it with books, notebooks, and papers.

"Hey! I'm not thrilled about this either!" MacArthur was throwing clothes into a suitcase. "But what can I do? We're just going to have to make it work. You know, I may be moving to the other side, but it's only fifty miles away. And besides, even if I moved halfway across the world, you saved my life. We're blood brothers! That means something, you know?"

David stopped. "Maybe we can take the train and visit once or twice a month or something. And when we play each other, we can stay over."

"Yeah. And David, I'd rather have one great friend like you than a million regular ones."

"Me too," David sighed. They finished packing everything but the clothes MacArthur would need for the next day, moving day.

The following morning there were tearful goodbyes as MacArthur, his sisters, and their parents hugged their friends. The Wells family was used to moving every couple of years, but some moves were harder than others. This one was harder. David and his parents were there, telling them that if they ever needed anything, they just had to call.

Finally, the moving truck was loaded, the family got in their cars, and MacArthur waved, grinning his goofy grin. David waved back with a heavy heart as he watched his best friend head for the Atlantic side of the Canal. He glanced at Sarah. Would he ever see her again? Although he was popular in the high school, even with some older girls, he hadn't had the nerve to ask her out. Maybe now he would forget her. But then, she *had* hugged him. *Oh my God! She's waving — at me!* He grinned and waved back until he saw MacArthur in the other car, shaking his head knowingly. He stopped abruptly and sought for something to save face.

CHAPTER 3

"Papa, can I drive home?"

"Si," and he tossed the keys to him. He had just gotten his learner's permit.

"Ah Dios!" cried Mama, as she got in the back seat. They laughed as she prayed all the way home.

9

Balboa High School had three times as many students as Cristobal High School; however, what Cristobal lacked in numbers, they more than made up by employing the best football coach in Panama. MacArthur was excited to work with him.

The two high schools were very competitive, and each had tremendous fan support. Football was a big deal in Panama, and the parents were as enthusiastic as the kids. With MacArthur on the team and Sarah a cheerleader, the Colonel and Jeanne never missed a game unless they had to fulfill a more important obligation.

The race for the championship that year came down to the final game between Cristobal and the Canal Zone College. David and MacArthur hadn't seen each other for two months, and since the game was going to be played at the College, MacArthur planned to stay the weekend with David.

As a sophomore, MacArthur had played in nearly half the games, but because it was the senior quarterback's last game, the coach let the championship be his night to shine. Although it was a great game and Cristobal won by just one field goal, MacArthur didn't get to play. He and David met in the parking lot afterward.

"Hey, Mac! Sorry you didn't get to play."

"Aw, Jason deserved it. He's a senior, so he's going out with a bang. Anyway, I have two years to show 'em what I got!" He noticed David's parents driving up to them. "Hi, Mama! Hi, Doc!" He jumped in the back seat with his duffle bag.

"Congratulations, MacArthur. How are you?" asked Elena.

"Just great. We've had a good season, and they let me play a lot, which was super. They worked me hard in practices too, so I feel really ready to, like, step up next year. The guy who is a senior next year is not as good as I am, so I know I'll get to play."

"Still our humble Saint Mac!" David chided.

MacArthur shrugged. "Hey, it's just the truth, Superman."

"I haven't heard that name in a while," said Ben, smiling in the rear-view mirror.

"Well, when you saved my life, that sealed the deal." MacArthur jabbed his friend in the arm.

"How could I forget with you reminding me all the time," said David.

"You are exceptional young men," said Ben.

"Yes, and we are expecting great things from you," added Elena.

"Well, you're going to see it, because David and I are going to change the world."

David burst out laughing. "Oh, really? And how are we going to do that?"

"I don't know. But we'll figure it out."

Once they were in David's room, settled in for the night, he asked, "What are the girls like at Cristobal?"

"There are lots of really cool girls, but I've only dated one that I really like."

"You mean, you've dated more than one already?"

CHAPTER 9

"Oh yeah. Like, about five."

"Five! I've only gone out with one this whole fall, and she's not really interested in doing anything but holding hands and necking."

"No kidding? You need to come visit me, and I'll set you up. I've gotten to second base twice."

David wanted to hear details but was curious. "I thought you were *saving* yourself."

"I am, but I want to know what I'm doing when I get there, if you know what I mean. Besides, all the kids are doing it, like, even my Catholic friends who go to mass all the time. You should hear some of the stories! And really, as long as we don't go all the way, we haven't really had sex. I think God's cool with that."

"Well, since God's not in the picture, all I care about is not getting someone pregnant. I have a condom in my wallet, just in case."

"So who are you trying not to get pregnant?" MacArthur laughed.

"Her name is Angela, and she has the most amazing body, but she won't go past first base. If I can't get her to second by Christmas, I'm going to break up with her."

"Why? Don't you like her?"

"Oh, she's nice, but it's too frustrating. I don't want to get to college and be a virgin. That's retarded."

"I guess you have a point, I mean, for an atheist." They were quiet for a while. MacArthur wondered if David had fallen asleep. "David?"

93

CONVERSION

"Yeah?"

"What do you want to do? I mean, do you know what you want to be?"

"I think I do! I just don't know how. I'm really interested in the whole Cold War with Russia thing, maybe because I was born in Cuba and my parents talk about it a lot. Remember, I did last year's research paper on the Russian Revolution." He turned on his side to face MacArthur and propped up his head with his hand. "I think it would be neat to be someone in government or some powerful organization and build a bridge between the Russians and us. I mean, don't you think if we got to know each other better, if we understood each other better, the whole Cold War would just melt away?"

"Oh God, you and your puns!" MacArthur groaned.

"That was an accident!" laughed David. "I didn't know what I was saying."

"Well, if anybody could bring world peace, you could. Everyone likes you. I'm too wild for something like that. People either love me or hate me. You're quiet and say the right things. I just, like, say whatever comes into my head, and it usually gets me in trouble."

"Oh my God! You know that?" David asked.

"Yeah! After being told fifty million times by my sisters. They're always telling me to shut up or calm down. The Colonel's thing is, 'Channel your energy in the right direction, Son,' but I know what he's really saying. At least my mom loves me just the way I am."

"Your mom loves *everyone*! Okay, so how can a wild man like you change the world?"

CHAPTER 9

MacArthur yawned, "I don't know. But it will be great when I see it, and I know it's going to happen...someday."

David yawned and lay on his back again. "Well, personally, *I* know you can convince anyone to do anything. Remember the time you got me to help you sneak into the girls' locker room and steal their underwear?"

"Oh yeah! That was insane! They were so mad, and they never found out who did it. That was, like, one of our best capers."

"Because we didn't get caught!" David yawned again. "We gotta go to sleep. Remember, we're going fishing with Papa, and Mama's gonna have breakfast ready in —" he looked at his clock — "ugh, five hours."

"It's all good. Night, Superman."

"Night, Saint Mac."

By the end of the weekend they realized they had not drifted apart at all. It was as though MacArthur had never moved to the Atlantic side of the Canal. As he boarded the train, he and David agreed to write more often.

In his Christmas letter, David told MacArthur that he had broken up with Angela and found a girl who was willing to go to second base. He was making straight A's and had finally figured out algebra. MacArthur didn't respond until the end of January.

> Dear David,
> Still a virgin, but it hasn't been easy! Seems like every girl I date has some part of the girl of my dreams, but I haven't met her yet. Got all A's except one B in

CONVERSION

algebra, of course, and I'm not playing baseball because I'm learning guitar and am playing golf. Love it!

And guess what? I was invited to join this really prestigious club called the 21 Club. There are always only 21 members, and it's for "outstanding" high school students. Ha! Ha! We each have a Latin American country, and the Club gives us access to government officials, like the ambassador of that country. I have Chile, and it is so neat! I want to visit there sometime. The ambassador had me over for dinner, and I got to use my Spanish a lot (Mama would be SO proud of me)!

The Club also has an interesting initiation — not at all like the Ordeal. They take you out to the bars and get you as drunk as they can! I had never been drunk before. It was really a blast for a while, but then I sort of checked out, and I don't remember how I got home. I woke up in my own bed (thank God!), and the Colonel was sitting next to me — yikes! I moved and thought my head was going to explode. That's when I started to remember. I thought I was in huge trouble, but he was pretty neat about it. He gave me something to drink and it tasted terrible, but it helped. For a while, though, I thought I was going to die!

The reason I'm telling you this is because we ended up having the best talk I ever had with him. He told me he didn't approve of what I'd done, but he knew

CHAPTER 9

I was getting old enough that he couldn't make some decisions for me. Then he told me that his brother, my Uncle Eddie, had been killed because he had driven drunk, and he didn't want that to happen to me. I knew my uncle had been killed in a car accident, but I didn't know that part. It was really heavy!

Anyway...I told him that I liked drinking but not getting drunk. I sure didn't want to feel like this again! He was relieved, and I told him I wanted to change the world for the better, but I didn't know how yet. Of course, what father wouldn't love to hear that! But honestly, I was sincere and he knew it. It was a great father/son moment! I know you've had that with your dad all your life, but mine hasn't been around much, so this was big!

Sarah's going to the U. of Virginia nursing school next fall. My time in the hospital had a big impact on her. Joanna is going to study in France, Meg is going to law school at Vanderbilt, and Rebecca was just hired as an assistant buyer at Macy's in New York, so it looks like I'll have the parents all to myself. I'll be like you!

Let me know what's happening on your side of the Canal.

Your BB&BF

(Blood Brother and Best Friend),

MacArthur

CONVERSION

During spring break, David visited MacArthur, who set him up with a girl he knew would go for him. They had fun, but all he could think about was Sarah. She wasn't dating anyone, seemed glad to see him, and David was overwhelmed — again. He thought he had forgotten her, but she looked even more beautiful. He loved her laugh, her gentle voice, and how small she was. He felt protective around her. He couldn't wait to get home from the double date so he could see her, but she had already gone to bed. MacArthur saw his disappointment and teased him. All he would say was, "Hey, she's not interested in me."

The third evening of David's visit, the Colonel called a family meeting. He began with, "I'm glad David is here, because I have some news that affects him as well as our family. I'm being transferred back to Virginia, effective May 1." He paused for responses of dismay, then looked his children in the eye, one by one, until there was silence. "Your mother and I will travel there next month, to find a house. MacArthur, I know you had high hopes of being star quarterback next year, but they have good programs in Virginia. And Sarah, don't worry, you'll graduate here. We won't move until the end of the school year." He looked wistfully at his wife and said, "I'll be a bachelor for a month."

"Like hell ya will," Jeanne shot back.

Their laughter broke the tension but not the sadness. MacArthur shook his head at David. "Here we go again!"

When they were alone, they determined to make the most of their remaining time together, doing all the things they loved to do.

CHAPTER 9

David especially enjoyed seeing the other side of the Canal Zone. The day he left to take the train back to the Pacific side, he said, "I've got an idea. Let's plan to meet at the next Scout Jamboree. I think it's in November."

"That's a long way off," said MacArthur vaguely. He had a funny look on his face, but before David could ask him about it, he said, "But listen, we'll see each other as much as we can before the move, visiting each other, like we've been doing."

"Yep." They shook hands, then MacArthur caught David in a bear hug. He stayed and waved as the train pulled away.

The race to the end of the school year made it difficult to exchange letters or a phone call. As soon as David was out of school, he rode the train to spend a few days with MacArthur and help him pack for the move. Elena sent fresh-baked cookies, and Ben sent toothbrushes, toothpaste, and dental floss, which made them laugh. The Colonel was in Virginia, but Meg, Joanna, and Sarah were there. With their help, Jeanne and the housekeeper had everything packed and ready for the movers, so David and MacArthur had time to party with his friends.

The final night, they talked well into the morning. It began with David deciding to tell MacArthur what he thought. "Listen, you don't seem to be as upset about leaving as I am. Frankly, it pisses me off."

"I'm sorry, bro, but I have to tell you something," began MacArthur.

"Oh no! Jesus came to visit again."

MacArthur laughed. "Oh yeah. I almost forgot. Well, this is

CONVERSION

kinda different. You know when my dad told us we were moving?" David nodded. "Well, the week before, I overheard him talking to my mom. I walked by their bedroom and heard him say that he's going to Thailand in August, and he might be gone a year. David, the moment I heard him say *Thailand*, I *knew* I was going with him. *Just me.*"

"What?"

"Yeah. He doesn't know it yet, but I am."

"How's that gonna happen? I mean, your parents will never go for it."

"I know it sounds impossible, but I know I'm going. I just know it."

David had a déjà vu moment. "Okay...like you *knew* your leg was healed?"

"Yeah! You get it!" MacArthur beamed.

"No! I don't!"

MacArthur's heart sank. "Either something is really weird-strange with me, or everyone else is dense. I mean, I feel like I'm nuts or everyone else is."

David wanted to laugh, but it wasn't in him. He suddenly felt empty and alone in the world. "This is just so...so.... I'm sorry, but it's crazy! I wish I understood, but then, I'm glad I don't! You were right about your leg, but Thailand? That's halfway around the world! And what do you care about Thailand?" He realized he was yelling in a whisper.

"Yeah! But isn't it cool? I've figured it out. Dad has to get me a tutor, because I don't know the language and I still have to go to

CHAPTER 9

school. And it'll be a real adventure."

David sighed. "When do you tell your parents?"

"I'm waiting until after the move. I won't unpack my stuff, because then I'll be ready to go when we leave in August."

"Jesus." David thought, *Wait 'til Papa and Mama hear this.*

"Listen, since I won't be able to speak the language, girls will be out, and I won't play sports because I won't be in a school, I'll have, like, eons of time to write. It will be like you're there with me!"

"Not really." David felt dejected, but he didn't want their last night to end on a sour note. "Well, I wish I could hide behind a chair when you tell the Colonel. Oh God — when you tell your *mom!*"

10

"Uh uh! Absoloootely not!" declared his mother.

The Colonel was furious with himself and threw his magazine on the coffee table. He should have been more careful in discussing his plans with Jeanne. That MacArthur had overheard him was disastrous. He had to do damage control and nip this in the bud. "Son, your mother is right. It's impossible."

MacArthur had expected this and steeled himself. "Look, I'm not crazy, really, and I know this sounds crazy, but I'm *supposed* to go with you, Dad. I know it in a way I can't explain. It has to be... like...God, because it doesn't even make sense to me."

That was it for Jeanne Talley Wells. She had grown up in the Bible belt and had never liked fanatic talk. She stood in that way that made MacArthur *and* the Colonel feel like they were two feet tall. "Ah cannot listen ta this any longah. Colonel, he's yowr son. Now *you handle* 'im." And she left the room.

The Colonel was quiet for a moment. He sensed this was a situation that could make or break his relationship with his son, but his wife's eyes had said, "You make my son stay with me! I've had to do without you too many years, and I only have him for two more, so keep him at home!"

"MacArthur, you are very intelligent and in some ways exceptional, but you are still a kid. I can't tell you why I'm going to

CONVERSION

Thailand — you shouldn't even know about it. In fact, I'm ordering you to forget it and never speak of it."

A wave of guilt nearly swamped MacArthur's resolve. He swallowed hard. "Sorry, Dad. I already told David."

The Colonel clenched his jaw. More damage control. "I'll fix that, but you've got to promise me that you will not speak of this again, with David or anyone else."

"Yes, Sir. I promise, but I'm still going with you."

"MacArthur, this isn't something *you* decide, and you can't be a part of it. Trust me on this." He paused. "I know we haven't had a lot of time together, and your wanting to go with me has caused me to think that I need to spend more time with you, but Thailand is not the time or place to do that. I promise we will do better after I get back. If all goes well, I may be back by Christmas, okay?"

"Dad, I want to spend time with you, but that's not the reason I'm supposed to go — at least I don't think it is…maybe it is…but… it's just…I *know* I'm supposed to go! It can't be impossible. It just can't!"

"Well, it is, and you're going to have to accept that. So unpack your things and get settled in. Football tryouts are next week. You have a lot to look forward to here." He returned to his magazine.

MacArthur realized he had to do something drastic. His parents were not seeing how important this was. He stood resolutely. "Sir, I'm not leaving my room or eating or drinking until you say I can go." He marched to the stairs and took two at a time.

The Colonel jumped up to follow him. At the bottom of the stairs he yelled, "Young man, stop right there." MacArthur didn't

CHAPTER 10

look back. "Come here at once!"

MacArthur had never defied his father to his face, and his heart pounded. He felt wretched, but it had to be done. He hurried into his room, locked the door, and sank down against it. He prayed, *Oh God, help me. Please tell me I'm doing the right thing. Please talk to my dad.*

Jeanne heard her husband yell and swear as she watered her flowers on the back patio. She came in to see what was happening. "Colonel?" She found him at the bottom of the stairs, fuming.

"I don't know what the hell has gotten into him! He's never acted like this — at least with me. Has he ever done this to you?"

"Done what?"

"Defied orders! Maybe it's hormones or he's just had it with my being gone so much —"

"What did he say?"

"He says he's not coming out of his room or eating or drinking until I let him go with me! Honestly Jeanne, I don't know whether to beat him...or be proud of him! He's either dead right or dead wrong — and I'm supposed to know the difference, for God's sake!" He was about to sit on the stairs, but she caught his arms and shook him.

"Well, Ahm not stumped at awl! He's mah son, and he's still a kid. He needs ta be home with me, not runnin' 'roun' the world with you, gettin' into awl yo scrapes. An' don't look at me like that! Ah've lived with you lonnng enough ta have some ideah what yo' up ta when yo' away!"

He couldn't help himself and smiled. "So you've figured it out,

CONVERSION

huh?" Her eyes filled with tears of frustration, and he knew he was in trouble. "I'm sorry. I know it's been hard." He let out a big sigh and put his arms around her. He hated seeing her cry. "Honey, let's give him some time. He'll get hungry soon and see things differently." He felt the tension go out of her body.

"Thaht's true — the powah of a maaan's stomach." She leaned her head back and smiled. He kissed her, and they felt better. Everything was going to be all right. Sure, MacArthur had eaten a good dinner, but by tomorrow noon their baby boy would be cryin' for his mama!

Two days later, MacArthur was still locked in his room.

They hadn't been able to catch him going into the bathroom, and they didn't want to speculate about that. The Colonel had given the order, "Leave him alone! He'll come to his senses or die!" But when he wasn't around, Sarah left water and delicious-smelling food at MacArthur's door. When she checked later, nothing was touched. She pounded on the door and cried out to him, but he remained silent. She wished Joanna was here. She could usually talk sense into him.

Each day, the Colonel had gone to work as usual, confident that the outcome would be as he expected. Before leaving for work the third day, he overheard Sarah begging MacArthur to at least drink something. Still, he was confident his son would break that day. He had performed enough interrogations to know how this worked. He sighed as he left the house. It was the third morning. If MacArthur had no water for over three days, his life might be in danger. Jeanne was a wreck and ready to call the fire department.

CHAPTER 10

Sarah's eyes were red from crying.

The Colonel had barely touched his breakfast, and his stomach was upset as he parked near his office. By mid-morning, staring blankly at the intelligence brief on his desk, he suddenly had the inexplicable but distinct impression that MacArthur had to go with him. He stood slowly, planted his hands on his desk, and stared out the window for a long time. *Oh God, Jeanne will never forgive me, and how can I justify this to the brass? Maybe this is what MacArthur means when he "knows" something. Or maybe insanity runs in the family!* He frowned and grabbed his suit coat, told his secretary to cancel his afternoon meeting, and hurried home.

MacArthur was sprawled on his bed, drifting in and out of consciousness. He wasn't sure he really heard a knock on his door. Then he thought he heard his father say, "MacArthur, you are going to Thailand. Come out. We have a lot to talk about." But he had been imagining that for a long time.

Please God, let it be true. He managed to sit up and sat still until the dizziness subsided. "Dad?" he rasped.

"Unlock the door, MacArthur. It's really me."

He stood slowly, leaning on his night table, then staggered to the door and grabbed the doorknob. He used his last bit of energy to turn the knob. It clicked, and as the door opened he began to fall back with it. The Colonel rushed in and caught him in his arms. He laid him on the bed and sat beside him, holding his hand, tears in his eyes.

MacArthur looked up at his father with compassion. "It's okay, Dad. Mom'll come around."

11

It was an incomparable early summer in McLean, Virginia, 1967. All of nature was singing, blooming, and birthing a new season. Winter coats were shed, children were outside playing in their neighborhoods, and MacArthur hardly believed that a dream of his was being realized in a matter of weeks.

He regained his strength quickly, because his mother had hired a "cook extraordinaire." Her name was Lois, and she was young and robust. She had grown up in a large family in the mountains of Virginia, where she had learned everything you could know about country cooking. She earned a scholarship to learn the culinary arts in Paris and could have her pick of jobs in some of the finest restaurants, but that did not suit her.

Lois was one of those "born agains" and knew her life's work was among families not institutions or restaurants. The moment she saw the advertisement for the Wells job, she knew that was where God wanted her to be. She assured Mrs. Wells that she was capable of serving the best cuisine to her family as well as the dignitaries that attended her fancy dinner parties. What MacArthur and the rest of the family noticed right away was that Lois had a knack of serving exactly what they wanted before they knew they wanted it. After a couple of weeks, Jeanne no longer saw the need to discuss menus with her.

CONVERSION

With Lois feeding him, it wasn't long before MacArthur was playing golf, writing songs on his guitar, and exploring his surroundings. He had lived in this area before, but he had been much younger. He and Sarah enjoyed visiting national monuments and exploring the Smithsonian. Their hearts swelled with pride at the amazing accomplishments of their country. MacArthur remembered the riot in Panama and what David had said. He knew America wasn't perfect, but he believed she was the best country on Earth.

He apologized to his parents and Sarah for putting them through hell, but he was firm that he would do it again in order to go to Thailand. His mother was the only one who refused to understand or be consoled. None of his old maneuvers worked, and he tried some new ones, but she remained aloof. Soon, his heart began to hurt. Besides missing her affection, he felt guilty for causing a silent war between his parents. He noted that nothing the Colonel tried with his mother worked either. While she watered and nurtured her colorful flowers around the outside of the house; inside, their home became a cold, dark place.

The men in her life did not understand that Jeanne's beloved mama's boy had disappeared. She didn't recognize the young man who seemed to have no problem leaving her before he had to. And she was furious with the Colonel, who was abandoning her without a child in the house for what might be a year. It wasn't right that he take him away — and into a potentially dangerous situation!

The Colonel couldn't make her understand, because he didn't

CHAPTER 11

understand it himself. He was familiar with the tug-of-war in his heart between duty and family; but now, he was torn between the commitment he had made to his son and his love for his wife. He had to trust that he was doing the right thing for all of them, as well as for his country, and so he immersed himself in what he did understand: every detail of the mission, which now included MacArthur's education and safety.

Other than his mother and sisters, MacArthur could only write David — and never mention his father's activities. The Colonel had a telephone conversation with Ben Parks, who assured him that any communication David had with MacArthur, before or during his time in Thailand, would not go beyond their family.

As difficult as it was to leave his wife alone for months, it was essential that he and MacArthur both return to her. The Colonel considered every contingency. After looking at all possibilities and devising the best plan — along with several back-ups — the next hurdle was to gain approval from his superiors. By the last week of June, he was ready and called a meeting.

The Colonel boldly outlined the details of his plan regarding MacArthur and issued an ultimatum: "If you want me to run this op, give me this. I know it's highly irregular, but as I've shown you, we can do it in a way that will not jeopardize the mission or my son's safety. There will be no extra cost to the government. I'll personally take care of all expenses regarding his time there. And gentlemen, he will receive training that might make him useful to our country in the future."

After a short discussion, they agreed to his demands. One

CONVERSION

general leaned back in his chair, folded his arms, and asked, "Do you have someone in mind for the tutor? He must have clearance. We can't take any chances. And MacArthur will also need a security detail that's cleared."

The Colonel had anticipated this and said, "I have the man."

Their eyebrows rose, and the same general asked, "Just one?"

"Yes," and the Colonel gave them a name. That was all he had to say.

That evening, he told Jeanne to have Lois plan for a dinner guest on the Fourth of July. She didn't ask who it was or respond in any way, which didn't surprise him. Lately, her attitude screamed, "I don't care! You're going to do what you want to do anyway!"

All of the girls were gone for the holiday week, and when he wasn't playing golf or his guitar, MacArthur was buried in books about Thailand and Southeast Asia. The house was so quiet and his mother so distant, he forgot it was the Fourth of July. He heard his father's car in the driveway and vaulted down the stairs to greet him. "Hi, Dad! Oh!"

"MacArthur, this is Reuben Katz."

"Nice to meet you, Sir." MacArthur held out his hand.

"I'm very happy to meet you, MacArthur."

What was that accent? The man's handshake was firm but not overpowering, and his dark eyes were bright — but there was something else there too. He couldn't put his finger on it. He studied the man carefully as he held the door for him and the Colonel. He was about six feet tall, olive-skinned, muscular, and much younger than his father.

CHAPTER 11

"Your father has told me about you, so you see, I have the advantage." MacArthur saw the sparkle in his eye and was captivated.

"Well! Look whaat the cat dragged in," said his mother, coming from the kitchen. Reuben held out his arms and she nearly flew into them. MacArthur had seen his mother react to other people this way, but then she took the man's large hands in her tiny ones and kissed them. She stood there for the longest time, shaking her head, tears running down her cheeks. Finally, she sniffed and looked at the Colonel, then back up at Reuben. "So yo' the one ahn'tcha?"

"Yes, once again I have the honor," replied Reuben with a smile.

She stood tiptoe and hugged Reuben again, patting him on the back, then turned to MacArthur with a look of sad affection — the first show of love in weeks. She put her hands on his face and kissed him. "Ah still don't wancha ta go, but the picture is decidedly diffrent now." Then she squeezed him like she hadn't seen him in years.

MacArthur's heart burst with joy as he hugged her tightly, but his mind was bewildered. *What was happening?* He looked at his father, and then it dawned on him. "*He's* going with us?"

His mother released him and said, "Yes, dahlin'. Reuben is yo' tutah and bahdigahd."

The Colonel continued, "And understand something: He's in charge. If I hear you've disobeyed him once, you're on the next plane home."

"Yes, Sir." He grinned and jumped right in. "Mr. Katz—"

"Please. Reuben."

"Reuben." He glanced at his father. "I can't place your accent. Where are you from?"

"Israel."

"Of course!" He clapped his hands as if he had missed an answer he had always known. He had never met an Israeli before, but he was sure this was exactly what they sounded like. "Hey, you just went through, like, a war, didn't you?"

Reuben's eyes flickered. "Yes, and we survived, thank God."

"Not only did you survive, you unified Jerusalem and took strategic territory," quipped the Colonel.

"Would ya like yo usual, Reuben?" interrupted his mother.

"No, thank you, Ma'am. Alas, I've been a complete teetotaler for many years."

"Well ah'll be a monkey's uncle! What brought that on?" she asked.

"Oh, I simply realized I couldn't be who I was supposed to be if I continued to drink." He shrugged his shoulders.

"Cold turkey?"

He leaned over toward her. "And it wasn't easy."

Jeanne didn't skip a beat. "Well then, how 'bout a soda or somethin'?"

"Do you have root beer?"

"We have *every* kinda beer, darlin'! Colonel?"

"I'll take the usual." He was smiling from ear to ear. His wife was back!

CHAPTER 11

She looked at MacArthur, who said, "I'll have a root beer too. Thanks, Mom."

As his mother hurried to the kitchen, MacArthur never adored her more. She didn't cook or clean the house like other moms, but she was loads of fun and a social genius. No one could entertain or throw a party like she could. The Colonel ushered them into the living room, but she had returned by the time they sat down. "Reuben, the yeas've been kind to ya, *despite* yo' sobriety."

He chuckled. "The years have made me older and wiser, I hope."

"How do you know my parents, Reuben?" MacArthur looked at his father. "You were never in Israel, were you?"

Lois brought a tray and served Reuben first. He took a sip of his root beer and said, "Oooh, that's good! Thank you." She nodded and smiled as she served the others.

"Ah'll answer yo' question," said his mother. "Ya know ya were born in Italy, wheh we were stationed at that very auspicious moment. So theh I was, tryin' ta take care a you an fo' little gals, with the Colonel comin' and goin' all the time. Then, he was gone 'bout a month to God knows wheh —

"And 'God knows where' was Israel," interjected Reuben.

She turned and wagged her finger at Reuben. "Which is what I figured out aftah *you* came crashin' through owr door ta save us awl — oh Lawd — I'm gettin' ahead a mahsef." She turned back to MacArthur. "Reuben's fathah, Yacov, which is how they pronounce Jacob, was charmin' and fascinatin'. I had the honah of meetin'm when he came to Italy to consult with yo fathah on some military

115

CONVERSION

mattah. Reuben was with'm, just a young man and so cute — but trouble, pure trouble."

MacArthur looked for Reuben's reaction. There was none.

"Well, sevral months latah, the Colonel left and said he'd be gone 'bout a week, which turned into two weeks. Evidently Reuben, bein' Reuben, got in a messy situation, which the Colonel sorted out with Yacov — and that's all they'd tell me. Anyhooo, because your fathah did this, Yacov's enemies became your fathah's enemies, and they wanted ta hurt 'im. Now this is how their thinkin' went: Because the Colonel saved Yacov's son, they were gonna kill your fathah's son, and guess who that was?"

"Has to be me — unless you and Dad haven't told me something," MacArthur grinned. It was great to tease his mom again.

The men smiled, but his mother shook her head and continued. "As luck would have it, Reuben discovahd theh diabolical plan, but Yacov and the Colonel were in a place wheh they could not be reached," she paused to roll her eyes, "so Reuben just hopped on a plane and litrally busted through owr front door! Ordahd me ta get you kids and leave without so much as a change of undahweah. Told all the hep ta go home until furthah notice, and off we went in this big, black truck-thing."

The Colonel smiled as he set down his drink and leaned forward. "The point is, MacArthur, you would not be here today and I might have lost all of you if Reuben hadn't acted quickly."

"Wow..." MacArthur turned to Reuben. "What happened to the bad guys? I mean, did you catch 'em?"

CHAPTER 11

"I went back to your house and intercepted them."

"What did you do to them?" MacArthur's eyes seemed to fill his face.

"I tied them up, and we had a nice conversation. They saw how foolish it was for them to harm your father or anyone related to him."

"That is so cool! Are you going to teach me that?"

Reuben almost choked on his root beer.

The Colonel's eyes narrowed. "I told you he would be a challenge."

"Dinner is served," said Lois.

"Your timing is impeccable, Lois," snorted the Colonel.

"Reuben, you will ado' Lois's roast lamb," said his mother.

12

Dear David,

    So much has happened, I don't know where to begin! And by the way, I think it's great that you're the starting quarterback for Balboa — and as a junior! Please say hello to everyone for me (especially Jennifer Westin! Ha! Ha!).

    News Flash: My mom did a complete about-face and said she was okay about me going to Thailand, because the Colonel chose this Israeli guy named Reuben to be my tutor and bodyguard. Well, I've spent the last week with him, and he is SO COOL! The first thing he did was ask me to make a list of what I was interested in learning and what I wanted to do while I was in Thailand. He said that I should write down anything — ANYTHING. So I did, and we went through my list, talking about each thing. It was great because he really took it seriously. AND, he didn't mark anything off the list! AND, he said that during the year I might change my mind about something or want to do something else (something I won't know about until I get there), and we could change our schedule. Of course, he said that our first priority was to cover

CONVERSION

everything I would be learning if I was in school here, so then I won't be behind when I come back for my senior year. We met with the vice principal at the high school to make sure we have all the right books and stuff.

Dad won't tell me a lot (as usual), but from what I can tell, Reuben must be a really top special forces guy in the IDF (Israeli Defense Forces). He was a captain at 23. A couple times I walked in when they were talking, and they stopped. I guess unless I join the army and become a tough guy like them, I will never hear their stories.

One time I heard the Colonel say something like, "... and if you hadn't been so drunk, you would have taken out their entire cache." And then Reuben said, "It remains one of my greatest regrets, but what can I do? I can only do better today." Then my dad muttered something, and they both laughed. Reuben said — and this is the kicker, "*Aman* will never let me go entirely." (*Aman* is the intelligence part of the Israeli military! I looked it up.) Then the Colonel said — get this — "You made the mistake of becoming their Samson" — and then — I was SO pissed — Mom came in, so they shut up.

So Superman, my new bodyguard is Samson! Ha! Ha! It's really weird because Reuben is strong, but he doesn't act like someone who will kick your butt (or kill you) if you get in his way. I think he's in his thirties,

CHAPTER 12

but he talks and acts like an old man. Since he doesn't drink anymore (and I guess he used to hit it hard), I can't get him drunk to find out his secrets, but I'm hoping he'll tell me more as we get to know each other better. Fingers crossed! I'll let you know.

We've got a couple more weeks before we leave. Mom's getting more emotional, and that's a drag. Sarah goes to nursing school at the University of Virginia the week after we leave. She's really psyched (and says hi by the way — ha!). It will be tough on Mom, but at least none of my sisters except Joanna are too far away.

Got to go — want to get this in the mail today. Please give my love to Mama and the Doc. As Mom would say, we all miss y'all!

>Your bb & bf,
>MacArthur

David folded the letter and put it in the shoebox he was using to collect MacArthur's correspondence. His father had suggested it. He and his parents were sworn to secrecy about the Thailand deal, which was really heavy, but it also made MacArthur's letters special. One day they might be valuable. David wondered why the Colonel wasn't being sent to Vietnam. Why was he going to Thailand? Maybe one day he would find out.

He missed his friend more than ever. There was something different about this separation. David had a foreboding that this

CONVERSION

Reuben person was going to cause a division between them. Still, whenever life was overwhelming, like today, he would pull out a letter and usually end up laughing, just picturing MacArthur's face and his goofy smile. He wished he was a fly on the wall and could listen to everything that was transpiring between him and the Colonel.

"Boys not much older than you are fighting in Vietnam. I'm glad you're not in the fight, but this is still going to be a test for you."

MacArthur frowned. He couldn't read his father. "What kind of test?"

"Trust. Obedience. I've no doubt you have courage, but by this time next year, Reuben and I will know if you can be trusted, if you can keep your mouth shut and put the safety of others before yourself."

"Dad, you sound like I *am* going to war."

His father's eyes seemed to bore holes in his eyeballs. "You are going to a very volatile zone. Why do you think Reuben is going with you?"

MacArthur nodded furiously. "Am I going to see things I shouldn't?"

"Some things. More importantly, some people. My team, you, and Reuben will be the only passengers on the plane, and you might recognize some of my men from Panama. That's where we trained for this mission."

"Okay. So...I'm not supposed to talk to these guys, I mean, even if I remember them?" He was trying to picture the various military

CHAPTER 12

men who had visited their homes while they were in Panama.

"You can say hello, period. The less you know, the safer you'll be. Since you'll sit with Reuben up front, that won't be too much of an issue, except when you get up to walk around. On these long flights, you need to get some exercise every couple hours."

"Will we fly straight to Bangkok? Don't we have to stop for fuel?"

"We're not going to Bangkok. We'll leave from Andrews. Brief stop at March Air Force Base near LA, an overnight at Hickam in Hawaii, then we'll stop in Guam to refuel before going on to the air force base in Thailand. Bring some good books to read."

"Dad, are you doing something like you did in Cuba?"

The Colonel's eyes flashed. "What the hell made you think I was in Cuba?"

"It was when we were in Virginia before. I heard you late at night, when I got up to get a glass of water. Remember, your study was close to the kitchen, and you were really ticked off. I peeked in and saw you talking on the gray phone."

"My God! Is listening to my conversations something you make a habit of doing?"

MacArthur was confused. "No, Sir. It just happened."

"Right. What exactly did you hear?"

"You said that you looked up and saw Cuban planes. You said the operation failed because the politicians didn't keep their word, that lots of good men died." He paused and took the plunge. "It was the Bay of Pigs, right?"

The Colonel shifted in his seat and cleared his throat. "Yes, well, I can tell you this much. Our plan was a good one, and the men I trained, ours and the Cuban freedom fighters, were some of the best I've seen. Those Cubans really wanted to be free. Unfortunately, at the last minute our air support never showed. This killed any hope of success. Most of those men either lost their lives or were captured, and God knows what Castro's guys did to them. The Bay of Pigs will always be a black eye in our history. And I have to say, it was a very bad day for me."

MacArthur was alarmed by the bitterness in his father's voice. "Are you sure you'll get what you need this time? I mean, are you doing some of the same stuff in Thailand?"

"This one's different. Don't worry. We have the support we need. I've made sure of it. And the Company knows better now."

"What company?"

"That's what we call the CIA."

MacArthur's eyes widened. "How long have you worked for them?"

"For a while."

"Are you a spy?"

The Colonel smiled. "Not everyone who works for the CIA is a spy, MacArthur. Again: The less you know the better. It protects you and me and everyone else. Okay?"

MacArthur smirked. "Need to know, huh?"

"Now you got it!" The Colonel patted him on the shoulder and started to leave the living room. He turned and asked, "I know you've read a lot about Thailand, but what do you find most interesting about it?"

CHAPTER 12

MacArthur didn't hesitate. "It's their desire to be free. Like us. Do you know they were the only country that managed to stay independent when all the other countries like Vietnam and Laos and Burma were under the thumb of a European power?"

"Yes, I did know that. And you're right. They are just as determined to keep the communists out too. They are real friends to us, and I want you to treat them that way. They may be different in many ways, and you may not agree with them on some things, but you can learn from them, and I want you to represent our nation well. Give them a good picture of the American people to remember, okay?"

"Yes, Sir. I'll do my best!"

One week later, it was time to leave. MacArthur had barely slept. He got up at 6 a.m., when a couple of army privates arrived in a truck to pick up their luggage and boxes. He was wary about giving them his guitar. He wanted to carry it on the plane with him, but the Colonel assured him that it would be handled carefully. Still, he had plastered the case with "fragile" and "handle with care" stickers.

Promptly at 7 a.m., a luxury sedan pulled into the driveway, and a sergeant got out. Rebecca met him at the door. "Hello, Sergeant."

"Good morning, Miss. I'm here to transport the Colonel and his son to Andrews Air Force Base."

"Yes, I know. They'll be right out."

Everyone was at home except Joanna, who had called earlier to wish them well and give the family an update on her adventures in

CONVERSION

Europe. She didn't seem to be homesick, but that didn't surprise MacArthur. She said, "Well Mac, we've always been the wild ones, haven't we?"

MacArthur smiled while his heart tugged. "I miss you, Sis."

"You too. Take care, and don't waste a moment!"

"I won't!"

He hugged Rebecca, Meg, Sarah, and then Lois, who stuffed some snacks into his carry-on bag. He saved his mother for last. She gave him a big squeeze, kissed his cheek, and then shoved him away. "Now go do whatcha gotta do and git home, heah?"

MacArthur saluted her. "Yes Ma'am!" He turned and walked to the car.

"And I betta get a letta every week!"

"Yes Ma'am!" he smiled over his shoulder.

He got into the car and watched his parents hold each other in a long, lingering embrace. For the first time, he felt the depth of his parents' sacrifice. He thought, *What gives a person the strength to risk never seeing the love of their life again?*

When they arrived at the airport, Reuben was waiting for them. "All secure?" the Colonel asked.

Reuben nodded and shook the Colonel's hand. "Everything has been loaded."

MacArthur was seeing a different Reuben — serious, impervious. "Then go ahead and board. I'm right behind you," said the Colonel.

MacArthur and Reuben left the terminal and walked toward a large prop plane that held both passengers and cargo. Reuben said,

CHAPTER 12

"We're flying Air America, which is the CIA fleet." He stopped and put his hand on MacArthur's shoulder. "From this moment, unless you are in a secure area, and I will define secure, you are not out of my sight. You will never walk behind me or run ahead unless I command you to do so."

"Yes, Sir."

They approached the stairs of the plane. "We are flying in a Lockheed C-130 Hercules —"

"Hercules! Cool!"

"I want you to learn the types of military transport, ours and the enemy's. Where we are going, you may see something we do not and it could be useful."

"Okay. I already know some of the names, 'cause I've been reading about the Vietnam War."

They walked up the steps to the jet doorway and were greeted by an older sergeant, who would serve as the steward on their flight. MacArthur greeted him as he turned to enter the cabin. All the seats looked like first class. Reuben directed him to sit in the first row to their left. As MacArthur moved to the window seat, he noticed a group of officers standing a bit down the aisle. A few looked Native American or Asian, some were black, and just two Caucasians. One looked like John from the Order of the Arrow. The Colonel entered the plane and the sergeant led the salute.

"We've got a long trip ahead of us, gentlemen, so be at your ease. Captain, you're with me." The Colonel sat in the window seat in the second row across from Reuben and MacArthur. A chorus of "yes sirs" filled the cabin, and all of the men sat behind the Colonel

CONVERSION

except the Native American captain. He walked to the front, leaned over, and held his hand out to MacArthur. "Did you find your knife?" he smiled.

Of course! It was Chuck! MacArthur jumped up, shook his hand and gushed, "Oh my God, Chuck! And I just saw John—"

"MacArthur," barked Reuben.

"Yes, I have my knife, Sir," he whispered, looking toward his small, carry-on duffle as he sat down. Chuck nodded and slipped into the aisle seat beside the Colonel. Reuben motioned MacArthur to place his carry-on under his seat. Besides his pocket knife, MacArthur's contained a small binoculars (a gift from David on his thirteenth birthday), a novel, his Bible, a book of crosswords, a travel Scrabble game, several comic books, a deck of cards, and the snacks from Lois. She had also put snacks into the Colonel's carry-on bag.

As they taxied to the runway and waited to take off, Reuben turned and said, "There will be times — many times I'm sure — when you can choose to resent me for being your shadow and dictator. I challenge you to think of this in different terms. This is not a game, where you try to outwit me and gain personal freedom; this is a war, and if you will listen and obey, you will learn how to survive. You might even flourish. In Israel, we must learn this as small children or we die young."

MacArthur blurted out, "Oh my God. I'm going to Thailand to become a real warrior! Reuben, I have to tell you something. You know my friend David?"

"You have spoken of him."

CHAPTER 12

"Well, that captain sitting with Dad was the guy who helped David save my life once."

"Tell me about this," said Reuben.

MacArthur told Reuben about the summer he and David went through their Ordeal at the Boy Scout camp in Panama. "We pretended we were great warriors, you know, but now, I think God wants me to become a real warrior. It must be part of my purpose. Can you teach me that?"

"What is your purpose?"

"Well...I haven't got all the details, but I know I have to change the world. Oh! I need to tell you about the light! When David and I were watching the riot in Panama City — do you know about that?" Reuben nodded yes. "Well, we were standing on this hill and got hit by this powerful light. It totally knocked us to the ground and got us laughing so hard that —" He slapped his head and slumped in his seat. "Oh crap! We promised we would never talk about it!"

Reuben chuckled. "Let me reassure you. This was a planned accident."

"Well I didn't plan it."

"No, God did."

Time stopped. MacArthur sat up and stared at Reuben. "What do you know about God?"

"Not a lot," Reuben smiled, "but what I do know is that there are times when he will get sneaky with us."

"Sneaky? I never heard him called that!"

"Hmm. Something will come up from your heart and out

129

of your mouth, and you have no idea how it happened. You say something profound, or the raw truth, and then you realize it wasn't you speaking. It was him, being sneaky."

MacArthur shook his head. "Boy, that almost sounds like heresy or something."

Reuben laughed and threw his head back. "Not for a Jew!"

"Oh, that's right! We have the same God, don't we?"

"Yes. And I believe we have the same messiah also."

"What? What are you talking about?"

"Was Jesus not a Jew?"

"Yeah...I guess so. I just never thought about it."

"So you see, I am a Jew who believes Jesus of Nazareth is indeed the Messiah of Israel."

MacArthur continued staring.

"MacArthur, close your mouth."

He pressed his lips together, but opened them immediately. "I...I...don't know what to say to that."

"Must you always say something?"

"I have no idea how I feel about this. I've never heard anything like it. I mean, Jews and Christians have been, like, enemies forever, haven't they?"

"This is a fact that loses power in light of the truth. Jesus is the truth to Jew and Gentile believers, making them one in him. I happen to be a Jew who came to the truth because Jesus saved my life."

"Really? He saved my leg!"

"Yes?"

CHAPTER 12

He told Reuben how Jesus healed his leg after the snakebite and then asked, "How did he save your life? Was it during the war you just fought?"

"No. It was years ago. He was there at my darkest hour."

"Is that why you don't drink anymore?"

Reuben smiled. "You are too perceptive. Yes, I stopped drinking only because he gave me the strength. I would be a derelict in the street or dead had he not saved me from myself."

"What do you mean? Did you try to kill yourself?"

Reuben frowned. "This is a discussion for later."

"Okay."

"But I will say this about your experience with the light. I believe God was affirming your purpose."

While MacArthur pondered these words, Reuben reached for his travel bag and pulled out a well-worn paperback. "Here is something I wish you to read. It will incite many questions, and we can discuss it."

MacArthur looked at the cover and read: *The Lion, the Witch, and the Wardrobe*, by C. S. Lewis. He turned up his nose. "Isn't this a kids' book?"

"There are no 'kids' books, MacArthur. There are only great books, good books, books not worth reading, and books that are so evil you best keep your eyes from them or they will twist your mind until you don't think right."

MacArthur had never thought of books in that way. He read for an hour and a half, when Reuben reminded him to get up and move around. And so began their travel routine of reading,

CONVERSION

sleeping, playing games, eating, walking up and down the aisle — and conversations about a myriad of topics incited by the C. S. Lewis classic. Did Lewis believe there was a time when animals talked like humans, or was he speaking allegorically? What was he saying about time? Was Aslan supposed to be Jesus and the witch Satan? And if so, what was he saying about them? Besides all the questions, one thing was certain: MacArthur loved the story and wanted to read the other books in the *Chronicles of Narnia* series.

They stopped at March Air Force Base to refuel, then the steward served them lunch on their way to Hawaii. Hour after hour, they flew over the Pacific Ocean. It was almost dusk when they began their descent. MacArthur looked down to get his first glimpse of the famous islands. They looked like monster heads popping out of the water. Soon they were on the ground at Hickam Air Force Base, and he felt like kissing the ground as his wobbly legs took him down the stairs to the tarmac. That night, he dreamed he was sleeping in a barracks.

"Wake up!" Reuben was shaking his cot.

"No more flying, please!" and he rolled over.

Reuben shook his arm. "Breakfast in ten minutes."

"Okay," MacArthur opened his eyes and realized he *was* in a barracks. He yawned. "Where's the Colonel?"

"He's taking care of business. You and I are going to the beach."

"Neat!" He jumped out of bed.

It was a perfect day. He felt like he had been sprung from a cage. They snorkeled. They rented a couple of boards and tried to surf. The only mishap was when MacArthur forgot his prime

CHAPTER 12

directive and ran down the beach to get a drink, leaving Reuben far behind. That was the end of the beach, but they had to be back at Hickam for dinner anyway. They were leaving for Guam early that evening.

MacArthur and Reuben ate at a different table than the Colonel and his men. MacArthur chattered on about his life in Panama, where he had discovered his love for golf, and how he and his friend David managed to stay friends when he moved to the other side of the canal. After reboarding the airplane, he slept during the flight to Guam. He woke up when they landed, long enough to walk the aisle of the plane a few times and eat a snack as he watched them fuel the plane in the dark. Soon they were in the air again, and he tried to sleep, but he knew they were on the final leg of the trip, albeit a very long leg. He yawned and turned to Reuben. "I forgot the name of the place we're landing."

"Udorn Royal Thai Air Force Base. It is one of the bases the US uses, not only to fly missions to Vietnam but to protect Thailand from communist insurgency. It is where the Colonel and his men will be headquartered. You and I will be lodged in a safe house not too far from the base, and your father will visit us from time to time. But he has probably told you this already."

"Not all. Can you tell me what they're going to do over here? Do you know?"

"The Colonel briefed me, and he has given me permission to tell you some things. But remember: Everything you see and hear that has any relationship to your father's mission is classified. You will not speak of it to anyone, not even David. Understood?"

CONVERSION

"Yes, Sir." He was excited to be there and certain he would keep all the secrets.

"I can tell you the general objective, which is to destroy supply lines of the enemy."

MacArthur's face fell.

Reuben chuckled. "First lesson of war: You can't fight with starving soldiers who have no ammunition. There are many aspects of war no one thinks about. They see movies with shooting and explosions, fighter jets swooping in and out, but they don't consider that all of this requires food, water, fuel, equipment, and vehicles. Eh? Cut off the supply lines, and you stop the aggression."

MacArthur nodded. "Oh! I see that. How are they going to do it?"

"They have a plan, and I can tell you this: I would not like to be figuring out how Colonel Wells is coming after my gun, my food, and my jeep!" Reuben leaned his head against the headrest and closed his eyes. He and MacArthur slept fitfully until the sun began to come up and they were in a slow descent.

They enjoyed a smooth landing at Udorn Royal Thai Air Force Base, but he and Reuben waited in the terminal for an hour while the Colonel met with some local officials on the base. They watched as the Colonel's men unloaded the freight section of the plane, sorting through it. A truck pulled up to the C-130, and they loaded MacArthur and Reuben's luggage, boxes, and crates onto it. Soon, the truck was gone, and Chuck, John, and the others picked up their duffel bags and walked to several waiting jeeps.

Finally, the Colonel appeared and motioned them outside the

CHAPTER 12

terminal, where a large sedan drove up. After the obligatory salutes, he introduced MacArthur and Reuben to their driver, Sergeant Mills, who said, "If you'll follow me, Sir." He continued in a low voice as they got into the car. "All of Mr. Katz's and your son's things are being transported to their quarters, and your overnight is in the trunk of the car. The rest of your things are being sent to your quarters on the base."

"Thank you," said the Colonel. "And Mr. Katz's request? Was that seen to?"

"Yes, Sir. It has been delivered."

13

Thailand enchanted MacArthur from the moment the airplane crossed its border. For a while, they flew over a large plain that looked dry and desolate, and he learned there was a drought in that area; but August was the rainy season, so most of the terrain was lush and green and often hilly or mountainous. As the airplane descended on the city of Udorn Thani and the base, he saw that some of the military barracks and housing were austere, but many of the buildings boasted the charming character of the region, on stilts with sloping decorative roofs and bamboo walls. What really struck him, however, was the vast number of fighter jets lining the runways.

When they deplaned, the hot, muggy air filled his lungs, and he knew he was in the tropics. *No different from Panama,* he thought. *Ah! That's why Dad trained there!* From Udorn Thani, they took a two-lane highway headed southwest for about five minutes, then turned northwest onto a dirt road. Several miles later, they turned onto what was a dirt driveway, which wound around some hills before arriving at a house that looked like a mixture of East and West. MacArthur was disappointed. It was not on stilts.

The walls were stucco, painted a coral color, and two large windows framed in green shutters graced either side of the dark wood front door. The roof was slanted tile, bordered by decorative

CONVERSION

eaves. Several steps led up to the bare front porch, which spanned the front of the house. MacArthur noticed a foreign model car and a motorbike parked on the right side of the house, and two bicycles leaned against the front porch. He got out of the sedan with his carry-on bag and stared at the austere structure. His father patted him on the back. "You're in the Army now, Son."

Reuben emerged from the other side of the car, while Sergeant Mills took the Colonel's overnight bag from the trunk. The front door opened and out stepped a beautiful Thai couple. They smiled and did the *wai*, the Siamese hello and goodbye, where hands are put together, as if in prayer, and the person bows slightly. Even bowing, everything about them was tall, straight, and dignified. Before his father or Reuben could say anything, MacArthur skipped up the steps, mimicked the *wai* with a grin, and introduced himself.

"MacArthur, meet Kau and Lawan, who will run the house and see that you are well fed. They will also teach you about the Siamese culture and what you should and shouldn't say and do. Listen to them, and you will stay out of trouble."

"Yes, Sir."

"It's good to see you both," said the Colonel, and he did the *wai*. "And this is Reuben Katz, who will serve as MacArthur's tutor and bodyguard."

Reuben did the *wai* also. "I am honored to meet you."

"Please come in and let us help you settle in," said Kau in perfect English. "I will show you your quarters while Lawan prepares brunch."

"It will be ready in an hour," added Lawan, also in perfect

CHAPTER 13

English. She entered the house, followed by Kau and the rest.

As soon as he was inside, MacArthur saw an entirely different picture than he anticipated. Confronting him was an exotic scene beyond two sets of French doors. The house was a U-shape that bordered a lovely atrium garden on three sides. They stopped to enjoy the view of flowers, lush greenery, and several trees. Then Kau said, "Please, come this way." He led them to the left, down the wide foyer, and at the end they turned right to follow him down a hall, rugs on the wood floors cushioning their feet. Despite the lack of windows, the bedroom hallway was nicely lit, the walls featuring colorfully painted murals depicting Siamese life. Three bedroom doors opened to their right.

Kau said the first bedroom was Reuben's, the second was MacArthur's, and the third was the Colonel's; but he led them directly to the end of the hall, where an open door revealed a bathroom. On the back wall was a soaking tub with a shower head rigged over it. A toilet occupied the corner to the right, and against the wall to the left was a metal sink, with a mirror hanging over it and a rough-hewn wood table alongside. Again, no windows, and the walls were painted a pastel green.

Mom and the girls — except Joanna— wouldn't like this, thought MacArthur, *but it's perfect for us guys.*

"Good job rigging this. Thank you, Kau," said the Colonel.

"You are very welcome, Colonel," Kau beamed. "I suggest you unpack before brunch."

"Good idea."

MacArthur walked through his bedroom door and grinned

CONVERSION

from ear to ear. The bedroom more than made up for the house not being on stilts. French doors led to the atrium garden, and to the right of the doors was a wooden desk with a window above. The desk top covered four drawers on one side and two bookshelves on the other side. On the desk was a small lamp and a clock. He stepped around his two suitcases and three boxes and opened the French doors, then quickly closed them when the sticky air washed over him. *Thank God for air conditioning*, he thought.

He turned to survey his room. It looked like all the furniture was made of dark bamboo. Against the left wall was a double bed with a bamboo headboard and pastel blue bedspread that matched the curtains at the window and French doors. On either side of the bed were night tables with tall, porcelain lamps painted with white elephants in a sky-blue background. Also on each side of the bed was a small blue rug on the wood floor.

On the wall to his right, across from the bed, stood a dresser with a mirror over it and a large wardrobe for hanging clothes and storing shoes and hats. He thought of *The Lion, the Witch, and the Wardrobe* and opened the doors expectantly. He frowned. No fur coats. Just towels, a blanket, and hangers. He tapped on the back wall just in case then closed the doors. As he turned he noticed a light switch by the door, and when he flipped it up, the ceiling fan began to turn. Whoever had furnished this room had thought of everything! That's when he saw his guitar case in the corner by the bed. "Thank God!" He rushed to place it on the bed and open it. He removed the guitar and examined it, then played a few chords. It had survived the trip without damage.

CHAPTER 13

He forced himself to put the guitar away and begin unpacking his clothes, books, and all the miscellaneous items he had thought essential for the middle of nowhere. He put the large box of stationery and package of ink pens in a desk drawer and made a mental note to write letters to his mom, his sisters, and David as soon as possible.

He slipped his suitcases under the bed and was breaking down the cardboard boxes when Reuben knocked and came into the room. "You have been busy."

"After so many moves, I've pretty much got the routine down." He slid the flattened boxes under the bed. "This room is cool. What's yours like?"

"My room is cool too," he chuckled, "except my color is green instead of blue. Let's see what color they gave the Colonel."

The Colonel's room was coral and otherwise identical. "Let's go eat!" He yelled as he clapped a hand on each of their shoulders and moved them into the hallway.

"Dad, I'm really surprised we have air conditioning. I mean, I'm not complaining! It's so much better than when we were in Panama, but how is this possible?"

"In return for allowing us to be here, we built a dam that provides electricity. Some of the houses now have central heat and air, and the irrigation from the dam also helps the farmers and makes our indoor plumbing possible."

"Reuben, can we go see the dam sometime?"

"Add it to your list."

"Cool!"

CONVERSION

They passed the French doors in the foyer and looked into the living area. There was a spinet piano on the wall to the right and a card table with four chairs just beyond it, in the corner. A beautifully carved chess set sat upon it. As they walked beside the piano, MacArthur played a little melody with his right hand. This was his mother's doing, most likely. She had insisted on piano lessons when he was younger, and she still loved to hear him play the songs he remembered.

He turned to see a fluffy yellow sofa with two wing chairs covered in a floral fabric that was predominately bright yellow. He glanced up to stare at a beautiful painting of one of the Siamese kings' expeditions to find a white elephant in the northern mountains. MacArthur had read that, to Buddhists, the white elephant represented the mother of Gautama Buddha, so the animal was highly revered.

The sofa was flanked by bamboo end tables with porcelain lamps and several books on each. Instead of looking to a television set, the furniture faced one of two sets of French doors, one for the living room and one for the dining area. Between these French doors was a comfortable chair and a tall, thin table with a telephone on it.

MacArthur looked past the sofa and end table and spotted a Magnavox stereo hi-fi receiver and turntable on the back wall. They sat upon a small cabinet filled with records. His gaze followed wires, which led to speakers planted at each end of the room.

"Reuben, what kind of music do you like?"

Reuben walked over to squat in front of the record collection.

CHAPTER 13

"Let's see what is here. Frank Sinatra. Duke Ellington. Ah! Beethoven's Ninth Symphony. One of my favorites."

MacArthur looked over Reuben's shoulder. "No Beatles or Rolling Stones?" Reuben stood, and MacArthur began to sing and gyrate, "I can't get no...sat...is...fac...tion."

Reuben looked at MacArthur like a scientist examining an alien being.

"Yes, well," said the Colonel, shaking his head, "let's honor Lawan by getting to the table on time."

A beautiful, painted screen separated the living room from the dining room. MacArthur sat in a side chair, Reuben across from him, and the Colonel at the head, of course. On the wall behind the dining table and chairs was another landscape painting of the mountains with a cascading waterfall. The table was beautifully set, with a centerpiece of fresh-cut flowers, cloth napkins, and china and silverware. MacArthur's stomach growled. It smelled like a Lois breakfast, and a wave of homesickness washed over him.

Lawan poured orange juice in their glasses, disappeared into the kitchen, and then brought out a platter of eggs and bacon. Kau brought a platter of buttered toast and cinnamon rolls and another platter of fruit. The Colonel thanked them, and after they had disappeared into the kitchen, he said grace and crossed himself. MacArthur did the same, and Reuben said, "Amen."

The Colonel noticed MacArthur was devouring the feast. "Slow down, Son," he said.

"Yes, Sir." He swallowed. "How long can you stay, Dad?"

"I go back to the base in the morning. I'm hoping I can return

CONVERSION

in a couple of weeks and stay for a few days. There's a nice stream at the back of this property that's full of catfish. Reuben, are you up for it?"

"Always." Reuben smiled then became serious. "But you know, you are old now, and I will outlast you."

MacArthur froze. He had never heard anyone talk to his father like this. And then, he had never heard his father burst out laughing like he did. Bewildered, he asked, "What's so funny?"

"MacArthur, I'm not sure I want you to know this side of Reuben. He can be quite the prankster."

"Come on! Tell me, please?"

Reuben shrugged his shoulders and smiled. "It is for your father to tell."

The Colonel wiped his mouth and threw his napkin on the table. "Well, my very first time in Israel, Reuben's father assigned Reuben to be my driver and guide. In the course of conversation, we discovered we both loved to fish, and Reuben asked if I would like to visit a special place he had found. I said I didn't know when we could swing it. My days were full and started early in the morning. So Reuben gets this twinkle in his eye — always beware when you see it — and says, 'We will go late at night. The fish bite better, and tonight there is no moon.' Needless to say, off we went.

"We drove for quite a while, and I had no idea where we were because I knew little of Israel then. Finally, we get out near the lake and bait our lines, waiting for a tug. The minutes go by. Nothing. After an hour, Reuben says, 'Sometimes they like singing,' and he starts to sing in Hebrew. He's putting *me* to sleep, so I don't know

CHAPTER 13

how this would get the fish to bite. Still nothing. About every fifteen minutes, which seems like every hour, Reuben keeps saying, 'I apologize. This is very unusual.'

"All this time, we're sipping beer. Finally, the sky begins to lighten and I say, 'Okay, I've had enough. I hate to tell you, Reuben, but this is the sorriest fishing hole I've ever been to.'

"He says, 'Giving up so soon?' And he starts laughing.

"'What's so funny?' I ask. Reuben picks up the fishing gear, still laughing, and says, 'Come with me.'

"We get in the jeep, go down the road a bit more, and stop at a big sign. It reads: Dead Sea."

"That's crazy!" MacArthur stared at Reuben. "You took the Colonel to fish in the *Dead Sea*? Oh my God!"

"Yes, I have to admit. I was young, arrogant, and — what your father omitted from the story — very drunk. The miracle was that we got home alive."

"And that I was able to get through the following day. I did appreciate that Reuben never told anyone. *However*, the following week, there was an anonymous cartoon in *The Jerusalem Post*. It was a simple drawing of a man holding a fishing pole, with the line in the Dead Sea, and the caption read: The American Dream."

"Oh God! That could mean a lot of things."

"Yes," said Reuben, "but only the Colonel and I knew the true meaning."

The combination of a full stomach, laughter, and all the excitement suddenly rendered MacArthur stultified. "Can I be excused? I think I need to lie down." The Colonel and Reuben smiled.

CONVERSION

"Sure," said the Colonel.

"Please tell Lawan how good the food was." He pushed back his chair, managed to traverse the long walk to his bedroom, and fell on his bed.

14

MacArthur opened his eyes and wondered where he was. A setting sun sent rays of light through French doors and magically lit a garden outside. *Thailand*. He sat on the side of his bed and stared for a moment. The clock on the desk said six o'clock. *Could that be right? Did I sleep for six hours?*

After throwing cold water on his face in the bathroom, he walked into the hallway and heard classical music coming from the living room. From the foyer, he saw his father and Reuben playing chess. Between the music and their intense focus on the game, they did not notice him enter the room. *Let's see if I can sneak by them.* He quietly stepped onto the living room rug and moved toward the dining room and kitchen. "Good evening, MacArthur," said Reuben, without looking up. "Did you think you could slip my notice?" He moved a chess piece.

"Damn. I wasn't expecting that," said the Colonel, looking at the board.

"I just thought I'd explore the rest of the house and the back yard." MacArthur paused. "Is there a back yard?"

"Yes," answered his father. "But don't be gone long. Dinner is in half an hour. And don't bother Lawan or Kau in the kitchen."

"Yes, Sir."

He moved quickly past the dining table and pushed the

CONVERSION

swinging door to enter the kitchen, which was an entirely different world. Something in a pot on a large charcoal brazier smelled delicious, and he was suddenly ravenous. Next to it was an oven that sat on a metal table. There was a small refrigerator, and in the center of the room was a large table for chopping and mixing. Baskets of fruit and vegetables were placed on it.

There was an industrial-looking metal sink, like you would find in a mechanic shop. Pots and pans hung in various places around the room, and a tall cabinet's right door was open, revealing shelves of glassware and dishes. Next to it was what resembled a chest of drawers. Light shone through three windows, about ten inches tall and two feet wide, like large eyes at the top of the wall on the atrium side. A ceiling fan whirred above him.

What really intrigued MacArthur, however, was the alcove to his right. There was a shelf with a smiling Buddha statue sitting on it, surrounded by flowers. To the left and right were doors. The one on the right was closed. *Wonder what's in there?* The door across from it suddenly opened and MacArthur got a quick glimpse of another bedroom as Lawan entered the kitchen and closed the door behind her. "You are hungry?" she asked, smiling.

"Yes, Ma'am. I promise, it smells great, but I haven't eaten any of it."

Her laughter was like beautiful music. "*Mai pen rai,*" she shrugged. "Dinner will be ready soon. Please, go outside and see." She gestured to the back door.

"Yes, Ma'am."

He noticed a large piece of metal, bigger than the door,

CHAPTER 14

hanging next to it, but quickly forgot this as he opened the heavy door. He could hear water rushing down the hillside in the stream his father had mentioned. A high, stone wall that extended from the outside walls of the house enclosed the back yard. One tall, iron gate at the back was the only exit or entrance. He definitely wanted to explore beyond that! But first, he walked around the lush green lawn, inhabited only by a few clusters of eucalyptus trees, the same kind that were in the atrium. Behind the wall of their bathroom, he was glad to see an archery target lying on three bales of hay. There were several long, iron rods next to a wooden crate. He tried to lift the lid, but it was nailed shut.

He walked back toward the kitchen and stopped to take a closer look at the atrium. The large opening between the kitchen and bathroom walls was filled by two avocado trees. *Yum. I wonder if Lawan knows how to make guacamole.* Then he walked over to a well-tended garden. A large window with a tiled awning that matched the roof of the house watched over the thriving plants. Presumably, the window was part of Lawan's quarters, which he had seen from the kitchen. *Were Kau and Lawan married?*

MacArthur walked to the formidable iron gate at the back and pulled the bar that locked it to the side. It was harder to pull open than he had thought, but he managed it and stepped through. The heavily forested hillside and warm, sticky humidity reminded him of Panama again. He walked toward the sound of the water and soon stopped to take in the beauty of the scene. What he had been hearing was a waterfall, higher up the hill, that cascaded into a gently flowing stream. He followed the stream a little way and saw

CONVERSION

that it ran parallel to the back wall of the house and down the hill. When he saw all the fish, his stomach began to churn, so he headed back.

Dinner did not disappoint. As Kau and Lawan served the soup, Lawan explained that instead of cooking American as she had for their brunch, she had prepared traditional Thai dishes. The aroma MacArthur had enjoyed in the kitchen was *guay teow*, a noodle soup with pork and a touch of lime. Next, Kau served a salad called *laab*, warning them, "The minty flavor is accompanied by a very spicy surprise." Lawan was delighted to find she was cooking for three who loved spicy dishes. The main course was called *panang*, a mild curry dish with shrimp and rice. For dessert, Kau served the popular mango sticky rice.

As the meal progressed, they asked Kau about what they were eating. What came from the garden? Where did he and Lawan shop for food? MacArthur listened intently, and his curiosity about Lawan and Kau grew. When Kau came to clear the dessert dishes, the Colonel patted his belly contentedly and asked Kau to come back with Lawan. When they came through the door, the three satisfied diners stood and applauded. Kau and Lawan beamed and did the *wai*, which the Colonel, Reuben, and MacArthur returned.

The Colonel moved toward the living area. "Well, MacArthur, now that you've explored the place, what do you think?"

"It's incredible."

They sat facing each other in the wing chairs, and Reuben walked toward the bedrooms. The sun was nearly set, and rain was pouring down in the atrium. The Colonel crossed his leg. "I will

CHAPTER 14

be leaving early tomorrow morning, so now is the time to ask any questions."

MacArthur moved to the sofa to sit close to his father and lowered his voice. "Tell me about Kau and Lawan. Are they married? Do they live in that room by the kitchen? And how do they speak such good English? How do you know them?"

"Well, that's a long story, some of which I cannot tell you, but Kau and Lawan are married and live in the quarters behind the kitchen."

"Do they have kids?"

"Three boys, but they're grown, the youngest in college. You may meet them while you're here."

"Where did they learn to speak English like that? Were they raised in America or something?"

"Lawan is from a wealthy family and attended a Presbyterian boarding school in Bangkok, where she learned English and Western ways. They encouraged Christianity, but she remained Buddhist. As you know, most Thais are Buddhist. She was also in a political club, and when she went on to Chulalongkorn University, she continued to study languages and was involved in political affairs. That is where she met Kau.

"He, on the other hand, grew up rough on the streets of Bangkok. When he was twelve, his father was killed in a bartering dispute, which was a great shame to his family. His mother worked as a maid for one of the foreign diplomats, and they weren't particularly kind to her, but they allowed her children to do odd jobs for them and eat the scraps from their table.

CONVERSION

"Kau saw how the better half lived and devised a plan. He became friends with one of the diplomat's sons and got him to teach him English and French. He made himself indispensable to the family. Any time they needed something, he would get it for them. Eventually, they realized how bright he was, and when he was old enough, the diplomat recommended him to Chulalongkorn, where he was accepted and excelled in his classes.

"He and Lawan met at an anti-communist rally, and a year later they were married. They have always worked for diplomats or government officials, so they are very trustworthy *and* excellent at their jobs."

"They seem great."

"Reuben will be in charge when I'm not here, but they are not servants. You can learn a lot from them. They are very aware of what is going on in their country and particularly in this region." He paused, took a deep breath, and leaned back in his chair. "What have you observed about the house?"

"Well, actually, I was kind of hoping we'd be staying in one of those houses on stilts, but…" MacArthur wrinkled his brow, thinking. "I just realized that the entire house is a stone wall, that goes on around the back yard. It's kind of a fortress, except for the front door and the windows and the back iron gate, so it's pretty secure."

The Colonel pointed to the entrance. "The front door is wood on steel, and the front window panes are steel bars. The iron gate and front windows and door have an alarm that Kau sets every evening, so the house *is* a veritable fortress. I just want to assure

CHAPTER 14

you that you are safe. Be on your guard at all times, but there's no reason to be afraid. You are in the best hands."

"Dad, what *is* the danger here? I mean, there's no fighting going on in this country, is there?"

He sighed. "The Communist Party of Thailand, or CPT, has tried to take over Thailand for decades. About two years ago, they began an all-out guerilla war against the Thai government. They murdered politicians and incited a lot of violence. They have factions around the country, and of course, the government arrests them when they can, but you can't be too careful. The CPT kill people who oppose them."

"Why are we here, really? I mean, here and Vietnam. I know the US has helped other countries when they got in trouble, but we're half-way around the world fighting someone else's war."

"We're helping them because the end-game of communism is *world* domination. They aim to take over the world, country by country. We didn't really understand this during World War II, because Russia was on our side and China was neutral. Plus, communism was a new concept. Then, almost immediately, Russia invaded Poland, East Germany, and Eastern Europe. Not long after that, Mao took control of China and patterned his rule after Stalin's rule of terror. Millions were slaughtered wherever communism spread, especially Christians and Jews, but also those who wanted to own their property and businesses and farms. We realized that we were dealing with an evil much worse than Hitler."

MacArthur frowned. "So, we just finished getting rid of one maniac who wanted to rule the world and several others popped up?"

CONVERSION

"Exactly. When the communists took the northern part of Korea and then invaded the southern part, we went in to stop them from taking more territory. That was the Korean War. Now, we're doing the same thing in Vietnam. If we don't stop them here today, they may be at our door tomorrow. We are doing this for them and for us, to ensure that free countries stay free."

MacArthur was thoughtful. "How do these guys get control of a whole nation of people who want to be free? It just doesn't make sense."

"In the beginning, communism sounds like a great idea. It's *communal* and everyone is *equal*. Everyone owns everything *collectively*. No rich or poor, just one class of workers, and each worker contributes to the welfare of all. So it begins when a leader of an elite group stirs up those who are poor and dissatisfied. They revolt, and the new leader dictates what everyone believes, speaks, and where they work. Furthermore, the government owns everything. There is no private property. If anyone disagrees, they are an enemy of the state and are tortured, sent to a labor camp, or executed. Millions in Russia, China, and Eastern Europe have been murdered because of their dissent, and once prosperous and beautiful countries like Cuba are now poor, oppressed dictatorships."

"Hmm…so some Thai citizens believe everything will be equal and perfect if communism takes over the world, and because we are against them, we are in danger."

"Yes. Just remember, most of the Thai people are glad we're here to help, but some are not. You and Reuben need to be tourists

CHAPTER 14

and keep a low profile whenever you venture out. Learn from Kau and Lawan how to act. Also, we chose this safe house because it was not only secure but, on the inside at least, it doesn't look like a prison. We hope you won't *want* to go out very often. And again, keep your ears and eyes open when you do. You might see or hear something we need to know."

"Yes, Sir."

"Let's get to bed."

They stood and walked back to their rooms in silence. Outside his door, MacArthur said, "Dad, David told me that the only people who like Americans are Americans, that other countries put up with us but really hate us."

The Colonel smiled knowingly. "There was definitely tension between us and the Panamanians, and I think that's what David was referring to. We built the canal and continue to ensure the Zone's safety, but some still resent our presence. It's the way people are. When you help those who can't help themselves, some are grateful and others get mad because your help makes them feel inferior and weak, even when you're nice and try to help them into a better way of life. And, of course, some Americans are just assholes and throw their weight around. That doesn't help."

MacArthur laughed at the last comment.

His father continued. "The main thing to remember is that nations act like the humans who control them, and humans can be good or evil — or both at the same time."

"What do you mean?"

155

CONVERSION

"Look at yourself. One minute you are helpful, kind, even *humble*. The next minute, you can be oblivious to others and run right over them with your own agenda."

MacArthur threw his head back and grimaced. "Got it. Nations are like people because people run them."

"Yep. Sleep well, Son."

The next morning Reuben was already at the table, talking with his father, when MacArthur joined them. "I was wondering. Can Reuben and I take a week and do some things on my list before we start school?"

"I defer to you, Reuben," said the Colonel.

Reuben turned to MacArthur. "You are excited and want to explore, but you must be patient and learn before we venture out. It is important to establish a schedule that you can easily return to after we leave and do tourist things. Yes?"

"Yes. But how many weeks before we can go out?"

"That will depend on you."

They heard a car drive up and MacArthur's heart sank. He was hoping for more time with his father, and the reality of being alone in a foreign land with people he barely knew suddenly hit him. *What was I thinking?* His heart raced as he stood and walked his father to the door, where his overnight bag stood waiting.

"Well, Son, I still can't believe you're here, nor do I understand it, but I have to admit, I'm glad. Be safe." He hugged MacArthur and said, "Reuben, you will be in my prayers with this one," he smiled and shook his friend's hand.

"Be safe, and we will see you in a month?" said Reuben.

CHAPTER 14

"God willing."

Then he was gone.

15

MacArthur was surprised that he enjoyed his daily routine. In the back yard that first afternoon, Reuben began, "You have expressed the desire to become a warrior. I know you understand obeying orders, but are you willing to make the sacrifices necessary to be a real warrior?"

"Yes, Sir!"

"Well, we shall see. There is a relationship between a goal and endurance. If your goal is selfish, endurance will be harder to sustain. If it is just you whom you are trying to please, it is easier to quit. Conversely, a goal to achieve good for others *and* yourself, especially those you love, inspires greater endurance. Your pain and suffering become an honor and even a joy."

"Geez, Reuben. You sound like a philosopher!"

"Do you understand?"

"Sure. I need to have the right reason for doing things, or when things get tough, I won't have the strength, well, maybe even the courage, to keep going."

"Correct. A warrior who has a clear mission for the good of all will endure to see the battle to the end." Kau brought out a table with a large pitcher of water and two glasses. Reuben led MacArthur over to the steel rods and the mysterious crate. The contents proved to contain smaller steel rods, nuts and bolts, and tools to construct

CONVERSION

a set of monkey bars.

MacArthur did most of the work under Reuben's supervision. As soon as they were finished, his charge jumped up to swing from bar to bar, making sounds like a monkey, then dropped to the ground in an exhausted heap. He looked up and squinted. "Reuben, I have one question."

"Only one?"

"You said I should have the right motive, and that includes the good of others not just myself, but this looks like something I did for me. I mean, I can't see you, Kau, or Lawan playing on monkey bars!"

"Ahhh. You have made a false assumption."

"What?" He stood to face Reuben.

"You have assumed they are for pleasure."

MacArthur's smile vanished. "What do you want me to do with them?"

Reuben jumped to grab the top bar and moved to the next and the next until he came to the end, then turned and came back the same way. He continued the cycle again and again as he spoke. "This you will do every day, beginning with five rounds. Next" (Reuben dropped to the ground and began to demonstrate), "you will climb to the top, move across the bars and down the other side five times. Finally, do ten pull-ups." (Again, he demonstrated.) "We will increase the number of each as you grow stronger. What do you think your goal should be?"

"Well, I guess to become strong."

"For what reason?"

CHAPTER 15

"Well…um…so I can do things I can't do without being strong?"

"What are these things?"

"I don't know. Like…lifting heavy stuff or climbing trees to get stray cats or…I don't know." Now he was frustrated as well as being tired and hungry.

"You are a warrior. What will inspire you to endure this exertion on the monkey bars?"

"Oh! So I can be strong enough to defend people, to save them!"

"And save yourself. A warrior is no good to anyone if he is dead. The only time a warrior would accept death is in the line of duty, to save others."

Kau came to retrieve the table and announced that lunch would be ready in fifteen minutes, time enough to shower and change.

> Dear David,
>
> How's football practice? Do you miss my unpredictableness? Ha Ha!
>
> After Dad left, I really thought, oh my God, what have I done? I'm in the middle of nowhere with people I hardly know. But so far, Reuben has been super. I told him about OA and our ordeal and asked him if he could teach me to be a real warrior. So everything we do is to make me into a real warrior! The first day, he had me build a set of monkey bars, not to play on but

161

CONVERSION

to get stronger.

Every afternoon, I spend an hour at least in physical training, and Reuben and sometimes Kau and Lawan do everything I'm doing and more. They are all so strong! I'm huffing and puffing and sweating, and they just breeze through. However, I can go five laps on the bars without stopping, and I think Reuben's going to increase it next week—ugh. He's also running me up and down roads and through the woods and all over the place — even when it's raining, which is half the time — and then he quizzes me on what I've seen. We do the same on bikes sometimes. It's like nothing in life is trivial anymore.

After training, I practice archery, and R. has me walking around and shooting at the target. He says eventually I'll be running and shooting! He's also teaching me to shoot a rifle and a pistol in the same way. I'm beginning to see why you like guns, but I still prefer my bow and arrow.

My brain gets a workout too. US history, geometry, biology, and English (grammar, writing, 19th Century literature) in the morning. The high school principal in VA gave us a reading list, and R. says I have to do one book every three weeks, two weeks to read and one week to write a report on it. The list is long, so we ordered fifteen books (just in case I read faster than we thought) to take with us. I wanted to start with

CHAPTER 15

Frankenstein, by Mary Shelley, but Reuben insisted I start with *A Tale of Two Cities*, by Charles Dickens. It's incredible! Have you read it? I can see why, because in History we're comparing the American Revolution to the French Revolution.

This is really hilarious. Reuben picked up the geometry book and broke out in a sweat! I asked him what's the matter, and he said geometry had always been a pain for him. Kau overheard him and said he'd teach me. He loves all kinds of math and is really great at it. He makes it easy to understand. He says he helped his sons that way. Anyway, R. was so relieved!

Being taught one-on-one is so neat, because we usually cover each subject in about a half hour and are done by lunch. Then Reuben and I listen to music and he's teaching me to play chess too. He's determined to make me love classical and jazz, and I have to say that some of it is really cool. One place we really jive is folk music. He's teaching me some Israeli folk songs that I can play on the guitar. And guess what? Lawan is not only a great cook, but she can really play the piano (forgot to tell you that we have one here). She joins Reuben and me sometimes and plays all kinds of stuff. She's also teaching me music theory, so I can write songs better.

After about an hour of music, etc., I do physical training for about an hour or more, then come in and

CONVERSION

shower. My free time is before dinner. After dinner I do homework and read. I don't even think about television, but it's in Siamese anyway. Kau and Lawan have one in their bedroom. I figure if anything big happens in the world, they will let us know (if they ever watch it).

I'm having some neat conversations with Reuben about stuff I'm studying. He asks questions that make me think HARD. He'll say stuff like, "Tell me how the Revolutionary War affects you today? How does it influence what you believe about life? About the world?" I mean, I never thought about history that way! Maybe it's because he's an Israeli and Israel plays such a big role in world affairs. I'm looking for a time when I can ask him about himself. Still don't know that much.

Got to go. Give my love to the Doc and Mama. I'm having a blast but miss you!

Your bb & bf,
MacArthur

"MacArthur, focus. Look at the board. Why did you bring your queen out?"

"Reuben, have you ever had a dream that's so real, it's like you're living it?"

"You have had such a dream?"

"Yes. Last night. I saw Dad being captured by the enemy. Then

CHAPTER 15

they shoved him in this hut and began to beat him and torture him. I don't even want to describe what they did. I just want to forget it."

"Get your Bible, please."

He was confused but obeyed.

Reuben motioned for him to sit beside him on the sofa and give him the book. He leafed through it. "Ah. Here it is. Throughout the Bible, God gave dreams to people for many reasons. The first dream mentioned in the Bible was a dream of warning. It is here, in the book of Genesis. Abraham had gone to another country, and his wife Sarah was so beautiful, he was afraid Abimelech, the king of that country, would kill him to have her; so, Abraham told everyone she was his *sister*. Now read here, Genesis 20, verse 3."

"'But God came to Abimelech in a dream by night, and said to him, Behold, thou art but a dead man, for the woman which thou hast taken; for she is a man's wife.'" MacArthur stared at the page. "So God warned Abimelech not to touch Sarah or he would die?"

"Yes. Now you must determine if this dream you have had is a true warning from God or an expression of deep feelings. Examine your soul. Have you been anxious about your father's safety the last few weeks?"

"Not really. I mean, I've thought about it, and sometimes I miss him, but I've been so busy. I haven't had time to be worried."

"If your soul has not been troubled, the next step is to ask another believer about the dream. You asked me, and in my spirit, I believe you have had a warning from God."

165

CONVERSION

MacArthur was horrified. "You mean, it's going to happen? He's gonna be tortured?"

"No, no. Be at peace. God told Abimelech to stay away from Sarah so he wouldn't die, and Abimelech obeyed and lived. God gave you a warning about your father and had you tell me so we could pray and stop the enemy."

MacArthur's face brightened. "How will we do that? Is that why you're teaching me to shoot and stuff? When do we leave?"

Reuben shook his head. "What did I say?"

"You said we should stop the enemy."

"I gave the strategy for stopping the enemy. What was that?"

MacArthur shrugged his shoulders in frustration, "I don't know."

"I said God gave you the dream so we could *pray* and stop the enemy."

"*Pray?* That's going to stop it from happening?"

Reuben tapped his fingers on the Bible. "We will pray according to God's Word and he promises to perform it. So…you pray first, then I will end our prayer."

MacArthur closed his eyes. He had never prayed with anyone like this, right off the top of his head and out loud. "Um. God, please keep my father, you know, the Colonel, uh…safe from the enemy or anything else that would hurt him. Amen."

Reuben continued, "Abba, we thank you that you placed your mighty angels around the Colonel and his men to keep them from harm. We thank you for giving them wisdom and information they need to perform their mission without mishap. Your Word says

CHAPTER 15

that no weapon formed against us will prosper, and we know you honor that promise for the Colonel and his men. In Yeshua's name we pray, amen."

As Reuben prayed, MacArthur's anxiety faded away. Eyes still closed, he breathed, "Wow...something's here."

"Some*one* is here."

MacArthur opened his eyes and stared at Reuben. "I've gone to church, actually, I've gone to two churches my whole life, and I've never heard anyone pray like that. Is it because you're Jewish? Do you know something Catholics and Protestants don't?"

Reuben chuckled. "No. Jews receive Yeshua as Messiah and follow him like anyone else."

"Is Yeshua the Jewish name for Jesus?"

"The Hebrew name."

"I like it. It's peaceful."

"How do you feel about your dream now?" asked Reuben.

"Super! I mean, I don't know why, but I just feel like everything's going to be okay."

"Good. Now, do you think you can focus on the chess board and tell me what possessed you to move your queen?"

MacArthur chuckled, and they returned to the game. He examined the board. "Oh man! Why did I do that? Can I take it back?"

"No. You must find a path out of the predicament in which you placed yourself."

Although MacArthur found a path out of his problem, he lost the game. Surprisingly, he wasn't angry but thoughtful. "Reuben,

167

CONVERSION

can we add something to our schedule?"

"It is quite full. Is it wise to take on another subject?"

"Well, since I'm not going to church, on Sundays will you teach me your kind of Christianity? Do you even call it Christianity?"

"Hmm. Historically, some Christians called Jews 'Christ killers.' Thus, many Jews take offense to the names Christ or Christianity. You would do well to use another name when speaking to a Jew about the Messiah."

"Well...but...didn't Jews crucify Jesus?"

Reuben was thoughtful. "Actually, the Romans did at the Jews' request. But MacArthur, for whose sin did he die?"

"Um. Everyone's."

"You speak the truth. We all put him on the cross, Jew and Gentile. So, to me personally, I do not take offense to the name Christ or being called a Christian. He is the Anointed One, Yeshua Hamashiach, Jesus the Messiah."

"Yeshua Hamashiach. Neat. I like that. So what about Sundays?"

"To study Scripture is always good."

MacArthur saw the glint in Reuben's eyes. "Great! Also, since we are really getting established in our schedule, can we go into town?"

"Yes. You have earned an outing. Let's show Kau and Lawan your list, and they can advise us."

16

As the rainy season was ending, Kau suggested they go to Bangkok. He and Lawan would be participating in the Buddhist festival of Kathina with their youngest son, who was at Chulalongkorn University, and they invited Reuben and MacArthur to join them. "It is the most important day except for the birthday of the Buddha," explained Kau.

"It would be an honor," said Reuben.

When they were alone, MacArthur asked, "Are we really going to their ceremony? I mean, isn't that, like, idolatry or something for Christians?"

"We will not participate. We will show respect for their beliefs and have an experience with them that will establish mutual respect. By showing respect for another person's religion, you invite them to show respect for yours. Then, in a bond of mutual respect, you can plant the seed of God's truth in their hearts and minds — as the Holy Spirit bids you."

MacArthur nodded and said, "Yes, Sir," but he wondered what "as the Holy Spirit bids you" meant. He would ask Reuben later. Right now, he was excited that he was going to see the great city of Bangkok. He had seen the movie musical, *Anna and the King*, and had read the books it was based upon. Now, he would actually see where it took place!

CONVERSION

Bangkok was called the Venice of Asia because it was a city of rivers and canals, which emptied into the Gulf of Thailand. The canals and rivers were like city streets, where various boats traveled from place to place. There were floating markets, and some people lived in houseboats. Kau hailed a water taxi to take them to the palace, as the whole compound was surrounded by water.

When he stood with Reuben, Kau, and Lawan before the royal palace, MacArthur was overwhelmed by the lavish wealth and beauty in each square foot. Gold and gemstones adorned every surface, and tall, golden spires pierced the sky. The lush grounds were immaculate and meticulously landscaped. After looking at the magnificent palace, they walked to the Temple of the Emerald Buddha, where Kau and Lawan were greeted by their son, Sunan. MacArthur liked him immediately.

MacArthur and Reuben watched while Kau, Lawan, and Sunan placed their gifts for the chanting monks and flowers to honor the Buddha. Reuben leaned over and whispered, "Who is their god?"

MacArthur thought about it. Buddha was a man not a god. He whispered back, "I guess they don't have one."

Reuben's eyes narrowed in sadness.

MacArthur rose to defend their friends. "But their lives are so good and they have such peace."

"Beware of paths that seem good but have no life in Yeshua."

MacArthur was uneasy. *Is Reuben intolerant because he's a Jew?*

As if Reuben read his thoughts, he continued. "Buddha's way to enlightenment is silence, nothingness, and attaining nirvana or perfection depends on the *follower*. Yeshua's way to enlightenment

CHAPTER 16

and perfection is made possible through *his own sacrifice* not ours. He is the only one who solves our sin problem. And when we say he is our Lord, he loves us and communes with us at all times. This is not nothing. It is everything."

MacArthur nodded, but he was even more unsettled. He had always liked the idea that all religions led to God. That was his conclusion upon earning the God and Country Medal in Scouts. Was Christianity really the only way?

When the ceremonies concluded, Sunan hailed a water taxi. Like his parents, he spoke English well, and MacArthur sat next to him in the back. He asked him what year he was in college. "I will graduate at the end of next year. My parents are not in agreement, but I would like to work in the United States for a time."

"Really? That's, like, how a lot of American students take a year off and backpack through Europe or some other foreign country."

"I did not know this was a common practice."

"Oh, it isn't really common, but some kids are doing it. My sister is in Europe, but she's on a work-study program through her college. Students do that too. Maybe Chulalongkorn would let you study and work in the US."

"That is not what I want to do, but I will explore the possibility. My parents might agree if I continued my education there."

MacArthur grinned. "I know what you mean. I could only come to Thailand if I had a tutor, so that is why Reuben is here." He didn't know how much Kau and Lawan had told Sunan.

"Yes. He looks an interesting man. He is American?"

"He is Israeli. Oh, but he's also a Christian."

CONVERSION

Sunan turned to look him in the eye. "How is that possible?"

"Well, Jesus was a Jew. Reuben says that if Jesus wasn't the Jewish Messiah, he wasn't anybody's messiah." MacArthur laughed, but Sunan didn't get the joke.

"What is this word, messiah?"

"It means 'the anointed one,' which means God's power is on him. In Judaism and Christianity, it also means the Savior and Lord."

"Ahhh."

"Do you know about Christianity or do you just study Buddhism?"

"My mother taught me Christianity so that I would not be ignorant of Western thought and manners."

"Hmm. I never realized Christianity was the reason I think and act the way I do, but I guess it is."

"It is a good way."

"Thank you. From what I've seen, Buddhism is also a good way."

"It is our way." Sunan suddenly seemed distant.

Sunan took them to his favorite restaurant to eat. Their meal was delicious, and Kau and Lawan delighted them with stories about him and his brothers. MacArthur noticed that Sunan easily laughed at his childhood antics and obviously loved his family, but there were times when a shadow seemed to cross his face. They said goodbye to him when they left the restaurant. MacArthur said, "Let me know if you come to the United States. We live in Virginia, which is where the US capitol is and so much more. Kau and … I

CHAPTER 16

mean, your parents will have all the information."

"Thank you." Sunan smiled and did the *wai*, and MacArthur responded in kind.

In the afternoon, Kau and Lawan took Reuben and MacArthur sightseeing, and MacArthur learned that he was a *farang*, or foreigner. He was grateful that Kau and Lawan didn't treat him as an unwelcome *farang*. After another wonderful meal, he asked if he could drive home.

"The driving age is eighteen in Thailand," said Lawan.

"It's just getting really old driving around the dirt roads by the house."

"What you mean is, you want to be on a road where you can drive faster," said Kau.

MacArthur flashed a smile and raised his eyebrows hopefully, but Kau, Lawan, and Reuben all answered, "No!"

Unlike most students, MacArthur looked forward to Saturday morning tests. He loved knowledge, but even more he loved to show off how much he knew. Because he answered nearly every question correctly for weeks, Kau and Reuben decided to ask more difficult ones.

Once in a while, they would ask him something they had not taught. This was meant to humble him, but MacArthur caught on and provided detailed and bizarre answers. His tutors had so much fun reading them, they made it a regular routine. This only made MacArthur pay attention more keenly, because in order to know what *hadn't* been taught, he had to know what *had* been taught.

The Colonel did not return for a visit until Thanksgiving, but

CONVERSION

MacArthur was happy being the center of attention in his new household of what he called "collective geniuses." When his father walked through the door, he declared somberly, "You will not be pleased, Colonel, that communism is practiced here."

His father looked askance at Reuben, who shrugged his shoulders and rolled his eyes. Kau and Lawan said together, *"Mai pen rai,"* which MacArthur had learned meant "never mind" in Siamese.

"You see, they are the powerful elite, and I am the proletariat, laboring away, doing everything they tell me to do, for the good of the whole household." Everyone laughed, and the Colonel hugged him tightly. One morning, MacArthur woke up later than usual and looked out his bedroom window. Across the atrium, he saw the Colonel, Reuben, Kau, and Lawan sitting at the dining table. He had learned that there was no sneaking by or sneaking up on any of them, but perhaps today would be different.

It hadn't rained, so he crawled through one of his French doors and crept along the wall of the atrium. When he was well past all the French doors on the other side, he stood and ran to the kitchen door. Yes! It was unlocked. He quietly opened it and tiptoed to the swinging door between the kitchen and dining room, pressing his ear to the crack.

He heard the Colonel say, "But this time I won't know how long. There are too many variables and the intelligence is ...." Silence. "I will miss Christmas. I know that doesn't mean much to you, but it will to MacArthur, so I have a surprise for him. It will help him to not get homesick."

CHAPTER 16

"Most of the time, he seems oblivious to his circumstances." Kau chuckled.

"Well, you know, when he was four he hit his head, so maybe something's loose in there." Laughter.

"If it is," said Lawan, "then what is loose should stay loose. It is a great asset to be able to turn a challenge to a positive end. He makes a good Buddhist."

"He's a good boy," said the Colonel. "I just wish we could get him to stop spying on us." With that the kitchen door began to swing toward him. MacArthur jumped back just in time and faced his father.

They were laughing again. The Colonel took him gently by the ear and led him into the dining room. He yelled, "Oh man! How long did you know I was here?"

Reuben smiled, "We saw you crawl through the garden."

"Okay, you have to teach me how to be stealthy like you guys."

"Not until the end of our time together. We want the upper hand as long as possible!" he answered.

He turned to his father. "Then tell me about the surprise."

The Colonel answered, "I have arranged for you and Reuben to visit Chiang Mai, which claims the first Thai golf course."

"You're kidding! For real? But I don't have my clubs!"

"They rent them, and I have hired a pro, who will give you instruction and play with you three times. There are also historic places to visit, so you'll stay for a week. It's the least I can do for not being with you during the holidays."

"Wow! I can't believe it! Thanks, Dad!"

175

CONVERSION

"Well, you've earned it. I wish I could be on the course with you, but duty calls, and your mother made me promise to do something special for you." The Colonel smiled, but MacArthur saw sadness in his eyes. He was reminded that he wasn't the only one who was missing his family.

That afternoon, they all went fishing in the stream beyond the gate, which resulted in a catfish feast that evening. Kau and Lawan regaled the others with stories of Thailand's history.

The next morning, the Colonel was not in his room when MacArthur awakened. Reuben was in the shower, so he walked over to the kitchen. No one was there, but he heard someone in the back yard. He opened the door and found Kau wielding the wicked-looking scythe back and forth, cutting the grass.

"Good morning, Kau. Is the Colonel gone?"

Kau stopped. "He was needed on the base. It was unexpected, and he didn't want to wake you."

"Oh."

"Would you please weed the garden." This was something he had asked MacArthur to do periodically. When Kau finished the grass, he came over to help with the last row of vegetables.

The back door opened and Lawan called out, "Breakfast in half hour!"

"Thanks Lawan!" MacArthur called back, and he noticed how Kau smiled and saluted her. She laughed and went back into the kitchen. MacArthur thought her laugh was like light, beautiful music.

"Kau, I would like to ask you a question, and I hope it won't

CHAPTER 16

offend you."

"You may ask. I *may* answer."

"Why are you a Buddhist?"

"It is my family's way and I believe the best way. When we are faithful to practice the ways of Buddha, we live a good life for ourselves and for others, and we ensure a good life, perhaps a better life, in the next life."

"So...you are absolutely certain you will have a next life?"

"We will have a next life until we reach nirvana."

MacArthur felt conflicted. *Maybe Reuben is right. Nirvana is not Heaven, and where's God?*

> Dear David,
>
> Today I helped Kau in the garden, and we talked about Buddhism. I studied it when I got the God and Country Medal, but it's different when you actually talk to someone who is practicing it. Kau and Lawan are neat people, and it's like they glide through life in a peace bubble. Makes me want to practice the ways of Buddha. What do you think of that? Ha!
>
> Was glad you beat Cristobal, even though I played there. In my book, you trump them, Superman. Sounds like you're falling in luv luv luv with Rita. What do Mama and the Doc think? I haven't talked to any girls here, but the Thai girls I saw in Bangkok were GORGEOUS.
>
> Guess what? The Colonel is sending Reuben and

CONVERSION

me to Chiang Mai (look it up on the map — it's in northwest Thailand). This is where they built the first golf course in 1928! and we are going to be there for a week! It's a neat city, so we'll be tourists and explore. I'm glad I'll be doing something I love to do. It will keep me from getting too homesick.

I'm sending you something for Christmas that I got in Bangkok. I hope you like it. You don't have to send me anything. Wait a minute. I take that back. Can you send me some of Mama's homemade tortillas, some dried pinto beans, and her recipe for bean burritos, salsa, and guacamole? We have two avocado trees with yummy avocadoes on them, and I want to show Lawan how to make Mexican food. Oh! And her recipe for empanadas! Man, my mouth is watering just thinking about them!

My sisters are all over the place, but Sarah's not too far from Mom at UVA. I've tried to write Mom every week, and every week I write a different sister. I'm just too busy to do more than that. Where are you applying for college? Have you decided? Reuben mentioned it to me last week. Good thing, because I haven't even thought about it yet! It would be great if we could go to the same college and room together. Think about it.... Superman and Saint Mac, together again! Ha Ha!

    Your bb & bf,

    M.

17

MacArthur and Reuben's memorable Christmas of golf and sightseeing was forgotten after events that transpired just before MacArthur's eighteenth birthday, January 30. For their Sunday Bible study, Reuben thought it appropriate to ask MacArthur to explain John, chapter 3, which was Jesus' famous "born *again*" message.

"So…Nicodemus is a Pharisee, a serious player in Judaism, who comes to Jesus at night so no one will see him, so…he's kinda chicken. Before he can even ask a question, Jesus hits him with, 'You must be born again to see, oh, *and* to enter the kingdom of God.' So Nicodemus says, 'What are you talking about? I'm supposed to get back in my mother's womb and be born *again*?' And Jesus says, …. Well…I know what he says…but the water and spirit stuff loses me."

Reuben began, "Yeshua says, 'That which is born of the flesh is flesh and that which is born of the Spirit is spirit.' So we know that this rebirth, this being born again, is not physical. It is spiritual. Does this make sense to you?"

"Yeah. Sorta. But I'm still not seeing it."

"It's good that Yeshua helps us. He says, 'You must be born again by the *water* and the *Spirit*.' Now what does water represent throughout the Bible?"

"Water is a symbol for God's Word."

CONVERSION

"Yes, so Yeshua says you need water, the *seed* of Scripture, to be born again. He also says you need the Holy Spirit. Now what did the Holy Spirit do in the first verse of Genesis?"

"He hovered over the Earth and brought it to life."

"Excellent! Remember this as you tell me how humans are conceived."

"What?"

"How is a child conceived?"

"Really? Okay. Well, the sperm from the man goes into the woman's uterus and fertilizes one of her eggs. Then the egg and the sperm form a baby, a new life." He paused. "It's a miracle, now that I think about it."

Reuben stifled a laugh. "Amen. Yeshua tells us that what happens in the natural must happen in our spirits, to be born again *spiritually*. Yes?"

"Okay...that which is born of the flesh is flesh — egg fertilized by the sperm, right? And so that which is born of the Spirit is spirit. Oh! God's Word is made alive by the Holy Spirit, just like the egg is made alive by the sperm?"

Reuben nodded. "Yes. Perhaps we hear, 'For God so loved the world, that he gave his only Son, that whoever believes on him shall be saved,' and the seed is planted." Reuben poked MacArthur's heart. "'On the third day, he was resurrected from the dead.'" Another poke. "God's truth is planted here, in your heart." Reuben began to poke MacArthur's chest rhythmically. " 'Believe in your heart that Yeshua rose from the dead and confess with your mouth he is your Lord, and you shall be saved.' "Seed, seed, and

CHAPTER 17

more seed, planted into your heart for the Holy Spirit to bring to life."

MacArthur stared at his tutor. Something was happening inside him. *That which is born of the flesh is flesh. That which is born of the Spirit is spirit. Believe in your heart...and confess with your mouth....* "Jesus is my Lord. I believe he rose from the dead. I...I know he rose from the dead." The words erupted from a place inside of him he didn't know was there. He sprang up, mouth agape, eyes wide.

Reuben convulsed in laughter and rolled on his side.

MacArthur laughed from deep within as he sank to the floor. He hadn't laughed like this since he and David were hit by the light in Panama.

When their laughter subsided, Reuben sat up and MacArthur sat cross-legged on the floor, staring at him. "Reuben, I'm...born...*again*."

"I suspected as much. And so, I must be with you in Heaven also?" Reuben shook his head.

"Yes. Oh my God! I mean, sorry, I guess I shouldn't say that anymore. But Reuben, I know I'm going to Heaven. I never thought you could know. I don't even know how I know, but I know!"

Reuben put his hand over his heart. "The knowing comes from the Holy Spirit, who now lives in your new, born-again spirit."

MacArthur grabbed his Bible from the coffee table, let it fall open, and read aloud, "'Who has known the mind of the Lord so as to instruct him? But we have the mind of Christ.'" He looked at Reuben. "I have the mind of Christ! I have the mind of Christ? This blows my mind!"

CONVERSION

"It will blow your mind, your *natural* mind."

"Huh?"

"You have the mind of Christ in your spirit, the eternal you, so you have the ability to think like God if you choose to do so. When you do, the Holy Spirit may use Scripture to challenge your old way of thinking. What your natural brain has thought to be true may not be true, eh?"

MacArthur shook his head. "Soooo revolutionary."

Reuben chuckled. "Yes. But most revolutionary is that your sins are forgiven by Yeshua's blood. You are a child of the Most High God. He is your Abba, Father."

That night MacArthur felt like he was reading his Bible for the first time. Every word was alive! Even when he didn't understand it, there was a presence there that assured him, "I will teach you." When he said his prayers, tears ran down his cheeks not because he was desperate to get something from God but because he knew him as Father.

He fell into a deep sleep and did not hear the phone ring at 3:27 a.m. Minutes later, Reuben was nudging him to get up and telling him to dress quickly. He went to the wardrobe and grabbed MacArthur's jacket.

"Are we going somewhere? What's going on? What time is it?" MacArthur was yawning and trying to focus as he dressed.

Reuben put his finger to his lips, indicating silence. He whispered, "A little more than half past three." He motioned MacArthur to follow him.

MacArthur's eyes slowly adjusted to the darkness as he

CHAPTER 17

stumbled behind Reuben. When they entered the kitchen, Kau came in the back door, closed it quietly, and pulled the metal covering over it, locking it in place. *So that's what that's for*, MacArthur thought.

They followed Kau to the alcove, where the laughing Buddha seemed to wink at them. The door to the right was open. They entered a small room, which became pitch black when Kau shut the door behind them. He turned on a low-beam flashlight, and MacArthur saw canned goods and other kitchen paraphernalia on shelves to one side. On the other side stood a tall combination safe. He stood before a ladder, which Kau motioned him to climb. As he did, he saw Kau take two rifles from the safe and close it.

When MacArthur got to the top of the ladder, Lawan took his hand and helped him step into the attic, but it looked like a bomb shelter. He wondered why it wasn't underground. After everyone was in the attic, Reuben pulled up the ladder and Kau put the ceiling boards in place. Then he closed the trap door covering them. He spoke in a low voice. "Sergeant Mills called. A CPT company was spotted near us, and our soldiers are moving to intercept them. We disconnected the phones downstairs and moved the car and bikes, so it looks like no one is here. The phone on the table is secure, but no calls in or out unless it is an emergency. They will call when it is safe to return below."

Reuben took a flashlight from a long table, pointed the beam down the eastern wall of the attic, and motioned MacArthur to follow him to a long cushion next to the eave. Kneeling down, he shut off the flashlight and opened a small door, then quietly closed

CONVERSION

it. "This is your station," and he waved his arm back and forth to indicate the eastern wall of the house. Turning the flashlight back on, he commanded, "Come," and they joined Kau and Lawan at the table. "All arms are here?"

"Yes," answered Kau. "And ammunition." MacArthur saw two klong jars next to the table, which had a ladle, canteens, and an ice chest on it. Next to them was a long box containing weapons, and he recognized the rifle and pistol Reuben was training him to use.

"Do I get a gun?" he whispered.

Reuben handed him the rifle. "Hopefully you won't need it, but if you see the enemy breach the wall, shoot to kill. Understand?" MacArthur nodded and swallowed hard. He confirmed that the gun was loaded and the safety engaged.

Reuben found his pistol and made sure it was loaded and the safety on. Then he put it on the table and took out a rifle and some ammunition. Kau and Lawan each took a rifle and ammunition. Then they turned off their flashlights so their eyes could fully adjust to the darkness.

"From what direction are they coming?" asked Reuben.

"The north," answered Kau, pointing to the back of the house.

"Do they know about this house?"

"Intelligence believes not."

"Then I will take the back, Lawan the front, and you the west wall?"

"Yes."

Lawan had filled four canteens with water from the klong jar and handed one to MacArthur, stuffing some beef jerky in the

CHAPTER 17

pocket of his jacket. "We don't know how long we will be here, but this will keep you for a while."

"Thanks, Lawan."

Even in the dark, she knew the look on his face and remembered when she had had the same look. She took another canteen, stuffed some jerky in her pocket, and grabbed a rifle and some ammunition. Patting his arm, she said, "You have trained well. You will do fine." Then she and Kau walked toward the front of the house, where they disappeared in the darkness.

Reuben put his hand on MacArthur's shoulder, which put him at ease for the first time since he was awakened. "Two important things. First, we pray." Reuben bowed his head. "Abba, be merciful to us and our enemies. We thank you for your protection and the courage to do your will in Yeshua's name. Amen." He lifted his head. "Second," he pointed to a small enclosure with a door located toward the back wall, "if we are here a long time, the latrine is back there."

"Won't that be noisy?" whispered MacArthur.

He smiled. "It drains quietly into a tank in the ground, like an outhouse."

MacArthur nodded, "Oh. Okay."

"Do not move unless you must. Stay alert, and do not fire unless necessary. Let us pray we will not be here long." He patted MacArthur on his back and turned to take his place at the back wall.

MacArthur laid on the long cushion and placed his rifle beside him. His stomach was in a knot again. Words he had read before

CONVERSION

bed floated through his mind: "Fear not, for I am with you." *He's here!* He relaxed. He could barely see Reuben lie down and open his lookout door, but his cushion was high enough for him to rest his head on his arm and have a good view through the small lookout window. The winter air was cold, so he was glad he was wearing his jacket — and he wouldn't be fighting mosquitoes.

All was still for a long time. Silently, he prayed, hour by hour. He prayed for the soldiers to stop the guerillas, and then he remembered Jesus' words, "Love your enemies, and pray for them." *Oh no! This is what Reuben meant when he said my mind of Christ would challenge the way I think about stuff. I don't want to pray for the CPT, but Jesus told us to.* His head dropped with exhaustion. He would think about this later.

He jerked at the sound of the first shot, which came from the north, beyond the back yard. He turned to see Reuben place the barrel of his rifle in his lookout. With a jolt, he scanned the eastern wall. More gunfire came from the north, but no one in the attic was firing. He eased his rifle into the lookout and reminded himself that besides the stone wall, the house was surrounded by a clearing of at least twelve feet. If anyone tried to breach the wall, they would be seen. *Oh God, let me see them if they come to my side.*

That's when he had the alarming thought, *Could I kill them?* He thought of Reuben, Kau, and Lawan. *Could I kill someone who was trying to kill them — or me? Is this what Reuben was talking about? The right reason?* He looked for any sign of movement and gripped his rifle, but he didn't disengage the safety.

The sound of gunfire began filling the air around him. He

CHAPTER 17

didn't know how long it lasted. It seemed like hours, and then it was sporadic. Finally, all was still again. After a while, he relaxed and put his rifle down beside him. *Thank you, Jesus!* He was almost asleep when he heard six gunshots in quick succession. They came from Reuben's station!

MacArthur grabbed his rifle and scanned his side of the house, but he saw no one. Again and again he looked. *Where are they? Show me, Lord!* The silence after that was the hardest part. It dragged on and on, and still no one in sight. He saw the first rays of the sun and wondered what time it was. *Damn, forgot my watch. Sorry, Jesus, for swearing.*

That night MacArthur learned one of the hardest parts of being a warrior: waiting and watching.

As the sun's rays pushed back the darkness, Reuben closed his lookout and walked silently toward MacArthur, putting his finger to his lips as he passed. He soon disappeared where Kau and Lawan had. Not long after, he passed by MacArthur again and returned to his station. And so they all stayed alert long past sunrise. MacArthur jumped when the phone rang. Reuben rushed quietly to answer it. Kau and Lawan also came running quietly.

"Yes…Two, probably dead in the back yard…Thank you, Sergeant." He hung up and said solemnly. "Thanks be to Yeshua, the entire enemy company is either dead or captured. They saw two break away and run through the woods toward us. Now they are lying in our back yard." MacArthur pictured the soldiers wounded and dying. Reuben had done that. Gentle and wise Reuben. The reality of war, of what it meant to be a warrior, was nothing like he

CONVERSION

and David had imagined. He felt like crying, but he didn't dare.

Kau and Lawan put their firearms in the box. Kau said, "I will unlock the gate." He opened the trap door and Reuben removed the ceiling boards, then Kau set the ladder in place, and down he went. Reuben told MacArthur to help Lawan then disappeared down the ladder as well.

Lawan and MacArthur checked all the stations to make sure the lookout doors were secured and nothing was left behind. When all weapons were in the box, they carried it to the ladder. MacArthur climbed down, and Lawan proceeded to hand him the practice weapons first, which he stowed in their usual place in the kitchen cabinet. He saw Lawan take two pistols into her bedroom, then she opened the safe and climbed up the ladder. MacArthur marveled at how agile and energetic she was for her age.

She handed the rest of the weapons and ammunition to him to store in the safe. "It was good this happened at this time of year. The attic is not pleasant in summer," she smiled. She was concerned that MacArthur was so quiet. She knew she must get him to talk. "Please, bring a basket to me."

Moments later, he was in the attic with the basket, and they were putting the food in it. "Are you hungry, MacArthur?"

"No." He descended the ladder, and Lawan handed the basket to him.

She came half-way down the ladder and put the ceiling boards in place. As she locked the safe, he still stood like a stone, just outside the door. "Are you weary?" She turned out the light and closed the door to the storage room.

CHAPTER 17

MacArthur put the basket on the table and slowly turned to her. "Have you ever had to shoot someone?"

She nodded. "Yes."

"Were you fighting the CPT, like last night?"

"It was in defense of my country." She began to put the food away. He could tell she didn't want to provide more details, but he pressed on. "I know Buddhists are to do no harm to anyone or anything. How do you deal with that?"

"You have said right. *Ahimsa* is the Buddha's principle of doing no harm to any person, animal, or thing. And in *shaolin*, our martial art, we are never the aggressor and always fight defensively. We are non-violent in all respects, but we make exception when we must defend our family, our friend, or our country from an evil aggressor."

"That sounds right. It feels right. I know Reuben would agree with you, because he has fought aggressors his whole life. I mean, Israel is surrounded by people who want to kill them."

Lawan looked aside. "As are we."

"Would you teach me your way of fighting...what do you call it?"

"*Shaolin*. Yes, I would be honored. But first, rest. I will come for you when the meal is ready." She did the *wai*, as did MacArthur, and she hoped he could rest peacefully.

> Dear David,
> Well, I turned eighteen. Now I'm legal to drive in Thailand. So much has happened, I don't know where to begin, but the most important thing — probably the most important thing in my whole life — is that I was

CONVERSION

born again! Now I'm really Saint Mac — ha ha! I know you don't believe in God or Jesus or any religion, but this is so real and so cool, I'm going to pray for you to get born again too. And get this — I KNOW I'm going to Heaven — I mean, I really KNOW it! And I want you to KNOW it too! Then we would KNOW we will be friends FOREVER.

And get this! Reuben baptized me in the bathtub! I had to scrunch down at one end, then he put the top of me under the water and lifted me up, and water splashed everywhere. It probably looked hilarious, but I'm still thinking about how it felt. It was really kind of profound.

Lawan is teaching me *shaolin*, which is the Buddhists' kind of martial art and is only used for self-defense. They're big on that. How's basketball going? Sometimes I miss being part of a team and being around kids my age. It's great being tutored, don't get me wrong, but it's like something is missing. I'm beginning to look forward to coming home and my senior year. How about the University of Virginia? I asked God where he wants me to go, and that was his answer. Why don't we both apply there? It's a great school — well, think about it.

Give my love to Mama and the Doc, and remember that I always pray for all of you!

    Your bb & bf,

    SAINT MAC (Yahoo!!!)

13

The first weekend in February, the Colonel visited for two days. For a belated birthday present, he allowed MacArthur to call his mom and each of his sisters long distance. They had to be up at odd hours to call when the others wouldn't be sleeping. Rebecca was loving her job at Macy's and said she had met the man she was going to marry, an amazing guy who loved dogs (a prerequisite for her) and worked where she banked. The Colonel said he looked forward to meeting him, in the tone of voice that meant, "We'll see just how amazing he is."

Meg said law school was hard. She studied all the time and her only social life was her study groups, but she was meeting some interesting people and still loved the law. Joanna kept speaking to them in French and had to be reminded that they did not speak French. She and her roommates were American but spoke French all the time. Of course, Paris was beyond anyone's imagination, and when she and her friends were not in class or working, they were traveling and exploring.

Sarah was trying to decide what kind of nursing she would pursue. She was leaning toward emergency medicine after volunteering at various hospitals since MacArthur's snake bite. It was then she discovered she enjoyed helping him and wasn't overwhelmed by his unbandaged leg. She told him the University

CONVERSION

of Virginia was the best place on Earth, which he was glad to hear.

Mom was not so good. MacArthur thought she sounded drunk. Although it was the cocktail hour in Virginia when they called, and she joked and laughed with them as usual, he could tell his father was worried. There had been a few times when MacArthur didn't like how much his mother drank, but she was so charming, even while drinking, that he had dismissed it. No one in the family had ever said anything about it, but now he felt the urge to pray for her.

At the end of his visit, the Colonel hugged MacArthur and left. As they closed the front door, MacArthur felt uneasy, then alarmed in his spirit. Even next day, he could not shake the feeling. As they finished their afternoon run in a downpour, Reuben said, "Today, during free time, we need to pray for your father."

"You've felt it too!"

"Yes. Let's meet in the Colonel's room after we shower. Bring your Bible."

MacArthur joined Reuben in his father's room and blurted out, "Reuben, do you remember that dream I had about my dad being captured and tortured?"

"Yes."

"Do you think that is what is about to happen? If that's it, why did I feel such peace before, but now I feel like something's wrong again?"

Reuben threw back his head. "Ah! Please forgive me, MacArthur. When your father was here last November, he told us he had nearly been captured. He said the enemy walked right by him and did not see him when they should have. It was a miracle, and I

CHAPTER 13

believe our prayers were answered."

"Wow. Why didn't you tell me?"

"I should have. It slipped my mind. I'm trying to break a habit of forgetting things God has finished. We should always remember the times he has demonstrated his faithfulness to us."

"Well…I forgive you, but what do you think is happening now? Why do I feel this…this….urgency to pray for him?"

Reuben took a deep breath and gazed at the atrium garden. "MacArthur, to show Yeshua to others and war in the Spirit, you must receive the most powerful gift Abba has given his children. Just before he ascended to Heaven, Yeshua's last command was to receive this gift. Here. Read these verses in Acts 1, verses 4 and 5. He also said this in the book of Luke."

MacArthur read the passage several times. "Okay. Jesus told them not to go anywhere until they were baptized in the Holy Spirit. What is that about?"

"When he told the woman at the well that rivers of living water would come out of her belly, he was speaking of the words of the Holy Spirit coming from our spirit and out of our mouth. This could be in preaching or teaching *or in various kinds of languages we do not know, some heavenly*."

"A heavenly language? Wow. What does that sound like?"

"It's what we call speaking in tongues."

McArthur shook his head in disbelief. "Isn't that what crazy fanatics do?"

Reuben chuckled. "Then you are looking at one crazy fanatic."

"You do it?"

193

CONVERSION

"Yes. When we speak in tongues, we are literally immersed in the Holy Spirit. In some translations, they call this baptism being clothed or filled to overflowing with the Holy Spirit. With your permission, I will pray for you this way."

"O...kay...."

Reuben placed his hand on MacArthur's back, a stream of unintelligible syllables coming out of his mouth. MacArthur instinctively closed his eyes when he felt the powerful presence of Jesus, in him and around him. After a minute or two, he perceived odd syllables in his own spirit and had the urge to speak them. He decided to try it. What he spoke sounded so ridiculous that he almost stopped, but for some reason, he kept speaking. The more he spoke these odd syllables, the more his spirit was filled with faith and joy, and then an extraordinary gratitude. Soon, it was like he and Reuben were soaring in the Spirit, worshipping God as one.

They prayed like this for several minutes. When they both stopped, Reuben said, "MacArthur, sometimes you will feel the Holy Spirit nudge you to begin praying in your prayer language, but sometimes you decide. Romans 8:26 says that when we don't know how or what to pray, we allow the Holy Spirit to pray through us. Jude, verse 20, says that praying in the Spirit builds our faith. That is why this is one of the most powerful gifts we have, especially when we are in a battle and feel weak."

MacArthur smiled like a child who had received a gift he never knew he wanted. As he prayed in tongues, he walked around the room, touching the few things the Colonel had left. They were like points of contact to his father. Reuben knelt at the bed and prayed

CHAPTER 13

fervently. MacArthur knelt beside him, and they prayed together.

After a while, McArthur stopped and sighed. "Reuben, my dad's going to be okay, but this time…it's going to be harder."

"Yes."

At dinner, Kau and Lawan noticed how quiet and solemn they were, but soon their weekly routine did its job and returned the household to normal. Lawan was impressed with MacArthur's progress in *shaolin*, and MacArthur enjoyed this new form of discipline. He continued to thrive in his studies and spent more time working with Kau in the garden in exchange for being allowed to drive the car on the weekly mail runs to the base. Kau stayed in the passenger seat, and MacArthur loved hearing his stories about his wild childhood on the streets of Bangkok.

"Kau, tell me how you and Lawan learned to shoot, or did you already know when you met her?"

"I will say nothing until you come back to the speed for this road."

"Oooo, sorry. I was just looking around and not paying attention."

"What do I say?"

"Be alert. Drive to stay alive!"

"Yes. Be scanning the road at all times." He sighed. "I carried a knife as a boy, in case I encountered a situation that required me to defend myself or someone with me. I learned to shoot with Lawan, when we received our training."

"I didn't know you were in the military."

"Not the military, but we received similar training."

CONVERSION

"Who trained you?"

"Now that would be telling."

A month later, Sergeant Mills was at the door. "The last contact we had from the Colonel and his men was two weeks ago. Because of their location and the sensitivity of their mission, we cannot send a helicopter or a large company of soldiers. The good news is that Captain Swallow did not deploy with them. The man is never ill, but he was vomiting and dangerously dehydrated when the unit had to depart, so the doctor forced him to stay behind. Because he has such a history with your father and this unit, he will be invaluable in locating them."

"Do you mean Chuck?" asked MacArthur.

"His first name is Chuck, yes."

"I never knew his last name. I just knew he was an Indian."

"He is also a first-rate tracker, which is exactly what we need right now."

"Thank you, Sergeant, for coming to tell us," said Reuben.

"I will call when we have good news." They shook hands and exchanged a knowing glance, but it was not lost on MacArthur. He knew that if there was more bad news, the Sergeant would come in person.

"Thanks, Sergeant." MacArthur shook his hand.

Reuben closed the door behind the Sergeant and turned to MacArthur. "God is already answering our prayers."

"Prayers we didn't understand when we prayed them."

"The Holy Spirit always knows what is needed. Sometimes he will tell us and sometimes he will not, but he always gives us peace

CHAPTER 13

when we pray his will."

"It's a miracle that even right now I have peace. I know everything's going to be okay."

"I believe so too, but let us continue to pray, especially for Captain Swallow."

A week and a half later, Sergeant Mills was at the door again. "With the help of latest intelligence, Captain Swallow found their trail, which ended abruptly. He came back to get more intel, and set out with two others, but we have haven't heard from them. They may be radio silent for security reasons, but I wanted to give you an update."

MacArthur was disappointed and tried not to be frightened. He thought they would have been found and brought to safety by now, but still, he knew Chuck would not rest until they were.

"MacArthur, begin your training. I will join you shortly."

MacArthur went from disappointment to frustration, but he knew from the tone of Reuben's voice that he should not argue. He sighed and stomped toward the kitchen. Reuben waited until he knew his charge was in the back yard before he spoke. "What can you tell me?"

"A huge caravan of arms coming from Hanoi was blown up near the North Vietnamese border. That was the Colonel and his men, and it would make sense that they would immediately withdraw and hide in Laos; but they should have contacted us from there. Captain Swallow tracked them to the mountains in Laos, near the North Vietnam border. He didn't know if they were captured there. When he got back to base, the intel he received was

197

CONVERSION

that, to our knowledge, they weren't; so, he decided to return to the trail with two other men. He believes they might be trapped, surrounded by the enemy and unable to contact us. He has a plan to extract them."

"Thank you, Sergeant." Reuben shook his hand and watched him leave. Then he joined MacArthur, who was performing drills on the monkey bars — and swearing.

"Is that helping?"

"Yes!"

"Good, then you can add ten rounds."

Enraged, MacArthur began to swear more loudly. Reuben went into the kitchen to get MacArthur's bow and quiver of arrows. Kau and Lawan were chopping vegetables, and Reuben repeated what the sergeant had told him. Kau was thoughtful. "Reuben, the band that was defeated near this house, at this house, were likely searching for the Colonel."

"Yes," he said solemnly. "That is why we are remaining within these walls until he and his men return."

Reuben found MacArthur breathing heavily, moving over the top of the monkey bars. He yelled, "Why can't you tell me what's going on? Obviously, something is happening, if I have to stay imprisoned in this house!" He dropped to the ground. "This is not fair! I'm his son, for God's sake, and old enough to fight in the damn war! If you don't tell me, I'll call Sergeant Mills and make him tell me everything!"

Reuben was relieved. The well-behaved, charming, and sometimes manipulative young man was finally releasing the fear

CHAPTER 13

and rage Reuben had sensed had been growing since the night in the attic. The realities of war were crushing his idyllic fantasy of a magical year in Thailand, where he would be transformed into the heroic warrior who would save the world.

"I will tell you what you need to know when you have finished."

MacArthur finished without another word, dropped to the ground, and joined Reuben, who had just sent an arrow into the bullseye of the target. MacArthur refused to be impressed, even if the man had first taken up a bow when they arrived in Thailand. As Reuben handed him his bow and an arrow, he demanded, "Tell me what I need to know."

"Hit the bullseye first."

"Easy." He pulled the arrow on the bow like he had done so many times. It flew and missed the center by six inches. "Damn!"

"Retrieve the arrow."

"Just give me another one."

"Retrieve the arrow."

He trudged to the target, grabbed the arrow, and returned in a fury. He nocked the arrow, pulled back, and released it. It landed six inches from the center on the other side. "What the f—!"

"Retrieve the arrow."

"God! This is stupid!"

As he retrieved the arrow and strode back to draw his bow, he knew he had to concentrate and hit the bullseye if he was to get what he wanted. He relaxed his stance, aimed carefully, and the arrow hit its mark. "There! Finally! Now tell me what I *need* to

199

CONVERSION

know." He kicked the grass and looked away.

"Look at me, MacArthur."

As the boy glared at him, Reuben stared into his angry eyes and said softly, "You need to *know* that Yeshua loves you."

The words were bad enough, but the compassion in Reuben's eyes quenched all arrogance, fear, and ire. Despite his best effort to remain hardened, MacArthur's heart burst. He fell into Reuben's arms and wept from the depth of his soul, and it had never felt so good. Reuben took a handkerchief from his pocket, and soon it was soaked through. MacArthur tried to wring it out, and they both laughed.

Reuben gathered the bow and quiver of arrows and he and MacArthur walked over to the bales of hay. As Reuben extracted the arrow from the target and placed it in the quiver, he sighed. "When I was not much older than you, I had the world in the palm of my hand. I fought hard, I played hard, I drank hard; and I did them all very well. I vanquished my foes and celebrated with wine, women, and song. Nothing was beyond my reach. When my father and mother said, 'You drink too much, you are reckless, you don't think about your future,' I scoffed and believed they simply wanted to control me." He sat beside MacArthur and leaned the bow and quiver against the hay bale beside him.

"Alas, on a raid in which we killed a terrorist leader, I met a woman. Nura. She was the wife of the terrorist, and it was my task to take her and her infant child to Mossad for questioning. The first time I saw her, she saw *me*, who I was to be, and I fell hopelessly in love for the first time. All the women I had known were like a bad

CHAPTER 13

dream in the light of her beautiful face.

"On the way to Mossad, she told me she knew she could trust me. Then she told me her secret. She was a believer in Yeshua. She wept for the lost soul of her dead husband, and she told me she was no longer Muslim, that she had embraced the Jewish Messiah."

"Good grief! How did that happen?"

"She read about him in her Koran and realized he was the true savior from sin and evil. She came to this realization days before she was to marry this terrorist, to whom she had been promised since birth. She decided to trust Yeshua and remain silent, but when her son Ahmed was born, she began to pray fervently for God to save her husband or deliver her in a way she could raise Ahmed to know her "Isa," as she called Yeshua.

"My heart was desolate. This beauty was sincere but crazy! I could not believe a Muslim could become a Christian. I changed the subject and asked her if she would tell all she knew about her husband's and his associates' plans, and she was hesitant. She said, and I will never forget it, 'I know their cause is evil, but I also know God loves them as he loves me, that Isa died for them as he did for me. I forgive them and pray for them to be saved, but I will help in any way I can to stop them from doing harm to innocent people. Please promise me you will do no harm to them unless it is to save others.'

"I pulled into Mossad, and I wanted to promise, but I knew I couldn't. I told her I would do my best. As for those I answered to, I couldn't speak for them. She said, 'I will pray for you and for them.' She smiled, looking so serene with her baby in her arms.

201

CONVERSION

"Nura provided good intel, and Mossad was grateful. We arranged for a new identity, with an apartment and a job far enough away to be safe from her family but close enough for us to protect her. Her family — and others — would kill her and take her baby. I volunteered to be one of her guards for the first months, until we were assured of her continued safety.

"She and I had passionate conversations about our differing views of God, life, and the struggle between Jew and Muslim and Christian. With Nura, there was no small talk. But Ahmed was a delight. And I loved that when she could not get him to sleep, I could. I would sing what my mother had sung to us, and he would close his eyes and go limp. The first time it happened, I thought I had killed him! But Nura laughed and placed him in his bed.

"I often came to her apartment with a bottle of wine. She refused to drink with me, and so we would argue, but once I stole a kiss. I wanted more, but she wanted a Christian husband. In a drunken fury, I told her if she really loved me, she would sleep with me. She fired back, 'If you loved me, you would commit your life to Isa and marry me!'

"I stormed out before my shift was over and took some days off, going on one of my benders, hitting my favorite bars and going home with various women. When I got to my apartment two days later, my father was waiting for me. He didn't tell me I reeked of liquor, which I did. There was just the look on his face. In Israel, we have learned to ask, 'Who?'

"He shook his head. 'The informant and her baby. When did you last see them?' I don't know what happened next. My father

CHAPTER 13

told me that I ran to the bathroom and vomited, then fell on the floor screaming. He knew I was one of her guards, but only then did he suspect how much I cared for her and the child."

MacArthur asked, "How did her family find her?"

"Her cousin traveled in his business and spotted her. He followed her and told the family where she lived. Her own brother…I can't speak the horror he did to her…and he took Ahmed."

"So, what did your father do when you, you know, were so upset?"

"Hours later I became conscious. My mother and one of my sisters were there. They didn't know what to do with me. They had never seen me like this. I had lost men and women in battle and family members in terrorist attacks. They had seen me upset but not inconsolable. I wept for a long time. I wanted to turn back time — and I hated God for all of it.

"My mother told me it wasn't my fault, but my father could not say it. He knew the timing. If I had stayed with her, I would have saved her from that monster. This is what I could not face. For months my heart raged against God. Like Adam, I blamed him for my own sin."

"Adam did that?"

"He said, 'The woman *you* gave me, she handed me the forbidden fruit.' We all say that. If we can't blame another human being, we blame God. We will do anything to release ourselves from responsibility for our sin, from the torment and shame of being wrong. Then we can maintain the lie that we are good and

CONVERSION

right without God's help."

"What made you change?"

"I went back to work, and my training saved me for a while. I shook my fist at this Isa of Nura's and decided he was evil. He had caused her death. He had played a dirty trick on *me* by introducing me to this Christian woman *he knew I would love*. I tried to forget her and hated every Christian I met. I associated all my pain with Christianity, which is easy for a Jew, eh?

"Then…the nightmares came. Night after night, in my sleep I watched families being tortured and killed in diabolical ways. When awake, I drank, thinking I could drown the darkness in my soul; but the nightmares persisted. I would wake in a cold sweat and grab the bottle. Alcohol dulled the pain…ah…but it did not kill it.

"In the final nightmare, I watched *Nura* being tortured and killed, but then another man appeared and the monster melted away, just vanished like the coward he was.

"Who was this man that a monster cowered before him? Of course, he was her Isa, the one she had loved. He took her hand and raised her, fully restored to life, glowing, more beautiful than ever. The door to Heaven opened and Isa picked up Ahmed. Nura caressed her child's face and looked at me, then walked into Heaven. Isa handed Ahmed to me, and I woke up."

"Wow! What did you do?"

"The first thing I did was throw out every bottle of alcohol and call an agent, who had once confided to me he attended Alcoholics Anonymous. I knew he could be trusted. It wasn't easy, let me

CHAPTER 13

tell you! I was very sick for weeks, and all I wanted was a drink. Months later, at a party, I felt good and decided I could drink again. I was standing at the bar, and I swear on the blood of Yeshua, the bartender, a stranger, looked at me and said, 'I thought you had had enough?'"

"You're kidding! What did you do?"

"I ran out of there and called my friend in AA. I felt like I had been saved from a fate worse than death."

"And you never drank again?"

"No. But that last dream haunted me. How to get Ahmed back? I saw no way. I could not kidnap him. By now he was over two years old. I found myself talking to Yeshua, telling him that he was asking the impossible. And then I would catch myself, 'Who are you talking to? You don't even believe in him!' The problem was… he was *answering* me."

"What? How? I mean, did you hear him speak?"

"In AA, there are twelve steps that are based on Scripture. In my words, the first three are: 1) Me in charge of my life equals insanity, 2) God is sane, and 3) I will let God restore me to sanity. Now, for a religious Jew, talking to God is no problem. But Yeshua, that's impossible; and yet, I knew *he* was answering me as I made my way through these steps in AA.

"Then, after a year being sober, I had that first moment of true clarity. Every meeting, we said "The Lord's Prayer." We Jews did not realize it was New Testament Scripture. It sounded like our Scriptures and did not mention Yeshua, so I memorized it because it was *shalom*, peace to me. Then one evening, as I said

CONVERSION

the words, they filled my heart. I knew that without Yeshua, I was lost forever. I, the mighty warrior, faced the truth: I was lost in all my sins without Yeshua's cleansing blood. He was Messiah. By the time I said, 'For yours is the kingdom and the power and the glory forever,' I was talking directly to him and changing into another man."

They sat in silence for a moment. MacArthur patted Reuben's arm. "What happened to Ahmed?"

Reuben smiled with a twinkle in his eye, the expression the Colonel had warned him about. "I entered into my most clandestine mission. I found he was living with the dead terrorist's brother and his wife. I observed them for months. He was now four years old, and I was satisfied they were good parents and at least not directly involved in terrorism.

"I prayed and asked Yeshua to show me what to do. It began with small things. Anonymously, I would have a toy, a game, or new clothes delivered to his home. When he was able to read, I would send books as well. Every month, he would get something from his Secret Friend. His family tried to discover who I was. If they caught any of the messengers, they offered large sums of money for information, but these men and women were trusted friends.

"When he was twelve, I sent a letter to his parents, still signing it Secret Friend —all typed, of course. I told them I would pay for him to go to a prestigious boys' school in England. They assumed what I had hoped. Since Ahmed's father had been educated in England, they thought, 'Of course! This Secret Friend is an old

CHAPTER 13

friend of Ahmed's father, most likely another Muslim emigrant who still lives there.' They made no connection to his mother and accepted my offer." Reuben smiled and looked at the sky. "So... Ahmed attends a British school that requires him to study Christian doctrine and go to a chapel service once a week."

"What about his Muslim religion?"

"They allow him to pray during the day and take him to a mosque once a month. His family is satisfied with that arrangement."

"Have you met him yet? Does he know you are his Secret Friend?"

"He knows me as...a tutor in literary studies. Your father knows this part of my life, which is one reason he asked me to be your tutor. Yeshua has indicated that one day I will tell Ahmed everything, especially the truth about his mother."

"Reuben, do you think you'll ever love anyone again? I mean, you're not *that* old."

"Not *that* old? Who shot the first bullseye today?"

MacArthur frowned, remembering his temper tantrum. "I'm sorry." He shook his head. "I don't know what happened. One minute I was fine and the next minute I wanted to kill you, which, now that I think about it, was a very bad idea."

Reuben laughed and put his arm around MacArthur's sagging shoulders. "You were angry because you were afraid. You felt powerless over your father's situation and forgot that Yeshua is faithful to his Word and loves you. And so, out came the colorful language."

CONVERSION

"Ugh!"

"You have repented, yes?"

"Yes."

"Rejoice! You are forgiven from Yeshua's cross. Now follow him closer."

MacArthur closed his eyes and took a deep, slow breath. "Father, help me to trust you more. I also repent for hating Reuben and treating him badly. Forgive me, Reuben."

"Done. And as to your father, Captain Swallow is searching for him and his team, so we must pray fervently for their trail to be found. The good news is that there are no reports of them being captured."

19

Every week Sergeant Mills would call to say they had nothing to report on the Colonel and his men, nor had they heard from Captain Swallow. But Reuben's story had effected a change in MacArthur. He knew he had to be more honest about his fears; otherwise, he would become angry and bitter, blaming God and everyone else for the challenges in his life. Right now, the challenge was believing God would save his father, while continuing to do what he was supposed to do each hour of each day.

Another challenge was writing to his mom, his sisters, and David. He couldn't tell them about his father's situation, which threatened to consume him day and night; so he filled his letters with details of his days, inserting jokes and interesting stories like he usually did. He knew they wouldn't be suspicious because he hadn't seen his father in over two months; after all, that was routine for his family. However, he was concerned they would think it strange that he and Reuben had not ventured past the walls of the house for some time.

He smiled at his solution. In each letter, he told them something he was learning from the Bible. He hoped they would see the light, but he also knew he was distracting them, even irritating them. David wrote impassioned responses espousing atheism, logic, and free will; his mother and Joanna and Meg

CONVERSION

warned him against fanaticism and cults. Only Rebecca and Sarah replied with no comment. Whatever impact his preaching was having in their lives, no one questioned his safety or asked about the Colonel.

In his struggle to remain hopeful, his free time was often spent in prayer with Reuben. These sessions nearly always included questions about spiritual warfare. "Reuben, you say praying in tongues can be spiritual warfare, and I know the Holy Spirit prays the perfect will of God through us, but that's like, on the offensive, isn't it? I mean, in spiritual warfare, what if we are attacked? How do we defend ourselves?"

"Go to Ephesians, chapter 6, verses 10 through 20. Read and tell me what you see."

MacArthur read the passage several times. "Well…you can only be strong in God's power not your own strength. And I guess we get his power by putting on *his* armor. Then we can stand against anything the devil throws at us. Oh, and our fight isn't with people but with the demons that influence them. Like Satan deceives the communists into thinking they are right to take over other nations and kill anyone who gets in their way. So, that means *our* fight is not with the communists but with the demons controlling them, spiritually speaking."

"This is good, what you are saying. We may pray in tongues or our language as the Holy Spirit leads us; and when peace comes, we know his will is done. We may not know how he will do it or when he will do it, but we know he will do it because we have prayed according to his Word and the peace of the Holy Spirit in

CHAPTER 19

our hearts. Go to 2 Corinthians, chapter 10, verses 3-5, and tell me what you see."

"Well…this says we don't wage war like the world does, and we use different weapons, spiritual weapons, which demolish evil strongholds. Um…these strongholds are not physical, like the walls of Jericho or the Great Wall of China. It says they are…uh…like a bunch of lies, thoughts and ideas that go against God's Word. So we have to watch what we think and make sure we are believing the truth and not the devil's lies."

Reuben thought a minute. "It is interesting that those who immediately recognize a counterfeit bill do so because they spend hours and hours studying the *true* bill. We are the same. In the Roman armor, the most important — and the first mentioned piece of armor — is the belt of truth. Did you notice this in Ephesians 6?"

MacArthur went back to the passage. "Oh…yeah."

"The belt stabilized the Roman soldier, and much of the rest of the armor rested upon it or was attached to it. Without the belt, the soldier was weak and vulnerable. So, praying in the Spirit must always be accompanied by study and meditation in Scripture. Then God's truth fills our eyes and ears and heart, and when the counterfeit appears and the lies are told, we sit straight and say, 'This is strange. These words don't ring true.' Like Yeshua when he was tempted, we speak the Scripture, the truth, to demolish the lies of the enemy."

"Oh! The sword of the Spirit is the Word of God! So whether we are attacking the devil or the devil is attacking us, the Word of God is our sword to overcome him."

CONVERSION

Reuben nodded thoughtfully. "MacArthur, Yeshua has given you a powerful imagination. Do not allow the enemy to use it, to build horrifying scenarios of what your father and his men might be going through. The moment you realize you are having thoughts along this line, stop and ask the Holy Spirit to reveal the verse of truth to tear it down. He often leads me to Psalm 91. I speak it, meditate on it, until all I see is the power and grace of God invading that situation."

More and more, MacArthur used Psalm 91 to pray for the Colonel and his men. Then finally, on the 19th of April, Sergeant Mills called to say they were safely back on the base! He advised Reuben to continue to stay in the house. That was all. They were relieved but knew there was more to the story.

Five days later, Sergeant Mills arrived at the house just after dinner. He asked to speak with everyone, so they gathered in the foyer. "The Colonel wants you to pack your things and be ready to leave by early Saturday morning. Reuben and MacArthur will be returning to the States with him and his team, and Kau and Lawan will be closing the house. I am here to pack the Colonel's things and assist you."

Kau did something MacArthur had never seen him do. He took Lawan's hand. No one had anticipated this abrupt departure. Thankfully, the next two days were a blur of decisions and activity. What to take home and what to leave? What was necessary and what was irreplaceable? He and Reuben decided to leave the monkey bars, and the hay bales and targets were carefully burned. MacArthur's practice rifle, pistol, and bow and arrows were packed

CHAPTER 19

for shipment almost as carefully as his guitar.

Very early Saturday morning, an army truck and two men came to load boxes, crates, and luggage. Sergeant Mills put the Colonel's few items in the trunk of his car, and then came the dreaded goodbye. Surely MacArthur would see Kau and Lawan again someday! Maybe Sunan could come to Virginia for school and they could all visit him?

Although it wasn't good form for a *farang*, MacArthur wept and hugged each of them. He thanked them for everything they had taught him, and he told them he loved them and would miss them. Kau's eyes glistened, and Lawan's cheeks were washed with tears. They did a final *wai*, and a moment later MacArthur and Reuben were waving to them from the back seat of the car as Kau, Lawan, and the safe house disappeared from view.

During the quiet drive to the base, MacArthur's sadness turned to hopeful anticipation at being reunited with his father, Chuck, John, and the rest of the team. When he saw them, however, he was shocked. Besides Chuck, they were gaunt and thin, like shadows of the mighty warriors he remembered. He embraced his father tearfully, feeling the bones in his shoulders and back, but his father seized him with the old strength. *Yes! He's still in there!* Reluctantly, they let go of one another. Then he shook hands with the others and hugged John, who smiled weakly and patted him on the back.

Chuck put his hand on MacArthur's shoulder and whispered, "Don't ask. Let him tell."

MacArthur nodded. "Thanks, Chuck. You were the answer to our prayers."

CONVERSION

"The Great Spirit led me." He stared into MacArthur's eyes. "I see you are changed."

"Well, I hope I'm better in a lot of ways. I know one thing: I have a lot more respect for what you and my dad do. I'm not sure I'm supposed to be a warrior like you, though."

"We are all warriors," Chuck answered.

"Time to get aboard," barked the Colonel hoarsely. Chuck hurried to help him, and Reuben motioned MacArthur to board the airplane before him. It looked like the same C-130 Hercules that had brought them to Thailand. As they sat in their seats, MacArthur was glad they were leaving in daylight. He wanted to savor every view as they left this extraordinary land.

MacArthur was quiet as he fastened his seatbelt and shoved his carry-on under the seat. When they were in the air, circling the area, he saw the safe house and tears filled his eyes again. When he had control of his emotions, he said, "Reuben, I still want to change the world, but I believe God is leading me in a different direction now."

"Yes?"

"Spiritual warfare instead of physical warfare. I mean, all the wars and fights and bad things that people do are because of sin; and like you say, only Jesus solves the sin problem."

"Are you a preacher now?" Reuben smiled.

"No!" MacArthur threw back his head and laughed. "I don't know how I'll take Jesus to the world, but I know I will somehow."

Reuben patted his hand. "One step at a time. One decision after another. Abide in Scripture. Pray without ceasing. This is how

CHAPTER 19

we walk in the Spirit and fulfill what God assigns us. You may not see it until the end of your life, but one day you will know what Yeshua has accomplished in you and through you."

"I'm bankin' on it!"

MacArthur did his obligatory walks during the long flights and only once was his father awake. He caught his eye, and the Colonel said, "Captain Swallow, would you give us a moment?"

"Of course, Sir." Chuck rose and smiled at MacArthur. He took a book and his coke and walked up the aisle to sit next to Reuben. MacArthur longed to hear what those two would talk about.

Once he was seated beside him, the Colonel turned and said, "Son, I've been worse and will be fine. I just need a few weeks of your mother's care and Lois' cooking." His voice was rough, but he was smiling.

"Yes, Sir." MacArthur leaned in to hear better.

The Colonel took a long breath and began. "After what became our last mission, we retreated into the mountains of Laos and realized an entire company was trailing us. We climbed higher and came to a stream, where we veered off down the mountain then stopped at what we hoped was the same stream. This time we got in the stream and hiked back up the mountain, hoping to lose them.

"A little over a klick upstream, John thought he saw the mouth of a cave. It was so well hidden, he almost missed it. That's where we decided to rest and see if we had lost them. Unfortunately, they sent half their company to hold vigil and watch for us just above the cave. It was a rock face with a strategic vantage point. So we

215

CONVERSION

were stuck there for weeks, on radio silence and living on little food and then just water."

"My God, Dad. Was there any water in the cave at least?"

"A trickle down a wall. We became very creative in catching it. Thank God, Captain Swallow found where our trail ended at the stream. He returned to base to get the latest intelligence and was drawn to the fact that part of that enemy company was camped at a certain spot on that mountain. He figured we were trapped near there.

"He devised a plan and set out with two men. When it was dark, the others would create a diversion by setting off explosives around the mountain, to draw the enemy away from us and the stream. Then they would return to the rendezvous point, where they left a truck and a jeep. Meanwhile, Captain Swallow moved up the stream looking for anyplace we might have taken refuge."

"Didn't the enemy see him?"

His father chuckled. "He wasn't splashing his way up. Chuck knows how to be invisible. As soon as he saw the cave, he stopped and waited until dark. When he heard the explosions and saw all but three of the lookout force leave, he made his move and took them out quietly. Then he found us in the cave and gave us what food and water he had. He helped us get to the road, where the other two guys were waiting to transport us back to base."

MacArthur put his hand on his father's arm. "Thanks for telling me, Dad."

His father looked him in the eyes. "Reuben told me you earned the need to know." Wearily, he leaned back and closed his eyes.

CHAPTER 19

MacArthur squeezed his bony arm gently and rose to change seats with Chuck.

He eased into his seat next to Reuben. "Dad just told me the whole story. It was brutal but they weren't tortured. Thank God for that."

"Yes."

"Um, did Chuck…uh Captain Swallow…say anything about the Great Spirit?"

Reuben smiled. "Yes."

"What did he say? Is his Great Spirit our Spirit?"

"I believe yes. He gave his life to Yeshua as a boy, but he honors the traditions of his fathers. Like me, he sees Yeshua in many of them."

"What do you mean?"

"I attend synagogue and observe the feasts with my family and Jewish friends. I even read Torah from time to time. Seeing Yeshua in the feasts is a revelation. Of course, they have no idea they are honoring Yeshua, and that saddens me, but the Scriptures declare that one day they will see him there also."

MacArthur wrinkled his eyebrows. "Are you saying that Jesus can be found in every religion? I mean, Nura found him in the Koran!"

"The Scriptures say that God is seen in all he *created*. He loves us and has left his handprint in his creation, even in our hearts. As the great deceiver, Satan perverts and twists what God says and created. The devil inspires people to form religions that may use parts of the Bible, but they never present God's truth in a pure way.

CONVERSION

And why does he do this? To keep us from knowing Yeshua."

"Ah. I get it! Jesus is the only one who defeated Satan."

MacArthur returned to reading the book Reuben had assigned for this month, *The Red Badge of Courage*. He was nearly finished and wanted to write his report before they arrived home. He was struck by the main character, Henry, whose responses to war were similar to his own during the conflict in Panama and the war coming so close to him in Thailand. He pondered how his view of the Vietnam War and war in general had changed and smiled as his book report formed in his mind. He would use the line from Shakespeare's *Henry IV*, which Reuben often quoted in their discussions: "The arms are fair when the intent of bearing them is just."

When they finally landed at Andrews Air Force Base, MacArthur ran into the terminal to embrace his mother and sisters. With tears of gladness, he hugged them and kissed them. Then he remembered and knew he had to prepare them. "Dad's okay, but he looks bad."

"What happened?" asked Joanna.

"I don't know," he fibbed, "but being with you is going to be what he needs to get better."

When the Colonel walked through the door, the women swarmed him with cries of joy and no indication anything was wrong. MacArthur's heart swelled. His mother was in top form, beaming as she threw her arms her husband. "Well, ah can see ya waisted away without me. Wouldn't expect anithin' else!" The Colonel laughed and squeezed her tight, and the girls encompassed

CHAPTER 19

the two with hugs and tears.

Reuben received almost as warm a greeting as the Colonel. As far as Jeanne Wells was concerned, he was the reason her son had come home in even better shape than when he had left. The sisters fawned over their brother. "My God, feel these muscles! You're as tall as Dad! And strong! Has our little brother become a man?" Reuben sighed and shook his head, praying it wouldn't make him insufferable. They still had a month of studies to finish.

MacArthur saw Chuck and motioned him to come. "Mom, you might remember Captain Swallow. He helped carry me down the mountain when I was bit by the snake, and he was a great help to Dad too." That's all he could say, but the women read between the lines as military families do. They hugged him and Chuck laughed, "I've never received so much love from so many beautiful women!"

MacArthur's sisters and mother hugged all the men on the Colonel's team and thanked them for their service. They greeted their families like they were their own. By the time Reuben and the family got to the house, the travelers were exhausted. Jeanne lovingly tucked MacArthur in bed, just like she did when he was a child. She found her husband fast asleep on their bed, still in his uniform. It was a familiar sight. She kissed him gently on the lips, removed his shoes, and covered him with a blanket. Her men were home and all was well. Life was fun again!

219

20

Jeanne Talley Wells was a perpendicular person. She often spoke and acted crosswise with what was assumed of her. Born into a prominent Mississippi family, she was expected to be a devout Presbyterian and an even more devout Democrat. With her sultry southern accent and her charming gift of hospitality, people did not expect to hear staunch opinions that ran counter to the stereotypes of the South, especially the Jim Crow South in which she was raised. The way most people resolved this conundrum was to simply say, "Well you know, Jeanne is a complicated person." They completely missed the obvious.

Jeanne was far from complicated. Her belief system rested on one principle: Life must be fun. Her belief in God was that he created people to have fun, maybe not with him but certainly with each other. She looked at the beauty and magnificent detail of the world around her and knew her Creator wanted his creation to enjoy life. Her religious beliefs rested on one simple truth: Jesus died for her sins so she could have fun and not worry about the hereafter.

Her marriage and family were functional because they had fun. Her social life was fulfilling because she had fun with people. She had a genuine curiosity and care for anyone who crossed her path, and most people adored her. Ironically, this is the gift that caused

CONVERSION

her to go perpendicular to her "raisin'."

Orphaned as a baby in 1922, the Judge took his granddaughter in and spoiled her without apology, hiring Viola to care for her. Little Jeanne adored her mammy, with whom she spent most of her time. It was not unusual for a child to be raised by a "colored," so Jeanne didn't question it — until she was five years old. She had often heard the word "niggah," but this time her ears heard it differently. Although it came from her grandfather's mouth, which wasn't unusual, he used the word to describe *Viola*.

"Ya know that niggah woman, Viola, who takes cah a Jeanne? Well she's ahmost too good fo a niggah. Too smaht. Uppity." Pause. "Yessiree. Not sho ah wahnt little Jeanne undah heh influence." Pause. "Well…I'll letchah know if I 'cide to git riddah heh. Thank yah."

Jeanne flew into her grandfather's arms, begging him not to send her precious Viola away. As the Judge's heart was completely at the mercy of his granddaughter's wishes, Viola stayed. And the Judge eventually had to admit that his granddaughter was better for it. He often consulted Viola when issues arose with Jeanne, and he found her advice surprisingly sound, even though she was an ignorant Republican like her kind was — and a fanatical Pentecostal besides. At least she couldn't vote.

The conversation that sealed Jeanne's perpendicularity would never be forgotten by either of the parties. She was fourteen, it was 1936, and the country was in the throes of the Great Depression. "Viola, don'tcha jest love FDR an all he's doin' fo us?"

"No, Baby. I don't much cah fo 'im or what he doin'."

CHAPTER 20

"Fo heavens' sake, why not? Ahn't all y'all Demcrats?"

"No, Baby. Demcrats da ones dat do da lynchin' an burnin'. Dey da Klan, Baby. Uh-huh. Jim Crow Demcrats ain't evah gonna see my kine equal."

Shocked, Jeanne blurted out, "But FDR isn't like that a'tall!"

Viola shook her head, eyes closed. "Hmm. He still see us as those as can't hep theyselves. Wansa put us on his dole an own us. Well, ah am raisin' you and my chillen ta know yo's free an have feet ta walk an hands ta work. Den yo can do anithin' da good Lawd tells ya ta do. It's tween him and you, not you and da govment."

"But isn't ouah govment good? Ahn't they jes tryin' ta hep?"

"Chile, my life's tole me, da mo govment hep, da mo ya don get ta 'cide yoself. Dey 'cide fo ya, which means dey don think much a ya. My kine jes got ta git edicated an 'cide dey *can* git it an den work hahd ta git it. Den, when dey gits it, dey can chuck ole Jim Crow in da pit a Hell wheh it blong!"

Viola was the one person who always told the truth, so Jeanne began to question everything her grandfather and her society told her. Was the Klan good or evil? Why were they so mean to the coloreds? And did the Democrats really want to help the coloreds or were they buying their vote?

Meanwhile, a history book she got from the library said it was the Republicans that pushed for freeing the slaves and had continued to fight for more rights for them. The Judge hated these "Republican Carpetbaggers," but knowing Viola and her people, Jeanne reasoned, it just didn't figure that the Republicans were in the wrong.

It wasn't long before Jeanne had had enough of Jim Crow

CONVERSION

Demcrats too. Viola and her family were a different color but that's where the difference ended. They were human like her — and some were smarter and better at some things than she was! She had no doubt they would grow up and throw old Jim Crow into Hell just like Viola said, and she was going to do it with them!

The first person she told about her secret secession from the Democratic Party was young Lieutenant Wells. He was not just a dreamy, Frank Sinatra lookalike; the moment she gazed into his eyes, she knew he would understand. She knew people. On their first date, she told him things she had never told anyone except Viola. Her instincts about the man were confirmed when he did the same. It was this foundation of trust — and Republicanism — that enabled a Catholic and Presbyterian to be deeply in love and live peacefully together.

The judge decided Viola's services were no longer needed when their baby girl married the Catholic Yankee and declared herself a Republican. He had accepted the marriage; what he couldn't abide was his granddaughter's new political views — new to him, that is. He blamed Viola and was furious with her. Jeanne asked Viola to stay with her and her new husband because Viola's husband Sam had been tragically killed in a tractor accident the year before. And when Lieutenant Wells and two of Viola's boys went off to serve in World War II, she and Viola formed a new bond as women. They thanked God and the military might of the USA that all their men came back in one piece.

Jeanne revisited these memories with tears as she quietly shut the door on her sleeping husband, back from another war. It wasn't

CHAPTER 20

until the Colonel regained his strength that she felt she could tell him her beloved Viola had passed into glory the end of January. She had been there, along with Viola's children and grandchildren, at the end. "Those Pentecostals make a time of it, fo sure, but she was the most remahkable woman ah've evah known. She had such a smile on heh face! An now she's with heh sweet Sam." She put her head on his chest and let out the sobs she had stifled for months. Some things just weren't real until she told the Colonel.

He held her tightly and winced that he had not been there when she needed him. He marveled once again at her incredible fortitude. Viola was not the only remarkable woman; she had raised one.

MacArthur had only met Viola a couple of times. She had moved back to Mississippi to be with her family when he was a toddler. But the minute his mother told him "the end of January," he remembered that that was just before he and his father had called her from Thailand. *That must be why she sounded drunk!*

Reuben stayed with the family for three more weeks to finish the school year. He and MacArthur discovered Lois had a strong faith and every morning the three of them would have prayer and a short Bible study in the kitchen. When it was time for Reuben's departure, it was another heart-wrenching goodbye. His last words to MacArthur were simply, "Live the truth, my boy, and stay in touch!" With that, he handed him a card with only a phone number written on it and gave him a bear hug.

To distract him from missing Reuben, the Colonel and Jeanne surprised MacArthur with a two-week visit to Panama; but

CONVERSION

MacArthur experienced culture shock there. His relationship with David seemed distorted, like the hall of mirrors at the fair. The boys were warm and friendly, and they were glad to be together, but there was a huge divide between them. The first night, David teased him when he said his prayers. MacArthur laughed like he always had, but inside he was grieved. The next morning, he arose early to read his Bible.

"Saint Mac is back in the Canal Zone, ladies and gentlemen! Everybody must be on their best behavior," David joked.

MacArthur closed the book and made the sign of the cross toward him. "Bless you, my son, for thou art a super man and must needs be good." As usually happens, their sense of humor eased the awkwardness between them. They went fishing and reminisced about their experience during the Order of the Arrow Ordeal. They met David's friends and some MacArthur remembered, surfing and jumping the waves at the beach. As the sun set, everyone was drinking and many were smoking pot around a fire. David and MacArthur stuck with beer.

"Have you applied to the University of Virginia yet?" asked MacArthur.

The expression on David's face looked odd in the light of the flames. He took a sip of his beer. "No. I'm sorry Mac, but I'm not going to college right away. I'm going to take a year off."

MacArthur couldn't believe what he'd heard. "What? Why? You don't need to 'find yourself,' do you?"

"No. I know what I want to do, but I'm just not sure how to get there, like whether the University of Virginia is part of it." He could

CHAPTER 20

see the disappointment on his friend's face and put his hand on his shoulder. "Don't worry! We'll still write and be in touch like we always have."

MacArthur felt uneasy. "I guess being blood brothers doesn't mean we agree on everything."

David laughed. "Like religion and sex and the war! What *do* we agree on?"

"That we're both great guys who are going to change the world, remember?" MacArthur seemed lighthearted, but he was confused and sad. It was true. How could they change the world together if they had different visions of how the world should be?

The next day, Elena fixed them empanadas to eat on the hillside of Quarry Heights. They climbed through the chain link fence — the cut was still there — and talked about the strange light and laughter. MacArthur frowned. "David, I have to tell you something. I know we said we wouldn't tell anyone else, but I told Reuben. I just blurted it out when I wasn't thinking."

David waved his hand and smiled. "Hey, it's cool. I told some guy about it one night. He was going on and on about how God was this and God was that. It pissed me off, so to shut him up, I said, 'Yeah, God hit me and my friend with a bright light one day. It was *neato keen*.' He had the weirdest look on his face," David laughed then frowned. "That's when I remembered we weren't going to tell. I don't think he believed me, though."

"Reuben said my telling him was a planned accident, that God meant it to happen, but I still felt bad that I didn't keep my word."

"Look man, if that's the worst thing you ever do to me, we're cool."

"Thanks. I feel the same way."

"Hey, is there anything you can tell me about Thailand that you couldn't in a letter?"

"Not really. There were a couple of intense times. I mean, I definitely saw the reason for bodyguards."

"You had more than one?"

"Well, Kau and Lawan were more than housekeepers."

"Neat. Did you see anyone get killed?"

"No." This wasn't a lie, but he remembered how Reuben shot and probably killed two CPT soldiers. Then he smiled and raised his eyebrows, "I did learn to shoot to kill though. Do you still shoot?"

"Yeah! Let's go to the range tomorrow. Hey, did you kill anyone?"

"No!" He rushed to change the subject. "And it's been a while since I've shot, so don't expect much."

Soon, they were saying goodbye again and MacArthur returned home. He told his parents and sisters that David was not going to college right away and assured them he wasn't thinking of doing the same thing. Then he asked permission to call Reuben, offering to pay for the international call.

"Y'all go on," said his mother.

"Just mind the time difference," said the Colonel.

He went into his father's study, closed the door and sat down at his desk to dial the number. "Hey Reuben. It's MacArthur!"

"MacArthur! Are you well?"

CHAPTER 20

"Yeah. I'm great. But I need to talk to you about something."

"I'm listening."

"I went to visit David, and it's just not the same. I couldn't talk to him, I mean, like, really talk to him like I used to. I'm not talking about what happened in Thailand. That's part of it. I mean, like, it would have been cool to tell him everything that happened there, but it's more than that. I, well, I just couldn't tell him anything about Jesus. I wanted to, but I just couldn't. I feel like I'm failing him. And I'm having the same trouble with my family. None of them believe like you and I believe, and they don't want to hear it from me. It just makes them mad. But it's the truth, Reuben! I know it's the truth." He paused. "Reuben, are you there?"

"Yes. I'm praying."

"Oh."

"MacArthur, there are some we *tell* about Jesus, but to most we must *be* Jesus. Show David and your family who Jesus is by the way you live. Did you pray when you were with David?"

"Yes."

"Did you read your Bible?"

"Yes."

"Did you treat him and his family with respect and serve them well?"

"Yes."

"It's a miracle. You were perfect."

MacArthur laughed. "I just feel like I should have done more, said more."

"MacArthur, faith without works is dead. Your faith means

CONVERSION

nothing if people do not see you doing what you believe, and when you live what you believe, that is the most powerful witness."

"Okay. I see that."

"Remember, you can't save anyone. You can only live as the Scriptures and Holy Spirit command you to live. Speak when and to whom God directs, and then watch him do his miracles. That is what I did with you."

"Ohh, yeah."

"I spoke as the Spirit led, and you wanted more."

"That's right! You did that. You poked me, man!"

He could hear Reuben laugh. "It was a Holy Spirit poking."

"Yes. Okay. I feel better. Hey, have you seen Ahmed?"

"Yes. He graduated and has a job in London. He is doing well, and I have told him everything."

"How did he take it?"

"Not well at first. He did not know his father was a terrorist or how his mother died. The parents who raised him told him his mother and father were innocent Muslims, murdered by Mossad. He is not yet a Christian, but he is not a Muslim either. His friends in London are mostly atheists and a few go to a Christian church now and then."

"So you are in the same boat with him as I am with David and my family."

"Yes, except my family nearly disowned me when I told them I believed Yeshua was our Messiah."

"Ooooo. That's serious."

"Yes. Well. There are few like me in Israel or in the world."

CHAPTER 20

"There's no one like you, Reuben!"

"That wasn't my meaning, but I thank you for the compliment. No, I was blessed to find a group of Jewish believers. We are few, but we are growing. When I am home, I am with them when I am able, and I feel their prayers when I am away. We protect each other because it is very dangerous to be a believer in Yeshua in Israel."

"I miss you, Reuben."

"I miss you too, my dear boy. Promise me something."

"What?"

"Promise me that wherever you live, you will find a group who believe, people with whom you can talk about Yeshua and study the Scriptures. Promise me."

"I promise."

"We are parting on a promise. This is good!"

"Thanks, Reuben."

"*Shalom*, MacArthur."

21

Dear Superman,

 Thanks again for the great time in the good ole Canal Zone. I'm disappointed about you not going to college, but I'm hoping you will eventually—and UVA would be a great choice!!! I'm applying this fall.

 Did you watch the moon landing! Incredible! Mom and Dad had some other families over and we sat glued to the TV. I'm still trying to figure out the real significance of it. With all these changes in our country — for good and bad — makes me want to change the world even more. I just have to figure out how.

 I'm still trying to understand what happened to the good ole USA while I was in Thailand — Martin Luther King Jr. assassinated in April (Mom and Lois were really upset about that) and in June literally watched the assassination of Robert Kennedy — surreal. Then all the antiwar protests and riots at the Democratic Convention this month. What a mess! I thought I left war behind in Southeast Asia, but it's like the war jumped into America.

 It's really odd, being at home and going to high school, but I'm excited about it. As I told you in my brief thank-you note (didn't have much to tell then), I met with the principal of the high school. He was impressed with what I learned over the year and told me about football try-outs that week. Now comes the good part.

I showed up hoping to make new friends and be a part of the team, but I really had to fight. I was nervous because I hadn't played for a year and had just thrown the ball with Dad a little. I think all through the try-outs I was praying, *Please God, help me!*

The first thing the coach did was line us up on the field, and what did he do? He introduced the new kid — me! Then he yelled, "What position do you play?"

I shouted back, "Quarterback, Sir!"

Well, the other guys laughed until Coach said, "Pipe down!" He looked me up and down — of course, noticing I wasn't the tallest guy around. "You play anything else?"

"Defensive back and split end, Sir, but I prefer quarterback."

"Our quarterbacks hit like everyone else, Son."

"Glad to hear it, Sir."

"Ooooo," the guys grinned, and I knew I was going to have to prove myself in a big way.

Coach said, "Then let's see what you got."

He had us do some strenuous warm-ups, and man, was I grateful for the physical training with Reuben. I did well in agility drills and was one of the fastest runners. Then Coach broke us into teams and began running

CHAPTER 21

plays. On my first one, I was on offense and took a hand-off from the quarterback. I kept my eyes on the oncoming tackler, who lowered his head to butt me — thank God! All I had to do was sidestep and stiff-arm the guy to the ground, and I buzzed on through the defense. This time, the "ooooo" was a little different!

When I was in the defensive line-up, I saw a kid who was obviously the full back. I knew by his height and weight that he was capable of running right over me. Sure enough, he got the hand-off and barreled toward me, so I charged in and at the last minute dove down and grabbed him just below the knees. That giant crashed to the ground, and this time I heard lots of "whoas" and "wows." Coach grabbed my belt — ha, ha — pulled me up, and said, "Great stick, Son. Great stick."

I thanked him and then went to shake hands with the full back. He turned out to be a real nice guy. I told him that I knew he'd crush me with that barrel of a chest, so I went low. I said, "I'm glad you're on *our* side!" He reminded me of Sammy, when we were all playing for Balboa. Those were the days, weren't they?

Then we had passing drills, and Coach picked five of us to try for quarterback. There was only one guy I knew I had to beat. He was pretty good and a lot taller than me. When it was my turn to quarterback in the line-up, I decided to risk it all and threw a long pass to a tight end. Thank God, he caught it and we both got slaps on the

CONVERSION

back. The next play, I faked a hand-off and then slipped the ball behind me to my new friend the full back, who cut through the defensive line because they were all looking at the guy they thought had the ball. I wish you could have seen it!

In the end, Coach (who I've come to like a lot) made that other guy (Nick is his name) and me co-quarterbacks. Nick is also a senior and at first was pretty upset. I told him I really understood why he might hate me and went out of my way to make friends. It wasn't long before we were laughing, but already I've learned he is nothing like you. He's cool on the football field but barely keeps his grades up in order to play, and off the field he's reckless and sometimes puts his friends in danger. He hasn't done that to me yet, but some others have told me some wild stories about him. Also, he is the leader of the popular kids in school, and of course, I'm popular — ha ha! — so, I don't just see him on the field.

I think I need to tell you about McLean, Virginia. It's a really rich, mostly upper class town. The kids just expect you to be wealthy, and there aren't any poor people to remind them how lucky they are. It only took me a few weeks to size up the different cliques of jocks, geeks, freaks, and some rednecks. And get this! The county passed a law that forbids secret societies, so of course the high school kids have one. I got invited but told them I just didn't have time. I knew it was

CHAPTER 21

something I shouldn't do. Also, if Coach finds out, you get kicked off the team. So no one talks about those who are in it.

Anyhoooooo. I'm enjoying being with other kids again and have met some really cute girls. No Mona Lisa yet, but I'm not in a hurry. And my classes are okay. McLean is known for academics, and the teachers are on prep school level. I'm glad I spent the last year being tutored!

Gotta go — write soon and tell me about your year so far.

Your bb & bf,

Saint Mac

MacArthur's senior year at McLean High School was proving to be a blur of vexation in the midst of success. While he did well in his classes and seemed happy co-leading the football team, the Colonel and Jeanne watched him struggle socially, which was not typical. Moreover, Jeanne had always been able to get him to open up to her, but this time he would not. What he couldn't tell them was that his new relationship with Jesus was at the center of his troubles. His Bible said, "Do not be drunk with wine, but be filled with the Spirit," but his friends were partying and getting drunk or high on pot almost every weekend. He went out with several girls he thought he liked, but he was shocked at how experienced they were sexually. There were things he used to do without question that now made him uneasy, and too many times he felt like he had

CONVERSION

crashed and burned. The words "repent" and "forgive" were taking on new prominence.

He tried to find friends in the youth group at his mother's Presbyterian Church, but they were more interested in dating and sports than their spiritual lives or the Bible. It was even worse at his father's Catholic church. From time to time he went to church with Lois. He loved their services, but there weren't many young people there. His hope for a happier future rested on getting accepted to the University of Virginia. A place that big certainly would have a group of believers like himself.

After two months of witnessing his son's distress, the Colonel announced that they were going to restore a car together. MacArthur was skeptical, but at a junk yard he fell in love with a beat-up 1958 Porsche speedster convertible. The Colonel had it towed to their garage, and Saturdays and sometimes Sundays after church, the two would scour junk yards and mechanics' shops to find parts and work on the car.

The engine needed to be rebuilt. The tires were good, but the body had suffered many dings and dents. The leather interior was covered with dust and grime but cleaned up beautifully, and only a few small rips had to be mended. MacArthur discovered his father knew a lot about cars, and if the Colonel didn't understand how to do something, he found a manual or they consulted a mechanic. In the process, MacArthur learned all about what would become his first automobile.

It took seven months, but the car was finally finished just before graduation. On graduation day, the Colonel handed him

CHAPTER 21

the keys to the Porsche and said, "This is your graduation present, Son."

"Wow! Thanks, Dad! This is the neatest present ever." MacArthur had sailed through finals, won a major golf tournament, and had been accepted to the University of Virginia. He graduated third in his class with his whole family plus Rebecca's fiancé Craig attending the ceremony. The Colonel was cordial to Craig, but Jeanne loved him at first sight and knew he was the right one for Rebecca. "Mah Gawd, Colonel, he may be a Luthran, but they ahn't so bad. Aftah awl, he's a Republican!"

After the graduation parties, the family drove to a lake house for a week's vacation. They hiked, swam, water skied, and sailed. They had a doubles tennis tournament at a nearby tennis club, and Rebecca and Craig were the winners, with MacArthur and Joanna a close second. At meals, they had lively and passionate discussions about their lives, their futures, the state of the nation, the war, and other hot topics.

MacArthur roomed with Craig and saw what Rebecca saw: a great guy with a bright future. They talked about their faith, and MacArthur was amazed that a "Luthran" had such a love for Jesus. He looked forward to their conversations each night and was relieved to discover that his oldest sister had chosen a guy who was a great deal more than just someone who liked dogs.

After the vacation, Rebecca and Craig returned to New York, where she was now a buyer of women's fashions at Macy's. She and Jeanne talked often, planning her wedding in August. Meg returned to Nashville to do a summer internship at a law firm. That left

CONVERSION

MacArthur, Sarah, and Joanna at home, each working summer jobs. MacArthur was hired to caddy and do odd jobs on the golf course at the Congressional Country Club, across the Potomac River. He met interesting and important people, and each night he would entertain his parents and sisters with his stories.

Most of the people he encountered were in the government, so the conversations inevitably turned to political issues. More and more, MacArthur was drawn to politics. He listened to everything his parents and sisters had to say, but he was forming his own opinions. He read articles by both Democrats and Republicans, while devouring the works of Francis Schaeffer and John LeCarré. Like most of his peers, he also read *The Godfather*, but his primary source for all beliefs remained the Bible. He talked to Reuben at least once a month, but sometimes it was difficult to find him.

At the end of the summer, Rebecca and Craig were married. Then Sarah left for Spain, where she would study a year abroad like Joanna had in France. She had found a nursing school in Madrid that accepted foreign students. Meg returned to law school, and Joanna drove to Michigan State to get a graduate degree in forestry. As exciting as Paris had been, it had shown her that she preferred outdoor adventure.

All too soon for the Colonel and Jeanne, it was time to take their baby boy to college. Jeanne rode with MacArthur in his Porsche, while the Colonel followed in the station wagon, filled with his suitcases and boxes. Once there, MacArthur registered and was given a map with his dorm marked by a red X, his dorm room number written underneath. The young man at the registration

CHAPTER 21

table pointed to the map. "You're in the corner room on the ground floor of the first-year dorm."

MacArthur looked at him quizzically. "You mean the freshman dorm?"

The young man smiled. "Here at UVA, we don't use freshman, sophomore, junior, and senior. We say first-year, second-year, etcetera."

MacArthur nodded. "Got it." He and his parents carried what they could, and MacArthur was the first one into his room. He dropped his suitcases. "What the...?!!"

"Hi, roommate!" David and his parents stood before him, grinning from ear to ear.

For a moment, the boys just stared at one another while their parents relished the surprise. In a moment, everyone was talking at once and hugging each other. MacArthur pieced together that David had enlisted their parents' help to surprise him. "I had the hardest time selling you that garbage about taking a year off! You totally fell for it, and then I felt bad that you felt bad. I almost told you everything."

"Oh my God! I can't believe it! This is so cool!"

The Doc's eyes twinkled. "We loved being on your side, when you so valiantly listed all the reasons David should go straight to college."

"Si! Si! What a passionate young man!" David's mother embraced him, laughing.

He looked at his parents. "And you knew all along?"

"Ahhhv course. Yo fahthah is not tha only coveht oprative in

CONVERSION

this family."

The Colonel shook his head and rolled his eyes. "Come on men, let's get the rest of MacArthur's things while the mothers *decorate.*" He winked at Jeanne, who began to open the box she had set on the unmade bed. She explained to Elena that she had always made each daughter's bed on their first day at college, and MacArthur was now the recipient of this important ritual. It was this gesture, of course, that ensured a successful four years.

By the time the boys and their fathers had brought all of MacArthur's belongings from the cars, both boys' beds were made and a few pictures set on their desks. The mothers were satisfied their sons would remember where they came from.

The Colonel treated everyone to lunch at the university cafeteria, where the food proved quite good. "But be sure to tell Lois that it's not as good as hers, and I'll try to keep my strength up," said MacArthur.

"Never going to beat Mama's cooking," said David.

"No...no...no!" His mother wagged her finger at him.

Then it was time to say goodbye. The parents were going to drive back to McLean and spend a few days visiting before the Parks returned to Panama. This would take the sting out of letting go of their boys. Still, the mothers had tears in their eyes and hugged the boys tightly for several moments. Jeanne whispered in MacArthur's ear, "Ya'll have some fun, ya heah? Don't study too hahd."

MacArthur squeezed her tight. "Don't worry, Mom. I will."

The fathers shook their sons' hands and took them aside for final words. The Colonel stared intently at MacArthur. "I have no

CHAPTER 21

doubt you will do well, Son. And I'll take good care of your car."

"Thanks, Dad. I wish I could keep it here."

"Take the time to get to know the campus. Plenty of time to venture out later."

"Yeah. It's cool."

He gave his son a hug and whispered in his ear, "And don't let your hair grow too long. That's an order."

They laughed, and soon the boys were waving at their mothers in the station wagon and their fathers in the Porsche as they left the parking lot. David cried, "Holy crap! Is that the old piece of junk you wrote me about? I guess I missed the Porsche part."

MacArthur nodded proudly. "Yep! And it's a beaut! I wish UVA allowed it. We'd have a blast."

"Yeah, that would've been so neat. Let's go back to the room and figure out our schedules."

"Good idea." MacArthur slapped him on the back. "Man, I can't believe you're here!"

The boys decided to go through fraternity rush, but they made it clear they came as a set. They did not preserve their friendship all these years to be separated in college. This, of course, had its challenges. David always found it hard to talk about himself, so answering question after question was trying. "Where're you from? Where'd you go to high school? What are your interests?" MacArthur, on the other hand, loved to talk about himself. To find a fraternity that liked both of them was difficult. There were only two houses that picked both of them in the last round, and they chose the one both of them liked.

CONVERSION

Dear Mom and Dad,

Well Mom, you told me to have fun, and that's what I'm doing. In fact, I have learned that when Playboy magazine judged all the colleges and universities on the best party schools, they said they were all amateurs compared to UVA — the professional party school! In other words, we know how to do it right!

Fraternity rush was a blast, and the parties are truly legendary — almost as good as yours, Mom — but a lot more rowdy. David and I pledged Phi Delta Theta, because we really like the guys.

As you know, UVA only has girls in the education and nursing schools, and David is dating a girl from the education school I don't like. I told him I didn't trust her, but he's continuing to go out with her, probably because she's incredibly pretty, so there's not much I can do except pray he sees the light. Or, if I'm wrong (and I don't think I am) that I'll see something different. I've met a couple of girls from there also that I really like and have had some dates. With no girls in our classes, we rely on the Phi Delt parties to meet them.

The antiwar types are getting more vocal, just like other universities. I'm glad I was in Thailand and got to know people like Lawan and Kau. I don't think these antiwar kids know why we're there. They just hate war — don't understand it — and some of them seem to hate our country too.

CHAPTER 21

David is the man on campus, and I'm kind of his buddy/mascot — ha! ha! He's on the football team, but I'm making a name for myself in intramural flag football. Mostly, I'm concentrating on my music. Which brings me to my big news — I've started a band! We're called The Decades. I play acoustic guitar and sing lead, my friend Jack is the drummer, Henry is our keyboard player, and Zaiah (short for Isaiah — he's from Jamaica) is amazing on electric guitar and sings harmony. Sometimes he plays dulcimer, which really adds a kick to the sound.

I'm taking guitar lessons at the music school and met these guys there. They're all music majors and great musicians, but I'm writing most of our songs. Jack is collaborating on some too. We're trying to figure out our sound and style. We're somewhere between rock and folk. AND, Phi Delt has hired us to play at their spring dance, so we must be doing something good!

Jack is a Christian and I've been going to church with him. The pastor is pretty good, but the music is great. No time for anything but Sunday service, though.

Don't worry, I'm studying too, and, as usual, doing a lot of reading on my own. I'm reading everything I can get my hands on about our founding fathers. I got the idea after staring at the statue of Jefferson at the Rotunda one day. I want to know exactly what they were thinking and what they saw America could become. Some of the stuff is really interesting! I'm amazed at how they talk about "Providence" all the time and obviously had a Christian view of mankind (humans being sinners and needing a Savior, I mean). I also want to see if they got something wrong, because I don't think we are becoming what they hoped we'd become.

David and I are looking forward to Thanksgiving. Who else will be there? Miss you!

    Love,
    MacArthur

22

Thanksgiving 1969 was tense for young men and their families in America, as President Nixon had announced he was reinstating the draft. Demonstrations against the USA's involvement in the Vietnam War were escalating, and before his death, Dr. King and other civil rights leaders had accused the military of purposely recruiting more blacks than whites. Thus, they devised a completely arbitrary method: a lottery. If a young man's birthday was picked out of the hat, he was called. This was a main topic of discussion at the Wells house, but David and MacArthur knew they would get a deferment as long as they were in college, so they weren't concerned.

David was grateful to be with MacArthur's family on Thanksgiving, but he was disappointed that Sarah was in Spain. She would come home for Christmas, when he would be with his family in Panama. He had never been able to shake his feelings for her, and the other girls he dated were an attempt to break free, because he couldn't see her in his future. He needed a woman who would light up a room and charm everyone in it to complement his shy nature. His parents had told him this. He was careful never to talk to them about Sarah. He was resigned to the fact that although she lit up a room for him, she was far too reserved — and religious. It could never work.

CONVERSION

The Colonel turned to David at the dinner table with a wry smile. "So David, MacArthur says he's having a good year. What do you say?"

David grinned. He knew exactly what to say. "Well, Sir, MacArthur has certainly been himself."

"Whoa! What happened?" asked Joanna.

"There is a political science professor who is notorious for expecting certain answers to his questions, and all of us comply because we want a good grade. So Mac stands up and proceeds to ream him out for it."

"No kidding?" asked Meg.

MacArthur shrugged his shoulders.

"What did you say?" asked Rebecca.

"Do tell! Do tell!" cried Joanna.

MacArthur smirked. "I said, 'You are convinced your position on this issue is right, and that is admirable; but it is not conducive to a good education for us.'" His sisters interrupted him with "ooooooo," and Lois peaked in to see what the commotion was about. MacArthur raised his eyebrows and continued, "I said, 'Unless you want UVA to be the College of No Knowledge,'" he waited until their outbursts stopped, "'you should be playing devil's advocate and encouraging a free discussion of all viewpoints. We are on a college campus that boasts statues of Jefferson and Plato, but we will get a bad grade if we don't agree with you.' Then I expounded on the opposite view of what I knew he believed."

"What was the issue?" asked Meg.

"Does it really mattah?" asked Jeanne. "Yo brothah would've

CHAPTER 22

taken an opposin' view just to make the point. An' good fo' ya, Son!"

"Way to go, Little Brother," said Joanna.

"Just like we taught you," smiled Rebecca.

"So what did the professor do? Did you get kicked out?" asked Meg.

"No! It was really hilarious. The guy actually laughed when I said, 'the College of No Knowledge'! He said his wife tells him the same thing. I mean, I was hugely impressed. Who even knew he had a sense of humor?"

"Yeah," David said. "You really lucked out with that one."

Back on campus, MacArthur and David joined their fraternity brothers in the TV room to watch the first two lotteries on December 1. Some upperclassmen were nervous and talking about going to Canada if their numbers were called. MacArthur turned to David. "You know, Dad suggested I join ROTC. Then, when I'm eligible for the draft, I'll be in a better position if I get a low number."

David shook his head. "Why? Just stay in college, do grad school or whatever to stay out of it."

It was true. He might obtain continuing deferments that way, but it didn't feel right. Still, he didn't want to get into another argument about the war, so he quipped, "No, I look too good in a uniform," and took a pose. David and the others began throwing pillows at him.

When Christmas finally rolled around, the Colonel saw to it that everyone in the Wells family was home, no excuses. He did

CONVERSION

this because Jeanne had been diagnosed with ovarian cancer. At Thanksgiving, she had told them she was having surgery the first of December. Nothing serious, just a routine hysterectomy. Even the doctors thought it routine until the biopsy report. After that, they did more tests, and then they scheduled exploratory surgery for the second week in January.

Being a strong military family and in good health, Jeanne's diagnosis was a shock. This was not the kind of challenge they usually faced. Meg, always the lawyer, ticked off the pertinent questions. Rebecca nearly cut off the blood flow to Craig's hand, squeezing it hard to remain composed. Sarah went to her mother, weeping, while Joanna hugged her father, who had maintained his military stoicism until then.

MacArthur was frightened and stunned. He stared at his mother and knew exactly what he had to do. Tears filled his eyes, and he took a deep breath. He had to tell her the truth one more time. He couldn't risk losing her for eternity.

It was several days before they were alone. His sisters had left reluctantly, especially Sarah, who wanted to stay and nurse her mother through the surgery. But in the end, Jeanne convinced them she did not want her illness to stop her children from pursuing their dreams.

The Colonel was at his office, and MacArthur was having lunch with his mother, when Lois caught his eye as she cleared their plates. She had been tearing up as she served the family during Christmas, but now she looked at him with a fire that said, "Tell her what I can't."

CHAPTER 22

"Mom," and he took her hand in his. "I know you think I've gone overboard with Jesus, but what if I haven't?" She looked intently at him and didn't say anything, so he continued. "Um," and he swallowed hard to remain composed, "I know I'm going to Heaven when I die. I mean, there is not a shred of doubt. And I want to know that whatever happens to you and me, we're going to be together forever."

"Ya know how ah feel, Sweethaht. Ya know ah don't believe that Heav'n or Hell stuff. Everybody goes inta the light an' finds out then. Ah don't think it's bad. Please, don't worry."

"But Jesus talked about Heaven and Hell. He said they were actual places. Are you really a Christian if you don't believe what Jesus said?"

"Hmm. Nevah thought of it that way."

"You want eternal life, don't you?"

"Well, doesn't everyone?" she smiled.

"It's so simple to get to Heaven. The Bible says that all you have to do is believe Jesus died for your sins and was raised from the dead—"

"Ya know I believe that."

"Yeah, and that's big. But then you have to completely surrender your life to him. Instead of just referring to him as *the* Lord, you make him *your* Lord, *your* Master. That's the part a lot of people have trouble with."

"Ah've heahd so many Christians use that as an excuse for theh bad behaviah. 'Gawd tole me ta do it!' Nevah set right with me."

"I know there are Christians who do that, but Mom, it's not

251

CONVERSION

about them. This is between you and Jesus. In the end, all that matters is: Is Jesus your Lord or do you choose to live your life without him?"

"Ah don't know…" He could see the doubt on her face.

"Mom, please," he pleaded, "don't let the mistakes of others keep you from knowing Jesus and knowing you will be with him — and me — forever." He dropped his head, no longer able to hold back his tears.

He covered her thin arms with his. He couldn't look at her. He knew he had said what he was supposed to say. All he could do now was pray softly in tongues and hope the seed planted would spring to life.

Jeanne recognized praying in tongues. Viola's people had done that. She remembered the comfort of Viola praying over her as a child and closed her eyes, soaking in her son's love and strength. What would become of her baby boy if she died? When she finally opened her eyes and looked at him, for the first time she saw the man. Then she saw someone else. She saw the Man who made him a man. MacArthur was going to be all right no matter what happened!

"Oh!" she gasped. "Jesus! Ah'm yours once an' fo' all."

MacArthur stopped praying and raised his head. "What?"

She sat straight, her tiny hands covering her heart. "Oh my! Ah feel so different…inside. Sorta free an' easy." She took his hands in hers. "And Son, I know that whateveh happens, we ah good."

Lois burst through the kitchen door, weeping. "Miss Wells, I've been prayin' for this for slong as I've been here. Praise the Lord and hallelujah!"

MacArthur returned to school knowing that his mother was

CHAPTER 22

okay. His heart was filled with hope that the healing of her spirit would bring healing to her body. Every day, he prayed for God to heal her.

MacArthur also returned to school in his Porsche. One of his Phi Delt brothers lived in a house near campus and had agreed to let MacArthur keep it there. Thus, not only was he known as David's best friend, but he was also the guy with the cool sports car.

> Dear MacArthur,
>
> I don't know what you said to your mother, but she is a different creature from the woman I married! At first, I thought it was good that she had a strong faith to see her through this illness, but she is saying things she would never say in her right mind. Only a crazy person tells people they need to give their lives to Jesus or they'll go to Hell!
>
> I've had upsetting calls from Joanna and Meg, and Lois and her crazy Bible study are only making it worse. I would fire her if she didn't do such an excellent job and your mother wasn't so attached to her.
>
> I blame you! You took advantage of your mother's weakened state and influenced her. Now she is embarrassing herself even with our friends. What were you thinking?
>
> Don't bother writing back to defend yourself. Just stop talking to her about it.
>
> Dad

CONVERSION

The first line caused MacArthur to chuckle because his mother was now his sister in the Lord, but his eyes stung with tears as he finished reading and folded the letter. He was late for band practice, so he jammed the letter in his pants pocket as he ran out the door.

After rehearsal, he handed the letter to Jack, who frowned and shrugged as he read. "This is the hard part. All we can do is pray for your dad and the rest of your family." He bowed his head. "Father, thank you for saving MacArthur's mom and for touching the rest of the family. And please give her strength to love her husband and be a witness for you. Thanks for putting Lois in her life too."

"Yes, Lord. Amen." MacArthur took the letter. "I don't know what I expected. I guess I thought my dad was the one who believed, that he was just quiet about it. Now I know, whew, that's not where he's at."

Jack smiled. "You really don't know how someone's going to react when you get serious about Jesus. I mean, do you know how many guys I've asked to go to church with me? You were the last guy I thought would ask if I knew a good church. Wow! That was a shocker!"

"Really?" MacArthur shook his head in disbelief. "I was kinda shocked a rocker like you said yes!"

"I just figured you were a frat party animal."

"And I thought you were a hippie."

They shook their heads in wonder.

"Well, thanks for praying for my family. I feel better. I'm ready to go out and party some more!" They laughed as MacArthur took his guitar and headed for the dorm. He had to hurry to get to the

CHAPTER 22

Phi Delt House for a meeting.

The Phi Delt House was the center of his and David's social activities. Of course, MacArthur did not tell his parents everything. There was beer in the vending machine and grain alcohol in every punch bowl. Cheap Sangria and bourbon were also favorites. It was not uncommon for girls to spend the night there, and those who were dating someone in the house were welcome anytime. David's girlfriend became one of their regulars. Then one night she came to a party with him and soon disappeared. He learned later that she had left with an upperclassman from another frat.

MacArthur stifled an "I told you so" and said, "Sorry, man. That sucks."

David must not have been too stuck on her, because he immediately started dating someone else. MacArthur liked this one better, but he still didn't believe she was the right one for him. He was praying for a Christian girl, who would shake him up.

Meanwhile, MacArthur had a steady girlfriend for the first time. He had been going to Jack's church for a month when he became captivated by one of the singers on the worship team, Sherilynn. He asked Jack to introduce him, and they felt an instant connection. She was living at home with her parents and working, while studying voice and piano. He loved her passion for truth, and they would have long discussions about the Bible. Some of the issues she raised were new to him, but examining their lives in the light of biblical principles was like water to his thirsty soul.

When they had gone out for several weeks, she introduced him to her family after church, and they asked him to join them

CONVERSION

for dinner. Sunday dinner with them became part of his weekly routine. By Thanksgiving, he realized he was madly in love with her, so when they returned to campus he suggested to David that they have a double date. It was time for her to meet his friends and family — and to be introduced to the Phi Delt House.

He prepared Sherilynn by telling her David and his girlfriend were atheists, and the Phi Delt house was like his mission field. He prepared David by telling him that Sherilynn was all about Jesus and spiritual things. He loved them both so much, it never occurred to him that they would hate each other.

They went to dinner and then back to the Phi Delt house for a party. The dinner went fine, as the girls wanted to hear the boys' stories about Panama. Then they went to the party and Sherilynn made a couple of cracks to David about his godless ways. This offended David's girlfriend, but MacArthur pulled Sherilynn away and said, "Let's dance."

Things didn't improve. "MacArthur, I'm not really comfortable dancing, especially to music that doesn't worship the Lord."

He stared at her. "I...never thought about this before."

"Really? It's all I think about, being a musician."

He listened to the lyrics of the song. "Ain't no mountain high enough...nothing can keep me...keep me from you." He laughed. "Well, you could hear this as nothing can keep me from God." He began to sing the refrain with the recording and point up as he danced, delighted with his new revelation of the song.

She tilted her head and rolled her eyes, unmoved, so he stopped and took her hand. They left the party, and that was the

CHAPTER 22

last one she attended with him. They proceeded to have a heated argument about some of the music his band was playing. She was challenging him again, but this time it hit a nerve. She believed that performing songs that didn't worship God was a sin. He asked her where that was in the Bible, and her answer was, "Sing unto the Lord a new song. The Psalm doesn't say to sing to the world what the world wants to hear."

When he got back to the dorm room, David wasn't there. MacArthur read through some of the psalms before turning off his light, then tossed and turned until David came in, stumbled across the floor, and fell on his bed. "I'm awake, so you can turn the light on if you want."

David flipped the switch on his desk light and sat up. "Where'd you go? We looked around and you were gone."

"Sherilynn wasn't feeling well, so we left."

"Look man, she's like…never gonna fit in at the frat. You know that, right?"

MacArthur sighed. "Yeah."

Now the shoe was on the other foot. David didn't like who MacArthur was dating, so they made a pact not to talk about it. MacArthur was in uncharted territory. He understood perfectly why David did not like Sherilynn. What he couldn't understand was Sherilynn's attitude toward David and his friends at the frat house. She continued to criticize them relentlessly: They drank and smoked and some slept around. They swore. And, how could MacArthur be best friends with an unbeliever? Even after he reminded her how David had saved his life, she remained hard-

CONVERSION

hearted toward him and treated all his friends coolly.

MacArthur decided to ask Jack about it. He was a country boy who had grown up in a Pentecostal Church like the one they were attending. "Why is Sherilynn so uptight about David? Honestly, I don't get it. If she had a good friend who wasn't saved, I'd try to be friends with her and lead her to Jesus."

"Well Bro, Sherilynn's really into purity right now. I mean, she sees everyone and everything in terms of how pure they are, because she doesn't want to get...uh, you know... corrupted or anything."

MacArthur scratched his head and frowned. "Are you saying she's got a perfect standard, and if you don't meet it, you're out?"

"Yep."

"Then why the hell is she going out with me?!"

Jack burst out laughing. "That's what I'm trying to figure out, Bro." He stopped. "Look Man, I love my Pentecostal background. Most of it is really good, but like all churches, you got problems. My kind tend to get so consumed with purity that they forget... excuse my words...they forget to smell their own crap."

"Whoa!!! Never heard that in church!"

"Well, there's purity and there's grace, and you got to know what applies to what."

From that time on, MacArthur became more and more aware that the preaching in their church centered on good behavior more than spiritual life. Reuben had always said that good behavior results from a close relationship with God, that people get it backwards when they make their good behavior the basis for their

CHAPTER 22

relationship with God. Now he understood what Reuben was talking about. He tried to discuss this with Sherilynn, but she just tousled his hair and said, "Honey, you are just too tolerant."

During Christmas break, they had talked often, even though MacArthur had to reimburse his parents for the long distance charges. Sherilynn was the first person he called after his mother gave her life to Jesus, then he called Reuben, who was back in Israel. The moment he heard, "*Shalom*," he smiled and his whole being relaxed.

"*Shalom*, Reuben. It's MacArthur! Long time no speak to."

He heard Reuben chuckle. "This is true, my friend. To what do I owe this great honor?"

"A miracle has happened! Mom made Yeshua her Lord yesterday!" There was only silence. "Reuben, did you hear me? Are you there?"

"Yes, my boy. I was thanking Abba. Please, tell me." And so MacArthur recounted everything that had transpired and how Lois was going to bring his mother to her Bible study, so he was confident she would be discipled and have a support group as she got over the cancer.

"What do the doctors say?"

"They're pretty negative, but now that she's saved, I'm sure she will get better."

"I pray so...I pray so. But whatever happens, we thank Yeshua that she is his. Now tell me, how is David? How is school?"

"Really great! I got all A's in my classes last semester, and David is eating up the Russian studies department. He loves it and is

CONVERSION

already pretty fluent in the language. He's still an atheist, but we put up with each other." He chuckled and took a deep breath. "And I'm dating an amazing Christian girl he doesn't like."

"Tell me about her."

"Well, she grew up in a Pentecostal church, and that's where I started going, where I met her. Oh! I forgot to tell you that I started a band. We're called The Decades. It's kind of a play on words for Jesus, who is the Alpha and Omega, beginning and the end, all time."

"Subtle."

"Yeah, and the drummer, Jack, is the one who asked me to this church — it's his church too — and introduced me to Sherilynn. That's her name. She's beautiful and has an amazing singing voice, and her whole world revolves around Jesus. I didn't realize how much I missed talking about the Bible until I started dating her."

"Ahhh. So you are in harmony."

"Ugh! I thought David's puns were bad! Yeah, I guess…I mean, she really wants me to quit The Decades. She's heavily into purity… but we do agree on the basics, and we pray together sometimes."

"I will be praying for both of you now." MacArthur heard some kind of commotion in the background. "I must go, dear boy. We will talk soon." And the line went dead. MacArthur wondered what "soon" meant.

One snowy Sunday in late February, Sherilynn suggested they go out to lunch instead of having dinner with her family. She was unusually quiet, and after they got in his car, she sat stiffly and gazed ahead as they waited for the car to warm up. "Look Mac,

CHAPTER 22

my whole life is about serving God and singing for the Lord. I get absolutely no pleasure from the world." She shook her head. "I just don't think we're on the same level spiritually. I mean, I really, really like you, but you're bringing me down." Her voice caught, and he reached for her hand, but she pulled it away.

His heart seized. "What are you saying? We believe the same things. We go to the same church. We both speak in tongues, for Pete's sake! I love your family and they seem to like me. I was going to introduce you to mine at spring break, when my mom is through with radiation and feeling better." He moved toward her, but she moved closer to her door.

She sighed, turned, and looked straight at him, tears in her eyes. "You're not the one for me, MacArthur. I know that. I guess I knew when you asked me to sing with your band. I mean, how could you even ask me that?"

"Is this about the band? You want me to quit the band?"

Now she was really crying. "No...it's more than just the band. It's everything. We're just not supposed to be together. I'm sorry, Mac. I don't want to hurt you, but we'll both get hurt more if we keep seeing each other." She got out of the car. "Sorry." She shut the door and walked away.

He didn't move, sitting in the car for a long time, in limbo. Finally, he put the car in gear and drove around aimlessly, wondering what had just happened. *Is she right, Father? Are we not supposed to be together? What an idiot! I didn't even ask you! I just assumed she was the one because everything was so great — well, almost everything. Maybe she's right. I'm not as spiritual as she is. Oh God!*

CONVERSION

What's the matter with me? It was long after dark when he walked into his dorm room, fell on his bed, and closed his eyes. The warmth of his coat was like a cocoon, and he soon escaped into a dreamless sleep.

He awoke with a start and glanced at his clock. It was after midnight. He winced when he remembered Sherilynn's words. His heart ached, and he began to weep. He would have to tell David. *Oh God, I'm one of those crazy Christians my mom was talking about! Please, don't let my stupidity give David another excuse to reject you!*

David opened their door and said, "Where've you been, man? I've been looking all over for you."

He stared at the ceiling. "Well, if you must know, Sherilynn broke up with me."

David sat at the foot of his bed. "Oh man. I'm so sorry. God!" His head dropped into his hands.

MacArthur knew David couldn't be upset about the breakup, so he sat up and faced him. "What's wrong?"

David put his hand on MacArthur's knee. "Look man, I don't know how to tell you this, so I'm just going to say it, okay?"

"Okay...."

"Your dad called about four hours ago. Your mom died."

MacArthur's ears began to ring. Surely he hadn't heard what he thought he had heard. He whispered, "What did you say?"

"Your mom died this afternoon. Your dad said it was sudden, even though they knew she was never going to get well."

MacArthur nearly jumped off the bed. "How could he say that! She *was* getting better! I talked to her just a few days ago! This can't

CHAPTER 22

be right! Why are you telling me this? Is this some kind of a sick joke?" His voice had a bite to it David had never heard.

"I'm sorry, Mac. I'm really sorry. But it's true." He stood to comfort him, but MacArthur ran out of the room. David felt helpless and collapsed on his bed. As soon as he returned, they would make plans.

MacArthur ran out of the dorm and continued to run until he had left the campus. When he had no more breath to run, he collapsed in the middle of a field, sobbing. *Why God? Why? She was yours! You could have healed her! I know it! And now she's dead. Dead!* He pounded his fists into the snow until they were raw. He seethed, *What does that say to David, to my sisters or my dad? What does that tell them about you? She stood up for you! She told everyone about you! And you let her die!*

Exhausted, he closed his eyes, and a bitterly cold darkness crept in around him.

23

Someone shook him. He looked up and saw a policeman leaning over him. "Wake up, kid. The party's over. Time to go home."

MacArthur took the man's hand and winced. His hands stung and he grimaced in pain as he flexed his near frostbit fingers. "What time is it?" He looked around, trying to locate himself in the dark. *What am I doing in this field?*

"Time to rise and shine, kid. Are you okay? Where do you live?"

"Um. The first-year dorm, UVA." His stomach growled, and he felt the hole in his heart that used to be occupied by his love for Sherilynn, for his mother. The ringing in his ears returned, chiming, "The good Christian girl ditched you. You're not good enough. God let your mother die because you're not good enough. Not good enough!" His life was a bizarre joke.

The officer patted his shoulder. "Come on. I'll give you a ride back."

He tried shaking his head to stop the ringing as he walked to the squad car. *Think. Okay. I need to call Dad and get home. Yes. That's what I'll do.* He kept putting one foot in front of the other.

When they were in the squad car, the policeman asked, "What were you doing out there, anyway?"

He sought for an answer that would stop the questions. "Uh…I

CONVERSION

don't know. I like to run when no one's around, and I ran until I got tired…um…so I just stopped to rest, and I must've fallen asleep. Kinda dumb, huh?"

"Oh, I've heard crazier than that."

The officer didn't ask any more questions, but he walked MacArthur to the door of his dorm room.

"Thanks, officer."

"Be safe, kid."

David was waiting for him inside. "My God. I know you're going through hell right now, but do you have any idea what you put me through last night?"

"I'm sorry. I've got to call my dad."

"No you don't, because I've been talking to him all night. At five this morning he said to tell you to come home as soon as possible. He was sure you were all right. I guess that's his CIA sense or something, because I didn't have a clue and couldn't find you."

"Sorry. I just ran…until I…." He dropped on his bed. "I need to get a shower and pack."

"I'm going with you."

MacArthur noticed one of David's suitcases was open on his bed. He wanted to hug him, but he knew he would burst into tears, so he sniffed and muttered a quick thanks. When he returned from the bathroom, David was gone. He dressed slowly, and as he tucked his shirt into his pants, there was a knock at the door.

It was Jack, who came in and hugged him. "I'm sorry, Bro, about everything." MacArthur disengaged and looked at him blankly. Jack had tears in his eyes. "Sherilynn called me. Then

CHAPTER 23

David called me. Wow, what a double-whammy. What can I do?"

"Nothing." He pulled a suitcase from under his bed. "I'm going home. Don't know when I'll be back. Tell the guys, okay?"

"Sure."

He watched MacArthur throw underwear and socks into his suitcase.

David walked in and shook Jack's hand. "Hi Jack. Thanks for coming."

"No problem, man." Jack turned back to MacArthur. "Is there anything I can do for you?"

"Find me a new church?" Jack's expression made him regret his sarcasm. "Sorry. No. Thanks for asking." He haphazardly folded shirts and pants and threw them in the suitcase.

Jack patted him on the shoulder. "Everyone at the church will be praying for you and your family, Bro."

MacArthur tensed. "Thanks. I'll see you when I get back." He refused to look at him.

"Okay. Bye." After Jack was clear of the dorm, he sighed. "God, help him." Not knowing what else to do, he prayed. He sensed a rough road ahead, but MacArthur was eventually going to be okay. In the days to come, he would hold on to this moment.

MacArthur and David carried their suitcases to the Porsche, which David had retrieved from their fraternity brother's house. "I'll drive, since I got a nice nap in the wilderness," said MacArthur sarcastically.

"Fine with me. I'm beat." David was so tired, he disregarded the edge in MacArthur's voice and fell right to sleep.

CONVERSION

About two hours later, he heard, "Wake up, David. We're here."

David stretched and yawned as they pulled into the driveway. No one came running out to meet them. They carried their suitcases into the house, which was quiet. "Where is everyone?"

Lois came through the kitchen door and burst into tears when she saw MacArthur. She hugged him tightly and said, "She went so peaceful...a smile on her face. An' now she has no pain...jest the best party she's ever been to!"

MacArthur forced a smile and nodded. "Where is everyone?"

"No one but you are here yet. The Colonel's at the funeral home, making arrangements. He's hardly had time to think, calling people. You know your mama. She expects a big send off!" She blew her nose.

MacArthur nodded again.

"Hi Lois," David extended his hand. "Sorry you're going through all this."

She took his hand and pulled him into a hug. "Your being here is so good. Are you boys hungry? I got pancakes, eggs, bacon, the works."

"Yes Ma'am. I'll take the works!" said David.

MacArthur turned toward the stairs. "We'll put our stuff away and be right down."

By the time they returned, the smells from Lois' cooking had ignited MacArthur's hunger, and he realized he hadn't eaten since breakfast the day before. As they devoured the food, the Colonel came in, eyes red. He shook David's hand, but hugged MacArthur tightly. "Glad you're home, Son." He didn't mention MacArthur's

CHAPTER 23

absence the previous night.

"What can I gitcha, Colonel?" asked Lois.

"Oh, just pile what they've got on a plate for me." He took his place at the table.

"Good. You need to keep your strength up for those girls. All you."

David perked up. "Uh…when are the girls coming in?"

The Colonel answered. "Joanna, Rebecca and Craig, and Meg are arriving at National on different flights, all about dinner time. They're going to meet up and take cabs. Sarah is not getting to Dulles until early tomorrow morning. She was pretty upset about how long it'll take her." It helped to talk about his children. He didn't feel so abandoned.

"I'll pick her up, Sir, if that would help." David glanced at MacArthur, expecting a "look," but MacArthur stared blankly, slowly chewing his food.

"Thank you, Son. Her flight arrives at 6 a.m. You can take the station wagon. Not sure how much luggage she'll have, and the Porsche may not have enough room." Lois put his plate down with a glass of orange juice. "Thanks."

"You're welcome. You boys let me know if you need anything else."

The Colonel took a sip of juice and cleared his throat. "The announcement will be in all the papers. Your mother would want the world to know." He took a bite of eggs, and they ate quietly. Forcing himself to eat was a habit he had formed long ago, but this time it was much harder. "The wake is Thursday and the funeral

CONVERSION

Friday. That will give people time to get here."

David said, "I talked to my parents last night. They're coming Thursday and leaving Saturday and will stay at a hotel. They know you'll have a lot of people here. Uh…if it's okay with you and Mac, I'd like to stay here to help."

"Fine with me, Son. Lot to do," said the Colonel.

He looked at MacArthur, who nodded.

It was a series of events that all concerned were sure made Jeanne Talley Wells dance through those pearly gates with joy. Tears and laughter flowed simultaneously as friends and family shared their favorite memories. And no one seemed to mind when Viola's family and others from the black community showed up and told a few stories of their own. In fact, many thought it a great tribute to this greatly loved woman.

The government told the family to choose a headstone for the Colonel and his wife at Arlington Cemetery, which was expected. What no one anticipated was that it was placed in the VIP section where President Kennedy was buried and the eternal flame burned. They chose a small but exquisite marble stone, and Joanna said, "It's little and cute, like Mom."

Because of the placement of the grave, *The Washington Post* published a half-page obituary about Jeanne Talley Wells. They wrote, "She championed women Republican voters of all races, first in Mississippi, which showed great courage, then in Virginia, and finally nationwide. She supported Dr. Martin Luther King Jr. and campaigned passionately for equal rights for all. Ms. Wells received full military honors, and the army chaplain offered a moving

CHAPTER 23

eulogy for a woman who had the heart of a reformer."

Jeanne's children thought she was buried in such a prestigious place because of their father's service, but he read her obituary out loud and set them straight. "Your mother," he said, "was the reason I could do my duty. I knew that whatever happened to me, she would be here to take care of all of you, that you would be all right. I also knew she would take action on issues I couldn't. It's only fitting that she would be so honored. And I'm sure she got a kick out of the fanfare!"

MacArthur was unusually subdued during the proceedings. He was happy to see Chuck and John and some of the others who had been with his father in Thailand. Reuben was unable to come, but he called and talked to both the Colonel and MacArthur. MacArthur only spoke with him for a few minutes and then promised to call him collect when he could talk longer.

David stayed by MacArthur's side except for picking up Sarah and spending one afternoon with his parents. He confided in them that he was worried about him. Mama asked, "How would you be if I passed? Eh?"

"I would be a wreck." He frowned.

"Si! You cannot expect MacArthur to be okay. He will need time to find a way to live without her in his life."

"Yes, Son. Just be his friend. Eventually, he'll come 'round and be his old, *mischievous* self."

There was a highlight for David, of course, when he saw Sarah emerge from the airline terminal. He jumped out of the station wagon and ran to help her. "Oh! David. I thought Dad…well, you know."

CONVERSION

"No...sorry... just me." He felt his face burning red as he took her bag.

"Thanks."

He put the bag in the back of the station wagon and took a deep breath. *Get a grip!* Then he ran to open her door, but she was already in the car; so he closed the door and ran around to slide into the driver's seat. "Did you have a good flight...or flights?"

"It was exhausting, and of course, I cried most of the way, but the stewardesses were so nice. I should never have gone back to Spain. I should have stayed home and...." Her voice caught. She took a handkerchief from her purse.

He drew a complete blank and panicked. *Oh no! I hate this! What do I do?* "Well...um...I don't know...it's a tough situation." *A tough situation! Good God!*

"Yeah." She blew her nose. "Um...how are you? How do you like UVA?"

"Oh, it's great. I'm on the basketball team and am learning to speak Russian. That's kinda cool."

She turned to stare at him. "That's more than cool. It's completely crazy. You're learning the language of our enemy."

For the first time, he glanced at her and almost could not turn his attention back to the road ahead of him. *Those eyes! Even crying, she's more beautiful than I remember!* He panicked again. *I have to say something!* "Um...well..."

"I mean, what are you going to do? Become a spy?" She giggled.

"No! I don't know. Um...I just...I've always been interested

CHAPTER 23

in Russia and thought it would be fun to learn the language. My parents think it's crazy too. I mean, we left Cuba to escape communism, and Russia sponsored Castro. Well…you know."

He glanced at her again. She was smiling. *Am I actually interesting to her?*

Sarah began to speak to him in Spanish, which would be translated: "Well, you won't be happy if you don't do what makes you happy. At least, that's what I believe. Actually, it's what Mom used to say all the time."

He answered her in Spanish without thinking, remembering her mother's warmth and charm. His heart ached for her and the family. "Wait!" He spoke in English and did a double-take. "We're speaking Spanish."

She giggled again, answering him in Spanish: "Silly. What do you think I've been doing in Spain? I started learning Spanish in Panama, so, how am I doing?"

He continued in Spanish: "You're doing fine. I didn't even notice…I mean…it was like being at home and going from Spanish to English with my parents." *This is terrible! The fantasy can't become real. Ugh!!!* He tapped his hand on the steering wheel.

"Gracias, David. That means a lot, coming from you."

Oh man! I wanted this, but I was hoping it would never happen. He wanted to force himself to answer in English, but it was just too wonderful to speak to her in his native tongue. He asked her what she did in Spain, other than speak Spanish, and she smiled. He had asked the right question, because she loved the nursing school in Madrid. "The staff and all of my teachers at

273

CONVERSION

Hospital Cruz Roja are wonderful...."

David's mind raced. *Oh God! I'm a goner. How am I ever going to forget her now?*

As it turned out, it was not difficult to relegate Sarah to the back of his mind after he returned to school with MacArthur. He had missed practices and one game, so he worked hard to get back in sync with the basketball team, even though he didn't play often. His girlfriend had found someone else while he was away, so instead of pining over Sarah, he scanned the landscape for what he really needed. He settled on a brunette he had met at a frat party. She was pretty, outgoing, and popular.

What distracted David most, however, was MacArthur's behavior. In McLean, he noticed that he wasn't reading his Bible every morning or praying at night. When he asked him about it, MacArthur said, "Oh, I forgot." When they returned to school, he never saw MacArthur reading anything but a textbook, nor was he going to church. Normally, this withdrawal from all things religious would have thrilled him, but his friend's goofy grin had disappeared. He was sullen and secretive, and when he did speak to David or anyone else, there was a bitter tone in his voice.

All these years David had hoped his friend would grow out of his religious superstitions, but he never wanted the light in him to go out. One day he ran into Jack as he was leaving their dorm room. He looked troubled and nodded hello as MacArthur yelled after him, "Look, don't worry about me! I'm fine! I'm just too busy to find another church right now!"

David found himself grieving his friend as his friend grieved his

CHAPTER 23

mother. He constantly reminded himself of his own mother and father's words, which sustained his belief that MacArthur would eventually snap out of it. He was glad the fraternity's big spring dance was coming up. The Decades were rehearsing a lot, which always lifted MacArthur's spirits.

The spring dance was a smashing success, largely because of The Decades. Everyone was talking about them, and they received invitations to play at different functions across campus. More and more, MacArthur spent his free time studying or with the band. Sometimes he came home late, often drunk, and sometimes he didn't come back to the dorm at all. David told himself there was no reason to be alarmed. MacArthur was finally having fun and letting loose.

Then the universe decided that their world had not been turned upside down enough. On Monday, May 4, he and David were eating pizza and watching the ten o'clock news on their small, black-and-white television set. "Police opened fire on 500 students and four students were killed on the Kent State campus in Ohio today...."

"Holy shit!" They both said at the same time and looked at each other, shaking their heads in disbelief as they listened to the news account. Not long after, a couple of frat brothers knocked on their door. "Guys, you gotta come. We're protesting, man!"

When they arrived at the Rotunda, students were streaming in, and some were trying to speak above the crowd. They accused the university of racism and gender inequality, decrying segregation and the fact that women were not allowed to attend UVA as

CONVERSION

undergraduates except in the nursing and education schools. Others were calling for an immediate end to the Vietnam War. Hundreds crammed the area, joining in protest. After a while, some marched to the president's home, while over two hundred broke into Maury Hall, the Naval ROTC building, and refused to leave. MacArthur, David, and their friends ran to see what was happening.

By the time they got there, the police were commanding the students to leave the building, which they refused to do. Then someone told David they were getting an injunction from the court, which came early that morning. The leader of the protesters decreed that they had made their point and did not think getting their heads bashed in would add to it, so they left the building peacefully.

Word spread quickly that no one should attend classes as a sign of protest, and David and MacArthur joined almost a thousand students in Old Cabell Hall to honor the fallen students of Kent State. The next day, William Kunstler, who had defended the Chicago Seven, and Jerry Rubin, social activist and antiwar leader, arrived to speak on the Rotunda. They incited the crowd to march again to the president's house and shout, "Burn it down!" David and MacArthur watched in horror until one of the campus leaders stepped up and took the megaphone. He said they had the wrong target for the antiwar effort. They should go back to Maury Hall and take the ROTC building again.

"He's trying to keep them from killing President Shannon," murmured MacArthur.

"And burning the mansion," said David.

CHAPTER 23

As they followed the noisy mob to Maury Hall, David yelled, "Mac, I'm having déjà vu!"

MacArthur had a grim expression on his face. "Panama 1964!"

"Only there's no Colonel Wells to stop this!"

MacArthur bristled at the mention of his father, remembering the dreadful letter he had written just weeks before his mother's death. "Did he really stop anything? As far as I'm concerned, the world's gotten worse on his watch!"

David almost stumbled. The MacArthur he had grown up with would never have said this. "Well, let's hope this doesn't go that far!"

When they got to Maury Hall, the protesters had occupied the building again. They heard a lot of damage being done inside, and then smoke poured from the windows. They found out later that the mob had lit a mattress on fire to carry out their threats of "Burn it down!" However, the mattress just produced a lot of smoke, which caused them to flee the building.

Protests and demonstrations continued throughout the week, and on Friday, the state police had had enough. They scaled the university walls and turned on the students and anyone near them with billy clubs. They arrested 68 students and bystanders (one turned out to be a pizza delivery man) and put them in a Mayflower moving van. None were charged and all were released, but now police occupied the campus. This only increased the students' anger.

MacArthur joined the outrage at the overreaction of the police and began to listen to David and other antiwar protesters with

CONVERSION

new ears. The sting of his father's letter, Sherilynn's rejection, and his mother's unexpected death informed him that the authorities in which he had faith were not to be trusted. If you were foolish enough to do so, you would be severely hurt. And so, he found solace in rebellion and wanton pleasure, his dream of changing the world replaced with a hedonistic vengeance to destroy all that was deemed good by the "establishment."

Although the campus calmed down, classes were cancelled. Students could take their final exams or accept their midterm grade as their final grade. Meanwhile, The Decades took advantage of the campus fervor to play as much as possible on the Lawn, and their popularity grew.

Before they knew it, David and MacArthur were moving out of the dorm and saying goodbye for the summer. David returned to Panama to work for a friend of his father in a large corporation, but MacArthur stayed near campus. He had no desire to go home and instead booked paying gigs for The Decades through most of the summer. They rented an old house in Charlottesville, and the band and a few other friends stayed there. Jack and the other band members knew MacArthur was slipping into a dark place, and they sought for a way to pull him out.

Whenever MacArthur thought about his mother, he discovered that alcohol dulled the pain. Smoking marijuana was even better. Occasionally, someone would offer him a snort of coke, which was a new and exhilarating experience, and speed was great to get you through a tough day. His own band members were not as interested in getting high or escaping, just drinking and smoking a

CHAPTER 23

little pot from time to time. Jack graciously bore their mockery for being the sober, designated driver.

Because of The Decade's schedule, the only time MacArthur saw his family that summer was the last week of July, during their summer vacation. He dropped in for a couple of days during the week, because the band had gigs every weekend.

His family was shocked when they saw him. Thinner and pale, his hair was past his shoulders and uncombed. He said his fingernails were long to play guitar. His jeans and sandals were worn, and he sported T-shirts with peace symbols and antiwar slogans on them. Craig saw him and laughed, thinking it was a joke, and called him the family hippie. He retorted, "I'm being true to myself, man."

Joanna tried to reason with him as they played a round of tennis. "What has happened to you? Your game is terrible. Are you getting any exercise? What are you eating, anyway?" He was so high, he didn't care that she was grilling him. He just laughed and told her he was fine.

She immediately found the Colonel. "Dad, this is worse than the Jesus stuff. At least then we could have a reasonable conversation and just disagree. But he is…I don't know…like in another world, and it isn't a good one. He reminds me of the kids on drugs. Oh God! I hope that's not what this is."

The Colonel hid his own anxiety. "Look, Sweetheart, I'll talk to him. It's probably just a phase he's going through, the same way he went through the Jesus thing. Don't worry about it. I'll take care of it."

CONVERSION

She hugged him. "Thanks, Dad. I've got to meet Meg. We're going on a nature hike so I can show her what I've learned. You want to come?"

"No thanks. I'll see you at dinner."

As he watched her jog away, he steeled himself. Life was hard enough when he had Jeanne to share it, but it was unbearable without her. In every situation with his children, he would turn to ask her what she thought or expect to hear her telling him what to do. Sometimes he thought he actually heard her say something. He walked to MacArthur's room and saw him strumming his guitar. He adopted a lighthearted manner and chuckled, "You know, Son, when I told you not to grow your hair too long, I think you misunderstood me."

MacArthur didn't laugh. He continued playing his guitar and answered, "What difference does it make? I mean, all the great bands have long hair. And I'm making good money. People love us. We're booked through the summer, and not just in Charlottesville. You should be proud of me."

"I am proud of you. I always have been. But frankly, I'm also worried. You don't look good, Son, and it isn't just the long hair. You don't look healthy. I hate to ask, but are you using any drugs?"

MacArthur stopped. "What? You have no idea what you're talking about! Not all drugs are bad for you. Some really help you understand yourself and life. I mean, besides sex, being high is like the coolest thing I've ever experienced."

"Sex? Getting high? Have you lost your mind? What drugs are you taking?"

CHAPTER 23

"This conversation is going nowhere." He put his guitar down and got up to leave, but his father pushed him back into his chair.

"You're not going anywhere until you tell me what drugs you're taking."

Whatever had not snapped in MacArthur's frayed emotional state exploded when his behind hit the chair. The father he loved and admired had disappeared into a sinister image of "the Colonel," the perfect symbol of the establishment and everything that was wrong in the country. He raged inside, knowing *this* man had ways to make him talk. *Let him try!* He leaned forward, his eyes like ice. "None…of…your…business."

The Colonel backed up, as though he had been slapped. He had seen this expression on the faces of the worst of humanity. It was a shock to see it on his son's. Instinctively, he came to attention. "Okay. If your life is none of my business, then you pay for it." He slammed the door as he left.

MacArthur spat on the floor where his father had stood. *Mom would never have let him do this! I'm done with him.* He grabbed his guitar, threw his few belongings in his car, and sped back to Charlottesville. *I'll show him. I don't need him or his money! I'll call Jimmy and make a million!*

24

The first of August, just before their second year began, MacArthur and David moved into a two-bedroom apartment near campus. MacArthur didn't tell David that his father had cut him off financially, but David observed that MacArthur had more money than usual and was impressed with how well The Decades had done during the summer. What alarmed him was MacArthur's appearance. David didn't like the hippie drug scene, and MacArthur looked gaunt and messed up, a sharp contrast to the healthy look he had maintained since Thailand.

The good news was that last semester's protests had accomplished one of their objectives. The University of Virginia had enrolled 350 undergrad women for the 1970-71 year. Rumor was that they had all graduated at the top of their classes. David was going to use this as an excuse to say, "Look man, you better clean yourself up if you want to get a date with any of *these* women." But before he could say anything, MacArthur cut his hair for ROTC and went back to wearing his preppie clothes for fraternity rush.

What David didn't know was that MacArthur was playing a role to mask his new life. Jimmy didn't want MacArthur to sell drugs; he wanted him to be the clean-cut, ROTC preppie he had always been. That made him the perfect courier. No cop would suspect him as he transported drugs from town to town and region to region.

CONVERSION

"Listen, kid. This is an all-expense-paid deal, and as long as you stay sober and show respect, you can...you know...dip into the shit yourself from time to time. We'll give you a car that won't draw attention. Only smartasses drive a Porsche." To MacArthur, this was the answer to all his problems. Free pot and pills when he wanted them, plus an income that covered far more than his expenses.

David wasn't suspicious about MacArthur's regular trips away from campus, because many of them were band gigs. Jimmy drew up a schedule to coincide with the gigs, but there were others that MacArthur covered by saying he and his new girlfriend, Jessica, were going away for the weekend. He had met her, ironically, through the ROTC drills early in the fall semester. Hit in the face by a huge, rotten tomato, he wiped the putrid mess from his face and saw her laughing, pointing at him, and yelling, "Take that, pig!" As he continued the drill, he couldn't turn his eyes away from her. She was short, slim, and blonde — just his type.

The next day, he realized she was in one of his classes, and the following day he asked her out. To his amazement, she said yes. Halfway through the semester, he had stopped having sex with anyone but her, even with the band's groupies. He also made her his partner in the drug business, discovering that she relished the idea of beating the system, having wild, drug-enhanced weekends — and making lots of money.

Jessica was not at all like Sherilynn. To her, anyone who had a brain was in charge of their lives and didn't need a god to tell them what to do. His frat brothers loved her. The band members, for the most part, tolerated her. Jack and MacArthur didn't write songs

CHAPTER 24

anymore; in fact, MacArthur didn't write anything the entire year. The Decades only played what well-known bands were playing and some favorites MacArthur and Jack had written the previous year.

David was busy with a hard academic schedule and sports. From time to time, he would become aware of an undercurrent of "something's not right" in his gut, but he was having too much fun with MacArthur to ponder his instincts. They joked and laughed like old times, regaling each other with their sexual escapades and general hijinks at the fraternity to ease the pressures of academia. Obviously, MacArthur had thrown off his Christian superstitions and was enjoying himself. Their friends thought it hilarious that he was still in ROTC. MacArthur often mocked the military and told wild stories of pranking his unit. It was his way of sticking it to the "man."

Altogether, David was having a fairly good year except for one fly in the ointment: Sarah was back on the UVA campus for her fourth year in nursing. He rarely saw her, but when he did, they would smile and sometimes stop and say a few awkward words (on his part). He was surprised when, a few days after spring break, she called and asked him to come to the house she was renting with three other nursing students. She needed to talk to him about something without MacArthur knowing. When he got there, she took him into a small sitting room. "Thanks for coming, David. Please, sit down. Can I get you something to drink?"

"No thanks." He removed his coat and walked over to sit in an old, high-back chair.

She closed the door and sank into a rocking chair facing

him. To his delight, she chose to speak in Spanish. "I'm worried about MacArthur. The whole family is. He didn't come home at Thanksgiving, and at Christmas only for a couple of days. Then, when I was home for spring break, I found out Dad had cut him off financially, that he hasn't given him one cent this year."

David looked stunned. "This whole year?"

"Yes."

He had to look away from her to think. "He didn't tell me." Memories raced through his head. "Um, I know Thanksgiving his band was playing somewhere. He said Christmas was fine, that he wished he could've stayed longer—"

"That's what's so bizarre. At Christmas he acted like everything was okay. He talked about his classes and his new girlfriend but… he and Dad never…I don't think they even had eye contact. Oh, and he avoided Lois, and they used to be thick as thieves."

"How did you find out he'd been cut off?"

"It was just Dad and me spring break. Everyone else had something going on. I asked him if there was something wrong between him and MacArthur." She stopped, looked out the window, and took a deep breath. "That's when he told me about cutting him off."

"What happened between them? Mac's never let on that there was anything wrong." He flashed back to the times MacArthur had made caustic comments about his dad and the military, but he had thought that was because he had finally seen the light about the war.

"Last July, during our family vacation, MacArthur looked awful,

CHAPTER 24

like he was sick. Dad asked him if he was using drugs. I guess MacArthur told him it was none of his business; so, you know the Colonel. 'Okay, if it's none of my business, no more money' or something like that." She looked down at her hands, which were clasped tightly.

David scanned the last year in his mind. *Shit! Mac has too much money if he's been cut off. His band doesn't bring in that much, and it has to be divided between them. I know he's been doing some drugs, but he's got to be dealing. And does Jessica know? Oh God! Maybe she got him into this.* He took a deep breath and tried to stay calm. "Look Sarah. I'm not sure what Mac is into, but I can see why you're worried."

"Can you talk to him? I mean, you probably know him better than we do, and I know he respects you."

"I'll try, but I don't know, he just seems so happy, like his old self." The minute he said this, he knew it was a lie. MacArthur had not been himself since his mother died. As much as David had disagreed with him on so many issues through the years, he knew the real MacArthur. This MacArthur was like a distortion of the person he had always known. Something was wrong.

"I'm at my wits end trying not to think the worst. And, well, all of us are still reeling from—" she winced and turned away.

He wanted so badly to take her in his arms and make her forget everything, make them both forget everything. It took all his resolve to stay in his seat. "Yeah. I know. I'm sorry. Um, I'll talk to him. I promise." He stood to go.

She jumped up to give him a brief hug, and his knees nearly

buckled. "Thank you so much, David. Anything you can do would be super." She burst out laughing. "Superman."

He shook his head and laughed half-heartedly. "Oh no! Don't call me that, please!" Hearing the name made him feel sad. MacArthur hadn't called him that in a long time.

He opened the door for her. She said, "Thanks. Um…will you let me know what happens, what he says?"

"Sure. I'll call you. It might take some time, though. Got two more basketball games."

"Sorry it hasn't been a very good season."

"Yeah…well….thanks for not saying we stink."

Her smile of gratitude stayed with him all week as he contemplated how to find out what MacArthur was doing. He decided to follow him. It wasn't difficult, because MacArthur lived in the moment and was always looking forward. He moved from one place to another with no thought to the trail left behind him.

And so David became the spy Sarah had jokingly accused him of being over a year ago. Every weekend MacArthur and Jessica went away, he borrowed someone's car and followed them. Each time, they drove to an old farm house outside Charlottesville and got into a Buick sedan with their luggage, which consisted of MacArthur's duffel and Jessica's big, grey suitcase. Sometimes, MacArthur took the suitcase into the house before putting it in the trunk of the Buick. Then they drove to another city and checked into a nice hotel. On Sunday they drove back to the farmhouse, took their bags into the house, then brought them out and put them in the Porsche.

CHAPTER 24

He tried to reason out of his worst fears. Maybe Jessica had a friend who loaned them the Buick so MacArthur wouldn't have to put a lot of miles on the Porsche. After all, it was old. But taking their bags into the house before loading them in the Porsche pointed to being a drug courier.

David tried to get MacArthur to discuss his weekends. He talked about where they went (not always where David saw them go). He never mentioned switching cars. After he had observed two identical weekends, David resolved that he had to find out what was going on in the farmhouse.

The following Saturday morning, he heard MacArthur slam down the phone in their kitchen and throw his overnight duffle on the floor. David was studying for a test and didn't want to stop, but he came out of his room. "What's wrong?"

"Jessica and I were going away this weekend and now she's backed out."

David saw the opportunity. "Hey, *I'll* go with you. The weather's great and we could do some hiking, camp out, maybe get in some shooting, like old times."

For a second, MacArthur looked like someone had just doused him with a bucket of icy water. But just as quickly, his expression changed. He smiled and shook his head no. "Yeah man, that's a great idea, but I really need to get away by myself and think. Um…, like…things are really strained with Jessica and me right now. I have to figure out what to do. You know how it is."

David tried again. "Oh. That's tough, but honestly, getting away sounds good to me too. Are you sure you don't need someone to

289

CONVERSION

bounce ideas off of?"

MacArthur grabbed his overnight duffle and was almost running to the door. "Thanks man. I appreciate it, but I really need to be alone."

David immediately called a friend to borrow his car. He ran as fast as he could to get it and sped to the farm house, parking far enough away so that he could see the Porsche arrive and the sedan leave. He followed at a distance, like always, and they ended up in Baltimore, at a Holiday Inn. There were enough people in the lobby so David could follow MacArthur inside. He was careful to stay out of MacArthur's line-of-sight and lingered by the table that offered free coffee. He overheard the concierge say, "Mr. Smith, you are in room 206."

When MacArthur got in the elevator, David ran up the stairs. On the second floor, he peeked out the exit door and was relieved that room 206 was almost across from the elevator, just two doors away from the stairway. He kept the door open a crack and heard MacArthur get out of the elevator and open the door. About an hour later, someone got off the elevator and knocked at the door. He had a large grey suitcase.

David cracked the stairway door and saw MacArthur at his door. A portly man entered the room barking, "Where's the broad?"

"She couldn't come. Just give me…" and the door shut.

A few minutes later, the same rough-looking man came out of the room. After he got on the elevator, David pondered what to do. He decided to wait and watch, so he wedged the stairway door open with his hat and hunkered down. Other than ordering room

CHAPTER 24

service, MacArthur stayed in the room all night.

The next morning, David awoke hearing MacArthur come out of his room. As soon as he heard the elevator doors closing, David grabbed his hat and ran down the stairs. He reached the lobby and ducked out the side door to the parking lot.

MacArthur came out of the hotel carrying his duffle and the large grey bag. So it wasn't Jessica's suitcase. Knowing she was a real clothes diva, David had assumed it was hers. Maybe this was why MacArthur was so angry she couldn't come. No one would think twice about a young woman having a large suitcase.

He followed MacArthur back to the farm house, staying well behind. After the sedan had turned onto the driveway, David drove past it and parked farther down the road, then doubled back on foot. By the time he had the house in view, MacArthur was carrying the large bag inside. David kept low and crept through the woods at the back of the house until he was near a large window. He heard MacArthur yelling, "…this handled!"

"You better, or we'll handle it for you." A man's voice. Low and grim. Not the same as the man at the hotel.

MacArthur: "Look Jimmy, I'm telling you: she's cool! She just had to study this weekend or she was going to flunk out. You don't want her to blow her cover, do you?"

"I'd like her to blow my cover," growled another man, and he heard others laughing.

The man named Jimmy said, "She's lucky this was a pick-up and not a delivery. Here's your cut. She gets nothing, understand? And we expect her back on the next run or she's out, and I mean

291

CONVERSION

out. Got it?"

"Loud and clear, thanks. What is the next run?" MacArthur didn't sound rattled at all.

"Philadelphia. Same place. Two weeks. Come here first to get the stuff."

"Okay. See you in two weeks."

David crept away from the house quickly and laid in the dense woods by the road until he saw the Porsche head back to the highway. When he was sure no one would see, he ran to his car, shaking. On the drive back to return his friend's car, he became irate. *How could Mac be so stupid? He's put his life in danger! He's put Jessica's life in danger. And just how much drugs are these two doing?*

He could hardly look at his friend when he returned to the apartment. He tried to figure out his next move. *How do I tell Sarah? Should I tell her? Should I go to the Colonel? The police?* In the end, he called his father, but he never mentioned Sarah.

"Hmm. This is a horrible shock, a terrible setback. I need some time. Give me a couple of days and call me when you can, okay?"

"Okay Papa. How's Mama?"

"Feisty as ever. She's taken up French cooking of all things, and so we are eating frog's legs and soufflés. I miss my empanadas."

David laughed. "I miss you. I wish you were here."

"Us too. We'll talk in a few days. And David…"

"Yeah?"

"Just act normal."

"Yeah. Thanks. I will."

Talking to his father didn't change the situation, but it made

CHAPTER 24

David snap back to life. He was able to talk to MacArthur and Jessica like nothing had happened, but he was also keenly aware that they were trying too hard to appear like a happy couple.

Three days later, David called his father when MacArthur was in class. "Hello, Son. You are not going to like what I am going to ask you to do, but for the time being, you must carry on as usual and act like you know nothing of MacArthur's activities. You must trick yourself into believing all is as it should be. Understand?"

"Yes, but you're right. I don't like it. He and Jessica are in real danger."

"And you will be too if you get involved. Listen to me. You must stay out of it. Immerse yourself in your schoolwork and focus your attention on…the cheerleader, eh?"

"But Papa—"

"No 'but Papa'. You must trust me. All will be well in the end. The semester is nearly over and you have finals soon, yes?"

"Yes. I'll be home in a couple of weeks."

"Call me if anything happens, but promise me you'll stay away from this."

"I promise. Kiss Mama for me."

"Of course. We love you, Son."

"I love you too."

David forced himself to call Sarah and tell her that he had talked to MacArthur and was satisfied he was not doing any hard drugs, just drinking and smoking pot now and then. He also told her that MacArthur was supporting himself through the gigs his band played. She didn't question it and thanked him profusely for

293

CONVERSION

the good news.

David had told lies to other women and felt nothing. This time, he felt dirty. He wanted to run to Sarah and tell her everything, but he knew that would only make the situation worse and put her in danger. He focused on doing what his father had instructed him to do: convince himself that all was well. When MacArthur and Jessica left two weeks later, he knew they were going to Philadelphia. He forced himself to study and then called Veronica, the cheerleader who had been flirting with him for weeks. She gladly spent the rest of the weekend with him.

It wasn't difficult to slide into a rhythm of self-deceit with final exams, papers due, and a new and exciting romance with Veronica; but as their second year ended, David was brought to reality once more. Students were celebrating on the Lawn, and a very high MacArthur was a ring leader. Somehow, he managed to find a fire hose and attach it to the nearest hydrant. Before they knew it, students on the Mad Bowl Field were screaming wildly as they were being pelted by the stream of water, and it wasn't long before the whole field became a chaotic mud slide.

The students were having the time of their lives, but the administration was not and called the police. Hearing the sirens, MacArthur dropped the hose and went running for the nearest dorm, where he was saved by some friendly co-eds. They put him in a dress, put bows in his hair, and applied makeup. Satisfied he would not be recognized, they gathered around him and accompanied him to the Lawn. The police were getting nowhere in finding the perpetrator. MacArthur walked over to David and some

CHAPTER 24

of his fraternity brothers. In a falsetto voice, he said, "I guess they didn't catch me, huh?" The response was just what he had hoped. He was the campus hero.

A few days later, David flew to Panama for the summer. He leaned back in his seat, closed his eyes, and relaxed for the first time in weeks. Unfortunately, his thoughts turned to MacArthur and crystalized, so he sat up and gazed at the lush Virginia countryside below. He took deep breaths and attempted to quell the foreboding that he was leaving his best friend in the clutches of another kind of snake.

25

MacArthur looked at Jimmy and smiled. "It's all good, man. I mean, she's on her way home and won't be back. She's sick of me and sick of UVA and just wants to go home and never return. I promise you, she won't be any trouble for you because she won't want anyone to know what she's been up to."

Jimmy eyed him coldly. "I like you, kid, but I've been in this business long enough to know you can't trust someone who won't talk face-to-face. You know what I mean?"

MacArthur had anticipated this. "I do know what you mean, Jimmy, and normally I'd agree with you, but these are special circumstances, you know?"

"Special circumstances? How?"

"Well, just think about it. After our last run, Jessica had to spend all her time studying for exams, and then she had to take her exams. The weekend her exams ended, her parents arrived to load up all her stuff and drive her home. I mean, this is true for both of us. School is our cover. If we had taken off like we were going away for the weekend during any of that time, it would have looked suspicious. And when her parents arrived to take her home, what's she supposed to do?"

"So you're saying she didn't come here face-to-face to keep her cover."

CONVERSION

MacArthur's face lit up. "Yes! Exactly!"

Jimmy did not reflect his elation. MacArthur hated that he couldn't read him. "Okay, kid. But don't bring another broad into this with you, okay? From now on, if anyone asks, and you're not on a trip with the band, you've got a favorite aunt who's up in years and needs you to move her furniture, got it?"

"Yes, Sir."

"Enough with the 'yes sir' shit! Get outta here! I'll see you next week."

MacArthur raced to the Porsche and jumped in. The summer was off to a great start. Jessica was safe and out of his hair forever! He grabbed his overnight duffle and stuffed a wad of cash in it. Jimmy had instructed him never to deposit his money in a bank. His funds had to remain untraceable and tax-free. Thus, he kept them in plain sight at all times, hidden on his bookshelf. He had cut a hole in a large, esoteric textbook no one would ever pick up and deposited his money there.

He decided to stay in the apartment through the summer. He had enough money to pay the entire rent. That way, when David returned they could have the same living arrangement. It provided MacArthur the freedom to come and go without anyone but David knowing.

There were times when he wanted to tell David what he was doing, but he had to protect him. And besides, the drug deal was just until he graduated and went to work. Then he could support himself legally and get on with his life. None of this would have happened, of course, if his father hadn't been such a myopic

CHAPTER 25

bastard. One day he hoped the Colonel would find out what he drove his son to do to get through school on his own. Meanwhile, when he had to be around the man, he acted the part of the good son and told him and his family what they wanted to hear.

Making drug runs and partying would occupy his summer, as The Decades had decided to take the summer off. Zaiah was in Jamaica, where he and his girlfriend were working with his family in their marina. He had confided to MacArthur, "Her parents are cool with me being black, but since she's white, well, I'll either be engaged or broken up or at odds with my family by the time I see you next!"

Henry was going to spend the summer at Meadowmount, a camp that trained string players and pianists who accompanied them. MacArthur thought this an odd choice for a rocker, but Henry was a piano major who loved accompanying other musicians. He had heard that a fifteen-year-old cello prodigy from China would be at the camp and told MacArthur, "This is my opportunity to accompany some of the greatest string players of our time, maybe of all time."

As for Jack, he was going to spend the summer exploring the Nashville country music scene with his brother, who was already living there and working as a fiddler and mandolin player for a recording studio. His brother had gotten him some gigs playing drums for the studio. He said, "It's cool, man. I'll be earning while I'm learning!"

MacArthur was relieved. With the band and David out of the picture, he could be at ease. The drug runs went smoothly all

CONVERSION

summer, and he made so much money that he had to get two more textbooks. He let his hair grow to his shoulders, but kept it respectable, and he met a lot of girls who were all about the sex, drugs, and rock-and-roll scene. One of them wanted to try LSD, so they tried it together.

Most of the trip was glorious, but as the drug began to wear off, every vision became a nightmare. He and the girl screamed and cried together, and yet his fears and paranoia only intensified. Finally, they fell asleep for hours. MacArthur awoke to find the girl had gone, and he was sure of two things: He would never drop acid or see her again.

The summer vacation in the mountains with his family was a yearly tradition he could not skip if he was to maintain his cover. Since the last summer had been a fiasco, he was determined to give his best performance this year. He cut his hair a couple of inches and ironed his preppie clothes. He stayed sober the week before and decided he would only drink beer in their presence. There was minimal withdrawal, but he was glad he was alone. He stayed in his apartment for three days, until he felt totally clear.

Unfortunately, the more clear-headed he became, the more he began to experience waves of mental anguish and emotional pain. He tried to distract himself by finding an archery and gun range. He had forgotten how much he loved the ping when the arrow left the bow and the plunk when it hit the target. The only drawback was that it reminded him of Reuben, whom he had never called after his mother's funeral.

His performance for his family was so good that he fooled

CHAPTER 25

himself. He knew he was being false, but the persona he was portraying was familiar and easy. He had a good time with his sisters and Craig, and he even engaged his father in conversation, deftly lying to conceal his real lifestyle and beliefs.

He returned victoriously to UVA and went immediately to a bar to celebrate, get drunk, and pick up a blonde. A few days later, he sobered up to do a run for Jimmy, and by the time David returned, his life of crime had kicked into a new normal. Jimmy had warned him not to let his guard down, but after a year of learning the ropes and successfully handling the Jessica mess, he was in complete control. He cut his hair short for ROTC and smiled when his commanding officer and unit were not happy to see him.

As juniors, he and David had a certain amount of seniority on campus, and they were able to take more classes that related to their majors. They were both in Arts and Sciences, but MacArthur was a Government Major with a minor in music and David was a Foreign Affairs Major with a minor in Russian. MacArthur got into a required first-year political science course he had not been able to take yet. The upside was that it would let him check out some of the new, first-year women.

The professor of the class was the one with whom he had had a run-in his first year. They had become friends, and he knew what to expect. The man orchestrated lively debates, which MacArthur relished. Ever since the political demonstrations his first year, the professors were more vocal about their liberal views and even less open to alternative beliefs, but this professor remained neutral. MacArthur liked to think he was responsible — even though he

CONVERSION

now agreed with the man on most issues.

The first day of the class, MacArthur came early and took a seat that allowed him to turn slightly and see all the new coeds walk through the door. He spied a couple of cute blondes and one stunning red-head. Then a tall brunette nearly stumbled into the room, laughing with her friend as she caught herself. Time froze when he heard her laugh and saw the most amazing smile he had ever seen. The moment passed as the professor entered and began his introduction, so MacArthur turned to the front and disregarded his reaction to her. He didn't go for brunettes.

In the third week of the class, the professor initiated one of his notorious debates. "Mr. Wells, choose a side and begin." MacArthur stood, knowing he offered the best answer to the question: What constitutes good government?

"Government is necessary for the good and welfare of society, and good government will always be comprised of a well-educated elite who have the wisdom and experience to know what is best for the masses. After all, the Bible itself maintains that people are basically sheep that need a shepherd. As long as the best-educated of society hold the reins of power, the people will have all their necessities met and live satisfying lives, because their government will provide them with everything they need."

As he sat down, someone raised their hand. The professor said, "What say ye, Ms. Miller?" The tall brunette with the radiant smile stood.

"I say that Mr. Wells has missed the entire object of good government. Good government encourages personal and civic

CHAPTER 25

responsibility and gives the people freedom to create and produce that which will serve society and make the nation strong and healthy. Good government encourages *self*-government and independent thought not mindless sycophancy. A government that is founded and maintained by a so-called elite is arrogant and narrow-minded and, as Mr. Wells evidently adheres to his Bible, he will remember that pride always leads to destruction. A government of arrogant elites will destroy a nation, but a government of good-hearted servants with common sense, a strong moral compass, and respect for their fellow citizens will cause a nation to flourish."

MacArthur slammed the door of their apartment, threw his books on the kitchen table, and fell face down on their old, worn sofa. David was eating a sandwich and reading a textbook. "God, the semester's hardly begun, and you're bent out of shape already?"

"I was shot down in my *first-year* poli-sci class. I mean demolished…by a *first-year woman*."

"A *first-year woman*? Jesus."

MacArthur pulled himself up and smiled.

David stared. He hadn't seen that goofy smile in a long time. "Why are you smiling?"

The smile vanished. "I would have been mortified if it had been anyone else but *her*. You cannot believe this…this…I don't know. She's not even my type! I have no idea why I'm attracted to her. I don't need this right now!"

"What's so bad about her?"

"She's first-year! She's probably a Christian! She might even be *smarter* than me. And she's tall! She's like this…awkward…I don't

303

CONVERSION

know…all-American girl, and I can't deal. I have too much going on." He couldn't say anything more. He'd probably said too much already. This girl had triggered something in him he did not want to face.

"Well hell, introduce *me* to this goddess."

"Hell no! One look at Superman and I'm toast!" He saw David's mouth drop open. "What's the matter?"

David swallowed. "It's…just been a long time since you called me that…*Saint Mac*."

MacArthur's face flushed. "Don't call me that. It's not who I am."

"Okay, okay. Well, I was never Superman either." His eyes twinkled as he folded his arms and leaned back. "So tell me, just how tall is this girl?"

MacArthur grabbed his books, stomped to his room, and slammed the door.

A few days later, David passed a Phi Delt pledge on his way home from class. He stopped and asked how his year was going. "Really good for the most part. The high point, of course, was when MacArthur got trashed by another first-year girl in my poli-sci class."

"Really? Who is this girl, anyway?"

"Her name's Erica Jane Miller, only her friends call her EJ. She's kinda different. Seems nice, kinda pretty, but too smart for me. See ya!"

"See ya!" David couldn't wait to tease MacArthur. As he approached the apartment building, however, he passed one of

CHAPTER 25

Jessica's good friends. She was crying. His stomach tightened. He entered their apartment quietly and saw MacArthur, sitting at the table, looking stricken. "Hey, what's happening?" He set his books on the table and sat down to face him.

"Jessica's dead."

"What? How?"

"She was crossing the street one night, and some guy hit her. It was a hit and run. They never caught him."

"When did this happen?"

"Last August, in her home town." MacArthur was clearly in shock. There were no tears. He had grown to despise Jessica, but she didn't deserve this; and the reality that he would get the same if he tried to leave Jimmy had struck him sober. A curtain had been pulled away, and he saw how foolish his plan had been. *How could I ever think I could leave?* was ringing in his head.

David clutched the table. He stared at MacArthur, who looked down, shaking his head in disbelief. This was the fear David had refused to consider: Jimmy would not let MacArthur go. His thoughts raced. *Please Mac, please! Talk to me! Talk to me, or I'm going to have to talk to you.*

Finally, MacArthur raised his head. He stared at David but did not see him for a second. Then he came to himself. "Hey, I forgot to tell you. I have to go home for a couple days. My dad needs me to sign some paperwork about his will or something."

"Oh. Okay. That's cool. When will you be back?" He was fishing for information but thinking, *This is good. He's going to see his dad. The Colonel will know what to do — if he tells him.*

CONVERSION

"Yeah, hopefully I'll get back tomorrow night, but if I'm not, can you just tell everyone that I had a family thing?"

"Sure man, that's easy." David grabbed his books, went into his room, and before he closed the door, he stopped. "You okay?"

"Yeah. It's a shock, but I'll be all right. Thanks for asking."

"Sure." He closed the door and pressed his ear against it.

MacArthur picked up the phone and dialed his home number in McLean.

"Colonel Wells."

"Dad."

"MacArthur! How are you?"

MacArthur knew his father's pleasure upon hearing his voice would be short-lived. "I need to come home, and I need you to call in sick tomorrow so we can talk."

The Colonel knew this tone of voice all too well, from operatives who were in danger or about to blow the lid off some diabolical plot. He was careful not to increase his son's anxiety. "Sure. We're due for a good talk. How soon can you be here?"

"I'll leave after dark and get there tonight."

"Great! Can't wait to see you. I'll have Lois make some sandwiches and we'll have a midnight snack."

"Thanks, Dad. See you soon."

"Goodbye, Son."

David waited until it was almost dark then came out of his room and knocked on MacArthur's bedroom door.

"Come in."

MacArthur was closing a larger suitcase than would be

CHAPTER 25

necessary for a trip like this. *Whew! If he was going to kill himself, he wouldn't have packed so much. Shit! What if he's going to run? No, he wouldn't have called his father. Or would he?* "Looks like you might be taking a long weekend."

"Yeah, I thought maybe, since I'm making the trip, I should spend a little time with the old man. I'll only be missing two days of class and one drill session, and it's still fairly early in the semester."

"It's cool man. Can I help you with anything?"

"No. Just...if anyone asks...tell them I had to go home for a couple days."

"Sure. Say hello to the Colonel for me, okay? And bring back whatever pie Lois has made. Mmm-mmm." He rubbed his stomach.

MacArthur raised his eyebrows and nodded. A few minutes later, he wedged the suitcase in the back seat of the Porsche. An eternity later, he was turning into his driveway. It was almost ten o'clock, and his father normally went to bed early, but all the lights shone brightly. The front door opened before he got there, and his father hugged him and took the suitcase.

"Whoa! You got a cannon in this?"

He followed his father inside and closed the door. "No. But it is kinda explosive." He thought, *David would have liked that one!*

Lois almost ran to him and hugged him so hard he thought he would pass out. "You been too much a stranger, and I can see you need some fattening up. Well, Sir, you've come to the right place! I left sandwiches in the fridge and there's a batch of homemade

307

CONVERSION

cookies already on the table."

He beamed at her despite himself. "Thanks Lois. Oh, and David says hi to you both, and I'm supposed to bring back one of your pies for him."

"I'll make his favorite." She turned to the Colonel. "You need anything else before I go?"

"No. You've gone beyond the call of duty staying this late. Please! Go home and feel free to come in late tomorrow. In fact, why don't you just take the day off."

"Are you sure you won't starve?" Her eyes teased.

MacArthur saw what his father was doing. "No, listen, I've gotten to be pretty good in the kitchen in my own apartment." He winked at her.

That was all she needed to leave happy.

MacArthur lifted the suitcase. "Can we go into your study?"

"Sure."

MacArthur followed and watched his father close the curtains on both windows. He laid the suitcase on the coffee table and opened it, moving some clothes aside to reveal three large textbooks. His father sat down in an armchair and watched as MacArthur opened the books to reveal hundreds of dollars in them. "There's three hundred seventy three thousand, five hundred sixty dollars, mostly in hundred-dollar bills. I made it as a courier for a drug cartel over the last year and a half."

His father never flinched. "Tell me everything."

MacArthur sat and tried to make eye contact with his dad, but soon jumped up to pace the room. "I met Jimmy at a party, after

CHAPTER 25

one of our band gigs. He asked if I was interested in making some extra money, but I said no. Then Mom died, and, well, it was too much. I drank more, smoked weed, and started using coke and speed when I needed them.

He stopped and looked at his dad. "Last summer, you knew and cut me off. I was pissed at you; but not anymore. If I'd listened, I wouldn't be in this mess."

"Go on."

"So when you cut me off, I went right to Jimmy, only he didn't want me to sell drugs like I thought. He wanted me to be a clean-cut guy no one would suspect was his courier. The money was good, and they also let me use some of the stuff myself, but I had to be sober when doing deliveries, so I think that's what kept me from destroying myself."

"That's debatable."

He winced and realized he was shaking. "I haven't gotten to the worst part. Jessica, my girlfriend last year, got involved. At first, we had a blast and made a good team, and Jimmy and all the guys thought she was great. But then she got a new roommate, who was pretty vocal about not liking what she was doing.

One night in her room, I said, 'I've got a surprise for you. It's really crazy.' And we acted like millionaires and smoked some really expensive coke I snagged from one of our runs. But it hit Jessica wrong and she freaked out. I spent the night and calmed her down, but in the morning, she said she was done. I thought she wasn't thinking straight; but she wouldn't budge.

"I was so pissed at her! We had a run the next day, and she just

309

CONVERSION

screamed, "Tell Jimmy I'm too sick to go!" She said she was going to go to the cops if I didn't stop nagging her. I tried to scare her, telling her Jimmy's guys would kill her if she didn't go. She was scared but still refused, and her roommate yelled at me to leave and not come back.

"Well, I did the run by myself and had to cover for her with Jimmy. Told him she had the flu. When I got back to campus, I waited a few days and went to see her. She looked better and agreed to finish the school year and then be through. So we did that, and she went home to Nebraska.

"I told Jimmy she was gone for good and wouldn't be a problem. I thought that was it." His voice broke. "But today I found out she was killed by a hit-and-run driver. I never told Jimmy where she lived, but I know they found her and killed her. I might as well have killed her myself."

He composed himself and forced himself to look his father in the eyes. "Dad, I'm finished with all of it. I'll go to prison if I have to, or maybe they'll kill me too, but I'm finished with all of it. I'm done."

"Sit down, Son. You're not done."

26

After Jeanne's death, the Colonel dreaded the end of each holiday with his children; but this past Christmas told a different story. He didn't have time to feel grief or loneliness after they departed; he was too agitated by MacArthur's behavior. How was he paying for his tuition, his living expenses? He didn't speak of outside jobs except the band gigs, but were they that lucrative? His stories did not add up. He also noticed that MacArthur avoided Lois. They used to have long talks, huddled in the kitchen with their Bibles. He had to face the fact that he was getting the same vibe from his son that he got from enemy infiltrators in his operations.

During spring break, Sarah voiced her concerns about MacArthur and was shocked to hear he had been receiving no financial support from him. She said MacArthur had always paid for their meals when they had the rare lunch or dinner, and he always had a lot of money in his wallet. They agreed she would confide in David and see what he knew. When Sarah called and assured him David was convinced MacArthur was only drinking and smoking pot from time to time, he still couldn't shake the uneasy feeling.

Soon it was the end of MacArthur's second year, and the Colonel decided to wait and see how he was during their summer

CONVERSION

vacation in July. Like Christmas, MacArthur dressed well and said all the right things, but there was a hollow sound to his words. Thus, a week after the vacation, he told Lois he was going out of town for two weeks. He handed her a check and said, "Here you go. You can take a much-earned paid vacation."

She took the check and stared at it, then looked up at him with an expression that always unnerved him. "You goin' after MacArthur?"

He was surprised, but he knew he could trust her. "What do you know?"

"I know he's not himself. He's in a dark, dark place. I've been prayin' for him, and I believe his very life is in danger." She paused and looked down, then decided to go on. "When I pray, I see him in a big, old house, out in the country, surrounded by large trees, and he's inside laughing with men who have fangs for teeth."

The Colonel was struck by this. "Please. Keep this to yourself." She nodded. "And…uh, I wouldn't mind if you did a little praying for me to sort this out."

"Yes, Sir." She smiled and waved the check. "Thanks for the vacation." As she left the house, she thought, *That man has no idea how many prayers have been flyin' up to Heaven since I came here to work.*

The Colonel packed a bag, rented a car, and spent the next two weeks tailing his son. By the time he returned, he had a full picture of the danger MacArthur was in. What unnerved him most, however, was that the farm house matched the description of the house Lois had "seen." He asked her, "Just how did you see that?"

CHAPTER 26

"Well Sir, the Holy Spirit showed me."

"Explain."

That evening, the Colonel heard a full explanation of the Gospel for the first time. He had always been a faithful Catholic, but now he was struck by the person of Jesus. He had worked with powerful people throughout his career, but now they were dwarfed by the presence and power of this God/man from Nazareth. Suddenly, he was desperate to know him like Lois knew him. Tears filled his eyes, and he surrendered his life to Jesus. Afterward, he asked Lois to continue to pray for God to give him wisdom.

During prayer a few days later, the Colonel knew he was to call his good friend at the FBI. He and Bill had known each other since college and had lunch periodically, but this time he asked Bill to go fishing on Saturday. As they sat on the dock of a lake that was deserted after summer, he told him, "I can give you the location of the farm house, some of their operations, and descriptions of some involved, if you can keep MacArthur out of this. My God, Bill, you know MacArthur. He's a good boy who just went nuts after his mother died. I was too blind with grief to see it."

Bill thought for a while. "Hmm. Okay. To do this by the book, MacArthur has to become our informant. We've just become aware of this group, and it would be great to have someone on the inside. Then, when it's all done, no one will know he's been involved illegally, and we can keep this off his record."

"Turning him is the tricky part. Right now, he's on top of the world," the Colonel snorted.

"Let me do a little investigating myself, and I'll let you know

CONVERSION

how to proceed. We don't want MacArthur running to tell them stuff that will get him and possibly your whole family killed."

A chill went down the Colonel's spine. "Damn! I'd rather be at war."

Two weeks later Bill invited the Colonel to go fishing. "We've had a break, but a tragic one. Evidently MacArthur had a partner for a while, a girl. It seems she wanted out, so she left at the end of the school year. From what her former roommate said, MacArthur was glad to see her go. Then last August, the cartel found her, living with her family in Nebraska. They killed her. Probably more than cleaning house. It was a message to MacArthur."

"How did you get this information?"

"We have agents posing as students at UVA, and agents in Nebraska reported their investigation of the girl's death."

"Of course."

"We instructed local authorities to list it as an unsolved hit-and-run until we pull in all the players. I pity that family. I hope they never know what their daughter was into." He paused. "Do you think, if we make sure MacArthur finds out what they did to her, it would shake him up enough to work with us?"

"If it doesn't, he's not the son I raised."

"Okay. Her roommate attended her funeral. It's only a matter of time before she tells MacArthur. If not, we'll *encourage* her to do so."

"So I just wait and hope for a phone call?"

"Yeah. From what you've told me and the time I've spent with MacArthur, my money is on him calling you first thing and spilling

CHAPTER 26

the beans. Then, just call me and we'll walk him through it. It won't be hard for him if he's got balls and a good poker face. The only difference in his routine will be reporting back to us. Then, when the time is right, we'll drop the net. We want to get the biggest fishies we can get." He jiggled his fishing pole and chuckled.

The Colonel recounted his side of the story to MacArthur, who wept and shook as he listened. The more the reality of his folly came to light, the more ashamed he became. The Colonel sat down beside him and put his arms around him. At first, MacArthur recoiled. He didn't want pity. But his father whispered, "Please forgive me, Son. I had no idea how you were suffering after Mom died. I'm so sorry I didn't help you."

MacArthur was stunned. And then, deep within his heart, he heard a voice he had not heard in a long, long time. "I love you, Son."

He grabbed his father and held on for dear life as a reservoir of grief poured from his heart. "I'm so sorry. Oh God! I'm so sorry. I miss Mom! It hurts so bad!"

When he was calm, the Colonel looked his son in the eyes and said, "You and I are going to be okay, but we have some work to do. Got it?"

"Yes."

"First, let's get you something to eat."

They ate the sandwiches Lois had left, and MacArthur drank a large glass of milk. The Colonel said, "We'll call Bill tomorrow and get started. For tonight, just rest. Oh, and Son...."

315

CONVERSION

"Yeah?"

"I want you to know that I got born again."

"What?"

His father smiled for the first time that evening. "Yep. Lois preached until I finally heard Jesus talking through her."

MacArthur was astonished. God had answered prayers he had prayed long ago! And he had done it while he was far away from him. "I can hardly believe this."

"Well, believe it. And I'm sorry I wrote you that letter after your Mom got her faith."

"It's okay, Dad."

"Thanks. Now I don't miss her as much, knowing I'm going to see her soon."

"Not too soon, I hope!" They laughed. "Dad, what time is it in Israel? Is Reuben *in* Israel? Do you know?"

"How long since you talked to him?"

MacArthur frowned. "Not since Mom's funeral. I never called him back. Does he know anything about this?"

"No. And you can't tell him. You are undercover. You and I are business as usual. Not Reuben. Not David. Not even a priest in the confessional. Understand?"

"Yes, Sir." It felt good to be taking orders from his father. Safe. Loved.

"Reuben is home. He should just be getting up if you want to call now."

"Thanks, Dad."

They hugged goodnight, and the Colonel went to bed.

CHAPTER 26

MacArthur sat in the study and dialed the number. It rang and rang, and when he was about to give up, he heard, "Katz."

"Reuben!"

"MacArthur! Is the dead raised?"

"Yes! I'm sorry for not calling you back. To be honest, I've been pretty out of it since Mom's death."

"Understandable."

"No, you don't understand. Reuben, I got mad at God and left him. My girlfriend broke up with me and then Mom died. I blamed God for all of it. When Mom got saved, I was sure she'd be healed of the cancer; but she died, and I did what you told me never to do. I blamed God and got totally angry and bitter. But... didn't he let her die? I mean, couldn't he have healed her?"

"You ask *the* question: Why did Abba heal your leg and not your dear mother? Let us not allow what we don't know to dictate what we do know: Abba loves us, and his promise to us is that by Yeshua's blood we are healed. He does not harm us or make us sick. He sent his Word to heal us. In this we must have faith. But sometimes...we make wrong decisions and remove ourselves from his healing hand, yes?"

"Oh yes! I understand that really well now."

"Mostly, we live in a fallen world, where sickness and tragedy come to us even when we have done nothing wrong. Sometimes, we don't know how to extricate ourselves from it. The good news is that our Abba loves us and does everything he can to help us. And, if we die, we are healed in Heaven and know all things."

"So I won't know until I get to Heaven?"

CONVERSION

"The Holy Spirit may show you before, about your mother, but in the meantime, he is here to comfort you and assure you that you will see her again."

"Maybe not."

"Excuse me?"

"Am I still going to Heaven? I mean, I *slammed* God. I said and did terrible things. I want to come back, and I heard him speak to me tonight, in my heart, but does that mean I can come back?"

"How long has it been since you read his Word or prayed in his Spirit?"

"Uh...a *long* time."

"Let me remind you of his promise never to leave you nor forsake you. He did not say, '...unless you become angry, spit on me, and do terrible things.' He promises to be with you *always*. MacArthur, his love for you is greater than your foolishness toward him."

"Wow. Um...Reuben?"

"Yes."

"I wish you were my roommate." He basked in the laughter that exploded from the telephone receiver.

"So, how is David?"

"He's good...I think. You know, I've been so crazy, I don't really know. He's the campus jock and seems to be in love with a drop-dead gorgeous cheerleader. Still Superman, you know; but somehow it never seems to go to his head."

"Ah yes. I wonder what his kryptonite is?"

"Right now I would say me!" He suddenly realized Jimmy

CHAPTER 26

probably knew about David too. He wanted to tell Reuben everything so badly. "Well, I mean, I haven't been the best roommate in a long time. I really need you to keep praying for me, so I can get my life back on track."

"On track. Interesting phrase. Yeshua says, 'the way.'"

"Yeah. If there's one thing I know for sure, his way is a lot better than mine!"

Reuben began speaking a language that was not Hebrew. Then MacArthur remembered. He was speaking in tongues! Though unintelligible, the words soothed his soul, and MacArthur was stirred to speak in his own prayer language. In a tsunami of gratitude for the overwhelming presence of the Father, he poured out his heart.

Reuben prayed in English: "Abba, MacArthur is facing great challenges and needs your wisdom and strength. Thank you for sustaining him in the months ahead, for giving him courage and endurance. Bless him with new friends who can encourage him in Yeshua and — ah!"

Silence. "Reuben? Are you there?"

"Yes. Who is this tall, dark-haired woman with a smile that lights my heart?"

MacArthur swallowed hard. "Erica Jane Miller. My nemesis. How do you know her?"

"I don't. Holy Spirit showed me." Reuben laughed. "So, she is trouble, eh?"

"Yeah. But I...well...I don't know what to do about her."

"Why must you do something? If Yeshua has brought her into

319

CONVERSION

your life for a reason, he will reveal it when the time is right."

Reuben chuckled.

"I'm glad you're amused, because I'm not."

"Oh, my boy, we are right back to where we started. Trust Abba. He has your best interest at heart."

"I know. Oh wait! Dad told me tonight that he got born again."

"Yeshua be praised!"

"Well, it just happened a little while ago. Please call him and catch up."

"I will do that."

"It's so great to talk like this again. I wish I had called you a long time ago."

"Well, we are here, and it is good."

"Yes, it is! Are you going to be in the States anytime soon?"

"I will call if that should happen. Be well, my boy, and let me know how things progress, yes?"

"I will. Bye Reuben. I miss you."

"I miss you too. *Shalom.*"

MacArthur replaced the receiver and bounded up the stairs to his room.

27

The meeting with Bill set the parameters for what turned out to be the rest of MacArthur's third year and a week into the following summer. The FBI wanted him to be out of school before they "dropped the net," which would better ensure his safety and give them sufficient time to gather information on the players and operations in the drug cartel. Bill stressed the fact that the more bad guys they rounded up, the safer MacArthur would be afterward.

"You'll continue to take the money and pay for your expenses with it, just like you have been. Then we'll arrest you with Jimmy and any others so the cartel won't know you turned. You'll spend some time in jail, but the prosecutor and the judge will be told you're our informant. The court will rule that because you're a first offender, you'll get probation with community service. Nothing will go on your record, and as far as the world and the cartel are concerned, you were a kid who strayed for a season but learned his lesson and went straight."

The only fly in the ointment was that ROTC required recruits to attend summer camp between their third and fourth years. Bill assured MacArthur they would do their best to wrap up everything before that, but if not, the Colonel knew MacArthur's commander at UVA. "I'll take care of it," he said.

MacArthur came to grips with the plan that would free him

CONVERSION

from the dangerous position in which he had put himself and others. Now that he was sober and his relationship with God restored, he found it excruciating to play the part of drug courier and party man on campus. He desperately wanted to find a church, hang out with Christians, and tell David and Reuben everything — and Jack. He knew Jack's prayers were one reason he was not dead. Instead, he was continually reminded of how far he had strayed into darkness.

To distract himself, he got the band together to play some parties on campus. At least he could laugh and joke with them and enjoy their music. He and Jack wrote another song, but he could tell Jack was wary of him, as he was still going out with lots of women, drinking, and not going to church. What Jack didn't know was that he took the women home early and had become adept at faking drunkenness.

In class, MacArthur continued to argue political issues as a passionate leftist. He saw goodness in their intentions, but more and more, as he secretly prayed in the Spirit and studied the Bible in the privacy of his room, he began to discern that their altruistic intentions masked a sinister agenda, something, perhaps, even they did not see. And then there was EJ. He couldn't seem to stay away from her, and every time she was near, he couldn't look away. He longed to show her he was not a heavy-drinking, pot-smoking, fornicating God-hater, but that was the reputation he had to maintain.

One day he saw her eating alone in the cafeteria, and before he knew it, he asked, "This seat taken?"

CHAPTER 27

"Now it is." She looked at him intently. "How are you, MacArthur?" But her eyes said, "Who are you, MacArthur?"

"Oh, uh, well, I'm doing fine. Hassling one of my classes…," and they talked about the political science department in general. He wanted to avoid issues on which they had disagreed in the past. Even in this informal setting, he marveled at how articulate she was, and yet her manner put him entirely at ease. He looked into her eyes and knew he was a goner. He admired her keen intellect, but it was her faith that made her beautiful. He stifled his laughter when she launched into a passionate attempt to bring him to "Jesus, the only one who can heal your soul." The pain from the consequences of his actions struck him again when he had to feign rejection of Jesus. And so, like Jack, she remained distant. He took solace in the knowledge that his friends remained safer this way.

David, on the other hand, had seen a marked difference in MacArthur the moment he walked into their apartment after visiting the Colonel. "What's happened to you? You must have had a good time at home."

"I did. I really did. I just needed time to work some things out with my dad. You know, we haven't been, well, on good terms for a while."

"Yeah. What was that about?"

"Oh, we got in a big fight the summer after Mom died. It was mostly my fault. I just didn't know how to deal with everything, so I took it out on him. But we had a good talk this weekend and worked it all out."

"Great! Your dad is not someone I'd want to be at odds with," he smiled.

CONVERSION

"You're right about that."

David wanted to ask more questions, but he didn't want to *have* to ask them. He wanted MacArthur to tell him everything. It surprised him when, in the weeks following, MacArthur continued the same routine of being gone most weekends. It was strange. He wasn't drinking or smoking pot, because when he came home from a party or a date, David could tell he was sober. He also wasn't talking about his sexual exploits. When David asked him about it, he answered, "Well, I guess I just started to feel like it wasn't right for me, so I'm going to try abstinence for a while."

"Good luck with that, man!"

MacArthur told David about the shooting and archery range he had found, and they went whenever they had time. It was great to be doing something they both enjoyed that didn't require much talk. Then the holidays were upon them. David was meeting Veronica's parents for Thanksgiving, so he wasn't there to witness that MacArthur and the Colonel were easier with one another. Meg, Joanna, and especially Sarah noted the change and spoke of it among themselves.

Rebecca and Craig were with Craig's family, but at Christmas they joined the Wells clan and announced they were expecting a baby. MacArthur desperately wanted to be completely open with them, but at least he could be himself for the most part. Playing this role felt like threading a needle, but every now and then his father would wink at him or give him a look to tell him he was doing fine.

The second semester was an exhausting grind. He rarely saw EJ,

CHAPTER 27

because they had no classes together. He focused his energies on his classwork and accumulating as much information as possible from Jimmy and the others without raising suspicions. Bill had coached him on this. His only truly good times were in his room, praying quietly and reading his Bible. Without fail, he would go in wondering how he could go on, and he would come out with renewed hope and courage.

When the semester ended and finals were over, David returned to Panama and MacArthur was by himself in the apartment. This time he dreaded living alone, but he had to finish what he had started. Then two days before he was to report to ROTC summer camp, the DEA stormed cartel facilities in the region. Millions of dollars of drugs were confiscated, and MacArthur was arrested with Jimmy and some others at the farm house. Bill got a full net of "fishies" to put away.

MacArthur was treated like everyone else until his arraignment, when the prosecutor and the judge played their parts. It was his first offense, so he received six months community service and probation, which stipulated he could have no contact with felons or any of his previous associates in the cartel.

The court also agreed to count as community service MacArthur's ROTC summer camp, because the recruits were already taking part in the tremendous clean-up after tropical storm Agnes. The storm brought devastating floods to Pennsylvania, particularly in the Harrisburg area. MacArthur saw first-hand how nature showed no favoritism in causing families to suffer, and the experience reignited his dream to find a way to help people.

CONVERSION

At the end of the summer, he joined his family for their vacation at the lake. Lois was there to cook for them and join in the fun. Rebecca was very pregnant and Craig very nervous. Being a nurse, Sarah was the one who calmed them. At dinner one evening, the Colonel rose to make an announcement, and concerned glances were exchanged. The last time he had done this, they had been told their mother was ill. Surprisingly, he said, "MacArthur has something to say, and what he tells you remains in this room."

News reports of the significant drug bust had been overshadowed by allegations that the Democratic National Headquarters had been burglarized and wire tapped by operatives of President Nixon's administration, so the family was unaware of MacArthur's arrest. When he finished his story, he tearfully asked everyone to forgive him for lying and putting them in danger, and to pray for him to forgive himself. Jessica's face still haunted him.

Meg and Sarah hugged him, while Craig smiled and shook his head in wonder. Eventually, they shook hands. Joanna slugged him on the arm. "What in God's name! Don't ever do anything like that again!"

"Don't worry, Sis."

An uncomfortable silence was broken when Rebecca quipped, "Well, thank God we won't have to explain to our child why Uncle Mac is not at family dinners."

Everyone laughed, and MacArthur smiled. "Thanks, Sis."

"Yes! Well." The Colonel coughed. "You are the trusted few. As long as the cartel believes MacArthur was loyal to them and then went straight, they should leave him alone. Still, some may make

CHAPTER 27

remarks or ask questions if the story ever breaks big. You cannot tell them the whole truth to defend your brother. Stick to what's public knowledge, capisce?"

"Yes, Sir," from everyone.

After MacArthur was back in his room, someone knocked on his door. "Come in."

Sarah came in and sat on his bed. "Have you told David yet?"

"No. He went back to Panama for the summer, and I couldn't tell anyone until it was all over."

"He knows, Mac."

"What?"

"After spring break, I asked him to come over and not tell you. I told him why we were worried, but this is the thing: When I said Dad had cut you off, he was really shook up. He said he'd see what he could find out, and I think he must have followed you for a while, because he didn't call me for several weeks. And if he followed you to the farm house and such, he must have known; but he called and said you were only drinking and doing a little pot. Why would he lie? I liked him. I *trusted* him."

MacArthur's heart sank. "Gee, Sis, I don't know. It doesn't sound like him. But as soon as he gets back, I'll ask him. Like Dad said, only our family and David, and probably I'll tell Reuben, but only they can know the truth...well, hopefully my wife someday."

"Oh my." She smiled and cocked her head. "Is there someone?"

"Probably not. She thinks...well...the very worst of me, so this latest will seal the deal. It would take a miracle of God to even get a date with her."

CONVERSION

"So she's at UVA?"

"Yeah. She'll be second-year."

Sarah smiled and patted his cheek. "Ooooo. Robbing the cradle, are we? You'll find a way. You're a charmer." Her gesture reminded him of his mother. She yawned and rose. "Got to get some sleep. Tennis tournament tomorrow! Looks like no one will beat Craig and Rebecca, 'cause they won't be playing!"

"You're right. You still wanna team up?"

"Yeah, but next year, you and Joanna. You're the only ones who can beat 'em."

"Got it. Sleep well — and don't think badly of David. I'm sure he has a good reason."

"I hope so. Night."

As she closed his door, he smiled. *She liked him. She trusted him. Can't wait to tease him about that!*

During the first weeks of the fall term 1972, UVA was abuzz with two news items: the massacre of Israeli competitors at the Summer Olympics in Munich, Germany, and MacArthur's arrest and sentencing. After talking with Reuben and offering his condolences about the slaughter of his countrymen, MacArthur had a more realistic perspective on his own difficulties. Still, he wondered if he was imagining expressions of disapproval as students passed him or friends said hello. Of course, there were a few who thought him a hero. That saddened him.

It was especially hard doing community service. Once a week for three months into his third year, with two other students who

CHAPTER 27

had been arrested for possession of marijuana for the first time, he picked up trash on campus. Luckily, he could talk to David. After they had stored their apartment furniture and moved the rest of their stuff into the fraternity house for their fourth year, MacArthur said, "Let's walk over to the garden. I have something to tell you, and I don't want anyone to hear."

They sat on a bench, and MacArthur told David everything, including his talk with Sarah. "So, why didn't you say anything?"

David looked straight ahead. "I know this is going to sound flimsy, but my dad told me not to."

"So he knows?"

"Only what I knew then. When I realized what you were into, I called him for advice."

"What did you tell him?"

"I told him about following you, about the drug running, and that you were using. I didn't tell him about my meeting with Sarah, though. I just told him I got suspicious and followed you a few times."

"Oh."

"He said that if I told you what I knew, I would be involved and put myself in danger, if I wasn't already. You have to understand. He took us out of Cuba to protect us and give us a better life. He saw what you were doing as a threat to me and the life he wanted me to have."

"I get it. But you need to talk to Sarah and explain."

"Sure."

"She's working in the ER at Martha Jefferson but living in the

CONVERSION

same house with her friends. Look on the bright side. You have an excuse to ask her out!"

David grimaced and stood, "Hey, I'm with Veronica." They began walking back to the frat house.

"Ah yes, the blonde bombshell with a brain."

"Stop it, or I'm going to ask EJ to be your date at the fall dance."

"Whoa! Don't you dare!"

"God, man, every time you hear her name you practically collapse. I've never seen anyone so stupid over a girl."

"Well, now you know the problem! She only knows me by my putrid reputation, which has just gotten worse. Then there's the fact that I haven't exactly been a good Christian. I don't think she even knows I'm a Christian."

"Never thought I'd say this, but even Superman can't help you with that one."

"Yeah, well, I put it in God's hands, and that's where it's going to stay."

"Hi MacArthur!" EJ and one of her roommates jogged past them.

"Uh, hi!" MacArthur squeaked. They had been so engrossed in their conversation, they hadn't noticed the sound of runners coming up behind them.

"It's a sign!" whispered David, raising his eyebrows.

MacArthur watched her run into the shadows of the evening. "I hope so," he murmured. Then he stopped and offered his hand to David. "Thanks for staying my friend when you knew I was a

CHAPTER 27

criminal."

David laughed and shook his hand. "Do you know how insane that sounds?"

"Yeah, I have some idea." He smiled and then became serious again. "David, you can't tell anyone ever. I mean, you can tell your dad about whatever's public, but nothing else. It's just not safe."

"Sure man. Your secret's safe with me. After all, we're blood brothers."

MacArthur smiled. "Yeah. But get ready. People who don't know the whole story, well, you can't defend me with the undercover part. You've got to say something like, 'Listen, I've known MacArthur a long time, and he's an awesome guy. Just watch, he'll land on his feet and astound the world.'"

David groaned. "No doubt about it, Saint Mac is back on campus, ego fully intact." But dealing with the religious stuff was a welcome relief compared to drug cartels and prison. And, of course, the goofy smile was back. That was the important thing.

When they got to the frat house, David went into the phone room to call Sarah.

"Hello."

"Sarah, uh…this is David."

"You talked to my brother."

"Yeah. Can we meet up some time?"

"Sure. What do you have in mind?"

"Well, I thought we could have a drink somewhere noisy, where no one will overhear us."

"I don't know. Someone might see us, and I don't think that's a good idea."

"Why?"

"Then we have to explain what we're doing there together. Wait a minute. Why don't you bring MacArthur. I'm his sister and you're his friend. We go way back. No big deal."

David's mind raced to find a fault with her suggestion. "Uh…well…I just don't know if it's a good thing for your brother to be in a bar, do you?"

"Oh, yeah. Right. I hadn't thought of that. I know! It's still nice outside. Why don't you and MacArthur pick me up Saturday about noon? I'll bring sandwiches and drinks and we can drive out to a park and have a picnic."

Ugh. Still with MacArthur. He forced himself to be excited. "Great idea! We'll be there." He trudged up the stairs to their room and told MacArthur the plan.

"That's so sweet. My sister needs me there to protect her in case you lose control."

"I told you, I'm with Veronica." At least, that's what he kept telling himself.

23

After MacArthur's ROTC training Saturday morning, they jumped in the Porsche and went to pick up Sarah. David took the picnic basket and helped her into the small back seat. They drove to a nearby park and found a picnic table, where they set out the food and drinks. David and MacArthur sat across from Sarah.

"This looks great. Thank you, God, for this meal, and thank you, Sis!" said MacArthur as he was about to take a bite.

"Yeah, thanks Sarah."

"So, spill it," she looked intently into his eyes.

He smiled and looked at MacArthur. "I followed our friend here, and when I saw what he was doing, I realized I was in over my head. So, I called my dad. He told me to stay out of it, because if I got involved, I would be in danger and possibly be implicated as an accessory. Basically, he told me to act dumb. Believe me, I wanted to have it out with you, Mac, but I knew my dad was right."

"He was," nodded MacArthur. "I wouldn't have listened. But you were surprisingly good at acting dumb."

David smirked and turned back to Sarah. "So I called you and told you what you and your dad wanted to hear, thinking that would keep you guys safe too. Although, now that I hear myself saying it, *me* keeping the Colonel safe is ridiculous. Anyway, I'm really sorry I lied to you."

"Okay." She frowned. "I wonder why your dad didn't call my dad?"

"He did."

Sarah looked puzzled and MacArthur put his can of coke down. "When?"

"I don't know. Sometime after he told me not to do anything."

MacArthur looked curious. "Huh. Dad never told me that part. Oh well. Maybe he just forgot or didn't think it was important. There was a lot going on the night I spilled my guts to him."

Sarah shook her head. "Dad doesn't forget details. He must've had a reason. We can ask him next time we're home." She grimaced. "Unless he can't tell us!"

David locked on her eyes intently, trying to stay calm. "So, we're okay?"

"Yeah." She patted his hand. "You're still my Superman."

MacArthur spit coke out of his mouth. "Sorry. Sorry. Just haven't heard that name in a while."

Sarah laughed and threw her napkin at her brother. David quickly changed the subject. "So Sarah, how's it going at the hospital?"

"The hours are long, but then I get a nice bit of time off every week. The ER sees all kinds of cases, which is interesting but sometimes heartbreaking. That's my biggest challenge. My emotions."

"Well, Sis, I'd rather have someone like you taking care of me than some old biddy who couldn't care less."

David nodded. "Me too. You're the one I'm calling every time I

CHAPTER 23

get beat up defending your brother."

Sarah laughed, then asked, "You guys thought about what you're going to do after you graduate?"

"Haven't you heard, Sister Sarah?" David put his arm around MacArthur and smiled mischievously. "MacArthur and I are going to change the world."

"Oh! So that's still on? I'm so glad I don't have to worry about the future."

And so ended any serious conversation. Long before he wanted their time together to be over, David was helping Sarah out of the back seat, handing her the picnic basket, and saying goodbye. He forced himself to get in the car and not watch as she walked into the house.

MacArthur started the car. "I have to say, I was really upset about something she said."

"What? What did she say?" David tried to remember anything in the conversation that had been amiss.

MacArthur dropped his head and shook it back and forth, then looked at him in anger. "Now you're HER Superman?!!!" He threw his head back, laughing.

"Oh God! Shut up! Just shut up and drive." He yelled above the roar of the engine, "I told you. I'm with Veronica!"

The ensuing weeks flew by with fraternity rush, football practice, ROTC, and classes. David was quarterback of a mediocre football team and wished MacArthur was still playing. He missed his "unpredictability." But MacArthur was busy finishing community service and, on top of his required classes, monitoring

CONVERSION

a computer class. He continually harassed his friends with the declaration that, other than Jesus, computers were going to radically change the way they lived their lives.

The Decades did a couple of parties at fraternities that still loved their songs, but they had decided not to continue except to jam now and then. The only mention of MacArthur's drug conviction came at the beginning of the semester. Zaiah asked MacArthur to meet him in the practice room. When he walked through the door, Zaiah greeted him with a dirge on his guitar, and Jack and Henry joined on drums and keyboard.

MacArthur shook his head and smiled. Then Henry stopped them and said, "We're burying the past, man, not you."

"Thanks guys. You're the best."

A couple of weeks after that, Jack came to the frat house and plopped on MacArthur's bed. "Hey listen, I know you've been wanting to try different churches. Have you found one yet? Because I just heard about one I want to check out. Sounds totally *bonkers*."

MacArthur watched him slap out rhythms on his thighs, teeth biting his lower lip, moving his head to music only he could hear. He wondered if all drummers were nuts like this. "What's the church?"

"That's the thing. It's St. James *Episcopal* Church. Episcopal! Some friends of mine have left my church to go there, talking about how great it is. They call themselves Charismatics and speak in tongues like Pentecostals, but they still do the Episcopal thing." He shook his head. "Sounds crazy, man. We gotta check it out."

Sunday service did not disappoint. Jack watched in wonder

CHAPTER 23

as the congregation operated in the gifts of the Spirit in sync with their rituals, something only the Holy Spirit could orchestrate — and something he hadn't seen in his Pentecostal church for some time. MacArthur was enthralled. They sang older hymns along with contemporary songs, people raising their hands in worship. When one particularly anointed song faded, everyone began singing in tongues. After worship, the pastor (called "rector") delivered a challenging, biblical message. And all of this occurred in the midst of an old, stately church that was packed with people of all ages and colors.

At lunch, MacArthur and Jack talked excitedly about everything they had experienced. They agreed they had to go back next Sunday. Then MacArthur knew it was time to tell Jack what had happened after his mother's death, everything except the undercover part and Jessica. "I just want to apologize for treating you so badly all those months. I wasn't mad at you. I was mad at God, so that meant I was mad at anyone, well, like you."

"It's cool, man. I knew you were in one dark, scary scene."

"Yeah, I know. It's funny. I thought I was so right, and I was totally wrong. I thought I had everything under control, and then something awful happened. It was like I woke up in a nightmare. But God pulled me out of the abyss, man, for sure."

"Yeah. You know what the Bible says about sin: It's fun for a while, then it bites you in the ass."

MacArthur laughed. "Jack, your translations of Scripture are so wild — but right on! And thanks for praying for me. Hey, next week, you wanna try the college class?"

CONVERSION

"Sure." He looked thoughtful. "Honestly, I've been looking for something more. I didn't know what until this morning. Those people were so on fire for God, and when we sang in tongues, well, I've never felt so…like we were one."

"Yeah. It was amazing, like we were really one body."

"You know, I think I've been trying to *prove* how spiritual I am instead of just *being* spiritual. Does that make sense?"

"Yeah. It's something I've been thinking about a lot, like I need to be doing that. Oh well, it sure was awesome."

"Amen, Brother!" Jack said pompously, then grew thoughtful. "I've been wanting to ask you. Are you still antiwar? I mean, you switched sides, like, drastically. I just wondered why."

"Most of it was this rage I had against my dad, you know, over the letter he wrote about my mom and the blow-out that summer. I hated him and everything he stood for. Swallowing everything the antiwar guys felt like slapping him in the face. I just hope Nixon makes good on his promise to end it, but in a good way, if that's possible."

That Monday David pushed through afternoon football practice and walked toward the Phi Delt house. He saw MacArthur walking out with an older man he didn't recognize. He was almost as tall as David, darker skin like his own, and curly brown hair to his neck. As usual, MacArthur was talking and gesticulating. The man was smiling and obviously enjoying MacArthur's company.

When David was about twenty feet away, the man saw him and stared at him, like he was looking right through him. David thought, *This must be Reuben.*

338

CHAPTER 23

MacArthur almost leaped in the air, crying, "Superman, meet Samson!"

Reuben extended his hand, "Hello David. It is like we met years ago."

David shook his hand and couldn't take his eyes from Reuben's. They were dark, yet dancing in a light that radiated his entire face. He caught himself and managed to say, "Yes, it is. What brings you to America?"

Reuben clapped his hand on MacArthur's shoulder. "To see this young man and spend some time with his father. Shamefully, I have not seen my good friends since before our dear Jeanne passed into Heaven."

David nodded. "Did Mac give you the tour of the house?"

"Ah yes," Reuben rolled his eyes. "I have had quite the experience. Reminds me of my youth."

"Can you have dinner with us?" asked David.

"No, unfortunately this is a short trip. I drove here from the airport and must drive to McLean this evening, but thank you for the invitation."

"You're welcome. Again, nice to meet you." They shook hands.

"I'll walk you to your car," offered MacArthur, who awkwardly slung his arm around the taller man's shoulders. David chuckled at the sight and walked toward the house.

When they stood by the car, MacArthur said in a low voice, "To continue what I was saying in my room, I didn't just do a lot of drugs and distribute them. I had sex with a lot of women. I mean, I know I'm okay with God, that he's forgiven me, but am I ruined for

CONVERSION

my wife? Reuben, this isn't funny. I feel really dirty."

Reuben's eyes shifted from amusement to compassion. "Forgive me. I know that feeling. But Yeshua's blood is a…marvelous mystery. First John 1:9 declares that no stain remains when his blood is applied. Abba forgives us *and* cleanses us. This you must believe, because he said it."

"Does this mean I don't have to tell my future wife about my past?"

"Yeshua forgives, but be led by the Holy Spirit. He will tell you what is right."

"Okay."

"Does this have something to do with the tall brunette?"

"Sorta. She doesn't know what really happened to me, you know, everything I told you. Other than Jessica being killed and putting David and my family in danger, she's the worst consequence of what you call 'my foolishness.' It's my own fault. I blew it with her."

"Have faith, my boy. Yeshua is still the doer of the impossible. Let's get in the car and pray."

In the car, Reuben turned to MacArthur and said, "First, I must give you the *scriptural* sex talk."

"O…kay."

"God designed sexual love to bind the man and woman together in their covenant of marriage. And, he designed it to be one of life's greatest pleasures. Thus, when you have sex outside of marriage, there is pleasure — but also great confusion comes. This is because you were also designed to be *one* only with *one*. You see?"

CHAPTER 23

"Yeah. I'm doomed."

Reuben smiled. "You are not doomed. Again, Yeshua's blood breaks all unholy bonds of the past and makes you new, as though you never sinned. Hmm. I see a shadow of condemnation and confusion still." He closed his eyes. "I believe you should name to Yeshua each woman you treated wrongly — even if she seduced *you*. Tell him you repent, and thank him for forgiving you, for forgiving her, and for breaking all unholy bonds between you."

And so MacArthur closed his eyes and began to present each woman to Jesus. He didn't know all their names. Some of them were just "the girl with long blonde hair and red boots….the girl I dropped acid with…." He found himself weeping over them, but he broke down when he named Jessica. "Jesus, I hope she knew you before she died. I didn't tell her. I knew the truth and didn't tell her. Father, please forgive me."

During this process, he became aware that, after each confession, he felt a little lighter inside and yet more agitated in his physical body. It was an odd sensation. When he finished, Reuben continued, "Now, look Yeshua in the eye and renounce the evil spirit of sexual immorality. Tell it to leave you forever."

MacArthur was nervous but spoke decisively. "Jesus, I renounce all sexual immorality. In Jesus' name, get out of my life forever!" He felt a heavy, dark presence leave his body, and joy filled his entire being. "Whoa! Reuben, that was amazing! Thank you!"

Reuben put up his hands. "I did nothing. Thank Yeshua."

MacArthur bowed his head. "Thank you, Jesus, so much. I consecrate my entire life to you." He blew his nose and looked up.

CONVERSION

"I feel like my brain just got cleaned, and my heart," he put his hand on his chest, "it's free. I mean, like, really free to maybe, really love someone."

Reuben smiled. "This is good. My spiritual father took *me* through this deliverance years ago."

"You have a spiritual father? Who is he?"

"His name is Derek Prince. He is British but has lived in America and spends time in Israel. He is a father to us few Jews and Arabs who have come to know Yeshua."

"Wow. You know, Reuben, you're *my* spiritual father," he paused, "although I generally refer to you as my rabbi and priest."

"I am honored. So. How do you see this brunette, uh —?"

"EJ. Short for Erica Jane."

"EJ. How do you see her now that your brain is clean and your heart is free?"

MacArthur pursed his lips. "Um, I have hope; but it's still in God's hands."

"This is good. This is very good. Now I must go." He reached out and hugged MacArthur tightly. "*Shalom*, dear boy."

"*Shalom*, Reuben." MacArthur got out of the car and watched him drive away. He wondered if the reason he was here had something to do with the massacre of Jews competing at the Olympics.

That Sunday, Jack and MacArthur joined the college students' Sunday school group. There were about thirty present, some from UVA, including Erica Jane Miller.

29

Thanksgiving 1972 was a joyous time for the Wells family after so much sadness and scandal. Rebecca and Craig arrived with three-month-old Jeanne, who never lacked attention. The family's grief, missing wife and mother, was ameliorated by the arrival of her namesake. As his children argued over who would hold little Jeanne next, they watched the Colonel dote on her. They were delighted to witness this side of him and wondered if he was like this with them as babies.

Joanna introduced them to Marc, who was quickly dubbed the gentle giant. The two had met the summer before, working in the Rocky Mountain National Forrest. Towering over her and everyone else, he was certainly no oaf. He didn't say much (she answered for him a lot), but when he did speak, he commanded the room with his deep voice. His insight into their sister — and that they adored each other — was so obvious, everyone loved him immediately. He spoke with the Colonel privately, and they were engaged to be married the following June.

David was finally at ease around Sarah. He thought, *After all these years, I can relax. Sarah's dating a doctor. I'm with Veronica. We're just friends.* They spoke in Spanish when they talked, sometimes cracking jokes even the Colonel and MacArthur had trouble understanding. He was shocked when Rebecca put the baby in *his*

CONVERSION

hands while she ran upstairs. Nervously, he was about to hand her to Sarah when Jeanne giggled and smiled at him. His heart melted and he joined the ranks of contenders to hold her for the rest of the holiday.

Each morning, MacArthur rose early to have prayer and Bible study with Lois in the kitchen. They were both surprised when, on the second morning, Meg asked to join them. Tearfully, she told them she had hit a low point her last year of law school. Out of desperation, one Sunday morning she drove out of Nashville and ended up at a little country church. The people made her so welcome, she felt she had found a home away from home.

"But then it started to be more than that. I began working at the law firm and the stress was so bad, I tried a women's Bible study and sometimes a prayer meeting. I've always been so intellectual, you know. I've heard all my life Jesus died for my sins, and my legal mind saw the sense in it. But one Sunday a light went on inside me. Jesus didn't just want to save me from eternal damnation; he wanted to be my *best friend*. Me! So I got born again, just like you've been talking about, Mac! Would you believe it?!"

"Yes!" cried MacArthur.

"Honey, not only do I believe it, but I have a question for you," said Lois.

"I know what you're going to ask," beamed MacArthur.

"Have you received the baptism of the Holy Spirit since you believed?"

"Yes! I have! It's SO crazy! My whole church does it. Do you speak in tongues too?"

CHAPTER 29

And so, when the Colonel got up to get his morning coffee and read the paper, he heard a cacophony of languages and laughter coming from the kitchen. Curious, he went to investigate, and soon there was a fourth prayer language added to the mix.

When Christmas arrived, it was a new day for the Wells family. Craig, Rebecca, and Baby Jeanne were with Craig's family on Long Island. Joanna was meeting Marc's family in Colorado. Only Meg livened up the holiday by bringing home her new beau to face the Colonel's scrutiny. Josh's family owned a large dairy farm outside Nashville and were long-time members of her church. After getting to know him, MacArthur whispered to Lois, "Looks like we've got another winner!"

By the middle of the week, Meg and Josh were engaged and would be married just after Joanna and Marc, sometime during the summer. But they wanted to have the ceremony in their church. The Colonel was gracious and struggled to be happy about the venue. "Well, I had thought all you girls would be married at home, like Rebecca, but at least Nashville isn't too far away. And, you agree on the church. God knows what Joanna and Marc will do. I didn't even ask if he was Catholic or Protestant!"

They all shook their heads. Neither had anyone else.

That evening at dinner, Sarah was quieter than usual and went to bed early, so MacArthur knocked on her door.

"Come in."

"Hey, Sis." She was in bed, reading a book.

He sat next to her. "Watcha reading?"

"*Northanger Abbey*, the only Austen I haven't read yet."

"Don't think I've read *Austen* at all, sorry."

She looked at him and frowned. "Why are you here?"

"I don't know. You seemed kinda down tonight, so I thought I'd check and see if you were okay."

She sighed and closed her book. "Are we next? I mean, are we expected to find the love of our life and get married in the next couple years? 'Cause I'm not ready. And anyway, there's no one in sight."

"No fireworks with the doc, huh?"

"Not so far."

"Well, I'm gonna tell you something I haven't told anyone but David and Reuben, and it probably won't make you feel any better."

"Spill it."

He smiled. Quiet little Sarah always shocked him when she talked like a gangster. "I've fallen madly in love with that second-year who knows all about my dirty past. Actually, I didn't feel good enough for her and had totally given up, well, really, on marriage; but then Reuben came to visit and, well, he said some things and we prayed about some things, and all the guilt and nastiness just went away. Now, I feel like God has given me the green light to ask her out."

Sarah's eyes grew big, again reminding him of his mother, beckoning him to tell her everything. "Who is this person?"

MacArthur described the first time he saw EJ, stumbling into the classroom, laughing at her own awkwardness. Her captivating smile and long legs. He told of their debates and how smart she

CHAPTER 29

was, and of the lunch where they had had "a moment." He said, "I went to the college Sunday school class at my new church and there she was. I think she was shocked to see me. I don't know. But you know me. I speak up a lot...."

"Oh, yeah."

He smiled. "But so does she! So I'm hoping she'll give me a chance."

"You're such an idiot."

"Well, thanks!"

"No. I mean, MacArthur, yes, you really screwed up, but you took responsibility and changed. She's seen that, hasn't she? And my God, you're you! You're cute and funny and a great guy. If she doesn't see that, she doesn't deserve you."

"Thanks, Sis."

"I just have one question."

"What?"

"How long are those legs? I mean, are you in love with an Amazon or something?"

"No!" They were laughing, but then his expression changed. "She's really close to my height, though, probably five eight or nine, just a hair shorter."

"And that doesn't bother you?"

"No. It's kind of cool, I think, like we're on even footing, no pun intended."

She put her hand on his arm. "Well, Mom used to say, 'No tryin' brings sighin' but tryin' brings truth.'"

He sighed. "I miss her."

347

CONVERSION

"Me too."

The next morning after breakfast, the Colonel asked MacArthur to come to his study. He shut the door, and they sat on the sofa. "Do you know what you're going to do after graduation?"

"Well, I've been praying about it, because my draft number is so low, I might get called up as soon as I graduate. I don't know why I haven't gone already, even though I'm still in college. You haven't pulled strings, have you?"

The Colonel shook his head no. "But I'm not arguing with the Almighty about it."

"Me neither!"

The Colonel frowned. "I don't think we'll be there too much longer. You can't win a war when the people oppose it and pressure their leaders not to fight it. Few politicians have the guts to see something through when public opinion turns against them."

"Are you saying we could win this?"

The Colonel looked away. "Yes," and he turned back to face him, "and that's all I'm saying."

"Well, I hope you're right about it ending, but ROTC means the army's still got me for two years after graduation, and I haven't exactly been their favorite."

"Now *that* I heard about."

"Oh. Sorry."

"Yes, well, you'll graduate as an officer. That's something."

"Yeah. It's no guarantee I'll survive Vietnam, though. I could do grad school to get another deferment, but…I feel like I'm not doing my part. Some of my friends have come back messed up, some

CHAPTER 29

stronger, but some didn't make it. I mean, my generation are doing their bit. Makes me feel like a coward."

The Colonel's expression was sad. "Sometimes it seems better to be the one who died instead of the one who survived, but it isn't. I've learned that. Wars will always be with us because every generation produces evil, power-hungry tyrants that will only be stopped by force. That said, I respect and mourn those who stopped them but didn't come home. I'll never forget them, and I'm grateful...so grateful. At the same time, I thank God I did come home and am here for you and your sisters, and now little Jeanne."

"We're glad too, Dad." MacArthur watched his father get up. "So basically, before I make any plans, I have to wait and see."

The Colonel opened the cabinet behind his desk, took out three large books, and dumped them on his desk. "I've been keeping these for you." He opened the book on top, revealing bundles of cash. "We forgot about these. The FBI doesn't know they exist, probably because the accounting books from the raid never mentioned you."

Looking at the books made his stomach churn. "Dad, I don't want any of that."

"It's your responsibility, Son."

"I know." He sighed. "Let me pray about it, okay? I promise. I'll get them out of your hair as soon as possible."

"Good." He put the books back in the cabinet.

As they walked out to join the others, MacArthur thought, *I'd like to burn them*. But he heard in his spirit, "Inasmuch as you did it to one of the least of these My brethren, you did it to Me." He ran

349

CONVERSION

up to his room, grabbed his Bible, and read the entire passage in Matthew, chapter 25. *His brethren. Did Jesus mean Christians or Jews or both?* He prayed, *Do you want me to give the money to the church, to a ministry, to Jews in Israel? What, Lord?*

The next day, Reuben called to wish them a Merry Christmas and see how MacArthur was doing. "Reuben, can I ask you a funny question?"

"I'm laughing already."

"You know what I mean. I, um, well…from when I got into trouble, I accumulated a lot of money, if you get my meaning."

"Yes."

"I think Jesus wants me to give it to Jews in need. Do you know of such a ministry or organization?"

"I do. It is a new ministry to bring Jews to Yeshua, and not just Jews in Israel. They call themselves *Jews for Jesus,* and your donation would help them print materials and support their evangelists."

"That's it, Reuben! But will they have a problem with how I got the money?"

Reuben roared with laughter. "Jews do not have this problem! But if *you* need Scripture, remember, the wealth of the wicked is laid up for the just, yes?"

"Ah, right! Okay. I have to clear it with Bill, the FBI guy, but go ahead and send me the address."

"They will be praising Yeshua," chuckled Reuben. "Now tell me. Have you asked your EJ for a date yet?"

"Oh my God! You won't believe what's happened." He told Reuben about his new church and seeing EJ there.

CHAPTER 29

"So, it's looking good for a date, yes?"

"Yep. I'm going to take the plunge when I get back to campus. I mean, I graduate this year, so if something's going to happen, it has to happen now. I've been thinking that she's got to finish school, and she has two more years. By then, I'll have finished my military service, whatever that's going to be, and provided I live through it — oh, and that she likes me too, of course—"

"MacArthur! Are you writing your future, or does Yeshua have a say?"

MacArthur laughed. "You're right. I need to slow down. I get it."

"You slowing down? Now there's a miracle."

30

MacArthur's twenty-second birthday on January 30, 1973, was preceded by two transformative events for the United States. On January 27, President Nixon made good on his promise to end the country's involvement in the Vietnam War. Unfortunately, MacArthur's hope for it ending well did not materialize. Many South Vietnamese, who were grateful for and fought alongside the US military, were killed by the invading North. Many perished in boats, trying to escape, and those who managed to make it to America or other countries often arrived dehydrated and nearly starved to death.

MacArthur thought of Kau and Lawan and the Thai people. What if they needed our help to thwart the communist invasion? And how safe were they now that Vietnam had fallen? He had corresponded with them regularly until his "fall from grace," and now he determined to write them again. He wondered, too, what Sunan was doing.

He was sad. America had never left a battlefield in this manner. And if what she left in the wake of her exit wasn't humiliation enough, her servicemen and women who fought so bravely came home to be mocked and scorned, vilified as "baby-killers" and "murderers of innocents."

This charge was ironic considering that just before, on

CONVERSION

January 22, 1973, the US Supreme Court ruled in the case of *Roe v. Wade* that women had a right to kill their babies in the womb. Abortion clinics opened throughout the nation, and within a decade, the total innocent lives taken numbered in the millions. Statistically, the most dangerous place for a baby became his or her mother's uterus. But most of the nation believed a fetus was a mass of senseless cells, so many had abortions and often paid a terrible mental, emotional, and physical price.

The abortion issue replaced the controversial Vietnam War as the most divisive issue in America, but *Roe v. Wade* escaped the attention of MacArthur and David and many other young men, who were no longer facing the possibility of going to the jungle to fight. For this, they were ecstatic, as were their families and friends. Although MacArthur faced two years of military service following graduation, he was heartened by the possibilities. Perhaps they would let him serve as an army chaplain.

When MacArthur returned to UVA early January, however, he could only think of EJ and hope. He was excited to discover she was in one of his classes. By now, he had a more conservative stance on most issues, and he knew it wouldn't be long before the leftist professors would be gunning for him. Conservatives were a small minority, so logically, they should support one another. That was his reasoning the first week of class when he took a deep breath, sat next to EJ, and asked. "How was your Christmas?"

"Great! Total pandemonium and good food. How about you? Were you naughty or nice?" The minute she said it, her face fell. "I'm sorry. I—"

CHAPTER 30

"No. It's cool. Compared to a year ago, I was really nice! Although, it was unusually quiet...." He was about to explain how some of his sisters were absent, when the professor brought the class to order.

He waited a couple of days to take another deep breath and call her. He said exactly what he had rehearsed: "I was hoping you weren't doing anything on Saturday night. I thought we could have dinner and go to a movie or something."

"Are you asking me on a *date*, MacArthur?"

He winced. "Yeeees."

"Why do you want to go out with me?"

Eyes wide. Panic. "Well...because I like you and...um..." *What?!*

"Let me explain my approach to dating. I'm not into frivolous relationships. Life is too short to date guys I'm never going to marry, some of whom may tempt me to sin or, in a weak moment, cause me to sin. I'm looking for my partner in life not a temporary fling. So MacArthur, what are your intentions?"

For the life of him, years later he still could not reckon how this came out of his mouth: "Erica Jane, I'm your man."

Silence.

"EJ? Hello?"

"What movie do you want to see?"

On their first date, they missed the movie and nearly closed the restaurant. EJ had always wanted to know why he was named MacArthur, then everything about his family. He reasoned later that this was probably because the one thing he learned about her was

355

that she was an only child. He felt especially good when she said, "You know, for the only boy and *baby boy* of the family, you don't seem to be *too* spoiled."

He returned the compliment. "Same for you. I mean, aren't only-children usually spoiled brats?"

She laughed, and he wanted to record it so he could listen forever. Whenever she smiled, he stared. Twice, he didn't hear what she was saying because he got lost in her bright, brown eyes. He never wanted to be away from her. More and more, his entire being longed for her.

Their second date, they made it to the movie, but during dinner he only found out she was from California and missed her dog. She asked him how long he and David had been friends, so the conversation was centered on the winding road of his relationship with his best friend and blood brother.

He thought their third date might not happen at all. The entire week, EJ was not EJ. He had never seen her like this, and it was more than a bad mood. In class, she was quiet and sullen, not wanting to talk, and afterward she made an excuse to hurry back to her apartment. When he called, her roommates said she was out. Thursday, he saw her between classes and she tried to avoid him, but he caught up to her and pressed, "EJ, I know something's wrong. What did I do? Please, tell me."

She kept walking briskly. "You've done nothing wrong. I'm just too busy. Maybe later."

"What about Saturday, Henry's recital? Can you still go?"

She hesitated. "Um...call me that morning, and I'll let you know."

CHAPTER 30

"Sure." He frowned and watched her walk away.

He asked her best friend if something had happened, but she was baffled too. Evidently no one had seen EJ like this.

All he could do was pray in tongues, because he had no idea what to pray. Then Saturday morning, when he called her, she sounded more like herself. "Sure. Let's go. Maybe the concert will do me good."

That evening, he decided to keep the conversation light on the walk to University Hall. He asked her about growing up in California, but she skirted the topic, saying, "Oh, you know, sun and surf and the Beach Boys, of course." Then she asked him about the recital.

The recital was of great interest to MacArthur because Henry was accompanying two of the soloists. Edward Elgar's Concerto for Cello in E Minor filled the first half of the evening, and the cellist was the Chinese prodigy Henry had befriended at Meadowmount. A standing ovation acknowledged his extraordinary performance, but MacArthur was also struck with Henry's artistry. As he played the orchestral part on the piano, he had an innate ability to support the soloist and coax the very best from him.

The second half consisted of various instrumental and vocal solos. In the final solo, Henry accompanied a mezzo-soprano, who sang the last song of Gustav Mahler's *Kindertotenlieder*. As they took the stage and bowed, EJ turned to the last page of her program, where the words to the song were translated into English. MacArthur leaned over and whispered, "How do you like this high-brow stuff?" She sat like a stone, her eyes pouring over the

357

CONVERSION

words. He wondered what had her transfixed and turned to read his program.

> Gustav Mahler
> *Kindertotenlieder*: Songs on the Death of Children
> *In diesem Wetter*: In this weather

Good God! No wonder she's gone catatonic. His heart sank. *God, help us!*

Soon after the turbulent beginning of the piece, EJ began to weep, so he put his arm around her; but her eyes stayed fastened on the singer. After what seemed an eternity of high emotion, the mood of the music softened, the storm waned, and a gentle lullaby emerged. EJ's eyes closed, tears falling gently on her blouse. MacArthur read the final stanza as the singer glided through it:

> In this weather, in this gale, in this windy storm,
> they rest as if in their mother's house:
> frightened by no storm,
> sheltered by the Hand of God.

Even Henry had teared up as he finished, and the audience rose to give the artists a standing ovation. MacArthur's arm came to his side as EJ slowly rose with him to applaud. When the musicians took a final bow, EJ turned to MacArthur and kissed him softly on the lips, then whispered in his ear, "Thank you for bringing me.

CHAPTER 30

This was exactly what I needed."

MacArthur had often imagined their first kiss, but this far surpassed his finest fantasy. As they exited the hall, hand in hand, his goofiest smile could not be contained. He was the happiest, luckiest — and most relieved — of men.

EJ squeezed his hand. "Let's go to the Corner and have some hot cocoa."

"Brrrrr. Sounds good." He put his arm around her and they walked briskly to the diner. It was their first comfortable silence, which lasted until after they had given their order to the waitress.

Still basking in the euphoria of her kiss, MacArthur stared at EJ. She looked away for a moment, then turned to face him. "I want to tell you something. No one knows except my mom."

He put his hand on hers. "I hope you know you can trust me. I'm an idiot most of the time, but I promise, I will never betray you. Unless, of course, you shoot my dog or something; that is, if I had a dog."

She smiled and squeezed his hand. "Okay Mac, I trust you." Their cocoa arrived, and she lifted her mug to taste the whipped cream topping as she waited for the waitress to leave. "I grew up in a beautiful place called Emerald Bay, which is a gated community in Laguna Beach. It's very affluent, but my parents are hard-working, good people, and they never spoiled me. They gave me a lot of freedom, though, mostly because I was a model student, valedictorian of my class as a matter of fact. So they trusted me, and I often betrayed their trust.

"I've always enjoyed being with people, and in my high

CONVERSION

school, well, you know the California stereotype. We partied at the beach or in posh homes, and we drank and smoked pot, fancying ourselves radical revolutionaries and progressive hippies." She took a moment to blow on her cocoa and take a sip.

"Having embraced my culture...I had sex with my boyfriend. A lot. Then he cheated on me, and a month later I got drunk at a party and had sex with someone else. To this day, I have no idea who he was." She paused and took a deep breath. "Two weeks later I'm nauseated, then I skip a couple periods, and it occurs to me that I'm pregnant. I have no idea what to do and tell my mom, who freaks out. She tells me not to tell my dad, 'cause it would kill him. Her words are etched on my soul: 'This is not going to ruin your life. Don't worry, I'm going to take care of it.' All I knew was that I trusted her.

"So Mom tells Dad that she and I are going to San Francisco for a weekend shopping spree. Next thing I know, I'm in a doctor's office on Friday night. He gives me a local anesthetic, and then," she bit her lip, "he literally sucks the baby out with this vacuum tube. It had only been a little over two months, but I could see the body parts going into this jar." Her voice became strained. "In the bloody mess were baby feet and hands, not just a mass of cells like Mom and the doctor told me."

MacArthur took her hands in his, barely aware of the knot in his stomach.

"The cramping was bad for about twenty-four hours, but I didn't care. I was just...dead inside." She squeezed his hands and let go to take a sip of her cocoa. He was about to say something,

CHAPTER 30

but she put up her hand. "Somehow, I got through my junior year. I tried to act normal so no one would ask questions. I didn't want my mom to go to jail. I didn't care if people found out about *me*, because I was worthless. I still went to parties and drank a little, to dull the pain, but I didn't date or have sex with anyone. I was a smiling zombie, and I applied to the University of Virginia because I thought if I went far away and was in a totally different environment, I might have a new life.

"That summer, I worked as a lifeguard on the beach at Corona del Mar, right up the coast from Laguna. I sat up on that tower, the paragon of heroic virtue, feeling like a complete hypocrite. By this time, I hated myself. I lived with the reality that I had allowed my baby to be mutilated and killed."

She looked at him, tears in her eyes. "Now the good part."

"I was hoping."

She smiled as she remembered. "I'm finishing my shift on the beach when I see this group of hippies singing songs I've never heard, dancing, and raising their hands in the air. I recognize a couple of kids from my high school, so I go over, and they tell me to sit next to them 'cause some guy is about to speak. His name is Chuck Smith, and he's so cool. He's talking about Jesus in a way I never heard in church. Within a week of hanging out with these so-called Jesus Freaks, I get born again, I mean radically saved. I join one of Chuck's churches, which is awesome, and get baptized in the ocean.

"Mac, when I prayed my first, real prayer to God, I literally felt him wash me clean. It was miraculous, like wave after wave of love and forgiveness. I ran home to tell my parents but, unfortunately, they didn't get it. They still don't. We love each other, but we're not close like we used to be, you know?"

"Oh yeah. I know. So…now I understand why that song tonight…."

"Yes! I saw Jesus holding my baby! I don't know if it's a boy or girl, but I know he or she is okay."

"Oh my God, that is…." His expression changed. "But why was this bugging you all week? What happened?"

She sat straight in what he had come to recognize as her "go to war" attitude. "MacArthur Wells, the Supreme Court just ruled abortion a *right* for all women, no matter what their situation, bending and twisting the Constitution in a way our founders never intended!"

MacArthur could only marvel at her.

"When I heard their decision on the news, what *I* had done crushed me all over again. I was so low, and I thought I had to stop seeing you because I just couldn't tell you." She leaned in closer. "Then tonight, Jesus used that song to heal me even more than before. My child is *okay*. We're *okay*."

MacArthur shook his head and chuckled. "Honestly, when I saw the lyrics of that song, just the title, I thought…well, I didn't know what to think except it was *not* good. Then you kissed me and I was *really confused* — but totally relieved."

"Then…you don't think less of me?"

"EJ, remember who you're talking to! Glass houses and all that." They both giggled with relief, and he grew serious. "If

CHAPTER 30

anything, I think much more of you."

"Well, there's more, Mac. Now I know I've got to fight this. This is going to destroy families. It not only kills the babies; it kills the souls of women who think it's okay, or those like me, who trust someone who believes it's the answer to the problem. If Jesus hadn't saved me and healed me, I wouldn't be talking to you right now. I'd be in a loony bin or worse. I have to speak out to help others. I know that. What I'm asking is: Can you go through this with me?"

She was resolute. He could see her standing in front of crowds, telling her story. Did he want a wife who spoke of such things in public?

Then he saw himself, resolutely announcing that Jesus had healed his leg when the bone was exposed, declaring he was going to Thailand with his father, and saying he was done with drugs if it meant prison or death.

He reached across the table and took her hands in his. "Erica Jane, I'm your man."

She smiled and leaned across the table to kiss him soundly on the mouth.

"Why Erica Jane, you have kissed me twice — in public — and not even asked permission. I'm quite flummoxed." But the goofy smile told all.

MacArthur paid their bill, and they began the walk back to campus. "EJ, I have something I need to tell *you*, something you cannot tell anyone, maybe until after Jesus comes back."

She stopped, put her arm around his neck, and looked him in

the eye. "MacArthur Wells, I'm your woman."

He put his arm around her waist and whispered in her ear. "I'm serious."

She released him. "Okay."

"You know when I was a drug courier and in a very bad place?" She nodded. "Well, this is the *whole* story. It started when my good, Christian girlfriend dumped me, and that same day my mom died of cancer. I basically shook my fist at God and…." As they walked, he told her about hating his father, his role in the drug trade, Jessica and her death, and confessing to his father. How he became an informant, and the judge made it look like he hadn't betrayed the cartel but kept his crimes off his record. "The most important part is that I came back to God, and he delivered me out of the horrible mess I made."

"I guess we're both messes he's fixing, huh?"

He stopped and faced her, holding her close. "EJ, I know this is only our third date, but I love you."

She grinned. "Well, since you know my sorry story, I guess the only logical response is to love you back."

This time, *he* kissed *her*.

31

David was happy for MacArthur, and he liked EJ despite her ability to rattle him. She had a way of looking at him, like she saw deep into his soul and liked him despite what she saw. Although she was one of the most intelligent women he knew, she wasn't snobbish or arrogant. It was odd, but her warmth disarmed him.

He had never seen two people more glued together in every way without having sex. How could they stand it? And it was making David's life difficult. EJ had her own room in an apartment with friends, and David had expected MacArthur to spend nights there, leaving David and Veronica the room in the fraternity house. Veronica shared a room with a girl in her sorority, who never went anywhere with anyone. David couldn't understand their friendship and often resented it. Veronica told him she was assigned the room with her and there was no getting out of it.

He and Veronica had talked about living together, but David and MacArthur had always planned to room in the frat house their fourth year. Plus, MacArthur was going through the post-drug phase, and David wanted to be there for him. In the end, they continued to use the same system they had used before EJ and MacArthur began dating. When Veronica's hair tie was on the doorknob, MacArthur slept on the sofa downstairs.

MacArthur introduced EJ to Sarah, then took her to McLean to

CONVERSION

meet the Colonel and Lois. Sarah saw how EJ loved her brother, the Colonel saw a young woman with sense (exactly what MacArthur needed), and Lois pulled MacArthur aside and said, "This one is younger than you in years but older in wisdom. You listen to her."

"Yes, Ma'am!"

"Yes, *Miss*, please. I'm not old or married *yet*." MacArthur noticed the twinkle in her eye.

"What's going on?"

She laughed.

"Are you *in love*?"

She grew serious. "Haven't told the Colonel yet, but I've met my man. He goes to my church and has a plumbing business, so I'll never have to worry about leaky pipes again!"

MacArthur hugged her and said, "I'm really happy for you, Lois." He let her go abruptly. "Does this mean you'll have to quit?"

"Heavens no! I won't leave the Colonel until God says! We'll work it out."

During spring break, MacArthur flew to California with EJ to meet her parents. At first, he was taken aback at the opulence of their lives. The two-story, sprawling home extended from the cliff by cantilever construction, steel beams driven into the rock and supporting the two decks overlooking the water below. After he unpacked his suitcase, MacArthur opened the sliding door of his bedroom and ventured out onto the balcony. Emerald Bay sparkled in the sun like the gem for which it was named.

EJ cautioned him not to make a hard pitch for Jesus to her parents but assured him she would stand with him if he saw an

CHAPTER 31

opportunity. As it turned out, they got along famously because her parents were ardent golfers. EJ played with them, even though walking around and hitting a ball was not her preference. She liked to run, often jogging and hiking with their dog.

Other than discovering their daughter's beau was an excellent golfer, what really sealed the deal was that MacArthur came from a military family. EJ's father had been a captain in the Air Force and flew with Jimmy Doolittle during World War II. Of course, he asked MacArthur if he was related to the famous general. Like the Colonel, he had a mostly favorable assessment of the man. He said, "Sometimes you need a bulldog to get the job done, even if he behaves like a jerk."

EJ and MacArthur stood on the upper deck one day, enjoying the gentle breeze over the sunlit bay. She sensed MacArthur was overwhelmed and said, "When my dad returned from the war, there were so many airplanes; so he bought a few and started an air cargo service. It became successful almost overnight, and he expanded his fleet to cover the entire US and eventually foreign cities. Mom was his bookkeeper and chief adviser until I was born, then she stayed at home; but he still consults her on major decisions. They're a great team."

"That's the way my parents were." He closed his eyes and raised his face to the sun. "Why are you an only child? I mean, it's obviously not because your parents couldn't afford more kids."

"When I turned three, they had been trying for a long time, so Mom went to her doctor. He found tumors on her ovaries, which resulted in a hysterectomy. Dad didn't want to adopt,

CONVERSION

because his family had had a bad experience with it; and by then, I was in school, so Mom turned her attention to helping others, volunteering as a candy striper. Now, she's running the entire service and is also a board member of the hospital. I think that's how she knew where to take me for the abortion."

MacArthur shook his head in wonder.

EJ stroked his back. "What is going through that amazing brain of yours?"

"Just...I'm staring into the eyes of the healing power of Jesus."

"So am I."

MacArthur wanted to scoop her up and take her to bed, but her father's face loomed before him. The Captain had given him a bedroom on the bottom floor on one side of the house, whereas EJ's room was on the upper floor near her parents' bedroom on the other side of the house. And, the Captain had told him that if he got up and walked the halls after lights-out, motion sensors would trigger lights both inside and outside the house. That way, of course, he couldn't get lost....

On the third morning, the sound of the surf woke him early. He dressed for a morning run with EJ and wandered down the hall, where the door of her father's study was open. It looked more like a library, and a crowded one at that. There were books floor to ceiling and stacks of books here and there. Most of the volumes were about war: the art of war, analyses of wars throughout history, causes of war, how wars can end, and personal memoirs of leaders in war.

As he skimmed one of the volumes, he heard, "Are you a reader,

CHAPTER 31

MacArthur?"

He turned to the Captain and grinned. "Not as much as you are, Sir."

"Well, help yourself to anything that piques your interest. Did you serve?"

"No, Sir. I have a low number, but it's never been called. I'm in ROTC, though, so I'll do two years after I graduate. I'm hoping to do them close to UVA, so I can see EJ as much as possible."

"Hmm. Two years is a long time."

"Yes, Sir, but EJ and I...well, I want you to know that I love your daughter very much, and I plan to marry her. I hope you will give us your blessing when the time comes."

"When will the time come, Son?"

MacArthur smiled, "Actually, that's something EJ and I have to talk about."

"What do we need to talk about?" said EJ, suddenly appearing in the doorway.

"When we're getting married."

Her smile disappeared. "Daddy, what have you been saying to him?"

Her father raised his hands in surrender. "Nothin', Darlin'. I'll leave you to it, MacArthur. Good luck."

For the first time, EJ was angry with MacArthur. "Why are you talking to my father about marrying me before asking *me*?"

"I'm sorry. I just assumed, I mean, the way we've been talking, how we feel about each other, that we're going to get married. Don't you?"

CONVERSION

"Of course, but I expected a decent proposal!" She saw how shocked he was and realized he was clueless. She relaxed. "Look, let's just forget this entire conversation took place, okay?" He nodded numbly. "And then one day, you can surprise me like you're supposed to, okay?" He nodded again. "Now, I'm going for a run. Are you coming?"

"Sure." He followed her upstairs, yelling to himself, *I need to talk to my sisters!*

True to her word, EJ acted as though the conversation had never happened, but it became the proverbial elephant in the room for MacArthur. As soon as they returned to UVA, he went to see Sarah. She was incredulous. "Where were you when Rebecca, Meg, and Joanna talked on and on about how they were proposed to? How did you not get the message that this is a major event for a woman?"

"Oh, yeah. I mean, no. I guess I must've tuned out — or I could've been on drugs." Sarah rolled her eyes at him. He asked, "What should I do?"

"You'll figure it out. Just keep getting to know her, what she likes and what she doesn't like, and then do something you know she'll like."

The semester was coming to a close and graduation lay before him. It was exciting, a relief, yet somewhat terrifying. Where would he be a year from now? David was one of the few who already had an answer. He had interviewed at the State Department, and his knowledge of Russia, summer corporate experience, and ability to speak the language secured him a job as an entry-level analyst on

CHAPTER 31

the Russian desk.

MacArthur thought his future had been decided by the US military when he was summoned to the office of his ROTC commanding officer. The man handed him an official letter and said, "You are honorably discharged with the rank of second lieutenant."

MacArthur stared at the letter, hardly believing what he was reading. "Sir, may I ask, how did this happen?"

"Son, this past year we've noted a considerable improvement, but it's no secret that you have generally been a royal pain in the ass."

"Yes, Sir."

"Your father had nothing to do with my decision, but he is who he is and I owe him, so I figure this will please him and get you out of the army's hair once and for all. Understood?"

"Yes, Sir. Thank you, Sir."

"Dismissed!"

He saluted him for the last time, turned, and forced himself to walk and not run out of the building. Then he ran to EJ's apartment and pounded on her door. He waltzed her into the hall.

"What's going on?"

He handed the letter to her.

"Oh my God! Does this mean you're done? No two years God knows where?"

He nodded. They stood and stared at one another for the longest time. No one was planning their future. They had no obligations. EJ was going to finish her degree, but now MacArthur was free to live nearby or....

"Mac, I have to study for finals. Don't you?"

"Yes."

"So, I'll see you, okay?"

"Right."

They turned and went their separate ways. MacArthur smiled and yelled over his shoulder. "Erica Jane, we have much to pray about!"

"I know. I know." Her laughter was music to his ears.

32

David sat at his desk, staring out the window, pondering his future. Spring was breaking through the late April showers, and the wretched basketball season was over. Playing sports at UVA was the second biggest disappointment of his college years, and he hoped that one day he would look back and be glad he had endured to the end.

The biggest disappointment was finding the love of his life. He went through his mental list again. Beautiful; in fact, Marilyn Monroe stunning: check. Intelligent, but not more than he: check. Vivacious and charming: check. Loves hosting and attending parties: check. Appreciates sports (even loves watching sports on TV): check. Shares religious and political views: check. Parents approve: check. Gets along with (or at least tolerates) MacArthur (and EJ too): check.

He loved all these things about her, so what was holding him back? Veronica adored him and would do anything for him. His parents had said that. Even MacArthur had said that. Many people had commented on how good they looked together, and it would be a plus in his new job to have a wife like her. Yet, he hesitated. Was he scared of making a mistake? Not with her. She was perfect. And he knew she was expecting a proposal. It was time to bite the bullet, set his doubts aside, and give himself completely to the idea

CONVERSION

that she was the one.

He went to the local jewelers to buy a ring. He knew she would love it. She loved anything that sparkled, and this one would light up her hand. He would get down on one knee and propose at the Phi Delt spring formal that Saturday night. It would be just what she would have dreamed. Veronica was all about spectacle.

Standing in her emerald green satin gown, he on one knee in his tux, the oooooooing finally died down so the crowd could hear her yell, "Yes!" Whooping and hollering ensued as he slipped the sparkling ring on her finger then rose to dip her and kiss her. And so, the dye was cast. He grinned happily. She laughed with tears in her eyes. The women gathered around to see the ring, while the men clapped him on his back enviously. MacArthur and EJ smiled and raised a drink to him, even though they both sensed something amiss.

The band began playing, and MacArthur worried that EJ was disappointed she hadn't gotten her ring yet, but she looked him in the eye and said, "Well, he did it perfectly for *her*. Dance with me?" MacArthur was relieved. Now he just had to finish final papers and exams and endure the graduation ceremony. Then he would be free!

Joanna and Marc had planned their wedding to coincide with MacArthur's graduation, so family and friends could attend both easily. At graduation, EJ met the rest of the sisters, and MacArthur watched as they chatted, their heads almost pressed together, laughing and glancing at him from time to time. David shook his head, "They've formed a new sorority: Phi Beta Mac."

CHAPTER 32

"Yeah, but I love it," MacArthur grinned.

"You ready to pop the question?"

"Yes! I've been ready since the day I first saw her."

David looked up at the sky. "Yeah. I felt the same way when I met Veronica."

MacArthur felt an ominous tug in his heart, but he had no unction to question David about his decision. And he reasoned that, although she wasn't the Christian girl he had prayed for his friend, Veronica was perfect for *him*.

The Colonel had invited family and a few close friends to the house that evening. David, his parents, and Veronica were there. Jack, Zaiah, and Henry dropped in with their dates or fiancés. The guests filled the back yard, enjoying the food Lois had prepared, including some of the dishes and desserts she had learned in Paris. Then MacArthur brought out his guitar and strummed it to get their attention.

Joanna cried, "The graduate is going to honor us with a song!"

MacArthur smiled and began to sing the love song he had written for EJ. Walking slowly toward her, the heartfelt melody and lyrics brought tears to her eyes. When the song ended, he handed his guitar to Jack and got down on one knee. He took a small box out of his pocket, opened it, and said, "EJ, you're the love of my life. Please marry me and make me the happiest man on Earth."

"Of course!" She fell into his arms, and then everyone watched him slip his mother's ring on her finger. The Colonel and his sisters were touched at how EJ loved it. It looked perfect on her hand. MacArthur turned aside to see Sarah congratulating David and

375

CONVERSION

Veronica. Veronica was beaming, holding out her hand and gazing at her ring. In that brief moment, David and Sarah shared a glance. That's when MacArthur knew David was marrying the wrong woman.

Later in the evening he said, "Hey David, I want to show you something in my room. Excuse us, ladies." As soon as he had closed the door, he took a deep breath. "You're the only brother I've ever had, and I want you to be happy. Remember that when I ask you what I'm going to ask you."

David frowned. "Okay."

"Why are you marrying Veronica when you are obviously in love with my sister?"

"What? No! You are taking all these years of teasing too far, man. Sarah and I have become good friends, that's all. It's a blast to speak Spanish with her, but I love Veronica, and she's the one I want to marry."

"Okay, man. But you're sure? Because this thing is, like, forever."

David chuckled. "Yes. I'm sure."

"Had to ask." He gave him a "bro hug" and reminded himself that Veronica was gorgeous and fun, and she and David agreed on everything. He and EJ would just continue to pray for them.

The following day everyone transitioned from graduation celebration to Joanna's wedding, which fittingly would be held in the beautiful gardens of Lewinsville Park. Because their mother was not there to guide the event, Rebecca and Lois had stepped in to help. Like Rebecca, Joanna was too tall to wear her mother's

CHAPTER 32

wedding gown and was happy to wear Rebecca's dress. With her wavy, blonde hair in an up-do, MacArthur was shocked at how beautiful she was. Growing up, she was his favorite partner in crime; now, she was something else altogether.

At the wedding, he looked at his sisters with new eyes. They had grown into amazing women. He was so proud of them, and he was even more grateful to God that both Meg and Rebecca were believers. He prayed Joanna and Marc would see the light too. He wasn't sure where Sarah stood.

A month later, Meg and Josh were married at their country church outside Nashville. So, when it was time for the Wells family vacation, the Colonel rented two homes on the lake. Sarah, Lois, and EJ shared a room, and the Colonel was with MacArthur. This time, the Colonel insisted Lois would join in the fun and only assist the girls in the kitchen if she wanted to. As Lois was not an assistant type, she trained a cadre of sous-chefs.

After the vacation with his family, MacArthur and EJ flew to California for an engagement party her parents were throwing for them. The Colonel accompanied them, and he and Captain Miller spent the first day sizing up one another, like two bulls circling the paddock. MacArthur, EJ, and Susanne breathed easy when they heard the men laughing in the study after dinner. They had in common an insatiable curiosity about man's proclivity to war. The next morning, a round of golf cemented their friendship and trust that their children would do well together.

EJ broke the news that she and MacArthur wanted to be married at their church in Charlottesville just before Christmas.

CONVERSION

They wanted the assistant rector, who taught their Sunday school class, to marry them and their church family to be there. Susanne was extremely disappointed. EJ patted her hand. "I know you always thought I would get married here, but please understand and forgive me."

"Of course." She sighed.

"Mom, we can still shop for my dress, do the invitations, and plan everything together."

Her mother's eyes lit up. "There's a new bridal shop in LaJolla that everyone is raving about. Let's visit there tomorrow. The party's all planned, so men, you can have a round of golf and we'll do some shopping. Then we'll have plenty of time to dress for the big celebration tomorrow evening."

On the golf course, the fathers got down to business. The Captain began, "MacArthur, what are your plans now that you're honorably discharged from the army?"

"I've applied for some jobs in Charlottesville. There are a couple of possibilities other than waiting tables, but I'll do anything I need to do to be with EJ. We've rented an apartment, where I'll live until we're married, then she'll move in. David and I saved all the stuff we had in our apartment, and he said I could have it. He and his fiancé are getting married in September, and she doesn't want our old stuff."

"Captain, David is MacArthur's best friend since they were twelve. We call him Superman because he looks like the comic book hero. And, he saved MacArthur's life once."

"Now that's a story I'd like to hear." Of course, MacArthur was

CHAPTER 32

thrilled to tell it, especially the part about Jesus healing his leg after he and David became blood brothers. The Captain said, "I don't know about you, Colonel, but I've seen some inexplicable things in my time."

At lunch, the Colonel launched another discussion. "MacArthur, tell the Captain why the army discharged you."

MacArthur stared at his father. "Really?"

His father nodded.

The Captain shifted in his seat. "I did some checking and was going to ask about that."

For once, MacArthur spoke briefly about his season of illegal activity and rage against the establishment. "The bottom line, Sir, is that my foolishness didn't cancel God's love for me; and I know I'm only here today because of him and the prayers of people who love me." He smiled at his father and hoped for a good response from the Captain.

"MacArthur, first of all, I'm sorry your mother isn't here. My condolences to you and to you, Colonel. Second, I'm glad EJ is marrying a man who has the sense to admit when he's been a moron and make things right. And third, in marriage, we men do tend to be morons from time to time. Just don't be *that kind* of moron again."

"Yes, Sir."

33

Almost a year before MacArthur and David's graduation, on June 17, 1972, five men had broken into the Democratic National Headquarters at the Watergate Apartments in Washington, D.C. The money they were paid was traced to President Nixon's re-election committee and eventually to the president and his closest aides. By May 1973, just before their graduation, the Public Broadcast System (PBS) aired two weeks of Senate hearings on the Watergate break-in, and David and MacArthur had to tear themselves away from their television set to study for finals and write papers. For months after, there was continuous media coverage on all networks. The beautiful Watergate Hotel became synonymous with an American scandal.

The end of September 1973, Watergate was forgotten for a moment as MacArthur stood up for David at his wedding to Veronica. Then, a week later, the country's domestic trouble was eclipsed by an international crisis. Before the news broke, the Colonel called to tell MacArthur that Egypt and Syria had led a coalition of Arab states in a surprise attack on Israel. It was Yom Kippur, the Day of Atonement, a holy day when all Jews were fasting in their synagogues. Depending on how long the war lasted and his involvement, Reuben might not be able to attend MacArthur and EJ's wedding in December.

CONVERSION

The world watched apprehensively as Russia assisted the Arab nations and the US assisted Israel. MacArthur was glad David was on his honeymoon, because they would have certainly argued over the conflict. David saw no logical reason to keep supporting a tiny nation that did nothing but incite trouble. MacArthur's biblical argument that God would bless those who blessed Israel and curse those who cursed her was nonsense to him. David considered the Bible a great blunder of mankind's overactive imagination. His dream was to forge peace between the US and USSR, and Israel was a fly in the ointment.

The world breathed a sigh of relief when the Yom Kippur War ended on October 25, 1973, without World War III erupting between the two superpowers. Reuben was free to participate in EJ and MacArthur's wedding. David was MacArthur's best man, and Reuben, Jack, Zaiah, and Henry stood up also. EJ's best friend from UVA was her maid of honor, and Rebecca, Meg, Joanna, and Sarah attended her. Little Jeanne was the flower girl, assisted by her Colonel Grandpa.

EJ's parents walked her down the aisle, and MacArthur said he thought he had died and gone to Heaven the moment he saw her. She was beautiful, head to toe, inside and out. Then, almost halfway down the aisle, he laughed out loud when he realized she was sporting a glittering pair of white running shoes. She gave him a quizzical look, so he pointed to her shoes. On the next stride forward, she lifted her skirt slightly and winked. Those who saw this interaction began laughing and pointing, so of course, the assistant rector commended the bride on her choice of wedding slippers.

CHAPTER 33

After the ceremony, the reception featured a live band; but the high point was when The Decades took the stage and performed a new upbeat song MacArthur had written for his bride. They regaled the crowd with a couple of their most requested hits, then all dispersed to dance with their dates or wives. MacArthur and EJ enjoyed every moment.

By the time 1974 began, the newlyweds were settled happily into their apartment. MacArthur was working two jobs, and EJ was studying hard. Some weeks later, David called to say that Veronica was pregnant. The future seemed bright for them all, even though the nation was still staggering from Watergate. EJ finished her third year, and the following August, President Richard Nixon resigned before Congress could vote on what might have been a unanimous impeachment. For the first time in her history, America watched her duly elected president — in disgrace and broken — wave good-bye and board an airplane to carry him home to San Clemente, California.

Vice-President Gerald Ford had already been sworn in as president and later pardoned his predecessor, a major factor in his losing the 1976 election to Jimmy Carter, the born-again peanut farmer from Georgia. Republicans and Democrats alike had high hopes for the country to heal after the years of scandal. Unfortunately, while MacArthur and EJ were enjoying a continuous honeymoon, the Carter Administration's honeymoon was cut short by disastrous policies that plunged the country into economic crisis.

Meanwhile, David became the rising star at the State Department. Those "in the know" dubbed him and Veronica one of the young power couples in Washington, D.C. It seemed their only

CONVERSION

misfortune was Veronica's series of miscarriages. They talked of adopting but never found the time. David's career and their social life were paramount, so although childless, they seemed happy.

MacArthur and EJ became known as a power couple of a different sort, and only by those who were the grateful recipients of their prayers. While EJ managed to remain at the top of her fourth-year class, she and MacArthur were also working with the National Right to Life Committee, formed by the Catholic Church in 1967 to fight the legalization of abortion. Now that it was the law of the land, their focus was to get *Roe v. Wade* overturned and save as many babies and their mothers as they could in the meantime.

MacArthur, EJ, and a few like-minded Christians in their church raised money to open a crisis pregnancy center, where a pregnant girl or woman could come for counseling, receive assistance after having her baby, or be connected with an adoption agency. As was his custom, MacArthur studied the issue thoroughly, always looking for the latest medical studies on the life of a baby from conception, articles giving insight into the challenges and fears facing a woman with an unplanned pregnancy, and medical and psychological studies on women who had had abortions.

EJ shared her story wherever she could, and her courage and compassion for others often brought healing but sometimes hatred from those who only saw a mother's will and not a baby's life. Many young women came to their apartment for a meal and prayer, some becoming dear friends even after they had given birth or had an abortion. They held a Bible study once a week for those who needed support. Thus, they gained a reputation in Charlottesville

CHAPTER 33

as a loving couple who provided a place of refuge for women who faced this life-changing decision.

They were shocked the first time a young man came to their door, shattered because his girlfriend had aborted their baby without consulting him. Neither MacArthur nor EJ had thought about the impact abortion might have on fathers. EJ's experience encouraged him that there was life after such a tragedy, and after that, they were always mindful that there were two parents involved in an unexpected pregnancy.

MacArthur held a series of jobs, partly on purpose. He believed God wanted him to write a common sense, practical book that would help people live happier, more successful lives. Therefore, he set out to rub shoulders with men and women from all walks of life. In various seasons, sometimes overlapping, he was a construction worker, a janitor, a bartender, a teacher, and volunteered in both the local veterans center and children's home.

In the spring, EJ graduated *summa cum laude*. At that time, they were ministering to a pregnant teenager and her parents, and the young girl asked EJ and MacArthur to adopt her child. Knowing this was the loving hand of God, six months later they held their precious son David in their arms.

When little David was three months old, MacArthur interviewed with a company that made discs for computer software companies. He jumped at the opportunity to be part of what he called "the coming personal computer age," and after three years of helping them become highly profitable, he had accumulated a good deal of wealth. He and EJ had just had a baby girl, Hannah,

CONVERSION

when they both sensed a big change coming. They talked about getting ready to move, and they sensed they would move to one of the western states, possibly California. MacArthur did not quit his job, but he began writing his book.

Little David and Hannah were finally asleep when the phone rang late one evening. EJ answered, "Hello. Reuben! It's wonderful to hear your voice! Where are you?" MacArthur motioned that he wanted to speak to him. "Tell me that again." She reached for a pen. "Okay. Thanks. He's right here and wants to say hello. Okay. I'll tell him. We miss you! *Shalom.*"

She replaced the receiver and turned to face her perturbed husband. "He didn't have time to talk. He'll call you when he has more time."

"Why did he call?"

"He woke up thinking about us and heard: Numbers 34:6." She reached for her Bible and found the verse. MacArthur looked over her shoulder and read aloud, "As for the western border, you shall have the Great Sea for a border; this shall be your western border."

They looked at each other in wonder. "EJ."

"Mac, did you ask him to pray about this?"

"No." MacArthur shook his head and took her in his arms. "We have to deal with this."

"I know. But it's hard. Except for my parents. They'll be thrilled."

"Do you think they'd take us in for a while, at least until I finish the book?"

386

CHAPTER 33

"Dad'll probably charge rent and require a weekly golf game. Mom won't care because she'll have her grandbabies under her roof."

"California, here we come."

MacArthur resigned his position at the company and cashed in his holdings. It was time to leave Charlottesville and the church family they loved so much. Their church had a large going-away party, offering prayers for safety and success. They sold their little house and put their furniture and some other items in storage near the Colonel's house in McLean, where they spent several weeks. Lois doted on them. She had married the plumber and had twin sons, who played with little David.

A few days before they were to drive west, MacArthur went into the city to have a final lunch with David. On the way home, D.C. traffic was not too bad. He crossed Chain Bridge back into Virginia when he noticed a black sedan behind him. It looked like the same one he had noticed as he had left the restaurant. When the road became four lanes on Route 123 to McLean, MacArthur slowed down and got in the right lane to see if the car would pass. It didn't. It stayed in the left lane and slowed down too. It appeared that he was being followed, and he noted there were two men in the sedan.

Before he could decide what to do next, traffic thinned, and the sedan suddenly sped up to come alongside the Porsche. MacArthur saw the man in the passenger seat point a pistol with a silencer, so he hit the accelerator and darted into the left lane, barely missing the sedan. From that moment, he darted through traffic to put as much distance as possible between him and his assailants. Thank

CONVERSION

God, he was in the Porsche and not the station wagon!

A road he knew well was approaching. It was full of curves and led up into the hills, so he took a hard right at the last minute and hoped to lose them. Later, he heard the screech of tires in the distance behind him and saw a black speck growing larger in his rearview mirror.

Should he try for the McLean police station or face them in the familiar hills? As a boy, he had explored every inch of these woods. His only weapon was his bow, which he kept on the floor of the back seat, but he couldn't use it and drive at the same time. And, the traffic in McLean might put him and others in more danger. He pulled off the road and drove swiftly across a field toward the woods.

He had gained a good lead on the sedan, and when he reached the dense forest, he stopped, jumped out, and grabbed his bow and quiver of arrows. As the sedan made its way across the field, MacArthur was disappearing into the woods. He stopped when he came to a tree large enough to give good cover and leaned against it.

Breathing heavily, adrenalin flowed and something old and familiar kicked in. He was running through the woods in Thailand and Reuben was calling to him, "Stop! See every movement, hear the slightest sound. Go on the offensive and strike before they see you."

He figured one man would try to circle around behind him while the other ran straight for him. They wouldn't be too cautious, because they didn't know he was armed. He nocked an arrow on the bow and slowly peeked around. He saw nothing, so he listened, forcing himself to relax and breath normally. When he heard a

CHAPTER 33

rustling of leaves, he again peeked and saw a gunman laboring up the hill toward him. He studied him carefully, pulled the arrow back, and aimed for the shoulder of the man's shooting arm. The arrow flew and hit its mark. The man screamed and dropped his gun. Falling to his knees, he picked up the gun with his other hand and fired aimlessly in MacArthur's direction, yelling obscenities.

Now the other attacker would know MacArthur was armed. He looked around the tree and saw the first man lying on the ground, hopefully unconscious or close to it. He had counted the shots and knew the man had used all his bullets. He turned to look behind him when he heard what sounded like a clumsy animal, circling to his right as he had anticipated. He took out another arrow and quietly nocked it, pulling the bow taut and scanning for movement in the direction of the sound.

A muted shot sounded and his right upper arm stung. He ducked around the other side of the tree as another bullet hit the tree with a thud. No movement. He listened. Then a voice inside him said, "Drop left!" In an instant, he dropped to the ground, saw the gunman, and released the arrow. It struck the man's leg, and he cried out and collapsed.

MacArthur nocked another arrow and cautiously approached him. The man had his hands on the arrow in his thigh, just above the knee, but it was proving too painful to remove. He screamed as he tried, then went to grab his gun when he saw MacArthur. MacArthur kicked the gun away and aimed the arrow at the man's groin. "The next one ensures you never enjoy a woman again. Tell me who sent you, 'cause I don't recognize you guys."

389

CONVERSION

"F— you!"

MacArthur drew the arrow back.

"Wait! Wait! Okay. Okay." He spat on the ground. "I'm supposed to say, 'Jimmy says thanks' before I put one between your eyes."

"He's out?"

"He's been out. God! Get this thing out of me!"

"Don't move." MacArthur took the arrow from his bow and placed it in the quiver, throwing both over his right shoulder. His right hand was covered with blood from his wound. Keeping an eye on his assailant, he took out his handkerchief and put the gun in the quiver of arrows. He helped the man stand up; and they began the trek down the hill, where the other gunman lay unconscious.

MacArthur let the man fall next to his comrade. He took his handkerchief and carefully removed the gun from the other man's hand, putting it in the quiver. "Stay here. I'll send an ambulance." Then he turned and walked away.

"You stupid bastard! You're a dead man! If I don't call Jimmy, he'll just know I'm dead and send someone else."

MacArthur ignored him and stumbled down the hill. Those guys weren't the only ones needing medical attention. He managed to get to the police station and tell the officer on duty what had happened before passing out. Hours later, he woke up in the hospital, his right arm bandaged and an IV on his left hand. EJ leaned over and kissed him. "Policemen came to the house and told us what happened. My God, MacArthur! What were you thinking?"

CHAPTER 33

"Well, I just did what Reuben trained me to do."

"So I need to chew *Reuben* out, huh?" she shook her head.

"You're awesome when you're angry."

"I think that's the drugs talking, but thanks."

"What happened to the two guys in the woods?"

"They're here. There are FBI agents outside their doors too."

"Too?"

"Honey, you're in danger until they catch Jimmy. He must have found out that you informed on him."

"Yeah, I want to know how." He squeezed her hand. "But I'm too tired to think about it. Did they find the guns?"

"Yes. Just rest. I'll be right here if you need anything."

As he drifted off, he mumbled, "For better or worse, huh?"

34

David stood over MacArthur's hospital bed and waited for him to awaken. He flashed back to another hospital bed in Panama, which seemed both ages ago and just yesterday. MacArthur opened his eyes. "Hi, blood brother. Want another go at it?"

"No. And you don't need me to save you anymore, not after what you did to those guys in the woods."

"Well, if you had been with me in the car, you would have shot 'em before we got to the woods."

David grinned. "True. So Jimmy's out and someone told him you're a rat. Are you going to have to go into witness protection?"

"God, I hope not. EJ says FBI guys are guarding my family until this is resolved." He closed his eyes. "The sins of my youth — ugh. If only I could go back —"

"Well, you can't," said the Colonel, who entered the room with EJ.

"Hi, Dad. Hey beautiful!"

David shook the Colonel's hand. "I'll go and leave —"

"No, David. Please stay. Sit everyone."

The Colonel closed the door. "You remember Bill, MacArthur? He is now with the DEA, and he believes they have a mole who has worked with Jimmy since he got out. Attempting to kill you is not the first murder Jimmy's been behind, and there have been two

CONVERSION

stings to bring him down, but he slipped the net each time. That's when Bill began to look at his team, and everything pointed to one agent. His investigation uncovered a large offshore account, so...."

David looked skeptical. "No offense, Colonel, but even if you arrest Jimmy and the mole and put them away, what guarantees do we have that Jimmy or someone else in the cartel won't try again?"

"That's where it gets interesting. Jimmy has become quite the dealer in human trafficking as well as drugs. Evidently he learned a great deal in prison. Bill thinks a girl caught his eye during one of his 'pickups' in Mexico, and he made it look like he saved her. She fell for him, married him, and they have a couple of kids, but he keeps them hidden from his colleagues."

"So Jimmy has a weakness," said David.

"He's very careful, seeing this woman only a few times a year. She tells everyone her husband died, Jimmy is her godfather — yeah, no joke — and the children have no idea he's their father. God knows what story he told her to make her tow that line, but I'm sure she is well provided for."

"How did you discover this?" asked David.

"It was a fluke. One of Bill's agents was coming home after an operation in Mexico City when he ID'd Jimmy in the airport. He had a couple of hours to kill and decided to follow him. He wound up staying two weeks."

EJ looked troubled. "You're sure about this?"

"Bill's guy was thorough. There's no doubt this is Jimmy's family. All they have to do is bring him in and show him pictures of agents outside the house and around his kids at the park, that

CHAPTER 34

sort of thing." He looked at MacArthur. "The deal will be that you and yours are not to be touched, or else the DEA will put his wife and kids where he'll never find them. If he turns and becomes their informant, they'll protect them. Then, after the heat on MacArthur goes away and Bill gets all the information Jimmy can supply, they'll put him and his family in witness protection."

"What about the two guys he sent after me?" asked MacArthur.

"Oh, Jimmy and his hit men will go away for a nice stretch, but Jimmy will see no one touches you, your family, or anyone close to you. He went to a lot of trouble to hide his family. He won't do anything to risk their safety or his ability to see them."

David studied MacArthur, who looked pensive. "What do you think?"

"I think I'm sorry I've caused all this. I suppose we're all under house arrest until Jimmy is caught."

"Correct," confirmed the Colonel. "And David, I've assigned someone to head the detail guarding you and Veronica. In fact, he volunteered for the assignment."

"I don't think I know anyone in the CIA except you, Sir."

"He's not with us. It's Reuben Katz."

"Reuben!" MacArthur's eyes brightened.

"Yes. Evidently he's on leave from Mossad, so he asked to be on your detail. A couple of my men will work with him."

"Wow. I'm really jealous, man," said MacArthur.

David smiled. "Now I get the rabbi and priest. We'll see how far he gets with me — oh God — and Veronica."

"Right! Now that's a conversation I'd like to eavesdrop on."

CONVERSION

EJ was still apprehensive. "I'll call my parents and tell them we've all come down with the flu and won't be arriving next week. Hopefully, Bill will nab Jimmy and get this resolved soon."

That week, the DEA mole confessed and helped them catch Jimmy in exchange for a lighter sentence. Jimmy readily agreed to the deal and to tell them everything he knew. He also agreed to be an informant until it was certain no one remembered MacArthur. To keep up appearances, he would do three years in prison and pay a hefty fine, which would circuitously make its way into an account for his children's college fund. MacArthur wondered what kind of woman had overturned Jimmy's criminal life.

After everyone was safe and before leaving, Reuben spent an afternoon with MacArthur. "You would have enjoyed our conversations. One night, David asked me about speaking in tongues."

"What? Why?"

"He heard you and was curious. 'What is the purpose of all that babel?' he asked. I showed him what I showed you in Thailand, how the first-century Church spoke in tongues and performed miracles, the result being that they turned the world upside down."

"How did he react to that?"

"He asked, 'Why is speaking in tongues so important now? What's the point?' I answered, 'It is what Jesus taught, that we must be indued with power from the Holy Spirit to be witnesses for him.'"

"Did he get that?"

"How could he? He does not believe. But then, he was *shocked*

CHAPTER 34

by what I told him next."

"What was that?"

"I gave him a short history of the Charismatic Movement, and he asked, 'Why have I never heard of this Charismatic Movement?' I said I believed it was because it spans all denominations. Even Roman Catholics and believing Jews like me speak in tongues, cast out demons, and heal the sick in Yeshua's name and authority. Most important, this powerful witness is a worldwide movement in which multitudes are coming to the Jewish Messiah. When I said this, for just a moment, he looked frightened."

MacArthur looked up. "Well, if I were an atheist, I would be pretty upset to hear something like that." Then he turned to Reuben. "I mean, that sounds like God is winning."

Reuben smiled. "Hmm. I sense there is more."

Two nights later, Sarah, Reuben, Lois and her family, and David and Veronica gathered at the house to celebrate the Colonel's 60th birthday. Meg and Josh flew in from Nashville, but Rebecca and Craig and Joanna and Marc were each expecting babies and could not attend. Reuben raised his glass: "To a man who is not only one of the best military minds of our time but also one of the best men of our time — and, he looks very well for his old age too!"

"Hear! Hear!"

When everyone was quiet, drinking from their glasses, Reuben continued. "And here's to their new life in the wild, wild West, obviously MacArthur's kind of place." Laughter. "Our love and Yeshua's blessings go with you always."

MacArthur and EJ made the rounds after dinner, taking time

CONVERSION

with each family member. Then Reuben joined them, followed by Veronica, sporting her drink and giggling. "MacArthur, Reuben is one of the most amazing men I've ever met, and I've met a few." She looked coyly at him. "If I wasn't married, you wouldn't have a chance. My God! You're like a modern Achilles or something, and I felt totally safe. I'm really going to miss you, except for your preaching." She smiled and kissed his cheek, then wiped off her liptstick.

"Thank you, Veronica. It was an honor to get to know you and David."

David walked up and put his arm around Veronica. "Reuben, I agree with everything my wife just said, except I don't find you that attractive. Seriously, thank you, and please come see us any time." They shook hands.

Hannah began fussing, obviously hungry, so EJ took her upstairs. Sarah followed her. She sat across from EJ as she nursed the baby. "I wanted to tell you something. Dad knows, and Lois, but I haven't told the rest of the family yet. I think I'll let him tell them after I'm gone."

EJ looked alarmed. "Gone? Where are you going?"

"When I was in Madrid for a year, I loved it there. I started going to mass with some friends from the nursing school, and one night Jesus visited me."

"Really?"

"Uh-huh. I was closing my bedroom door when he appeared behind me and put his hand on my back, so I didn't see his face. He said, "I'm giving you endurance to wait patiently for the

CHAPTER 34

blessings I have for you, because you care for those in need in my name."

"What a promise!"

Sarah nodded. "Well, it's strange, but it's only been recently — actually, when you and MacArthur told me you were leaving Charlottesville — that I remembered this. Suddenly, I knew I was supposed to leave too, that I was to go back to Spain and work, probably in a Christian medical clinic or medical mission."

"Do you know anyone there?"

"Yes. Some of my friends from the nursing school there. I've already talked to them. They are in an organization called Opus Dei, lay ministers who serve God by serving others. It's an official part of the Catholic Church, but its members can be married or single, men or women. I like that. I feel I fit there."

"Sarah. I'm perplexed. I didn't know you were a believer in Jesus."

"Well, I leave the evangelism to MacArthur."

"Ah, yes," EJ smiled knowingly.

"But I've always loved him, even as a little girl. And when MacArthur became a zealot, I listened. After Thailand, he talked like Jesus was his best friend. Then, about a year ago, I was visiting Dad and talked to Lois."

EJ threw back her head and laughed. "Whoa! Talking to Lois usually seals the deal. Look how she led your dad to the Lord."

"That's what *really* shocked me. *Dad* was talking like Jesus was *his* best friend!" She shook her head in wonder. "Well, after Lois showed me about being born again in the Bible, I drove back

CONVERSION

to Charlottesville and couldn't even listen to the radio. I told Jesus I was his and would follow him the rest of my life. And EJ, something happened inside me. I was completely content. You know, I had always felt lonely, different, like the black sheep in the family. Everyone else was married, having kids. But now I'm happy, at peace with my life."

"I know exactly what you mean, because the same thing happened to me when I got born again. And then I met MacArthur...."

Sarah laughed. "Say no more!"

"But Sarah, what you're doing sounds perfect for you. It really does. I'm just sad you'll be so far away."

"Well, so will you."

"Oh, you've got me there!" she nodded.

"It's going to be hard on Dad. Meg and Josh and Joanna and Marc are only a plane ride away, Rebecca and Craig a train ride or quick flight, but still. I feel bad for leaving him."

"We feel the same way. But the Colonel still has his work — whatever that is! And he has a lot of friends and Lois and her family. It's not like he's going to sit in his study and be depressed."

"I know you're right. He'll soldier on like he always has. It's one of the things we love about him. I just have to trust God."

"Yeah, it's funny how everything in life comes down to that one, simple thing."

That night, as EJ recounted her conversation with Sarah to MacArthur, in mid-sentence, he jumped up and ran to Sarah's room.

CHAPTER 34

An hour later, he got in bed and EJ murmured, "You okay?"

"Never better."

"So you and Sarah are good?"

"I'd say so. Left her praying in tongues."

EJ turned toward him. "No kidding!"

"Yep. My sister is baptized in the Holy Spirit, praise God! Now I just have to work on Joanna and Marc and David and Veronica—"

"And the rest of mankind. Go to sleep, Mac. Even Jesus rested."

35

President Carter's policies had plunged the US economy into crisis, and Christians especially learned a valuable lesson: Just because a person is born again doesn't mean they're the right person for the job. Although he achieved his dream of brokering what became a temporary peace between Israel and Egypt, this legacy was overshadowed by double-digit inflation, soaring gas prices, fuel shortages, and nearly 20 percent interest rates.

The state of the economy was the primary reason MacArthur and EJ moved in with her parents. It was not the time to buy a home, especially in California, where home prices had risen nearly 80 percent more than the national average. And the journey from Virginia to California proved costly. Many gas stations had no gas or long lines to obtain a ration of gas, thus MacArthur and EJ shortened their driving times per day and made certain they would spend each night in a city large enough to have fuel for their station wagon and the Porsche.

President Carter's worst bequest to the world, however, was his policy toward Iran. The Shah was often difficult and cruel, but he was enacting significant economic reforms to raise the standard of living for all of his people, and women were being educated and becoming professionals. Still, Carter desired a change in leadership and favored an exiled cleric by the name of Ayatollah Khomeini.

CONVERSION

Through back channels, Khomeini promised Carter even more reforms; unfortunately, they were not the reforms President Carter had in mind.

When revolution came and the Shah fled for his life, the Carter Administration flew the Ayatollah Khomeini back to Iran. The new leader immediately deprived women of education and any profession outside the home, enslaving them to their fathers and husbands and enshrouding all but their eyes in burkas. Then he allowed a group of students to storm the American Embassy and hold hostage US diplomats and citizens. The Carter Administration sought a diplomatic solution in what marked the beginning of a new wave of Islamic extremist terror across the globe.

Carter's failures in leadership caused considerable suffering for most Americans, and this lit a fire in MacArthur regarding his political interests. But first, he had to complete his book. He wrote every day except Sunday, and the family endured the "clack, clack, clack" of his typewriter coming from the Captain's study. Within a year, he had finished *Help Yourself*.

"What, exactly, is this about?" asked the Captain.

"It's, I believe, something new and probably revolutionary. The book addresses every area of a person's life, beginning with their body, then their thinking and their emotions — which are closely related — then their relationships, their profession, and finally their spiritual life. It challenges them in each area on several levels."

"Which are...."

"First, to realize that their life today is a result of their decisions yesterday. To change their tomorrow means making different

CHAPTER 35

decisions today. So, the first challenge is to be completely rid of the blame-game and take responsibility for yourself. No matter what was forced upon you in the past, you own your life and each decision you've made, are making, and will make. Only then can you change your life for the better."

"Self-government," said the Captain.

"Yes. And the second challenge is opening the mind and heart to new possibilities, alternative ways of seeing yourself and your life. In each section of the book, I present a series of questions. The answers help define your Point A and Point B, where you are now and where you want to be."

"In other words, you can't get to Point B without recognizing how you got to Point A, right?"

"Yes. And, you can't leave Point A without establishing a Point B as your goal."

"Ah. True."

"The third challenge is internal change. People can't expect to improve their lives without being *willing* to change, and that means changing their underlying desires. They can't move from Point A (discontent) to Point B (where they want to be), unless they *truly desire* to leave Point A *and truly desire to work toward* Point B."

"So you're saying, if I want to quit smoking, I have to change how I think about it."

"No. It's not thought. It's motivation. How badly do you *want* to quit?" MacArthur asked.

"Uh...not as badly as I want to smoke!" laughed the Captain.

MacArthur threw up his hands. "Exactly! Well, when your

CONVERSION

desire to quit trumps your desire for nicotine, you can change. You can change your lifestyle and move from Point A/smoking toward Point B/not smoking."

"Hmm."

"The final result is that you get on track. Every human has a right path for them, and getting on that path and staying on that path is the key to their personal success and happiness. You make decisions that keep you moving forward in accomplishing your goals and realizing your dreams in every area of your life. You stay *on track.*"

"I know exactly the moment I get off track, as you say, because I feel it in my gut and everything begins to go to hell."

MacArthur nodded vigorously. "I have the same experience, and I believe most people do. What this book does is encourage us to recognize those moments and get back on track as fast as possible, doing minimal damage to our lives and the lives of those around us. Ultimately, as more and more people get on track, our society improves. The world becomes a better place." He took a deep breath. "This is true not only for individuals but for families, businesses, communities, and even nations."

The Captain frowned. "What about the spiritual part? Do you tell everyone they're going to Hell if they don't become a Christian? That's not going to sell many books."

MacArthur smiled. "Many people consider spiritual life a private matter, but that's the beauty of a book. I can get personal because it's just an author and a reader. And, like the other chapters, I simply present facts and encourage them to make the

CHAPTER 35

best decision for their life. Of course, I believe the facts cry out a resounding, 'Jesus is *the* way, *the* truth, and *the* life, and no one comes to the Father *but by Him*.' But no one can force another person to believe. As you know, that's between them and God."

The Captain tilted his head with a suspicious glint in his eye. "Something tells me I've just been preached to."

MacArthur laughed.

"Well, thank God. Have you seen the light, Captain?" They looked up to see EJ, grinning in the doorway of the study.

"Now, now, Daughter. Don't press. Don't press." He stood, kissed her on the forehead, and left the room.

MacArthur shrugged his shoulders. "He asked me what the book was about."

She sat on his lap and put her arms around his neck. "Oh. And you managed to tell him in just one day. I'm impressed. You're growing, Mac!"

"Between you and Jesus, how could I not?" He kissed her until they heard squeals. Little David pulled on their hands and Hannah grabbed their legs, telling them to stop and play with them. They managed to stand, and EJ took David in hand as MacArthur swung Hannah on his shoulders. He said, "I didn't tell your father one thing, though."

"What's that?"

"This book is going to be a best seller."

The look on MacArthur's face told her it wasn't *his* idea, so she smiled and said, "Okay...wonder what changes that will bring?"

Within a year of being printed, *Help Yourself* was in demand

CONVERSION

in every book store, and MacArthur's publisher sent him on a nationwide book tour, which included interviews on local television programs and a couple of national talk shows. As he began writing a second book, he launched *A Week to Help Yourself*, a seminar that took people through the book, using exercises and games that facilitated making good decisions in each area of their lives. He was determined to get to know and personally help as many people as possible, and in the final session of each conference, he took questions and comments from the participants. The results proved significantly positive, and soon corporations, churches, and some cities invited him to come.

By the time *More Ways to Help Yourself* was being printed and sold, he and EJ had accrued a good deal of wealth, which excited them for two reasons: They could give more to those in need and ministries they supported, and they had saved enough to buy their own home.

It had been their dream to live in a beach house, and several became available in Malibu. The third one they walked into felt like home. The sellers were desperate and agreed to lower the price considerably if MacArthur paid in cash. Several weeks later, the deed was in their hands and they moved in. They threw a big "thank you" party to God and all the people who had prayed for this miracle.

Not long after the move, EJ was interviewed by a women's magazine. The interviewer was taken aback by her answer to the question, "How has your husband's success affected your marriage and family?"

CHAPTER 35

"I believe the effects of MacArthur's success and his travel schedule would destroy us if we didn't have our relationship with Jesus and the support of our church family. When I start feeling sorry for myself because Mac's not here, I have friends to pray with me and someone in the church can either fix the problem, tell me who can fix it, or help me fix it."

She laughed. "One time, our son got carried away with his little wooden tool set and there were holes, all about so high, along the family room wall. My girlfriends came over, and together we managed to patch the dry wall and paint it. When we finished, we had a pizza party and celebrated with our families. It was great."

"Sounds like a wonderful church."

"It is. Our pastor is one of the best Bible teachers I've heard, and our worship services are so powerful. We've seen many people healed of incurable diseases, and every service people give their lives to Jesus. The best part is that our kids love their Sunday school. If Mac or I say we're too tired to go to church, the kids mutiny."

"Now that's impressive! But there must be a strain when you spend so little time together."

EJ shook her head. "We don't allow ourselves to be apart long enough for that to happen. MacArthur and I are very careful about our schedules. When we are apart, we talk every day, and he always talks to the kids. And when we're together, we appreciate each other so much more."

MacArthur Wells was becoming a household name as the Carter Administration tried in vain to free the hostages in Iran and

CONVERSION

couldn't seem to stop rising inflation. EJ and MacArthur remained involved with the Right to Life movement and several other charities where they saw first-hand how people were struggling. They campaigned for California Governor Ronald Reagan in his 1980 presidential run and were delighted when, on January 20, 1981, he was sworn in as the 40th president of the United States.

That same day, after 444 days in which the Carter administration could not achieve a diplomatic solution, the US hostages in Iran were suddenly released. The American people were stunned. Maybe it was true: Reagan was "the new sheriff in town" no enemy wanted to cross. The hostages were overjoyed to be reunited with their loved ones after their horrible ordeal, America began to heal, and EJ and MacArthur began to sense the next step in their lives.

The following weekend, MacArthur was walking on the beach and greeted his neighbor, the nightly talk show host Johnny Carson. They had a short but friendly conversation, and a week later MacArthur's literary agent called to say he was booked to do *The Tonight Show* the following month.

On February 11, 1981, after a brief discussion of the success of his books and seminar, Johnny Carson asked MacArthur, "Well, tell me, MacArthur. You're fairly young. Where do you go from here?"

He answered, "I've always been concerned about the well-being of both individuals *and* our nation, and I believe I can help more people by becoming involved in government. Well, actually, as part of the government, I want to work to diminish it, so government is less intrusive, especially in businesses. I've met creative, smart

CHAPTER 35

people *in the slums* who have great ideas and big dreams, but they take one look at all the red tape and bureaucracy involved and decide to stay on welfare."

Carson drummed his pencil on the desk, raised his eyebrows, and said, "So, are you running for office?"

He smiled that goofy smile that so many had come to love. "Thank you for asking, Johnny, because I wish to announce that I'm running for the United States Senate here in California." The audience yelled and stood to their feet, applauding. The cameras scanned the audience as Carson chuckled.

When the noise died down, MacArthur turned to him and said, "I believe it's time our nation considered new and better ways of doing things. We need a breath of fresh air and common sense in Washington."

More applause. Carson nodded his head, but his expression was skeptical. "A breath of fresh air. Okay." He scratched his neck. "And you believe a best-selling author can do this in *our Congress*?"

"Yes, Sir."

Johnny loosened his tie and raised his eyebrows to the camera. The audience laughed.

MacArthur joined in the laughter then said, "Well, Ronald Reagan was an actor. Many of the founding fathers were farmers, businessmen, or physicians. I've been a janitor, a teacher, construction worker, and many other things before I became an author and conference speaker. I know what a lot of people go through to try to make it in this country."

"That's quite a resume."

411

CONVERSION

MacArthur leaned over the desk. "Johnny, I don't need to go to Washington to become rich and famous even if I wanted to. I want to work hard for a few years in Washington, making changes to open up the future for all Americans and their children, and then come home. It's time to shake up the lifers, the powerful Washington *elite,* who too often pass laws and regulations that put a foot on the necks of good, hard-working people — while putting money in their own pockets."

Carson leaned toward MacArthur to mimic him. "MacArthur, you're my neighbor, and we don't live in the slums. Are you not one of the *elite*?"

The audience rumbled, "Oooooh."

MacArthur smiled and shook his head. "No. We're not elites, Johnny. Elites believe they are better educated and more intelligent, and that gives them the right to tell everyone else how to live their lives and run their business. What gets *me* excited is helping someone else realize their dreams. And *you* do *your* part by giving us a good laugh along the way."

"Well, thank you, MacArthur. I wish you the best." He looked at the audience, "And you heard it here first, folks!"

And so MacArthur's campaign for US Senator in the 1982 California election began with national media coverage.

36

"My God! Did I just hear what I think I heard?" Veronica set her glass of wine on the coffee table and flashed her fiery green eyes at David, who sat staring at the television set. "David?!" she pressed.

He smirked. "This is classic MacArthur."

"Jesus Christ! Did you know he was going to do this?"

David shook his head. "Uh-uh."

"Why aren't you upset? I know he's your friend, but he's a right-wing stooge! We sure as hell don't need another one of *them* in Washington." She took a drink then sighed. "Do you think he can win?"

"Honey, if MacArthur's doing this, it's probably because 'God' told him to, and unfortunately, that also could mean 'God' told him he'd win. Did you see his face? He was resolute, and every time I've seen that look, what he said would happen happened."

"Oh shit! You're kidding?"

"Sorry, but that's MacArthur. He *knows* things, and there's nothing you can do about it. He acts like a five-year-old, and then something impossible becomes possible. You almost have to believe there *is* a God pulling the strings, because there's no way he pulls it off himself."

"Well, pardon me, but I'm not falling for that God crap.

CONVERSION

Reagan's bunch has put him up to this and are probably bankrolling the whole thing. How are we gonna handle it? Everyone in Washington knows you're his best friend, and I don't want to be 'disinvited' because of it!"

"Calm down, Veronica! You've got nothing to worry about. MacArthur and I have never hidden the fact that we disagree on many issues, *especially* religion and politics. All our friends know this."

"You're right. Of course you're right. I've just had too much to drink and am running off my mouth…when I should be using it for far more pleasurable pursuits." She kissed him seductively and began walking towards the bedroom.

David turned off the television and followed her.

In January 1983, MacArthur was sworn in as the junior US Senator from California. When the microphones were shoved in his face, he thanked God and everyone who had helped him, particularly his wife EJ, "who, by the way, is expecting our third child!"

David called to congratulate them, and Veronica sent a gift. Then the power couple of Washington turned their attention to hosting their annual Valentine's Day costume party. It had become a gala extraordinaire, and this year David was Mark Antony to Veronica's Cleopatra. David watched his wife glide around the ballroom, regaling their guests. She looked striking in a black wig and gold lamé dress, which was still talked about in the social column of *The Washington Post* several days afterward.

CHAPTER 36

On the first Monday in March, David called to tell her he was running late. She sounded relieved. "That's fine, Sweetheart, because I'm running late myself. Just starting dinner."

He arrived home an hour later, and this is what he told the police: "I came in the house and something smelled good, so I started toward the kitchen. But I glanced in the living room and couldn't believe what I saw. Veronica on the floor, and blood everywhere. I tried CPR, but I couldn't get a pulse; so I called 911. Then I noticed that the television and all the stereo equipment were gone. My God, she would have given them to them!"

He called his parents and then MacArthur, who was in Washington and came immediately. He wept with him and stayed at his side while the police and ambulance did what they needed to do. Then he insisted that David spend the night at his apartment. David never returned to his house. After having it scrubbed clean, he sold it furnished except for a few of his personal things and moved into an apartment near his office.

He carried on with his work at the State Department, but it was several months before he began attending parties and going out with friends. It was a long time before anyone saw him with a date. He was in no hurry to marry again, much to the consternation of many young women in the nation's capital.

When MacArthur was in town for congressional sessions, they had lunch every week if their schedules allowed. "Do you honestly believe the common man has the depth of understanding and knowledge to decide what is best for him and his family, not to mention that many are hopeless victims of classism, racism, and

415

CONVERSION

gender biases?" demanded David. "You know how ignorant most people are. You've seen the shows that go out on the streets and ask people who was president when the slaves were freed. Some of them say George Washington and some JFK! And don't get me started about economics or foreign affairs."

"They may say George Washington or JFK, but they understand right and wrong, doing a hard day's work, paying their taxes, and what it means to be free. I've spent years talking to all kinds of citizens, and I've learned that most of them learn as much from their experiences in life as they do in school. And you'd be surprised what even high school dropouts are reading!"

David was tired and didn't want to argue with his friend. "How're EJ and the kids?"

MacArthur's face fell. "I won't lie. It's harder than I thought it would be. Caleb seems to be okay with me whenever I'm home, but he's only six months old, so I can only hope he continues to be good about it. David and Hannah pretty much understand why Daddy is away. You know, now that I'm older and wiser, I have a lot of empathy for my old man, having to leave us so much."

"Yeah. I've thought about that too. The sacrifice of public service," mused David.

"How are you? It's been over a year."

"Oh, some days are good. Some are crap. More good now."

"Don't let the pain beat you! Find the purpose. Get the understanding. Then you can defeat it and be a better man."

David laughed. "Okay, Mr. *Help Yourself.*"

MacArthur laughed and raised his hands in surrender. "Guilty

CHAPTER 36

as charged. But you know, I just want you to get past this and be happy. I mean, you're Superman! I'm sure you're saving us all the time, and we don't know it. You deserve to be happy."

"I don't know about that."

"Hey! I almost forgot! EJ's parents are throwing a big bash for her 30th birthday. It's at their house in Laguna next Saturday. Why don't you come to Malibu and spend some time with us and the kids. You'll go to the party and meet my crazy and ignorant friends. And, you can add more color to that natural tan of yours."

David smiled and moved his food around with his fork. "You know, that actually sounds good."

"EJ and the kids will love seeing you." MacArthur reached in his pocket. "Here's your official invitation. The party's on Saturday evening, so we'll probably bring the kids and spend the night at the Captain and Susanne's —"

David started to laugh. "The Captain and —"

MacArthur rolled his eyes. "I know. Sounds like a rock band. But that's my wonderful in-laws. So we'll drive back to Malibu the next day. I hate to miss church, but our pastor and his wife and a lot of our church family will be at the party, so we'll have that time with them — and you'll get to meet them."

"I'll look forward to *that*."

David arrived a day ahead of the party, and little David and Hannah crawled all over him. He had forgotten how wonderful it was to play with them, but a wave of sadness almost swamped him when he wondered what his own children would have been like.

The party was a huge success. EJ couldn't stop smiling, and

CONVERSION

she cried when MacArthur gave a corny but moving toast. "You're my true north, even though you brought me west...but seriously, I savor every moment with you, as though it was the only moment we would ever have together. Here's to forever with Jesus!"

David was pleasantly surprised that the "church family" proved to be a lot of fun and didn't preach at him. He was touched when many said they had heard of Veronica's passing and had prayed for him. Pastor Eddie, a short, round, jovial sort, quipped, "You know a lot about the Bible for an atheist."

"Well, I was raised Catholic, and I've been around Bible-thumping St. Mac for most of my life; so I've picked up a few things. Besides, it was important to me to be a knowledgeable atheist. I wanted a good reason for my beliefs."

"Now that is something I'd like to hear."

"It's simple. I'm an empirical person. I believe what I see with my own eyes. Your God is not known by our physical senses and thus must be a creation of your imagination."

"Then, you don't believe you're an eternal spirit?"

"Show me my spirit. You can't. When I die, I die."

"Hmm. What does that say about the value of your life?"

"Exactly! We must make the best of our time on Earth, ensuring a better world for our children and grandchildren, because that's our purpose and value."

"I certainly agree with that, but there's so much more! We weren't created to be merely physical and terminal; we are eternal spirits with the capacity to know and love the Creator of the universe...uh...forever. Now that's some value and meaning!"

CHAPTER 36

"I'm sorry, it just sounds like a fairy tale to me."

He grinned kindly. "Well, we'll just have to pray harder for you."

David laughed nervously, shook his hand, and excused himself. He found MacArthur on the upper balcony by himself, pensively watching the waves hit the beach as the sun began to set.

"Beautiful view."

MacArthur smiled. "Yeah. And a wonderful life. I want that for you, you know."

"Yeah. I know." His eyes narrowed and he was suddenly serious. "Don't move, Mac."

MacArthur instinctively followed David's orders and froze, but said through clenched teeth, "Is this a joke?"

"No joke. There's a yellow jacket on your neck."

"Can you get it off?" he whispered.

"Don't worry. I'll get it." David took his handkerchief from his pocket and walked behind MacArthur, slowly bringing the handkerchief close to the wasp, and then moving swiftly to capture it.

"Ouch!"

"Shit! Sorry Mac. I don't know how I missed it! Ugh. Hold still. Let me get the stinger out." He pulled it out with his handkerchief, which he then waved over the rocks below. "Let's get some baking soda on it right away."

In the kitchen, the caterer helped them immediately. "I'm allergic to them damn things," he said, as he mixed the soda and water and something else David didn't recognize. "Here you go," and he dabbed a blob of the concoction on the site of the sting.

"Wow, that was some mixture. The pain is completely gone!

419

CONVERSION

Thanks, man!" MacArthur hugged the caterer.

An hour later, MacArthur and EJ were in the lower floor family room when David walked up, put his arm around EJ, and said with a frown, "My boss just called."

"How did —"

"I left this number with my secretary just in case. The White House is working on a project that needs my immediate attention, so I'm afraid I have to catch the red-eye back."

MacArthur put down his drink. "I'll drive you to the airport."

David shook his head. "No need. I've called a limo service we use. They're on their way."

EJ looked up at him, "The kids will be so disappointed, but we understand about duty calling."

"They aren't the only ones who are disappointed. Happy birthday and thanks so much for inviting me." He kissed her cheek and gave her a hug.

"You go save the world from Russia and communism and all that bad stuff, okay Superman?"

He smiled. "I'll do my best."

"Love you, man." MacArthur caught him in a bear hug.

"Love you, too. We'll talk soon."

David was in his office Sunday evening when he received the first phone call from EJ. "David, MacArthur's in the hospital. They aren't sure what's the matter with him. Some think it's a bad reaction to the yellow jacket sting; others think it's a freak virus."

"What are his symptoms?" David asked.

CHAPTER 36

"He had a cough this morning, which was really bad by this afternoon. Then he started having trouble breathing, so we brought him here. Pastor Eddie met us," her voice cracked. "David, something terrible is wrong, and I have a bad feeling."

"I'll be there as soon as I can."

"I would love that, but you can't do anything, and I know you're needed where you are. Besides, I called the Colonel and his sisters to ask them to pray, and you know how they are. Everyone but Sarah will be here by tomorrow. The clan will fill our house." Her voice was shaky, not at all like the tower of strength he knew.

"Are you sure?"

"I'm sure. You know MacArthur. He loves being dramatic. He'll probably be perfectly fine tomorrow, and the whole family will be mad at *me!*"

"Okay, but call me the moment there's any change, please."

"I will. Love you, David."

"You too." He put down the receiver. A wave of fear and then nausea began to take hold, so he shook himself and focused on the task at hand.

The second call came Monday afternoon. EJ said MacArthur was on a breathing machine and in and out of consciousness. She broke down and asked him to come. "I'll get there as soon as I can, EJ, as soon as a plane can get out after this snowstorm. Tell him I'm coming, okay?"

"I will." She left the nurses' desk and resumed her post by MacArthur's bed, leaning in to whisper in his ear. "MacArthur, David's on his way." She gazed gratefully at Pastor Eddie and Meg,

421

who were praying. Rebecca, Joanna, and the Colonel were holding on to each other. Sarah was still en route from Spain and would probably not get there in time if the doctor was correct in his prognosis.

"So you called David?" the Colonel asked.

She nodded. Pastor Eddie's wife entered the room and held her for a while. Then EJ turned back to MacArthur, holding his limp hand in hers. Suddenly, he opened his eyes. Because of the breathing tube, he couldn't speak, but he looked at her with such love, she nearly collapsed on the bed. She thought she heard him say, "Good-bye for now, Beautiful. I love you. Love our kids for me." Then he closed his eyes.

Dr. Ross came in and examined him. He was the specialist who had been with them from the moment MacArthur was admitted. "Folks, I wish I had better news for you. We can't find anything that would cause a complete respiratory failure, and now his liver and kidneys are failing. We're doing everything we possibly can; but frankly, we really don't know what we're fighting. I'm a man of prayer myself, so Pastor, keep praying. In the meantime, you need to prepare yourselves."

"Oh God, I wish Sarah was here," moaned Rebecca.

"I do too, Sweetheart," said the Colonel.

They circled the bed, holding each other and weeping, praying, trying to find some ray of hope in the overwhelming sense that there was no hope.

It was a little after 6 p.m. when an alarm sounded. Dr. Ross and two nurses hurried into the room. A nurse turned off the alarm,

CHAPTER 36

and the doctor's face was grim. "Folks, I'm so sorry. There's no brain activity, and his pulse is imperceptible."

EJ stared at him for what seemed an eternity. Finally, she nodded. He slowly removed the breathing tube, and they heard MacArthur exhale his last breath.

The other nurse removed the IV line from his hand. Dr. Ross said, "Take all the time you need," then he and the nurses left the room. Pastor Eddie and his wife wept and embraced each one, then left also.

MacArthur's family stared at the face of the one they thought indestructible, touching him, crying in pain. The Colonel kissed him on his forehead. "Goodbye, my dear son. Say hello to your mom." His voice broke, and the sisters held onto him. Finally, each sister kissed MacArthur and said their good-byes.

"I want some time alone, if you don't mind," said EJ. They nodded and hugged her on their way out.

As the door closed, she laid down beside MacArthur, put her arm across his chest, and kissed his cheek. "Father, I don't understand." She stroked MacArthur's hair and his cheek, now growing cold. "He's my man, remember? I'm his woman." She lay her head on his chest and sobbed, "Please, Jesus! This makes no sense! It's not right. Help me understand. Please, help me."

She cried until she was drained of emotion, then arose from the bed to take one last look. In her suffering, a sweet peace surrounded her, somehow comforting her. She kissed him tenderly, then walked out of the room, thanking Dr. Ross and the nurses for all they did.

CONVERSION

"We will hold him in the morgue here until you make arrangements with the funeral home," he said gently.

"Thank you. Thank you all."

37

David placed his cup on the newspaper and forced his eyes to meet Reuben's gaze. "MacArthur was assassinated. And I know who did it."

Reuben's eyes flashed. "How do you know this?"

"Because I was there."

"Are *you* in danger?"

"Yes, but not the way you think."

"You are safe here — no bugs — so tell me what I need to know to help you."

"What you need to know is much less than what I need to tell you."

Reuben cocked his head and looked at him circumspectly. "You are sitting in one of my safe houses, David, saying our dear friend has been murdered. I have all the time in the world."

David noticed the gun case on Reuben's desk. He sought for any alternative but this and could find none. "Okay." He took a deep breath. "As you know, I was born in Cuba. What you may not know is that my father was Russian KGB and my mother was a Cuban revolutionary. They met in an underground meeting with Fidel Castro during Batista's reign. My dad's cover was dentistry, and he told everyone he pumped his clients in Batista's government for information so he would know when to leave, before the

CONVERSION

revolution. He *was* listening, but to gain intel for *Fidel*."

Reuben sat back in his chair but remained expressionless.

"My father and mother did such a good job, the KGB put us on a freedom boat for Miami to become US citizens. The idea was to live in a strategic military location, where we could continue gathering intel. In Panama, the military came to Papa for dental work and, as luck would have it, Colonel Wells arrived when I was twelve. He was one of the commanders of the Bay of Pigs invasion, so…a major target. Some of our relatives died stopping that invasion. We hated him, but instead of killing him, my father was to gain his trust and gather as much information as he could. If he could turn him, even better."

Reuben scoffed. "He would be more likely to turn a cat into a mouse!"

"Yes…well, since the Colonel's only son was my age and lived in a household of women, with a father who was gone much of the time, MacArthur would be an easy mark for me to befriend, gain access to the household, etcetera. They were right, well, almost." He paused to drink his tea and gather his thoughts.

"My parents raised me to be a quiet but likeable deceiver, the perfect spy. The quiet part was my nature, but occasionally the lying was difficult. I had to remind myself that I was part of something noble and great. We were forging a just world government in which all people would be equal. My parents thought it would happen quickly and violently, like it did in Russia, China, Eastern Europe, and Cuba; but after Kennedy's blockade forced Khrushchev to keep his missiles in Russia, they again abandoned a bloody revolution

CHAPTER 37

and continued their slow, subversive strategy.

"Khrushchev's 'I will bury you' speech." Reuben's face was inscrutable.

"Yes. I was proud to be a part of defeating the evil US from within by befriending MacArthur. By the time I met him, I knew how to be the affable friend to whom you could tell anything. Whatever any of the military or diplomats' kids told me, I only told my parents. My friends learned that their secrets were safe with me. I was not only a likeable liar; I was a trustworthy one."

Reuben raised his eyebrows.

"My training was that children in free nations are programmed by their parents to believe lies and superstitions. I was the lucky one. My parents taught me the truth. Capitalism was an evil that bred selfishness and greed. Religion was an opiate to subdue the masses and enslave them in a sadistic morality. Only communism would bring true freedom, equality, and peace to the world.

"Ultimately, in our socialist global order, children would be taught these truths by the state. This would ensure *lasting* peace and prosperity. US public schools were already educating children to understand these principles, as we had placed our people in universities across America for decades. Our professors were teaching those who taught the next generations."

Reuben shifted in his chair. "Okay. Let's leave the indoctrination and return to your role."

"Of course. Sorry. My biggest obstacle was MacArthur himself. I genuinely *liked* him. He was so…outlandishly himself, freer than any kid I'd ever known. I envied his ease to be who he was

CONVERSION

in any situation. Even when he was making a fool of himself, he was *himself*. Of course, there were times I wanted to strangle him; but most of the time...being with him, the great times we had... well, the idea that he was being programmed by anyone seemed foolish."

"And the light during the riot in Panama?" asked Reuben.

"Oh, yeah. That was the first thing I kept from my parents."

"There were other things?"

"Yes. I never told them how much I came to love MacArthur and his family." David rolled his eyes and shifted in his seat. "And I *never* told them about Sarah."

"But a marriage to Sarah might have given you even more access to the Colonel and what he was doing."

"Maybe, but the KGB were looking at the long term. She didn't fit the description of the woman they wanted me to be with, someone who would share my ideals but remain ignorant of my true loyalties. Most of all, she had to capture the spotlight while I did what I needed to do in the shadows. Sarah was too quiet, genuinely patriotic, and a devout Christian besides. It was impossible.

"On the other hand, Veronica was perfect, growing up in a progressive school in New York. She applauded taking prayer out of public schools as a kid! No moral hang-ups. Socialist... feminist...atheist. She believed the Constitution was out-of-date and the founders, well, not as smart as some people thought. A true Democrat leftist and our kind of woman right to the end. But the end was...bad."

CHAPTER 37

Reuben cocked his head. "How *did* she die?"

David shook his head. "She had me fooled. God, she would've made a terrific spy. If my handlers knew what she was up to, they didn't tell me. She secretly remained close to her roommate in college, Daphne, a woman I couldn't stand; and back then it was obvious Daphne hated me too." He paused to sip his tea, then winced. "All these years they were *lovers*, and I was oblivious. Then one night, I came home to hear Daphne screaming, 'Leave him or I'll kill you both!'

"She was pointing a gun at Veronica in the living room. Man, I had never seen Veronica scared, ever. That shocked me almost more than what was happening. Daphne turned to me and snapped, 'You are the stupidest of men.' She laughed and waved the gun at me. 'Your beloved wife *killed* every one of your babies.'

"At first, I didn't understand what she was saying. It didn't make sense, because we had never had any babies to kill. I asked her what she was talking about, and Veronica yelled at her to shut up; but Daphne hissed, 'Not miscarried, idiot. Aborted.' I just kept staring at her, trying to process all this, and she screamed, '*My* dear V never got close to having one of your brats!'

"Veronica was furious. She told her they were through and screamed at her to get out. Daphne just went insane and shot Veronica several times before I could grab the gun. As she ran out of the house, I almost shot her in the back; but I had the presence of mind not to. I verified that Veronica was dead and called my handler. She and her guys disposed of the gun and made it look like a burglary gone wrong."

"Your handler is a woman?"

"Yes, since college."

"Anyone we know?"

David took a deep breath. "Miss Lila Jenkins."

Reuben remained inscrutable.

"You know about her?"

He waved his hand. "I cannot say."

"Well, Lila's guys also took care of Daphne. The following night they drove to her apartment, and as far as the world knows, she hung herself because, as her note said, she couldn't face life apart from her lover." He took a drink. "Then I played the grieving husband."

"You had no love for Veronica?"

"There were moments when I convinced myself we had something, but she was always part of the mission." He shrugged. "I played the part. I guess she did too. She was incredibly sexual, which was nice, but I knew she wanted power and money more than anything. I was the means to that end. And that was okay with me. It made us even in 'the grand deception.' Equal partners."

"And the abortions?" Reuben's tone was kind.

David shifted uncomfortably. "I support abortion, but since that night, every time I think about what Daphne said, what Veronica did, it sickens me. I don't know what to do with that." He smiled sardonically. "Maybe I'll get some counsel from EJ."

Reuben growled.

He shook himself. "Sorry. Habits." He cleared his throat. "Well, meanwhile, back in Panama...I was lucky to save MacArthur's life

CHAPTER 37

from the snake bite. I mean, it would have been a gross failure if my first big assignment died! Then I became his blood brother, and my father indicated it was a sign I would be involved with him for life. It's a Russian thing. But before I could begin to fathom that, MacArthur freaked me out with his leg being healed. He freaked everyone out."

He was suddenly irate. "I was trained to control and influence, to manipulate, and in every attempt to do that, MacArthur made that impossible!" He drove his fingers through his hair and resented the smile on Reuben's face.

"I thought I might be done with him when he moved back to Virginia, but then he maneuvered himself into going to Thailand; so I was told to maintain the relationship and get as much info as possible. Frankly, I was astonished. For someone who shot off his mouth all the time, I couldn't get him to tell me anything! I wondered why the Colonel never tapped him for the CIA, especially after *you* trained him."

"He didn't want that life for him."

David sighed. "That I understand. When he returned from Thailand, even more religious, again, I thought I was done; but it seemed MacArthur had truly become my life's work."

"You say you wanted to be done with him, but did you *train* yourself to want that?"

David bit his lip, tears stinging his eyes. "I had to stay mad at him to keep from slipping. My insides got…torn up. I mean, he really was my best friend. I hated myself for it, but that's what I…I guess the real me…if there was a real me…felt."

CONVERSION

"Undercover work demands deception to reveal truth. It is painfully paradoxical, and it can scar the souls of all involved."

"Yes." David took some comfort in knowing Reuben understood. "After Thailand and you, MacArthur wasn't as open with me, and I wasn't sure how much I was missing. Then his mom died. It was hard, but her dying was a good thing for me, because Mac turned away from the Jesus crap — sorry — and got angry at his dad and his country. I enjoyed him again…well…for the most part. I could tell some kind of spark was gone, but we had fun, and he was open with me, almost like before Thailand."

Reuben creased his brow. "Did he divulge what happened in Thailand?"

"No. For some reason, he kept whatever promise he made to you and his dad to stay mute. But with his rebellion, my parents and Lila thought it was time to turn him, even point him to the CIA to be a double agent. I mean, he was disillusioned of everything he had believed, and he really got into the antiwar, anti-American, socialist agenda. I was about to introduce him to Lila when he got tangled up with the drug cartel!

"I called my father, and he called the Colonel. The Colonel thanked him and said he would handle it. It was one of those times my father earned some trust, but the Colonel was uncannily good. There were times when I wondered if he knew about us."

"There were suspicions."

"Do you know if he ever acted on them?"

"You will probably get to ask him yourself."

David frowned. "Right. Well, Lila wasn't happy, but I was glad

CHAPTER 37

when Mac managed to extricate himself from the drug mess, and it was fun to watch him go nuts over EJ. The problem, of course, was that she replaced me as his best friend." He stretched and looked at the ceiling. "I couldn't believe them. They had something...I didn't want that with *Veronica*, but it made me want...*that*. And EJ...she's not just smart. She's spooky."

Reuben quipped, "A godly woman is...as you say...spooky."

"Hmm."

David took a moment to take another drink and ponder his situation. Despite betraying his parents and everything he had believed, he was relishing his first act of being fully honest. And Reuben seemed to pull the truth out of him. "So Jimmy gets out of prison and almost kills Mac. God, did I get busted for that! Then he and EJ move to California, he writes *Help Yourself* and gets famous.

"We liked that he was working himself into some influential circles, but we hated his book. Basic self-government and Christianity. Makes communism impossible. A perfect society requires the masses to be dependent upon the state not a fairy-tale God or their own wits."

He caught himself. "Of course, I never said I was a communist or a Marxist, because my cover at the State Department was to find a way to bring the superpowers together. My *actual* mission was to neutralize US fear of the USSR so the USSR could eventually take over from within. And so I hammered away at social problems and decried capitalist corruption. But Mac knew socialism requires a totalitarian regime. We had some noteworthy debates about this. God, he was a great thinker. One time —"

CONVERSION

Reuben's telephone rang. "Excuse me, David. I must answer." He disappeared into the bedroom, closing the door. David automatically stood and walked quietly to the phone on the desk, aware of the gun nearby. He caught himself before lifting the receiver and instead walked aimlessly around the room, trying to reconcile the reality of his past training with the reality he had entered the moment he began talking to Reuben. Hearing Reuben's footsteps, he quickly returned to the sofa.

Reuben sat down, smiling. "Forgive the interruption, and please, continue."

David wondered, *Is he smiling because he knows I didn't pick up the receiver?* "You know, Lila still wanted to turn MacArthur when he was deep into the drug business. She said she could blackmail him and control him forever if he didn't want to go along with us. She had friends in the mafia who would back her up. In fact, she had Jessica killed to drive MacArthur into her arms; but that was a strategic error. He ran to the Colonel instead and became an informant for the FBI.

"Did you know this?"

"Not the informant part. Neither did Lila. We both misread MacArthur. He was a bigger Jesus freak than we thought. I mean, we have plants in seminaries proposing that Jesus was a socialist and even a communist…you know, 'sharing all things in common and helping the least of these.' So many Christians think they can be religious and also communist. But true Jesus Freaks don't buy it."

"Unfortunately, I can't agree with you. A true believer can

CHAPTER 37

be ignorant of the context of these passages. They miss entirely Jesus' identification with his own and his endorsement of private ownership and free markets. Thus, they are deceived."

Out of habit, David dismissed what he was hearing and moved on with his story. "Well, MacArthur went a different direction than Lila and I anticipated. He came clean, married EJ, wrote the books, and became a senator. The only reason he was elected was because he followed Reagan's playbook and criticized Carter." He chuckled. "Now there's a man who had no idea how great he was for us. We love these liberals who think they're being so open-minded and altruistic. I mean, he gave up the Panama Canal *to a communist* for Christ's sake! That was a huge victory! From that day we knew we could shut America out of a vast amount of world trade in a moment's notice."

Reuben frowned, and David thought, *Maybe I finally hit a nerve.*

"Our only disappointment in Carter was racism. We always thanked the founding fathers for slavery. It never takes much to get people of all colors stirred up about it again and again. Few know the true history. Unfortunately, Carter was a southerner and didn't want that dirty laundry thrown in his face, so he generally avoided the issue."

Reuben interjected, "No, his greatest transgression was bringing Ayatollah Khomeini to Iran, launching a new era of terrorism."

"Yes! And with his domestic policies tanking the economy, Americans were angry, afraid, and demoralized! Just what we wanted. You know, destroy all faith in America's founding, especially the Constitution and Judeo-Christian belief. With all

CONVERSION

these false restraints gone, there arises a complete lack of respect for law! Then crime escalates, riots ensue, and the great American Republic collapses into chaos, just begging us to step in and establish order and equality."

He realized the fire of his upbringing had overtaken him and stopped. "But then, too many Americans still wanted freedom more than a controlled, stable society, so in came Reagan, and we were back to slow and steady subversion."

Reuben raised his eyebrows. "Communists play chess not checkers."

David nodded. "I was glad whenever MacArthur was in Washington for the congressional sessions. We'd try to have lunch every week." He paused and shook his head, then swallowed hard to maintain control. "There was no one like him. He'd passionately disagree with me, and then he'd hug me goodbye and smile that goofy smile. No matter what happened, I was his best friend. His loyalty unnerved me."

"David, why was MacArthur assassinated?"

"Unfortunately, he followed Reagan in making Russia the main issue. Some people on the intelligence committee were aware that his father was CIA, and they befriended him — and one of them is one of us." He cleared his throat. "He realized Mac had come by some information that...well...enabled him to put two and two together about some of our *projects*...and *me* being a part of those projects."

"KGB projects."

"Yes. I realized things were getting serious when Mac and I were

CHAPTER 37

gonna have lunch a couple of weeks ago. I called to say my meeting was running late, and he said he'd meet me at my office. I walked in and found him going through my calendar. He closed it and covered perfectly. Every month, he had put a star on the 30th, his birthday, and written 'so many months before St. Mac's Day.' God, he was funny. But it was my job to suspect him, and I did. I just didn't tell Lila."

"You sensed he was in danger?"

"Yes. It wasn't long before I got a message to meet her. I almost threw up when she told me my cover was blown unless MacArthur was taken out. She said his popularity was also a problem. No matter what the liberal media did to sabotage him, like harping on his arrest and involvement with drugs, people loved him for his honesty." He glanced at the picture of MacArthur in the paper while taking a drink. "So...she said that KGB wanted me to take care of him, because I could get close to him and no one would question it."

For the first time, Reuben's face was fully expressive: horror and rage.

David forged ahead, hoping Reuben wouldn't kill him, automatically calculating how he could get the gun before Reuben did. "Lila tried to sweeten the deal. She said that being a good-looking, eligible widower, and then losing my best friend, the popular senator, would inspire sympathy and a lot of media attention. It would be easy for our 'friends' to eventually promote me to secretary of state or even president." He took a chance and looked Reuben in the eye. "You are probably aware that the State

CONVERSION

Department has employed many of us for decades."

"Yes."

"I called my father. He had been briefed and told me I had to do it, but I could tell he was shaken. I heard Mama crying. You know, we were spies, but we weren't without feelings. I believe my parents never thought I would face such an assignment, even though they made sure I was trained for it. We were just informants and influencers. I think they also had developed an affection for the Wells family."

"You will soon discover how much of your belief is true."

David caught the bite in Reuben's tone. "Yes, I guess I will." He looked down at his feet. "I didn't sleep that night. Told myself this was what it cost to bring about a perfect world, that the end justified the means. It's simple and logical: People who oppose universal equality and global government must be eliminated. Sacrifices are necessary to have peace on Earth."

"Actually, only one sacrifice."

Reuben's gentle reference to Jesus on the Cross irked him. Again, he brushed aside his words. "Mac was marked for death. If I didn't do it, someone else would. So I decided that EJ's birthday party was the perfect place, especially since you weren't going to be there."

"Hmm. But I sense things would not have gone differently had I been there."

David nodded. Then his eyes became fixed. "I'm alone with MacArthur on one of the balconies overlooking the bay. I tell him not to move, that there's a yellow-jacket on the back of his neck. He

CHAPTER 37

automatically freezes. I know he trusts me. I whisper, 'Don't worry. I'll get it.'

"I move behind him and reach into my coat pocket to draw out my handkerchief, uncapping the small ricin injector hidden in it. Then I inject him. Of course, he jumps, thinking he's been stung. I tell him to be still so I can remove the stinger, while hiding the injector in my handkerchief. Then, I shake it over the balcony. The evidence silently falls to the rocks below and is washed away."

He avoided Reuben's gaze and stood to walk to the window. "Later that evening, I told him I had to get back for an important meeting and —" he almost choked and cleared his throat — "he hugged me. I knew it was the last time I would see him. No one questioned the red mark on his neck, and the next morning he had a nasty cough. It was just dumb luck that the caterer mixed something odd into the baking soda concoction. I knew we could point to him if anyone suspected foul play.

He shoved his hands in his pockets. "Back in DC, I burned the handkerchief and checked in with Lila. I tried to think about anything but MacArthur. And then, after a couple of horrifying calls from EJ and not being able to get to him because of the snowstorm, yesterday evening she called to tell me he was dead."

"Why are you here, David?"

Reuben's tone sent a chill through his body. He took out his handkerchief and blew his nose, but the tears kept coming. His voice was hoarse and strained. "I don't know. I want to die. I want to live. But if I live, I can't live like this anymore." He turned. "Have you ever had to kill someone you loved?"

439

CONVERSION

"No, thank God."

"Is that something you would do?"

"Yeshua would tell me what was right."

"Well, he isn't an option for me." He turned back to the window.

"David, why are you *here*?"

David watched new snow falling gently, lightly. Then he closed his eyes. "Last night, as my comrades and I were celebrating my rite of passage, something happened. I heard a voice, like someone whispered in my ear, 'What kind of government emerges from those who murder the innocent?' Time stopped. I saw the evil I was a part of. I knew I was finished, and that I had to get to *you*. You would know what to do."

He continued to stare out the window. "God, the snow is so white, so pure. Makes you think everything is…fine…like there are no people like me in the world."

Reuben sighed heavily. He rose slowly and joined him at the window. "I will tell you why you have come." He put his hand on his shoulder. "I forgive you, David, and God forgives you."

David turned on him. "Don't waste your religious bullshit on me! I murdered my best friend, a husband, a father. I killed an incredible human being! Deal with that!"

"How do you wish to deal with it?"

"I'll face the consequences of my actions."

"You believe that if you go to prison for life or are executed, you will clear your account and purge your soul of all guilt and shame?"

"Of course not! Nothing I do will ever make up for what I've done."

CHAPTER 37

Reuben noticed the lights go on at the church. "Close your eyes, David."

David obeyed. He heard Reuben praying softly in a language he didn't recognize and smirked inside, *Probably tongues*. But he jerked to attention a moment later when he heard Spanish, and then Russian.

By the time Reuben stopped speaking, David had begun to shake inside. He opened his eyes and turned to him. "I didn't know you spoke Spanish and Russian."

Reuben put his hands in his pockets and looked him in the eye. "I don't."

David snarled, "How did you know what happened before I was born?"

Reuben shrugged his shoulders. "What happened?"

Although the shaking increased, David was adamant. "You said, in Spanish, 'I knew you in Mama's womb. You were in trouble, and I took the trouble from you.' You didn't see this in some Mossad file?"

Reuben shook his head no.

The words poured from his mouth. "We never talk about it with anyone, because it was too close to a miracle! Mama was pregnant with me, there was a problem, and she and Papa were frightened they would lose me. She had been told she could never have children, but she had *me*."

"Yeshua has been looking out for you."

He sensed he was breaking apart inside but pressed on. "Then you said in Russian, 'You have been deceived, but now you see the truth. I am the truth, and from this day, you will live in me.' And you swear you don't speak Russian!"

Reuben looked at him intently. "I do not."

David rubbed the back of his neck and tried to calm himself. "You said I was deceived. I know it's the truth but...."

"Truth is not a concept, David. Truth is a person: Yeshua. Jesus the Messiah. You know the truth because you are not hearing *me*; you are hearing *him, the Truth.*"

David felt his inner being collapsing. He knew he would either live or die in the next few moments. "Reuben, is this forgiveness, this being…how do you say it?"

"*Shalom*. Whole. Nothing missing, nothing broken."

A sliver of hope rose in his heart. "Is this possible, even for me?"

Reuben walked to his desk.

David eyed the gun case and knew he was going to die.

Miraculously, Reuben picked up a worn Bible instead and sat on the sofa.

"Come. See for yourself."

33

That night, David slept peacefully for the first time in his life. The boy and man he was had died. He was brand new. *Shalom*. He had no idea what would become of him, but he knew his future was in the best hands. And the words in Reuben's Bible resonated in his spirit: "The goodness of God leads us to repentance. The goodness of God…the goodness of God…."

When he awoke the next morning, he remembered what had transpired the last few days and grieved violently for the loss of MacArthur. Waves of sorrow washed over his soul as he saw the depths of his sin against God, MacArthur, everyone who loved him — and even Veronica. He felt the trauma he had caused those he loved, especially Sarah. Then, just as he thought he would be swallowed in darkness, a strong arm pulled him up and bathed him in forgiveness and love. *The goodness of God. Oh, the goodness of God!*

When he smelled something good, he got up and dressed. He and Reuben sat down to have a late breakfast, but first Reuben blessed the food and prayed for wisdom to advise David.

David could only thank God and shake his head in wonder. "If I've gone mad, I want to stay mad."

"I know this logic!" Reuben laughed.

"You know, Reuben. I'm not the only one who's been converted."

CONVERSION

"Who?"

"The United States has also been converted, but not to truth, justice, and the American way. They just don't see it yet. Maybe this is what MacArthur has been talking about all these years, that we must change the world."

"My boy, now you know, only Yeshua can convert people from darkness to light, and so it is with nations. He wants both. People and nations. He says this. All we can do is our part, pray fervently, and watch him work."

"Okay. I see that."

"So. Next for you?"

"I'll turn myself in to the Colonel. Tell him everything. I just hope one day everyone can forgive me for what I've done. Reuben, they will either execute me for treason or turn me into a double agent. I don't mind dying now, knowing I'm going to Heaven and I'll see Mac again, but…I don't know…I don't think that's supposed to happen."

"My experience is that Yeshua prepares us for our next step even when we don't know it."

"In other words, right now I don't know what I'm trained for?"

Reuben chuckled. "Abba has this notion that we must take one step of faith at a time. Why? So he can surprise us in each move. And, in the end we are in awe that he got us exactly where we needed to go."

The phone on his desk rang. He walked over and answered, "Katz." A moment later he leaned on the desk and then fell into his chair. Long silence. "Yes, beloved, I'm here. Yes. Please." He began

CHAPTER 33

to weep and raise his hand in the air. Longer silence. "He's with me. Yes. Yes. It was my greatest test. It is true. Would you like to speak with him? David." He set the receiver on the desk and returned to the table, where he sat and stared, weeping quietly.

David dreaded talking to EJ but put the receiver to his ear. "EJ?"

"Don't freak out. It's me. I'm alive. Jesus sent me back because we're not through."

David stood like a statue. "Good God!" He looked at Reuben, who was now laughing and crying at the same time. "Is it really you? Are you okay? You aren't sick?"

"No, man. I'm better than ever." MacArthur's voice resounded in David's head, and yet he could hardly believe he was hearing him. "I'm alive and well!"

David broke. "I'm sorry Mac. I'm so sorry."

"You're sorry I'm alive?" MacArthur laughed.

"No! I'm sorry I...I killed you." He flinched at his confession. "Did you know I killed you?"

"Yes, but not until I was in Heaven and Jesus told me."

"Oh."

"He also told me you'd be his by the time I talked to you. Reuben said that's true. Is it true?"

David chuckled wryly. "Didn't you believe Jesus? I thought he was *the* Truth!"

"Oh my God, you must be converted because the old David would never say that!"

"I know! I can hardly believe this conversation. It's so bizarre on so many levels. My God! You're alive! Wait!" He turned to

CONVERSION

Reuben. "What does this mean legally?"

Reuben shrugged his shoulders and blew his nose. MacArthur said, "Look, can you and Reuben come out here? My dad's still here. Then we can pray and figure out what we're supposed to do."

"Reuben, he wants us to come to California."

Reuben rose and walked to the desk. "Let me speak to him." David handed the receiver to him. "My boy, who knows you are alive?"

"Only EJ, her parents, my dad, and my sisters. Oh, and a few at the hospital."

"*Only* them, eh? Who knows about David?"

"Just EJ and my dad, and he's arranging a private jet for you. It makes sense, you know, David going to New York to take the flight with you."

"Once more, we have stumbled into Yeshua's perfect plan."

"Yes! Put David on again, please."

"Hah! A moment with Yeshua and you're giving *me* orders! Shalom." Reuben's face beamed as he handed the receiver back to David.

"Yeah."

"Listen David, Dad told me to tell you to operate as usual. You simply went to New York to fly out here with Reuben. Nothing suspicious about that, right?"

"Right. Tell the Colonel...tell him I look forward to speaking with him."

"I will. Love you, brother — now my blood brother in more ways than one!"

"Yes! God, I love you too. See you soon."

CHAPTER 33

MacArthur hung up the phone and hugged EJ, drinking in the smell of her hair. His mind raced through all the twists and turns they had traversed together in just a decade. He had known his book would be a success and change many lives, and he had known he would be elected senator. He knew these things the way he knew his leg was healed from the snake bite. But what happened to him on the balcony with David was a complete surprise. He thought he had been stung. By the time he realized he was dying, there was no time to think about how he had become ill. His sole concern was for EJ and his three children.

When his physical body died, he traveled upward to stand at massive gates of pearl. He was stunned at their majesty. There was nothing like them on Earth. But they faded from view when he saw Jesus, and he ran into his open arms. Their conversation was brief, but Jesus told him everything he needed to know. MacArthur never wanted to leave him, but Jesus said he must return. He heard EJ calling out, "MacArthur Wells, come back to us!" Over and over, louder and louder, she called to him.

EJ had gone home Monday night surrounded by an inexplicable peace yet grief-stricken. She fell asleep on MacArthur's side of the bed, breathing his scent and weeping. That night, she dreamed she and MacArthur were playing on the beach with their *four* children, two boys and *two* girls. She awoke Tuesday morning, saying, "We're going to have another girl, *and I'm not pregnant!*"

She dressed quickly and went to nurse Caleb, all the while praying in tongues, her faith growing, pondering the dream. The

CONSERVATION

verse that resonated in her spirit as she prayed was what Jesus said to Martha before he raised her brother Lazarus from the dead: "I am the resurrection and the life. I am the resurrection and the life."

After dressing Caleb, she found the Colonel alone in the kitchen, sipping his coffee. "Colonel, take Caleb and dry your eyes because MacArthur is coming back to us."

He put his mug down, stared blankly at her, and took his grandson. "What?"

She kissed him on the cheek and talked fast. "Jesus still raises people from the dead, Dad, and I believe he wants MacArthur to come back. So pray, okay?"

"Yes, Ma'am."

She ran out the door, admonishing him, "And don't tell anyone. I'll let you know."

The door closed, and he looked at Caleb. "Oh God, I hope your mom's not gone mad." The child giggled and tried to grab his nose.

At the morgue, the attendant pulled out MacArthur's body and unzipped the body bag to expose his head and chest. EJ swallowed hard and let her purse fall to the floor. As soon as the young man was gone, she put her hands on MacArthur's dark, cold cheeks and closed her eyes. "I thank you, Jesus, that you are the resurrection and the life. So MacArthur, come back! We are supposed to have another daughter!" Then over and over she yelled, "MacArthur Wells, come back to us!"

When he gasped for air and sat up, EJ stepped back and just stared at him, eyes wide, mouth open. MacArthur whispered hoarsely, "You called, EJ?"

CHAPTER 33

She laughed and threw her arms around his neck. "Oh my God! Thank you, Jesus! Oh my God!"

MacArthur hugged her tightly. "It's okay, Beautiful. It's okay. I'm okay now."

She pulled away and looked at him, touching his face, moving her hands up and down his arms. "Your color is...."

"Green?"

She laughed again through her tears. "No. It's just...a moment ago you were *gray*. You've been dead for over twelve hours." She looked at him like she had never seen him before. "What happened to you? Oh my God. This is...." He pulled her close and whispered that he had talked to Jesus, who had revealed David's treachery, which would lead to his conversion. She pulled away. "Of course. Everything makes...but I never, ever would have...I mean...oh...in my spirit...I kept...I mean...wow...he—"

MacArthur put his finger to her lips and grinned. He had never heard EJ stutter. Never. "I know. Me too. But no one can know about David until we talk to him and he talks to my dad, okay?" She nodded.

39

When the morgue attendant returned, it took him some time to adjust to the situation. EJ and MacArthur could not suppress their laughter. When the young man was finally composed, EJ asked him to bring MacArthur a pair of scrubs, and MacArthur asked him to call Dr. Ross and the hospital administrator. "Just tell them they are needed because a very challenging situation has occurred in the morgue. Please don't tell them or anyone else about this," said MacArthur.

The administrator arrived first. He scratched his head and sent the morgue attendant for MacArthur's chart. He rigorously questioned the story he was being told. After all, MacArthur was a politician, and politicians went to great lengths to get media attention. "I will agree only after talking to Dr. Ross."

The look on Dr. Ross's face was proof enough. He was beside himself when he saw MacArthur alive and well. He examined him and found nothing wrong. Only a small scar on his neck and a bruise where the IV was inserted in his hand remained, which he noted on the chart. The morgue attendant couldn't stop shaking his head and grinning. The hospital administrator kept repeating, "This is wild. This is just beyond, well, anything."

Dr. Ross said, "I've seen some miraculous things, people being cured when there was no medical explanation, but I never thought

CONVERSION

I'd see anything like this." All three agreed to keep silent for two days, which would give MacArthur time to contact his family and decide how to break the news to the public.

After EJ had left the house, the Colonel was deeply concerned. He called her parents and asked them to come as soon as possible. He told them she had gone to the hospital to make arrangements and would probably need their support when she returned.

Little David and Hannah had not been told of their father's death. No one felt it was their place to tell them. Thus, they merely thought it was party time at breakfast when both their parents walked through the door and pandemonium ensued. They shrieked with delight when their father scooped them up and hugged them tightly, squirming and laughing when he vowed never to put them down.

The Colonel declared, "I don't know what has given me greater joy, that my son is here or that my daughter-in-law has not lost her mind." Later, Sarah arrived and burst into tears when she saw her brother, hugging him and laughing with the rest.

Amidst their merriment, the telephone rang, and Meg answered it. Her eyes grew big and she said, "I'll get her for you, Sir." She pressed the receiver to her shoulder and began waving frantically for everyone to be quiet. "It's the governor for EJ."

MacArthur broke out in a knowing grin, and EJ's parents took the children outside. When everyone was quiet, EJ said, "Hello, Governor. Yes, Sir. I understand. I will give you my answer in a couple of days, if that's acceptable to you. Yes, Sir. Thank you, Sir. I

CHAPTER 39

do too." She hung up and faced MacArthur. "My goodness, I'm not sure you should come back. The governor wants *me* to fill your seat until the next election." There were shouts of, "Hear, hear!" and "It's your time, EJ!" from the sisters.

Later, in the privacy of their office, MacArthur told his father about David. The Colonel shook his head, but he didn't act too surprised. EJ joined them and called Reuben, and then MacArthur spoke to him and David. The Colonel arranged for a private jet from New York for the following day, after the snow had been cleared from the runways. When MacArthur offered to pay the cost, the Colonel smiled wryly. "You can use your life insurance."

MacArthur's mouth dropped open. It seemed odd that the full reality of dying and coming back to life didn't truly strike him until that moment.

Knowing their church family would be bringing food, EJ called Pastor Eddie and requested that they wait for a day or two. She would explain later. At the Colonel's request, she called a reporter they trusted and told her that she was planning a memorial service, but because MacArthur had such a large family, it would not take place for several days. When she had more details, she would let the reporter know. Thus, the world and his enemies thought MacArthur was no more and turned to other issues.

The next morning, Rebecca, Meg, and Joanna happily flew home to their families. MacArthur asked them to tell only their spouses until they heard he was alive on the news. "This thing has to be handled carefully, you know. I mean, some people are just going to freak out and others aren't going to believe any of it." He didn't tell them the real reason for silence was David.

Sarah was the only one who stayed. She had arranged to take vacation time, thinking it would help her through her own grief by helping EJ with the children for a while. Now, she was ecstatic and beyond grateful to God that her brother was still with them, and she was going to have a true vacation with him and their family.

When the Colonel met David and Reuben at the airport, he greeted them warmly. Reuben asked him to fill in the details they had not heard. David listened quietly, blowing his nose from time to time. When they reached the beach house, EJ and MacArthur held onto David and Reuben, all of them weeping for joy. EJ explained that her parents and Sarah were with the children on the beach.

David looked beyond the sliding glass doors and searched for her. She was sitting in the wet sand, her long auburn hair in a neat braid down her back. Caleb sat in front of her and they laughed as the small waves splashed over their legs.

MacArthur followed David's gaze and said, "Let's go to our office, where we'll have privacy when the kids come in for lunch. EJ's got burritos and chips and all kinds of goodies in there."

When everyone was seated in the office, David turned to the Colonel, "Sir, before I say anything, I want you to know that I will do whatever you tell me to do." The Colonel nodded. David took a deep breath and began. "As you know, I was born in Cuba...."

EJ held MacArthur's hand and squeezed tightly from time to time as they listened to David's story. He related only what he needed to tell them. The intricate details of his years of spying

CHAPTER 39

would be for the Colonel's ears only. When he finished, the Colonel stood to stretch his legs. "I need more sustenance."

Reuben asked the Colonel, "What is David's legal status?"

"He's guilty of treason and murder. The question is, David, what do you want to happen?"

"I'll do whatever you tell me to do, Sir."

"No, Son. That's not how this is going to work. You've done everything you were commanded to do since you were born, and I commend your obedience and loyalty; but now, for the first time in your life, you have the opportunity to make a decision without handlers or KGB or parents. No more Mission MacArthur or Communist Party. For this moment, it's just you and your God."

Even Reuben was shocked at the Colonel's words. "Are you saying you're willing to forget everything you've just heard?" And the Colonel knew Reuben's eyes were asking, "Will you pass up an intelligence asset we all dream of?"

"No, but David needs to know his next step before I decide how I'll proceed."

Susanne knocked on the door and poked her head in, saying, "Kids have eaten, and we're all taking naps."

"That's great, Mom! Thanks. We'll see you after," said EJ. Her mother paused and smiled at MacArthur, then blew him a kiss and closed the door.

David could hardly speak. "Thank you. Thank you all for not... stringing me up." He looked at MacArthur and spoke brokenly. "Other than my genuine love for you and your family, there's been only one constant in my life, something I've never been able to

455

shake, something that was mine alone." He glanced at MacArthur, "You've always known it, but," he turned to the Colonel, "I have to pray and think before I say more. Thank you, Sir, for giving me this opportunity. I don't deserve it."

He offered his hand to the Colonel, who took it and gave him his military brotherhood hug. "Son, you've been programmed for over thirty years, but God has brought you here. Take the time you need." He patted him on the arm. "But stay close, okay?"

The others laughed and embraced him, saying things like, "It's going to be okay...we love you...God'll show you what you need to do."

"Uh, Mac," David hesitated, extended his hand, and whispered in his ear, "Thanks for staying my friend when you knew I was a criminal."

MacArthur laughed and hugged him. "Returning the favor, man. Returning the favor."

EJ yawned, "I'm going to get some Z's while the kids are sleeping." Reuben and David helped her pick up what remained of their lunch and take it to the kitchen.

The Colonel motioned MacArthur to stay, and they sat down again. He leaned in and asked, "What was David referring to, when he said there was a constant he could never shake?"

40

Sarah tried to nap, but her body had not adjusted to California time; so she arose and walked down the hall to the kitchen for a drink of water. As she approached the office, she heard her father say, "David in love with Sarah? How did I miss that?" She froze.

"I don't know, Dad, but he's loved her ever since we met, I mean, that's what he was talking about, you know, the only constant that was his and no one knew. I used to tease him about it, but my guess is that he couldn't be with her because the KGB wanted him to be with Veronica. And I don't know if we should even tell Sarah. I mean, how would she react, or any of my sisters feel, about David being the one who killed me? I don't even know how she feels about him *without knowing* he's a spy and an assassin. Do you?"

"No. She's my *quiet* daughter." He frowned. "Except when she's speaking Spanish it seems." He sighed and shook his head. "David is in a dangerous place. Frankly, I'd be thrilled if she became a nun."

"I get it. It's just…now that David's a Christian, well…it changes everything. I mean, look at me, sitting here with you, a miracle. If God did this for us, what does he want to do for David, for Sarah?"

"Hmm…you have a valid point, but this is my baby girl we're talking about."

"I know, Dad, but I just pray God has a miracle for them. I can't help it. EJ and I have always thought they belonged together.

CONVERSION

Unfortunately, the only option I can see for that to happen, I mean, assuming Sarah *wants* to be with him, is for him to be a double agent. How dangerous would that be?"

"Actually, he already sees you regularly. They expect that. So it would be easy for him to get information to us, providing you wanted to be involved too. But let's not get ahead of ourselves. You know, we've discussed how there's an entirely different attitude with Reagan in office, and I sense that something big is about to happen on the Russian front. That might affect David's future."

Sarah had heard enough. She quietly hurried to her bedroom and closed the door. Lying on her bed, she revisited every time she had encountered David, growing up and as an adult. Could what MacArthur said be true? David a spy... *Oh my God! I asked him that once!* ... her brother's assassin ... now a *Christian* ... and yet all these years loving *her*? Her mind was whirling, so she closed her eyes and prayed in the Spirit until her whole being was at peace.

Then she listened.

She didn't stir until little David and Hannah burst through her door to beckon her to dinner. With them in tow, she greeted David and Reuben with hugs. Did she imagine it, or was David's hug especially strong? Throughout dinner, she noticed he was more animated and at ease with everyone — and how he looked at her. Had he always looked at her this way? She had to fight the urge to run.

When he addressed her in Spanish, it put her more at ease. They laughed about how Little David, who was five, and Hannah, who was three, were the only ones who were not surprised that

CHAPTER 40

their father had had a visit with Jesus in Heaven.

Soon after dinner, the Captain and Susanne drove home, vowing to keep MacArthur's secret until he and EJ decided how to tell the world. The Colonel and Reuben took a walk on the beach, and MacArthur and EJ began putting their children to bed. She nursed Caleb, who fell asleep in her arms, while MacArthur read to them. After Caleb was asleep in his crib, they tip-toed out and Hannah and David ran into their parents' bedroom. By the time MacArthur and EJ arrived, the two were faking sleep with loud snores. Of course, this was an open invitation to be tickled.

Eventually, they all rested on the bed, holding each other and saying their prayers, thanking Jesus for having such a good time with Daddy. Then, it was time to take David and Hannah to their rooms and tuck them in for the night.

Meanwhile, Sarah and David were left to do the dinner dishes. He asked about her life in Madrid. She described her work at a medical clinic for the poor, then said, "I'm considering becoming a nun."

David was rinsing a dish. She saw him hesitate for a moment, then he shrugged his shoulders. "This doesn't surprise me. You've always had a big heart."

She paused as she wiped the table. "I know I sent a note, but I was very sorry to hear of Veronica's passing. Are you doing okay?"

David loaded the soap in the dishwasher and closed the door. "Yeah. We didn't exactly have a great marriage, but it has been a difficult...adjustment."

Sarah hung the dishcloth to dry. David started the dishwasher

CONVERSION

and said, "I'm going to get some air. Want to come?" He looked hopeful.

She panicked. "Thanks, but I have a good book I want to get back to."

"Sure." He smiled weakly and walked out onto the terrace. The sun was floating slowly toward the edge of the ocean as he fell into one of the large deck chairs, exhausted.

She stared at him for the longest time. *Oh Lord, give me courage.*

David turned to see the Colonel and Reuben walking down the beach. He leaned his head back and closed his eyes. *Wonder what they're talking about.* The waves of the ocean calmed him. *What now, Lord? Like the Colonel said, it's just you and me. I'll do anything you ask.*

He vaguely heard the terrace door slide open and close behind him. *MacArthur, coming to do a post mortem.* He smiled at his pun, but he was too tired to say anything or even look around. Still, his heart was filled with gratitude that his friend was alive…and forgiving.

He gasped when two slender arms slid around his neck, and he froze when he realized to whom they belonged. He dared not breathe for fear he was dreaming.

She whispered in his ear, "A funny thing happened on the way to the nunnery."

David clasped her hands. "Sarah. There's so much you don't know."

She hugged his neck and said in Spanish. "My dearest man, I know everything."

CHAPTER 40

He gently loosed himself from her embrace and stood to face her. "What do you know?"

She came to him, placed her hands on his chest, and looked up at him with tears in her eyes. "I know what you've done, and I know the real you."

David hung his head. "Well, that makes one of us."

She put her hands on his cheeks and raised his head. "You are the blessing Jesus promised me years ago."

"What?"

She giggled. "I'll tell you about it in the next fifty years or so."

David Parks had the uncanny ability to discern if someone was telling the truth, and at that moment he saw the truth in Sarah's eyes. He grinned. "So…no nunnery?"

She shook her head.

With trembling arms he lifted her, felt her arms encircle his neck, and they were engulfed in the joy of their first kiss.

Epilogue

As the final fingers of light stretched across the ocean to warn of events soon to shake the Earth, generations of warriors rested in the miracle of being together. The world was entering a time of continuous and accelerating birth pangs, groaning for new life, and these warriors — and many others like them — were its hope.

Historical Note

Many people reviewed the manuscript before it was published, and we determined there was a lack of knowledge about the Charismatic Movement, even among Christian readers. Some found it hard to believe so many Christians were baptized in the Holy Spirit and spoke with tongues in our story. However, from the late 1960s through the early 1980s, it was not uncommon for entire families and even congregations to receive this "Promise of the Father."

The Charismatic Movement was a season in Church history, when Christians from all denominations received the baptism in the Holy Spirit, speaking in tongues and moving in the gifts of the Spirit. As some pastors and congregants were expelled from their denominations for this life in the Spirit, the "non-denominational" churches that are common today were formed.

Here is the wonder of the Charismatic Movement: The words of Jesus in John 17:21 manifested! "…that they may all be one; just as You, Father, are in Me and I in You, that they also may be in Us, *so that the world may believe that You sent Me*" (John 17:21 NASB). Catholics, Baptists, Methodists, Presbyterians, Episcopalians, Lutherans, and many others were united as one, and people around the world saw that God had sent Jesus to save them. Multitudes were converted to Christianity.

A reawakening of the Church in the manner of Pentecost is what the devil and those he controls most fear.

Acknowledgements

Our heart-felt gratitude goes to:

George and Linda Dany and Dave Albanese for their recollection of all things Panama in the 1960s.

John Pojman for his knowledge of the Order of the Arrow.

J. R. American Horse for his expertise in building a tipi.

A. J. Albanese for knowledge of World War II, Korean War, Douglas MacArthur, Central Intelligence Agency, Bay of Pigs, and Cuban missile crisis.

Tom Teetor for knowledge of military and intelligence operations during the Vietnam and Cold Wars.

The Reig family (especially Jose's cousin) for their knowledge of nursing schools that accepted foreign students during the late 1960s in Madrid, Spain.

Emily Nydam, who loaned her copy of *Mai Pen Rai Means Never Mind: An American housewife's honest love affair with the irrepressible people of Thailand,* by Carol Hollinger. This delightful memoir gave us a sense of Thailand during the 1960s.

All those wonderful first-readers who corrected our misspellings and gave invaluable advice and encouragement.

About the Authors

R. J. Albanese graduated from the University of Virginia and became the vice president of marketing for a new and highly successful computer software company specializing in artificial intelligence. Later, he left that company to attend Rhema Bible Training Center in Tulsa, Oklahoma, and after that he did mission work in Central America and worked in crusades around the world. He returned to the United States to work with his father's law firm, doing title work until he retired.

Always active in his church, Ron taught children for twenty years, and he still teaches whenever he's given the opportunity. He participates in prayer teams and also performs various acts of service in his church. He has written or co-authored four other books: *Who You Are and What You Should Be Doing*, *The Meaning of Life*, *The Meaning of Life for Kids: An Adventure for All Ages*, and *The Meaning of Life for Kids II: Living in Super Power*.

Ron is married and has a daughter and step-daughter. You can contact him through his website: www.rjalbanese.com

E. T. Sherman graduated from Northwestern University and worked as a legal assistant until she married and had two children, a son and a daughter. She left the legal field for Christian publishing, working as a developmental editor, acquisitions editor, and editor-in-chief. Employed by publishers and later as a freelancer, she has helped many self-publish and has edited or ghostwritten over 250 books, which include authors from various denominations and theological persuasions. She co-authored *The Meaning of Life, The Meaning of Life for Kids: An Adventure for All Ages,* and *The Meaning of Life for Kids II: Living in Super Power.*

Elizabeth ministered with Native American Christians and was an instructor at Two Rivers Native American Training Center in Oklahoma. For a season, she published Native American Christians as Perfect Circle Publishing, Inc. In churches she has attended, she has worn many hats: choir member, worship leader, drama team, teaching and caring for children, preaching, teaching Bible studies, prayer ministry, and serving those in need.

Elizabeth's children are married, and she has five incredible grandchildren. She can be contacted through www.rjalbanese.com.